God Loves Us

An Achim Jeffers Novel

By

Josiah Jay Starr

2nd Novel in the Achim Jeffers Series

Spirit of 1811 Publishing, LLC
New Orleans, Louisiana
www.spiritof1811publishing.com
"Our Story. Our Family."
God Loves Us
An Achim Jeffers Novel

By: Josiah Jay Starr
Spirit of 1811 Publishing, LLC
Alliance of Independent Author Member

Spirit of 1811 Publishing
New Orleans, Louisiana
www.spiritof1811publishing.com
Copyright © 2022 by Spirit of 1811 Publishing

Library of Congress Control Number: 2022913325

Paperback ISBN: 978-1-953102-08-9
Hardback ISBN: 978-1-953102-09-6
eBook ISBN: 978-1-953102-10-2
Audiobook ISBN: 978-1-953102-11-9

Editors: Kimberly Rose
Cover Art: michaelstar

Dedicated to my beloved homie Derek Johnson.
Until we meet again cousin.
And when we do, have that Sega Genesis controller ready.

Contents

Chapter One

Strong Bullfrogs In Juffair

Jessica has started to lend a quiet voice to her inner complaints. After our New Year's Day party, I sensed that the uncertainty of our relationship has begun to wear her down. From the moment her pregnancy test came back positive. I knew her support for my career at Robert Charles would start to falter. Now, her co-existence with my duties as a counter-racist hitman have morphed into something more akin to simmering animosity. Our loving relationship has devolved into a contentious cold war. Jessica now hates what this career demands of me, while I was all too committed to performing this labor of love.

I wouldn't need a damn fortune teller to predict this outcome. This was heading towards me having to choose between God's path, and the black woman I loved dearly. Early on, Jessica told me she believed in us. When we first started, she made me feel like she supported this mission the Lord had chosen for me. Back then, she was a rider and was more than down for the cause. Nowadays, it isn't hard to catch her anxious spirit whenever I mention Robert Charles.

Annoyed with Jessica's snarky email, I tossed the cellphone onto the table before loosening my bow tie. Having to deal with her silent insecurities was beyond frustrating. Searching for some sort of mental reprieve, I grabbed the sweaty cocktail glass and forced down more than a few swallows. After all, I was in a damn bar, and there is no better place in the world to try and push away life's tribulations.

My eyes probed the darkness of the cocktail lounge, aching for any distraction I could find. Yet, my attempts to occupy my mind were futile. The loneliness of the bar forced me to watch three drunk Arab men awkwardly dance to old school hip hop. Here in Bahrain, my only company happened to be my scolding hookah bowl and this melted drink.

This entire bar was way too cheesy, with its nineties style strobe light and long panel mirrors hanging from the ceiling. The whole layout felt like it was pulled out of a corny P. Diddy music video. Even in a deeply pious country like Bahrain, everyone wanted the swag of Black Americans. All over the world, it was fun to imitate Black Americans while not actually getting treated like a Black American. Frustrated by their phony appreciation, I took a small puff of my grape mint hookah, and blew the anger out of my lungs.

Despite Jessica's childish tirades, I constantly had to remind myself that this was her first pregnancy. The sudden turbulence of life can become overwhelming once the impending responsibilities of parenthood take root. Yet, a shot of luck has been stirred into our double expresso. Thankfully, I've had the opportunity to experience this wild journey of parenthood once before, so it's my duty to guide Jessica as best as I can.

During my first marriage, the harsh lessons of fatherhood taught me that underneath the bright glow of raising a child, sat a world of daunting realities. It's not just the many sleepless nights that come along with infants, it's the fact that outside of your love and comfort awaits a world eager to misuse them. Foremost among them is the fact that no matter how much love I poured into my son, that love alone wasn't enough to protect him from the sharp jaws of Systemic White Supremacy. The day my son was brutally executed by that White demon, a piece of my heart was forever wounded. I guess watching Jessica glow with the same inner life that my slain wife once had…has made me a bit more detached this time around.

The bloody experiences from my first family, have forced my spirit into this state of numbness. I find myself a little reluctant about blindly enjoying life's moments. Deep down, I knew it was the horrifying presence of this numbness that was starting to worry her. Jessica would prefer that I smile and pretend it all away, but that isn't who I am, at least not right now I'm not.

"Achim…are you sure you're ready to do this again?" She asked.

"Why do you live in the past so much, baby?" Jessica would often demand.

Even from the comfort of this sofa inside of the Grand Juffair Hotel, my mind replayed her nervous voice, asking me those two pointed questions. The questions alone weren't of a concern, instead it's my cold answers to them. In all honesty, I didn't know if I was ready to go through all this madness again. If our enemies found out that the Chief Counter-Racist hitman for Robert Charles, had a whole damn family…that fact alone would easily become a death sentence for everyone I loved. Years ago, I had failed as a black man. I failed to protect my first family and I'd be damned if I doomed Jessica to that very same fate.

"Excuse me, my dear. Would you like another drink sir?"

She was naturally attractive and extremely sexy as she pointed at my empty glass with her broad smile. Her eyes blazed through me, summoning my wonder to the godly beauty of our biblical ancestors. The tortured sounds of her rough English fighting through that heavy Ethiopian accent, tugged at my self-awareness. It was obvious that English was not this woman's preferred language. Who knows where this East African lady learned her English? To survive in this world dominated by White Supremacists, black people needed to be resourceful.

After inspecting my empty glass, I handed it over to her before springing upwards towards her eager ear. Noticing me, she quickly leaned down and met me halfway. I felt her purposely rub her breasts up against my arm as I closed in, teasing me with a forbidden feel. Her eyes were ready to accommodate, so I knew it was best that I avoided them.

"Yes, I'll take another drink, sister." I spoke over the bar's corny music.

"I'll have a Blue Bullfrog, and please tell the bartender to go easy on the ice this time."

With a half-understanding nod, she shot me a cute smile before scurrying away. As my waiter and the Arabic bartender talked, I saw the bar's front door swing open. A small group of young white men walked inside the lounge. All of them were wearing stares that longed for excitement. Sporting dark dress pants and long sleeve shirts, they all flossed shiny necklaces and gold pinky rings. Unlike the more modestly dressed Arabs, each one of these corny looking white boys was loud and obnoxious. Even from my sofa, I could tell that these young men were all U.S. Marines, most likely stationed at the Navy's 5th Fleet Command in Juffair.

The presence of U.S. Service Members in Bahrain is omnipresent and unmistakable. From the bubbly nightclubs, five-star restaurants, lavish jewelry shops and gourmet weekend brunches, Bahrain has an extremely active night life. Despite huge cultural and language differences, U.S. servicemembers eagerly spend their money everywhere. There is no doubt in my mind that this group of barely drinking age young men had come here to cure a spell of boredom. As the group found lounge chairs for themselves, the front door once again opened and my overanxious partner wallowed into the dark lounge. His light-yellow long sleeve shirt looked half wet, and his brown skin shined with sweat. With his hairy chin and unmanicured line up, I could tell that he hadn't bothered to visit the barbershop I recommended to him. From the discomfort in his spirit, I knew my partner was rushing himself. When the door closed behind him, our eyes briefly met. It only took a millisecond to see the lack of poise blossoming within him. He was under pressure, and instead of meeting the challenge with confidence, Anthony was allowing self-doubt to grow its roots.

His lack of self-confidence was the main reason Aunt Rita and her Robert Charles counterparts demanded that I supervise this whole Bahrain operation. Several months earlier, Anthony had badly botched a lucrative hit in Oregon, allowing a murderous member of the Hound Boyz to escape his grasp and flee to Ukraine. Robert Charles has a reputation for delivering justice to our paying customers, so Anthony's failure to kill the racist bastard was not just embarrassing, but it was bad for business. I personally believed Anthony's Caribbean Island upbringing was failing him. He was superb at taking orders and executing a set plan, but when things got fluid, he tended to struggle. Making a snap decision in a critical moment was certainly not his calling card.

Robert Charles' leadership believed Anthony needed more seasoning before he could operate independently. Jessica wasn't thrilled that I was forced to go back out for field work again. My days as a boots on the ground assassin were supposed to be over, but Robert Charles thought it best to pull me out of moth balls until Anthony was ready for primetime.

Looking confused, he quietly found himself a seat near the well-lit bar and pulled out his cellphone. After watching him type away, I felt my own phone vibrate on the marble tabletop in front of me. Within two minutes, Anthony had already made two errors that were all too common among inexperienced operators. For one, I knew he had been trailing too close behind that group of white Marines. There was no logical reason for him to come into the bar right after they entered. That, coupled with his decision to sit at the bar, where everyone with two eyes could see him, pissed me off. Now, I felt the need to grab this situation before it spiraled beyond the scope of his limited capabilities.

"Is he already in here? I wanna make sure I didn't miss him," Anthony texted.

"Calm down. Remember, confidence is king." I texted back. "Control the situation or the situation will control you."

"First, get up and find a seat away from the bar. Do it before the waitress notices you and comes over to take your order," I followed up.

Anthony took in my text messages, then dumped his phone into his pocket. He obediently rose from his seat and slowly made his way across the room to a corner set of lounge chairs. Now, he was in a much better vantage point to see everything happening around him. With a slight head nod, I acknowledged the prudence of his choice.

Moments later, the Ethiopian waitress arrived with my freshly squeezed Blue Bullfrog. Without hesitating, I took a test sip and tasted mixed alcohol faintly masked by a sweet blast of citrus. This was a grown man's drink; light weights need not apply. You only needed one Blue Bullfrog to hold you over for the rest of the night, and that too was part of my plan. Before the waitress could leave, I handed her three U.S. twenty-dollar bills and told her to keep the change. I watched her brown eyes explode with happiness as she quickly calculated her tip. Visibly appreciative, she leaned down and teased my cheek with a respectful kiss before offering a flirty smile.

"Thank you, my brother. Thank you so much, my love," she spit out in her rough sounding English.

"You are very kind and very handsome. I know you. You are a good man."

"If you want another drink sir, just let me know, OK. I take care of you, OK," she continued.

Pleased, the waitress winked before walking over to Anthony. As the two introduced themselves, the bar's front door opened again, and I instinctively knew who was about to enter. Three elegantly dressed Eastern European whores walked inside. They were followed by a short white man with a long brown ponytail. The pale skin of the women instantly drew gazes from the sexually curious Arabic men in the bar. Brimming with the self-confidence that automatically came with their status as white women, the ladies of the night made their lounge entrance an eye-grabbing one. Behind them, the short white man began to dance clumsily to rap music. He struggled to stay on beat while walking, making him look like a damn goofball. All of them knew they were being watched, and they undoubtedly relished the attention.

The group walked over and sat among the young marines, allowing me to positively identify the white bastard, as our target. Jared Spillers was a high-priced scumbag lawyer from Northern Virginia. In Black circles, he was well-known for his trademark ponytail, brash legal approach and his reputation for representing some of America's most loathsome White Nationalists. Due to his preferred clientele and the boat load of Anti-Black litigation he presented to the Supreme Court, Jared found himself on Robert Charles's shit list. For years, we monitored Jared and kept tabs on all of his activities and associations.

Back in the United States, he was a man on the run. The state police in Virginia had a warrant out for his arrest. He was the lawyer for a White Extremist accused of hanging a black fourteen-year-old several years ago. Law Enforcement officials had discovered evidence that Jared knew the well-hidden whereabouts of their primary suspect, a White Identity Extremist named Trevor Hancock. Unwilling to surrender his client to the cops, Jared instead decided to blow off a federal subpoena and took an impromptu vacation to the Middle East. For weeks, he's hid himself here in the Kingdom of Bahrain. Aside from drinking at bars and paying for whores, he usually keeps himself inside his plush hotel room.

Frustrated with the police's reluctance to find Jared, the mourning family of the black teenager contacted Robert Charles. Once the family signed the check, Robert Charles executives assigned the task of locating Jared to Anthony and I. Our mission was to use all reasonable means to convince the man to reveal Trevor Hancock's secret whereabouts. Due to Anthony's prior screw up, this meant that I would have to leave my pregnant girlfriend in New Orleans, and take a long flight over to Bahrain.

Now, I was here in this dark lounge smoking hookah and drinking way too much, while Jessica was back home silently marinating in her insecurities. On the other end of the bar, Jared looked alive with joy as he bought drinks for everyone at his table. If you didn't know the guy, it would be hard to imagine that this fun-loving white man was on the run for obstruction of justice.

I watched the drinks continue to flow as my waitress served them round after round. The young Marines' voices got louder with each sip, challenging the DJ's rave music. Jared's expensive whores seemed to enjoy teasing the young Marines. More than a few times, I noticed the sly ladies cleverly teasing the horny soldiers with hand rubs and naughty stares. Even if white women weren't my cup of tea, I had to at least admire how shrewdly these ladies operated.

Finally, the moment Anthony and I had waited for arrived. Jared rose up from his seat and his legs began to wobble. He awkwardly tried to keep his balance before his body tilted forward in a drunken stumble. Sensing this, one of the young soldiers reached out to catch Jared, but his useless attempt was way too late. Jared's left knee crashed into the wooden lounge table, causing a wave of alcohol and ice to spill out beneath them.

"Fuck me!" he cursed.

"Hey waitress! Somebody made a mess over here, so you're gonna need to mop this up and bring us more drinks."

With panicked urgency, the Ethiopian waitress scrambled over, whipping out her long wash towel upon arriving. While the ladies of the night and their young thirsty subjects scurried away from the growing pool of liquor and ice, my humble African waitress obediently dove to her knees. With light chuckles, the group teased Jared with shaded smiles and hazy eyes. They all were much too inebriated to suffer within their own embarrassment. These were white people, and even on the Islamic Island of Bahrain, whiteness means living life without any notion of remorse or regret.

"Hurry up with the mop job. The floor doesn't need to be perfect. Just pick up our glasses and go get our refills," Jared vented.

Shaken by his abrasive tone, the waitress jumped up from the floor and nervously stared at him. Afraid to challenge him and risk getting herself deported, she attempted to say several words of pitiful English before dashing away with a mountain of fear. The group laughed as she departed, openly teasing her heavy accent and menial manner. Inside my soul, I could feel my black rage reaching its apex. If it had been part of our mission to kill Jared, I would have done so with an abundance of joy. A murderous fantasy of slitting his throat began to play out in my mind. It would be orgasmic to witness the life God had gifted this snow roach, get snatched away by my hand.

Jared clumsily unbuttoned his sleeves before turning around towards the bathroom. As he stepped forward, both of his knees buckled and he crumbled to the floor. Somehow he caught himself, bracing his fall with an extended arm.

Everyone in the bar noticed his fall, and not one person bothered to help him to his feet.

"I'm fuckin alright! I just need to go take a piss….and then I'll really get this party poppin!" He loudly proclaimed while waving his black card in the air.

In a cringe worthy display of misplaced bravado, Jared stood tall while everyone watched. He performed several drunken and offbeat dance moves before letting out a loud shout of personal satisfaction. Everyone in the bar, from the wealthy Arabs to the indentured Ethiopian servants, tried hard to suppress their soft chuckles as he stumbled towards the restroom. No matter how harmful their behavior, no one dared to correct these White Supremacists. It's much too easy for others to simply make excuses for them or try to pretend away their misbehavior. Pissed at his pathetic display, I took my glass and finished off my drink with three large gulps.

Unfortunately for Jared Spillers, his White Privilege was about to meet Robert Charles. Within my world, White Privilege carries zero weight. After exhaling a long white cloud of smoke, I glanced over at a pensive Anthony, giving him the signal. Summoning his confidence, he rose from his seat and slowly walked passed my table after placing his empty beer bottle next to my glass. As the music blasted and Jared's entourage poured out on the dance floor, Anthony slipped into the restroom unnoticed.

When the restroom door swung shut behind him, I immediately spotted the DJ. He was a shaggy looking Russian expat, with an insatiable taste for anything pertaining to Black American culture. Despite looking like he was in his early twenties, the Russian man loved to dress like a late-90's rapper, sporting oversized pants and faded soccer jerseys. The

DJ found my gaze and returned a bright smile while fading his corny rave music into the Three 6 Mafia's song, Tear da Club Up. He increased the volume and the mounted speakers sent vibes of excitement pulsing throughout the bar. Instantly, everyone near the dance floor burst into action, letting out loud shouts as they performed pathetic renditions of popular Hip-Hop dances.

My plan appeared to be falling into place rather nicely, so it was time to get a move on. I took one last puff of the grape mint hookah before removing the plastic mouthpiece, dumping it into my pocket for safe keeping. Using a wet napkin, I wiped down my empty glass and Anthony's beer bottle, erasing our fingerprints. My next pressing task was to secure the restroom. Looking over at the bar, I found my exhausted waitress and waved for her to come. With a genuine smile, she eagerly trotted over to me.

"My hookah bowl is all ash, so I'm about to head out," I informed her.

Confused about my intentions, I watched her eyes widen as she innocently motioned towards her lips with a tightly balled fist. Amused by the awkward hand signal, I tried to contain my childish laughter, but failed. I couldn't make out the sister's English, but her eyes told me she was asking if I needed a refill. I laughed, shook my head and told her no, insisting that I was fine. Without hesitation she kneeled down, picking up the scorching hot bong with her bare hands before giving me a soft kiss goodbye.

With my waitress gone, I paced over to the DJ booth and examined his equipment. There were no stacks of vinyl records, just his thick laptop plugged into an old school mixer. His light blue eyes seemed to glow in the darkness of the bar, as his head wildly bounced to the beat. Pulling off his huge earphones, he reached over, offering me a handshake. I accommodated his request, but his uncaged excitement caused me to second guess our agreement.

On the back of his hand, I saw a crude tattoo of a scorpion outlined in blue and yellow ink. I recognized the prison artistry that was typical among all Russian members of organized crime. The Kingdom of Bahrain is overrun with a wide assortment of Eastern European trash. From the hotel owners, club managers, bouncers, bartenders, pimps, prostitutes and DJ's, the shadowy presence of the criminal underworld is pervasive here. Reaching into my pocket, I pulled out a small envelope and handed it to him. His eyes grew serious as he peeled back the flap and peered down at the stack of hundred-dollar bills tucked away inside.

"That's the first half up front…. just like we agreed," I clarified. "You'll get the second half once I'm done."

Visibly pleased, he leaned over, embracing me with a one-armed hug like we were besties. I felt the warmth of his vodka scented breath as he whispered into my ear with his heavy accent.

"When you're done, you must come to my flat tonight. We will smoke a mountain of Kush and get fucked up, I promise you. Bring your partner too. I'll have all the beautiful ladies ready for you both."

"I'll even bring that pretty African waitress you've been flirting with," he stated with a devious sparkle in his eye. "She gives good head and will please you for sure."

"We can do a lot of business together my friend. We will make a good team. This is only the beginning, I promise you.

Bahrain is our spot homie, together we can run this place. I promise you."

I played him off with a phony laugh, giving him some dap before heading off towards the restroom. There was no way in hell I intended to stick around and smoke weed with this bastard. I'd be an idiot to trust a white criminal like him. The only thing this pale faced gangster could do for me was honor our damn agreement and make sure no one entered this restroom.

Despite my initial concerns, the Russians had done a great job spiking Jared's drink. It took me a while to convince them that I wasn't here to make trouble. A stack of cash mixed in with a few kilos of rare contraband from Columbia was enough to convince these white thugs to play along. I could tell that the DJ had done a little research on me after our initial meeting, which is why I gave him a fake name. The second time we met, he was more suspicious, so he made me promise that I wouldn't kill anyone. Being a man of faith, I looked him in his blue eyes and made that promise, yet everything about that interaction caused me to second guess his real intentions.

I pushed open the restroom door and my nose was wildly punched by the sour smell of hot shit. Two toilet stall doors were shut, while the third hung wide open. In the first stall, I could see Anthony's ugly dress shoes with his pants dangling down above them. In the stall next to him, I saw Jared's fine leather shoes and heard him grunting heavily. The sounds of his loose stool splashing into the watery toilet, echoed throughout the restroom. Satisfied, I flipped the lock on the bathroom door, convinced that the Russian laxative had begun its work. Then I walked over to the sink and started washing my hands. Hearing the signal, Anthony flushed his toilet and exited the stall.

In his hand he held a long syringe, filled with a truth agent cooked up by a Robert Charles chemist. As I rubbed my fingers underneath the cold running water, I peered into the mirror and watched as Anthony gathered his strength before blasting open Jared's stall door. In one quick motion, Anthony grabbed Jared's long hair, jerking his head to one side and exposing his meaty neck. Before he could react, Anthony jammed the sharp needle into his neck and compressed the syringe. For a few seconds, he tried to scream, but the DJ's loud music and my running water muted Jared's whimpers for help.

Still holding him down, Anthony looked back at me wearing an adrenaline-induced smile, eagerly awaiting my approval. Without words, I shut off the water and dried my hands with several paper towels before wiping away my fingerprints. As I tossed the drenched towels into the trash bin, I felt my cellphone vibrate inside my pocket. Pulling it out, I looked at the screen and noticed it was Jessica. After silencing the phone, I slowly walked in front of the stall and stared down at a sleepy-eyed Jared. Seeing his once tense body go limp, I knew the truth agent had begun to run its course.

"You only have two options here" I explained. "The first option involves a lot of pain and certain death. The second option entails you giving my partner the answers he's asking for."

"If you choose option number two, none of your clients will necessarily know you helped us. You'll just wake up in your bed tomorrow morning and your white associates won't know a thing."

"But if you're silly enough to choose option number one….if you go that route…well God help you and your young daughter," I conveyed.

Jared's lazy eyes seemed to come alive when he heard me rattle off the school and home address of his thirteen-year-old daughter. In a loss for words, Anthony and I watched as tears ran down his blood red cheeks. He was in a bad spot, and he knew it.

"You've got two minutes, Anthony," I instructed. "Get the address from him and clean up once your done."

I unlocked the bathroom door and made my way through the dance floor to the bar's entrance. Stepping outside, I was immediately greeted by the midnight heat of Bahrain. Instantly, I felt my skin began to sweat as the smothering humidity engulfed me. Grabbing my cellphone, I unlocked it and connected to the lounge's Wi-Fi. After opening a browser, I logged onto 6zeros.net, a social media platform designed and built by friends of Robert Charles. After scrolling through the site's discussion forums, I accessed a secure communications thread only available to those approved by Robert Charles. Clicking on Jessica's username, I typed an instant message and hit the send button.

"Hey baby," I sent.

"I see you're still awake," she sarcastically replied.

"Whatever you're doing on your little vacation over there…. you need to finish it up and get back home right now."

Looking at my watch, I noticed it was near mid-night in Bahrain, which would have made it around lunch time in New Orleans. After wiping sweat from my forehead, I unbuttoned my collar, preparing myself for Jessica's rant.

"This will be our last night here," I responded. "I should be heading to the airport real soon."

"Well, when you land be ready to get right to work," she cryptically wrote. "We both will be on the clock. We'll need to follow up on some work we did for one of our favorite clients."

"What happened, Jessica? Is everything alright?" I sent.

"Achim, just browse through the Cookout section on 6zeros when you get on the plane. That ought to be enough to get you up to speed before you land," she replied.

Fully understanding her coded message, I sent Jessica a goodnight emoji and patiently waited for a response. She never sent it, so I placed my cellphone back inside my pocket before leaning up against the wall. When Jessica resigned from the NOPD, we both decided to open our own Private Investigation business. Aunt Rita supported the venture, providing us with a large loan which we used to purchase a small commercial office in downtown New Orleans. I fully believed in the idea, thinking it was the perfect cover. I could conceal most of my activities as an assassin, behind the legitimacy of being a P.I.

Ironically, our favorite client happened to be the Chief of Police, Superintendent Mark Spann. Better known publicly as Pokey, Mark Spann took over as Chief of NOPD after the White Nationalist scandal became public. I hadn't known Pokey for long, but he seemed to be an honest cop, and not just the typical boot licking Boule types we normally see in high places. Pokey didn't look the part at all. He was a big jolly brother from very humble beginnings. Yet, behind his overweight exterior, was a black man that could correctly read the streets. Having grown up in the bowels of the 7th Ward, he knew his people and understood their daily challenges.

He begged Jessica not to resign from the force. Given the situation he was inheriting at the NOPD, I could hardly blame him for not wanting her to leave. Pokey needed good cops and Jessica was one of his best and brightest, but neither of us trusted the situation. There was no way he could guarantee her safety in a police department that was still stained by corruption and overflowing with Race Soldiers with an axe to grind. From a distance, Jessica and I committed ourselves towards helping Pokey, but that help would have to come with a certain degree of detachment.

Whenever Pokey needed a trusted ally to investigate a sensitive NOPD issue or provide the unvarnished truth, Jessica and I got the call. For us, the pay was good, but the access to power was even better for Robert Charles. He had no idea who I really was and who I truly worked for, and I wanted to keep it that way. For now, he only needed to know that I was the co-owner of Silent Endeavors Investigative Services.

In the back of my mind, I was always worried about Pokey somehow catching wind of my ties to Robert Charles. For that very reason, my real job as a Counter-Racist Hitman had to remain hidden. As I scanned through the trending threads on 6zeros, I could only hope that my cover hadn't been blown.

While my private worries pulled my attention away from the mission, the bar's front entrance swung open. Heavy bass accompanied a nervous looking Anthony outside. He was rubbing his hands feverishly and even from a good distance away, I could smell his lemon-scented hand sanitizer. Several small red drops of blood were visible on his sleeve, and the crotch area of his brown dress pants was wet. Then I noticed the bleeding scratch below his left eye. Looking at my watch, it finally dawned on me that he was five minutes late.

"What the hell did you just do?" I instinctively asked.

"He woke up, Achim," Anthony murmured in his Bahamian accent.

"The shot wore off. I had to inject him again to keep him quiet. Now he's sitting in that stall unconscious and struggling to breathe."

He pulled the vial out of his pocket and handed it over. Feeling its lack of weight, I immediately knew he had emptied it. Anthony had used the entire bottle on this damn guy. One injection was more than strong enough to put a grown man out for a whole day, yet Anthony had used the entire vial, which held three full shots. If Jared Spillers lived to see the sunrise in the morning, it would be a fuckin miracle. This was the kind of trouble our greedy Russian counterparts wanted to avoid. If pushed up against a wall, I knew they would rat us out to the Bahraini authorities, if they didn't end up killing us themselves. It was time to execute a contingency plan. We both needed to get the hell out of dodge, and fast.

"Anthony, did you at least clean up?"

"Yeah, Achim. Everything's sanitized," he replied. "I wiped down everything I touched. That's why I'm running late."

"How about the address? Were you able to get it?" I followed up.

"Yes, Jared gave me the address before he passed out. Trevor Hancock is hiding in Buffalo…."

"Alright, you can fill me in later," I loudly broke in. "We better get a move on."

"First we go to my hotel," I laid out.

"We'll both change clothes and pick up my luggage. I have two plane tickets on standby. The earliest flight leaves at 1:30 AM. So if we hurry, we can fly outta here and probably be in Amsterdam before the medical examiners find your needle marks on Jared's neck."

I turned and slowly walked towards the parking lot, allowing Anthony to jet in front of me to unlock his doors. In total silence, Anthony drove us to the Gulf Hotel and we went straight to my room. Within eight minutes, we were walking out of the lobby wearing different attire and carrying my bags. As we pulled away from the hotel, I looked at my watch to check the time. It was now twenty minutes past midnight. The bar would be closing at 1AM and if the employees hadn't already discovered Jared's body, they would within the next ten minutes for sure. If Jared was indeed dead inside that stall, our Russian hosts will probably spill the beans and the Bahraini police will begin searching for us any minute now.

"Don't speed or break any laws, but we really need to push it," I advised. "The sooner we get through Bahraini Customs, the better."

Anthony nodded and gripped the wheel. He pushed down on the accelerator and we coasted through the narrow streets of Bahrain. Within five minutes, we had arrived. The late-night emptiness of the local airport was to our ultimate advantage. Ten minutes after arriving, we ditched the rental car and checked into our flight. Fifteen minutes later, we both passed through security and turned in our visas to customs.

Our contingency plan was well-thought-out, prudent and most importantly, working.

As we walked to our gate, my cellphone vibrated, so I pulled it out of my pocket. It was a call from our Russian friend. I ignored the call and proceeded on without a thought of answering. Minutes later, my phone once again erupted with noise, this time a long series of angry text messages. After opening the first two, I got his point and saw no need to continue reading his rant. Our Russian friend and his gangster bosses were rightfully pissed, but I didn't give a damn.

The Bahraini police force and U.S. Embassy Officials were crawling all over their bar and asking all sorts of questions. A White American citizen had been killed, so someone had to take the blame and that person wouldn't be me. As I powered off my cellphone and boarded the plane, I felt secure enough to order a cup of coffee before we hit the runway. I kept my damn promise and I hadn't personally killed anyone. The dead white American was all their problem now, not mine.

These European bastards are infamous for recruiting among the poor countries of Africa, flying young Ethiopian women into Bahrain and stealing their passports and visas. Once they have them, they withhold pay, sexually abuse them and control their ability to return home to safety. All of this is a human rights violation, and just another form of quasi-slavery. For me, this is a small taste of Black justice. The culture vulture DJ should count himself lucky that I allowed him to live.

"Achim, why does my ticket have such a long layover in Amsterdam?" Anthony asked from the seat behind me.

"Because I suspect someone might be looking for two black assassins traveling to the U.S.," I answered. "It's a precaution, just in case the Bahraini government is on to us."

"If we split up, they will only arrest me. You can stay in Amsterdam and switch identities before traveling back home to finish this job."

"Our customer has paid Robert Charles handsomely for our services. So, we need to be sure one of us makes it back stateside to deliver the results they paid for."

Reaching into my carry-on bag, I pulled out a small leather pouch and handed it to him. Inside were government documents and a U.S. passport with another false identity. Along with the documents were instructions and a list of black owned safe houses in Amsterdam.

"Hang around Amsterdam for a day or so. After you catch up on some sleep and put food in your belly, fly to that address Jared gave you. When you locate Trevor Hancock, kill him. If any white collaborators try to help him escape, kill them too," I instructed.

Without words, he took the pouch and buckled into his window seat. Within minutes, the lights in the cabin were dimmed and we were airborne. Once our plane lifted into the dark sky, I felt a sense of victory wash over me. Now my worries immediately returned to the crisis awaiting me in New Orleans.

At cruising altitude, I logged into the plane's Wi-Fi service and searched through the local news back home. Most of the articles were benign, involving the typical fare about local politics, festivals and traffic issues. After scrolling down, I found a national news article that caught my attention.

Clicking on the link, I was only able to read the banner before an embedded video began to play.

"Three Suspects Shot During Record-Breaking Drug Bust In Chalmette," the headline read.

The video buffered momentarily before coming into focus. I immediately heard the ominous sounding voiceover by the local news anchor. As the footage played on, I noticed it was video of a crime scene. In the video, a long piece of police tape flapped in the wind as an NOPD police unit sat still with its bright lights blasting. The video then cut to images of spent bullet casings laying on a cracked sidewalk. Behind the police tape, I recognized the old brick warehouse as plain clothed detectives strolled out of its entrance carrying bundles of evidence bags. Then the image changed, displaying still photos of three Asian men. Underneath the pictures were their names and ages. All of the Asian men had been killed in a shootout with an NOPD SWAT team. The news anchor reported that several NOPD officers had been wounded, but their injuries were minor. The video cut to an interview and I immediately recognized Pokey's wide face, as he stood tall in his freshly ironed uniform.

"Today, the NOPD has confiscated over 300 million dollars' worth of opium. Removing these illegal drugs from our streets will go a long way towards cleaning up this city," he proclaimed.

"This is a proud day for all of us in the NOPD. Our hearts and prayers go out to those SWAT team members who were wounded. Interacting with dangerous criminals is always risky. Our city is grateful for the dedication and selfless sacrifice of our law enforcement professionals."

The video abruptly cut to paid advertisement, so I scrolled down and scanned the entire article. A few months ago, Pokey had asked Jessica and I to investigate activities at this very warehouse. Asian gangsters were pretending to use the warehouse to store seafood caught by Vietnamese commercial fisherman. While legitimately storing catch, the warehouse also acted as a storage facility for all kinds of illegal contraband that had been smuggled into the country via the Gulf of Mexico. Using the lawless Southwestern corridor of Louisiana, Asian fishermen would rendezvous with illegal Mexican Shrimpers to onload bales of opium before sailing back to New Orleans. The entire drug traffic pattern was extensive, and I believed it all originated from somewhere in Asia.

After receiving the evidence from our investigation, Pokey raided the warehouse and now three Asian men were dead. In the back of my mind, I couldn't help but to think that somehow, he had made a grave mistake. Arresting Asian criminals and confiscating their dope was one thing but killing them in a botched raid attempt was completely another. All over the world, Asian gangsters are notoriously violent. This sort of bold enforcement action would certainly cause more violence in the future, especially if crooked NOPD officers were involved.

I powered down my cellphone and tried to catch a nap, but thoughts of Jessica trapped my fatigue. The oncoming effects of an impending hangover also kept me wide awake. All of the mixed alcohol in the Blue Bullfrog seemed like a good idea going down, but now, I found myself beginning to regret the decision. Aside from Pokey's raid, I spent most of the flight staring into the darkness of the cabin, wondering if marrying Jessica was the safest thing for me to do right now. A big part of me wanted to marry her. There was no denying my love for this woman. Every time I looked into Jessica's brown eyes, my soul moved. This relationship was beyond the simplicities of sexual attraction. Jessica added to me. Her quiet encouragement drove me to seek higher quarters, not just for myself, but for the both of us. Yet, the nightmare of witnessing my late wife's bloody execution still haunted me. There would be no way I could guarantee her safety, especially if we were legally married.

She failed to realize the gravity of my past and its tremendous effects on my present. The business of killing White Supremacists for Robert Charles had turned a lot of dangerous people into mortal enemies. For years, I had sustained myself in this lonely life by avoiding any and every attachment. Hell, as a hitman, emotional attachments are one of the first things I looked to expose in order to trap a target. Now, I was sitting in this cramped middle seat trying like hell to convince myself that I could survive in this line of work with a whole family.

The hours slowly melted away and our plane touched down on the runway. As we taxied to our terminal, the flight attendant turned on the bright cabin lights and my assaulted eyes screamed for cover. Glancing behind me, I saw a groggy looking Anthony unbuckling his seat belt. He had undoubtedly been beating himself up over the mission, thinking he had screwed up somehow. Waving my hand to get his attention, I motioned for him to lean closer.

"You did good," I offered. "From here on out, you shouldn't need me anymore. That was the best lesson I could have ever given you."

"Always remember, a smart man merely plans for his success, but a genius has contingencies if things fall apart. You must find a way to give yourself a chance in every battle Anthony, just in case things don't work out as planned. In our business, things never go the way you plan them. You need to bend events towards your will with foresight and bold action."

The cabin door opened and we all filed out into the airport terminal. Following the signs, I made a left towards my next gate while Anthony turned right, heading to the customs area. Nothing appeared out of the ordinary. No one was following me and security in the terminal was light. It was my guess that our Eastern European thugs hadn't talked or that Jared had somehow, managed to survive. Either way, paying them could go a long way towards concealing our secret and making amends.

After buying a bottle of water and taking some Aspirin, I found a seat near my next gate. I took out my cellphone and logged into my international bank account. With a few finger swipes, the final half of my payment to our White European gangsters was transmitted, along with a final message.

"I took the liberty of adding two zeroes to your final invoice. I trust that this bonus might help subdue any anguish your admirable service may have caused you. Have a great life."

With that, their payment of $1.00 was sent to them before I blocked their accounting string and transferred my remaining cash into a separate Robert Charles savings account. If they weren't mad before this, they would surely be incensed by my trickiness now. But hey, fuck'em, at least I let them live.

My time at Amsterdam airport came to an end, so I boarded my plane. The plane flew me across the Atlantic Ocean with the rising sun chasing close behind. After a layover in Atlanta, I finally landed on the sweet soil of New Orleans. Seeing the magical city appear below me, sent familiar chills running down my spine. No matter where I traveled or how long I had been gone, for some strange reason, New Orleans just felt like home.

Walking downstairs to the lower level, I entered the baggage claim section and found her patiently waiting. She was wearing her Sunday's best and her hair was twisted and held up with bobby pins. Her small belly bump barely protruded past her unbuttoned jacket. From the bulge on her right hip, I knew she had to be carrying her Springfield 911. Until I saw Jessica, I hadn't realized how much I missed her. No matter how exhausted I felt, the awe-inspiring splendor of her brown eyes always seemed to give me a boost. I had only been gone a week, yet seeing her stand there in the full beauty of motherhood made the absence seem like ten years.

"Hey baby." I offered while leaning in for a hug.

"Hurry up and get your bags so we can go," she softly snapped.

I'd only been home a few minutes and Jessica was already blazing hot. Once her snarky words left her lips, I watched her face tense up as she turned her gaze away from me. She was pissed and we both knew why. Wounded by her reaction, part of me wanted to lash out at her, but I decided it was best to quietly take my lumps. Holding my tongue, I plucked my luggage from the conveyor belt, and we walked outside to our SUV in awkward silence.

As I loaded my bags into the trunk, Jessica gingerly slid behind the wheel. From her muted grunts of pain, I knew that her back and feet were bothering her. It had likely been a long night for Jessica, filled with painful cramps and bouts of nausea.

"Let me drive, baby," I offered.

"No, I got it," she answered. "Plus, we're leaving here and going straight to church. Aunt Rita needs you to talk some sense into Pokey's ambitious ass."

"So, we're going to church service right now." I retorted.

"I've been flying all day and I'm not even dressed. Let me call Aunt Rita and tell her that I can go visit Pokey tomorrow after he gets off work."

"No way, Achim. Aunt Rita wants this done today," she declared.

"Pokey just shot a campaign ad for Governor Lewis that's going to air during the Democratic Convention next summer."

"Both the Governor and the DNC have gotten really chummy with Pokey, and there using this whole Asian opium bust to boost the Governor's street cred in the black community."

"Because of it, Pokey is getting all kinds of media exposure. Aunt Rita wants us to make sure he doesn't find himself too close to these white politicians. She's worried and she's not in the mood to wait around, Achim."

Jessica merged into highway traffic and we both went silent. I understood Aunt Rita's concern. Governor Lewis happened to be a presidential front-runner and clearly intended to use Pokey's status as a black police chief to boost his poll numbers among black voters. Although I had no beef with the man, Governor Lewis's shrewd tactic had the potential to harm Robert Charles. When Democrat and Republican opponents perform opposition research on Pokey, my name would surely come up. That had to bother Aunt Rita, because it sure as hell worried me.

If Governor Lewis's opponents caught wind that he had associated himself with a man that had ties to a group of black assassins, the media fall out would be sensational. Pokey's jets had to be cooled or we risked being outmaneuvered by our enemies.

"Alright. Let's go do it," I sighed.

"You act like you really have a choice here," Jessica blurted out.

"When Aunt Rita calls, you always go running, but when I need something from you…. I get crickets."

"Come on, Jessica! Aunt Rita's money is the only thing keeping our P.I. business afloat right now," I countered.

"Plus, I still work for Robert Charles. Aunt Rita is still my boss….and she's your aunt. You have no damn reason to be jealous."

"When I need my child's father, why do I find myself having to compete against my aunt," she loudly responded. "Aunt Rita still sees you as her go-to hitman, Achim. That's my only issue."

Jessica turned into the parking lot and found an open space. We both entered the church and followed a soft-spoken usher. Even from outside the door, we could hear the rumbling voice of the Pastor, who was in the middle of his sermon. Self-conscious about my appearance, I wiped the crust out of my eyes and moistened my lips. Three rows from the front, we found Pokey sitting next to a focused Aunt Rita.

Jessica and I scooted down the pew, squeezing into seats next to them. With nodding smiles, they both acknowledged our presence. Aunt Rita and I shared a light embrace as I whispered underneath the brim of her colorful Sunday hat. My words were enough to inform her that our mission in Bahrain had been a success. Unmoved by the news, she barely flinched before returning her ears to the Pastor's sermon.

Pokey gave me a handshake that failed to conceal his inner confidence. I could sense that he had become a much more emboldened man during my absence. Now, he was a nationally recognized figure; a black politico that had an elevated voice within the white media.

"Hey, Achim," he whispered with his deep voice.

"I got something big coming up and I gotta have you on my team."

Pokey leaned back and looked into my eyes while holding my hand in a vice grip. This gesture wasn't simply a friendly request. I knew from the serious look in his eyes that he was willing to beg if he had to. Whatever this request happened to be, it was clearly important to him. With a polite smile, I nodded my head and gently tapped Pokey's shoulder.

"God Love Us," the pastor blasted from his pulpit. "That's what we all must humbly ask."

"In this day and age….Satan has purposefully polluted the meaning of the word…love."

"Today, love means accepting lies and denying the truth."

"Today, love means making excuses for sin, all in the name of finding common ground with the devil."

"Today, the devil walks right into church's and instructs you to disobey God! These days, love means you must reject God's guidance, and embrace the ways of the world."

"Well, folks….I may die alone on this hill, but I challenge the world's definition of what the word love really means!"

"Our Bible gives you the greatest demonstration of what love truly is…and that's telling those you love the hard truth," he blazed on.

"For better or worse, God has always been honest with us. His messengers were honest with us. His son was honest with us. His disciples were honest with us…They didn't sugarcoat or deny truth to appease the world….in fact, the world killed them for telling the truth and showing us what the word love, truly means."

"In the Bible, the world tormented them for telling the truth. These days, the world will shame us all for telling the truth!"

"Today, our neighbors will forsake and curse us for daring to tell them the truth. Are we really ready to continue to love our neighbors, brothers and sisters?"

Half of the congregation stood up from their seats and clapped wildly, while the other half simmered in quiet discomfort. As the Pastor hammered home his Biblical points, I felt myself missing my old life in the ministry. Since the day the terrorist murdered my family, I hadn't missed my church, but standing there and feeling the Lord's spirit caused me to swim in old memories. God's truth will move you to action, if you're willing to hear and accept Him.

The pastor tapered off his sermon and coolly slid into his closing remarks. I watched as both the organist and pianist calmly climbed into seats in front of their instruments. The church grew quiet as the old ladies and deacons instinctively grabbed their purses and wallets.

"Before we take our love offering today," the Pastor calmly explained.

"We need to recognize Brother Mark Spann, better known among our family as Deacon Pokey."

"We've all seen the recent news reports of the fine work our Police Department has done under his guidance, and we thank the Lord for that," he continued.

"Deacon Pokey has done such a great job cleaning up the NOPD, that our Governor has asked him to become an official spokesperson for his Presidential Campaign."

The congregation erupted in hand clapping and loud praise. Pokey was filled with emotion as he was convinced to his feet. The look on Aunt Rita's face was obvious. I knew she hated the idea of Pokey getting involved in national politics. Yet, the high-profile drug bust and all the national media exposure only served to wet Pokey's dry beak. He had tasted relevancy, and Governor Lewis's promise of more cameras was an addiction he wouldn't easily kick. Feeling himself, Pokey leaned in close and whispered into my ear.

"I'm gonna need you bruh. We're going to the big ballgame and I gotta have a shit hot investigator like you to give me an edge out there."

Chapter Two

Beauty Of The Cape

The seconds rolled by without the interruption I was expecting. Instead, I was chained to impatient wonder as the cold blue waves crashed into the rocky shoreline. By my count, my enigmatic host was already twenty minutes late. Heck, if I got up and left, he could hardly be upset with me at this point. After all, being punctual was supposed to be polite protocol among the Asians, especially when you request a meeting with a White man like me. The complimentary plate of Bluefin sushi was empty, so the only good reason for me to sit here, had officially exhausted itself.

Notions of executing a hasty exit dominated my thoughts as I watched the young bartender approach. He was a Black South African of ancient tribal bloodline. His pace was brisk and his face was stained with apprehension. In his hands, he nursed a freshly stirred Bloody Mary, evened out with a mint twist. From the anxiety in his eye, I suspected my host must have called him and ordered another round.

"Sir, your host would like to apologize and offers you another drink free of charge," he humbly offered in impeccable English.

"I can assure you that your host will be here shortly and begs for your continued patience."

He placed the drink in front of me, before cautiously departing. Not trusting the situation, I pushed his drink away before reaching into a hidden coat pocket to adjust my sidearm. Life experience had taught me that it's always the nervous Blacks that set you up. When the bartender finally disappeared, I discreetly pulled my gun out, quickly placing it on the table before tossing my newspaper over it. You can never be too careful in this part of the world. Nothing is ever as benign as it appears. Underneath the contrasting realities of white excellence and black incompetence, flows a river of spilled blood. In South Africa, a person is either comfortably swimming in that blood, or painfully bleeding into the damn river.

Looking out from my beachfront view, I could see the vastness of the Atlantic Ocean as it swirled eastward. The rocky beach below was half-filled with giddy vacationers. All of them were enjoying the early morning sun, after wading in the cool seawater. As a child, my father would fly us all to his summer yacht in Coastal France, before we'd sail south toward Cape Town. Spending our summers in South Africa was once a valued family tradition. However, after our parents passed, none of my self-righteous siblings have made an honest attempt to reignite our old tradition.

It had been over two decades since I last visited Cape Town. All of the new sights and sounds remind me of the weird stories my father would recite. He would always scare me with his tales about the dark savages that lived out in the bush. My old man would tease that blood thirsty Africans wanted to steal young white children. They would cook and consume our skin in some ancient ritual that was supposed to spiritually empower them. As a nervous young boy, his wild stories were terrifying. They left me awake at night and caused me to cling to my mother's hand during our walks through the city. As I got older and stronger, my late father also told me stories about the deadly sharks lurking off the country's coastline. Man eating Great Whites were known to hover close to these Cape Town beaches, waiting for an opportunity to score an easy meal at the expense of an unwitting swimmer.

I loved those stories, and always fancied myself as one of the dangerous sharks and never the unfortunate victim of my father's imaginary savages. For me, vacationing in Cape Town had become a valuable life lesson. It served to remind me that my people were in control, and not some dark boogeyman cowering behind a leafless bush. Like the deadly shark, I was the ultimate source of fear and awe in this realm. I swam through the waters of this planet without a thought of mercy. My life is dominated by instinct and survival, swimmers beware.

The old memories pleased me, so I leaned back into my chair and relished the moments. As the rising sun cast a blinding glare off of the ocean, I saw the patio doors swing open. A small group walked out towards my table, so I examined them as they closed. The group consisted of three Asian men and one fashionably dressed lady. The three serious looking men arrived at my table without any sort of formal greeting. From behind their designer sunglasses, I knew they were sizing me up, anxiously waiting for me to make a wrong move. They abruptly motioned for me to stand before one of them performed a rough frisk of my outer garments.

Mildly offended, I swallowed my pride and gazed over the paid muscle, looking directly at the finely dress woman.

To my surprise the Asian lady didn't blink, instead, she took my challenge to heart and stared me down with remorseless eyes. She was a unique woman, with plenty of sex appeal, mixed in with a hint of danger. Her outer femininity and elegance cleverly hid a streak of ruthlessness that was buried deep within her. I could tell from her body language that this woman was in charge, and she was calling all the shots. This was no ordinary Asian woman; she was in fact, my host.

I quickly erased the notion of my host having to be some greying old Asian man and accepted the reality that stood in front of me. Without protest, I allowed her bodyguards to pat me down, stretching my arms out to my side to accommodate. The men finished their search and moved away from the table having satisfied themselves. In the back of my mind, I made note that they failed to find my handgun, which remained hidden beneath the newspaper. Not wanting to draw attention to the gun, I smiled at my host before pulling out my own chair and politely offering it to her.

"Please have a seat Ma'am," I offered with a traditional Ojigi bow.

Turning on the sexy, she shot me a wordless smile before strolling up to the chair to confidently claim my seat. Mildly impressed, I found another seat across from her and situated myself. Before she could begin, the African bartender nervously walked up to the table, asking us if we required beverages.

"No, we won't be needing any drinks," she declared in perfect English. "Please allow us a moment of privacy. Your work here is done."

She reached into her expensive purse, pulled out a brown envelope, and placed it next to the newspaper. Then she looked at her bodyguards, giving them a hand wave, before they obediently followed the scary bartender inside the building. While stroking her hair, she looked at me and at that very moment I knew this ruthless lady was full of lust. I could literally see her undressing me with her eyes and mentally enjoying a fantasy of me thrusting inside of her.

Life experience had taught me that White men like me, are a delicacy for Asian women. I lived in Singapore long enough to know when these women were offering me an open invitation. Most men think Asian whores are the riskiest, but the truth is that the rich ones are more aggressive. I couldn't tell you the number of times I went to a bar empty handed, only to go home with some wealthy virgin that was supposedly saving herself for marriage. This lady in front of me looked no different from the other women I had conquered. Putting on a show of respect, I removed my Brent Black hat, placing it on the table before purposely running my fingers through my stringy brown hair.

"Aside from being well-recommended, I see that you are also very cultured," she began.

"The designer hat, the custom-tailored clothes, matched with your modest yet exclusive jewelry....Tells me you're a man of excellent taste."

Looking into her eyes, I ignored the bait and instead held my tongue. If she wanted to fuck, she had made all the wrong moves. Some desires are better left unsaid, to remain in the realm of enticing curiosities, until the moment is right. Determined to outwit me, she continued to wait for a response with a flirty grin. My next move would be to continue to dismiss her interest in complete silence. So, I grabbed my Bloody Mary, taking a sip before slowly swallowing while staring her down, adding to our awkwardness.

"My name is Zhilan," she finally relented. "Please allow me to personally apologize for my tardiness."

"As you can imagine, meeting you is not my only business in Cape Town. Prior to this meeting, I had to catch up with an old associate. It was not my intention to keep you waiting, so I do ask for your forgiveness."

"Can we get to the point, lady?" I rudely broke in. "Let's cut out the small talk and get straight to it."

Her transition into another tactic was a boring one. I could care less if having to kill some poor chap caused her to be late. None of that involved me, so it didn't damn well matter. Sensing my impatience, she smiled, picked up her brown envelope and placed it in my lap. She was smart enough to realize that I hadn't stayed here because I was desperate for attention, sex or money. I sat here waiting because I was a pro and that's what pro's do. Zhilan had given me an informal interview, and I had passed.

"The last thing I want to do is burden an absolute treasure, such as yourself, sir," she cleverly slipped in.

I opened her envelope and pulled out a high-definition photo. Underneath the image was the target's name and title, but I didn't need to read it. I recognized the face and was able to figure out the entire backstory behind this meeting. Zhilan and her gang are an open secret throughout the criminal underworld. When she started selling her dope across the globe, junkies began showing up in morgues all over the place. To say that her opium is barely cut, is an understatement. The purity of her product is unprecedented and that alone has created all kinds of problems. There are a lot of jealous competitors out there and each of them are pissed that Zhilan has made it her business to intrude upon their turf.

Looking down at the photo, it wasn't hard to envision a jealous competitor manipulating this person into doing their dirty work for them. Drug dealers using slight-of-hand tricks to eliminate competitors was part of the business, yet something about this situation felt a tad bit different. Looking up at Zhilan, our eyes instantly met and I could tell she was examining me for my initial response. I knew better than to show my hand, so I dramatically flipped the photo upside down and gently placed it on the table next to her.

"Recently, one of my family members was fatally ambushed by cops in Louisiana," she loosely described.

"Aside from the loss of a dear relative, this man seems intent on disrupting my business in the U.S.

"My family is very small. We are fiercely loyal to each other."

"To threaten one of us, is to threaten us all…and we are a family that does not tolerate threats… I'm certain a man in your position, can sympathize with that sentiment."

Grabbing her purse, Zhilan opened it before reaching inside. I watched as this beautiful woman unveiled a silver 3032 Beretta, before matter-of-factly placing it on the table next to my gun. Reaching inside again, she pulled out a nearly empty pack of Asian brand cigarettes and coolly sparked a flame. After slowly exhaling a cloud of smoke, she turned and once again looked into my eyes, attempting to gauge me out. Unable to suppress my laughter, I let out a muted chuckle. This woman knew exactly what she was doing.

"Can you kill this man?" She bluntly asked.

I stared at the upside-down photo while my mind considered her question. My entire life had been devoted to the art of eliminating targets. I had been the lethal instrument of cruel betrayal between partners in crime. If a customer failed to make good on a debt, I was paid handsomely to deliver the final invoice upon them. When governments or otherwise reputable organizations needed a mortal threat erased, they would travel off the grid and hire me. All of my work is bloody and done in public. My clients didn't just pay to have someone killed; they paid for a message. Giving each customer their bold statement was my calling card and I absolutely loved it. Yet, to protect my passion, I needed to be careful and deliberate.

In this business, too many clients approach me with their illogical delusions and wishful thinking. They want me to be their damn easy button, someone who can make all their prior mistakes disappear. Drug kingpins like Zhilan are usually the worst culprits. Most of the time, they don't have enough common sense to maximize the peace of mind my services offer. All too often, I'd give them the price tag or explain the consequences of their request, and they'd suddenly grow cold feet.

Yet, this lady was different. She had seemingly considered all the ramifications and appeared willing to stand in the middle of the fury that would surely engulf her once this was done. For Zhilan, this job was about passion, and not just the self-interested business of crime and money. She had made a show out of placing her gun next to mine. The woman knew my pistol was sitting there the entire time, and didn't even bat an eye. She was on a mission, and if that mission compromised her life, she thought nothing of it. This pretty lady wanted a war, and her genuine passion had captured me.

"Yes, I can kill this person," I whispered.

"But if I do this job, I'll have to hide away forever. I'll never be able to work again."

"That means, this job is going to be extremely expensive for you."

While gauging her reaction, I grabbed the photo and slid it back inside the envelope before placing it in her lap. A smiling Zhilan took the package, engaged her cigarette lighter, than put the flame underneath a corner. She held on until the very last moment before tossing the burning envelope on top of the sushi dish. We both watched puffs of thick smoke rise from the plate, as the remains of the colorful photo turned into charred ash.

"How much do you want?" she whispered. "And how does all of this work from here on out?"

"For starters, Three hundred and fifty million US dollars," I explained. "All in cash, transferred to banks of my choice, in amounts that I specify."

"You'll pay half now and the other half upon completion."

"How many people know of our meeting today?" I inquired.

"Outside of my loyal bodyguards…just me and you," she softly answered while peering over at the black bartender.

"Anyone else who has seen us together today, will be made silent…once we agree."

"Good," I relayed. "Keep it that way. Never refer to our agreement online, in emails, on cellphones, to partners or family members."

"If any word of this agreement leaks, I retain the right to abort the mission and I'll keep your initial payment. No refunds."

"My liaison will contact you upon receipt of the first payment with certain details. From there, all communication between us will happen through him…or her."

"When this goes down, you should stay away from Southeast Asia. Find a place to vacation until the hoopla dies down. After this is done, the authorities will likely want to bring you in for questioning. So it would be best if you remain in a remote location. Be sure to pick a place where U.S. extradition is challenging."

"I must warn you…this will be a life changing event for you and your business," I seriously cautioned.

"My services will only provide you a thin layer of plausible deniability. You should expect that every law enforcement agency in the world will crawl up your ass with a fine-tooth comb once this is done."

"Do you agree to these terms, and can you handle the backlash?" I asked.

She didn't need to say a word. Zhilan's pretty eyes turned into stone as she looked at me with a resolute spirit. The price tag and repercussions of this didn't mean a damn thing to her. At that very moment, I knew that this was how my illustrious career as a contract killer would come to its end. Picking up my hat, I placed it back on my head and slowly rose from my seat.

"When everyone in the whole world sees what we've done and they start chasing after me, where will you hide yourself good sir?" She asked while purposely crossing her long thin legs.

"Sadly, I will be far away from you." I shot back.

"And that, my lady, is a massive shame."

Reaching into my pocket, I opened my wallet and laid a handful of money on the table next to her. Underneath the dollar bills, I buried my private business card, which contained a temporary email address. Looking down into her enticing eyes, part of me wished we had met each other on different terms. The sexual curiosity within me captured my thoughts. Within them, I hid away the vivid mental fantasies of feeling her skin and sucking her tiny erect nipples.

"Use that money to buy yourself a strong drink, my lady. Have a stiff one and give all of this a little more thought before fully committing," I advised.

"You have six hours to email me. If you don't respond within that time frame, I'll leave Cape Town and you'll never be able to summon me again."

I picked up my gun, slipping it into my pocket before tipping the brim of my hat. Without saying goodbye, I walked away from the table and headed for the exit. After climbing into my jeep, I energized my cellphone before pulling away. Driving down Beach Road, I felt a sense of nostalgia while zooming in-between the vast ocean view and tall palm trees lining the street. Even if she didn't meet the deadline, it was refreshing to have visited a country that had been such an integral part of my childhood.

Mindful that she could have one of her slant-eyed minions following me, I decided not to go to my berthing and instead, took a lazy drive about the city. Seeing old decaying buildings that were once bright beacons of success during my childhood, brought back forgone memories. On a whim, I exited the freeway and turned towards the towering mountains, driving down the old street where my family's vacation home was located. When the familiar surroundings of yesteryear came into view, I slowed, pulling over to the side of the road. I got out of the jeep and huffed it up a steep walkway until I found my family's old vacation home sitting amongst a collection of other government owned houses.

Standing in front of the building, I felt a sense of remorse as I examined my family's old property. The rusted iron fence sported a thick pad lock, securing a horror of disappointment behind it. Tall weeds and overgrown trees partially concealed a structure that had been neglected for over a decade. Brown panels of plywood covered the windows and the house's scorched roof was in ruin. Decades ago, this house had once been a palace of elegance. I can still remember my brother and I running around the front yard, seeing who could kick our soccer ball the farthest. When it got too hot, our loving mother would order us inside and spoil us with glasses of fresh lemonade before allowing us to finish our day with a dip in the pool.

Those were the days when we were a close family. Everything in this damned world was exactly as it should have been. Now, this house is owned by the savages. These thieves stole everything that was meaningful to us, ruining the greatness my ancestors had built. No longer able to suffer the agony, I turned away from the horrifying sight and bottled up my anger. Getting enraged wouldn't do me any good. For all I knew, this could be the exact reason Zhilan wanted to meet in Cape Town. If she knew the right people and spent the right amount of cash, she could have possibly found out enough details about me to at least discover my father's name.

Having our meeting in the very country that illegally stripped my father of his land, was indeed a clever bit of context. Forcing me to walk among the Black savages that had set this house ablaze, was smart. Like her, I understood when the line between humanity and the uncivilized had been crossed. When the uncivilized fail to follow our rules, the only proper way to restore order, is bloodshed. She wanted to meet with me in her quest for revenge and security, but in a funny way, she may have been offering me the same solitude.

While walking back to the Jeep, I made sure to check my surroundings before climbing behind the wheel. I was all alone, and there were no suspicious cars or idle watchers. If her goons had been following me, they must have long since given up. Grabbing my phone, I punched an address into the GPS and dialed up directions to an old friend's house. As I hit the ignition, the cellphone let out a sharp ring. After unlocking my screen, I was able to find the new email and noticed the address. It was from Zhilan and the content of her message was short, but clear.

"No need to wait any longer, handsome. Let us both have this dance," she cryptically wrote.

I responded to her message, sending her three routing numbers, along with specific dollar amounts to be transferred to each account, all of which totaled one hundred and seventy-five million dollars. Now it was time to put serious thought into the successful completion of this job. As my Jeep zoomed past traffic, I began to envision how I wanted this whole scenario to play out. She is no doubt expecting something memorable and horrifying, so I needed to provide the maximum amount of terror.

I pulled the Jeep into my friend's driveway and parked before ringing the doorbell. Even from outside the door, I could smell the rotten stink of kitty litter pulsing from within his house. Connor had always been a bit filthy, while I was a paranoid germaphobe. I had thought long and hard before deciding to stay in his home, but using his spare bedroom offered me one less problem.

I heard the loud footsteps of Connor approaching the door. With labored breathing, I could hear him cuss in frustration at having to abandon that comfortable spot on his recliner. After unlocking the door, he cracked it open and peered outside.

"Fuck, mate," he murmured in relief.

"Why didn't you just use the damn key I gave you?"

"Because I wanted you to get off of your fat ass and smell the odor that's pouring out of your house," I blasted.

"The smell hit me as soon as I climbed out of the jeep. You gotta do something about this Connor, it's terrible and it's embarrassing. You'll never attract a good woman living like this."

Connor swung the door wide open and the first thing I noticed was his coffee-stained shirt. This was the third day in a row he had worn the bloody thing without taking a shower. His tight underwear suffered because of his fat belly as it screamed for attention. They too were stained, colored with the dried marks of shit and urine.

Blowing me off, he walked back towards the living room, so I followed him inside and found a cleanish spot on his long couch. Several cats scurried away as I politely knocked them away with my hand. Not missing a beat, Connor unscrewed the top off of his bottle of Wild Turkey and took a small sip before plowing back down into his faded gray recliner.

"I'll be needing those passports and documents I asked for," I proclaimed.

"You got my money?" he sarcastically replied.

"Once I have the money, you'll have the documents. These documents don't make themselves, and I'm not in the business of working for free."

"I have every cent I owe you," I responded. "When I see my paperwork, you'll see your cash. You know how this works, Connor. So get off of your lazy ass and get my shit, will ya?"

Annoyed by my insistence, he pulled himself up, huffing and puffing as he labored into his study room. Connor was allergic to work, but there was no better forger on this side of the Atlantic. His skill at producing phony documents was only rivaled by his lust for anything greasy or drowned in garlic. There was no denying that we were opposites, considering our upbringings. He came from a lower-middle class family, while I had grown up wealthy. I was his loyal customer because of our longstanding friendship. Our relationship stretched back to our days playing youth soccer together in Cape Town's summer leagues. He was one of the few men I could trust, mainly because I knew he had zero ambition. He was more than happy sitting on this nasty throne and governing his kingdom of spoiled cats.

Connor ripped open the study room door and walked back into the living room carrying several sets of documents. After tossing them at me, he dropped down into his recliner.

"It's all there, just like you asked," he relayed with an annoyed sigh.

"I dug up the false names from several nursing homes. They'll pass an initial inspection, but if someone does a deep background check, you'll get flagged pretty quick."

I reviewed the documents, inspecting them for obvious errors, finding none. All of the photo ID's looked real, including the ones were I disguised myself as a woman. Satisfied with his work, I walked into my room and opened my luggage bag. After removing a few items, I found my stash of cash and counted out Connor's money. As I stored my luggage, I felt my cellphone vibrate. Before I could pull the phone out of my pocket, it shook two more times.

There were three separate messages from my banks, each one of them asking me to accept a transfer of funds for fifty-eight million dollars. Lowering myself down to the edge of the bed, I logged into each bank and authorized the transactions. One of Connor's spoiled cats waltzed into my room and began to rub herself against my leg while I finished up the business. Repulsed by the cat's disgusting fur, I promptly kicked it in its stomach, before heading towards the living room. The cat scurried away in pain, hiding itself underneath a wooden lampstand.

"No way, tricky little girl. Don't try to snuggle up and make friends with me now. You'll starve to death before I buy your ass a can of cat food."

Before sitting on the couch, I handed Connor his cash and watched him slowly count the bills until he reached the magic number of ten thousand dollars. Pleased with his bounty, he shoved the money into a small pocket on his recliner and turned his attention back to his TV. Lively images of South Africans dancing and shouting among a large parade of bright red EFF T-shirts dominated the screen.

"These EFF monkeys think they will scare us Whites out of South Africa," Connor uttered. "Well, I don't scare easy mate."

"They got another thing coming if they think I'm about to run. My ancestors came here and built up this country with their bare hands. I'll be damned if we just turn it all over to these animals."

"You guys have to hold down the fort here in South Africa," I chimed in.

"If you run and let these savages have their way, blacks all over the world will smell blood and they'll follow suit."

The news anchor switched topics and transitioned into a story about the Presidential Race in America. Footage began to roll of an overweight black man in a police uniform walking down the street. As the anchor began her lead in, I read his name and saw it was Mark Spann, Chief of the New Orleans Police Department. The man better known as Pokey, grabbed my full attention and my mind once again exploded with ideas.

"Apparently, the whites in the U.S. think allowing their blacks to tell them who to vote for is somehow OK," Connor joked.

"They've got lots of problems over there. Some of them are even having talks about paying the Blacks reparations."

Purposely ignoring Connor, I pushed my thoughts into the possibilities. It was one thing to complain about the state of the world and another to get off your fat rump and change it. Our great ancestors had done what was necessary to capture our future. As a recipient of their blessings, it is my obligation to pass down this advantage to the next generation.

"Do you wanna play a board of chess?" Connor asked while pointing towards the gaming room.

"No, not at the moment," I lamented. "I'm gonna step out and get some fresh air. I'll clear my nostrils a bit, then come back to beat your ass."

Stepping outside, I sat down in my jeep and pulled out my phone. With a quick browse through my contacts, I found the name I knew I needed. I hadn't talked to Alex in months and I was sure this out of the blue call would be received with a good amount of trepidation. The last time we conversed, I quietly blew him off, not wanting him to suffer the indignity of hearing me dismiss his pleas for help. Alex is a proud white man, and white men like us ought not suffer the trauma of having to beg at the feet of anyone

Now the tables had turned. As I pushed down on the call button, I scratched my brain to remember the details of his previous request. The phone rang and after four long rings, someone picked up on the other end.

"Hello?" a confused Alex asked.

Years ago, we befriended each other while competing in dog sled competitions in Southeastern Alaska. Alex was a solid guy and one of the more reliable White Nationalists I'd ever met in the States. Most of the Neo-Nazis, Klan Members or White Identity Advocates I met in the U.S. were all just attention junkies. None of them were willing to do the hard work that was mandated to maintain absolute control over their own state.

Like me, Alex is hard-nosed and dedicated. He's a highly effective Ghost Skin with more than a handful of successful missions under his belt. During my time in Alaska, I witnessed him and his brother Rickey, beat a native half to death for petting one of his sled dogs. The native was only saved by Alex's drunken decision to urinate in the man's mouth, instead of kicking out the rest of his teeth. Aside from his commitment to our cause, he was a reservoir of back channel connections within the Federal Government. This aspect of Alex's portfolio was what I needed the most. What worried me was the price he would surely demand for his convenience.

"Hey, Alex," I answered. "You know who this is, and you know I need a favor. What's it gonna cost me bud?"

The phone grew silent, so I let my blunt words sink in. The seconds passed and I could hear him on the other end chuckling to himself. He still felt the sting of my rejection and I knew this was about to cost me big time.

"How about this," he started off. "You do what I asked you to do before, and we'll call it even."

"It doesn't need to be flashy. Just make sure it gets done and whatever favor you need, you'll have it."

For me, there was no consideration. I needed Alex. He was my best and most reliable contact in the United States. Without his support, I'd be pissing in the wind, and I'd never make it out of New Orleans alive.

"I'll take care of it," I agreed.

"But I'll need you to arrange a shipment from our Russian friends." I added.

"The items I want, are hard to find and even harder to ship. Let's send them to our old stomping grounds over in Prince Rupert. From there, I'll need to travel to New Orleans, Louisiana."

"If you can make arrangements for your contact to service my needs in Canada, I'll make sure everything goes smoothly from there."

"Yes," Alex quickly responded. "I love a challenge. The more difficult, the better."

"Just so you know, I live in Arizona now. Once you leave Canada, make your way south and we'll meet up like old times."

"Good," I jumped in. "Because I'll be using you as a liaison between me and my customer."

"Keep her in the dark as much as possible, and I'll make it worth your while with a bonus on the backend." I instructed.

"If she gets squirrelly, let me know. We'll pull the plug and both disappear."

"No problem," he agreed. "Sounds like we got a deal."

"It's been years since we were chasing each other on the powder. I must say man, it's really good to work with a real brother in arms," he insinuated.

"You can tell me how much you appreciate me when this is finished," I broke in. "After the smoke clears, we'll celebrate over a bottle of sparkling wine."

After ending the call, I sat in the Jeep for about thirty minutes, putting the finishing touches on my plan. It would be best to start this later in the fall, when all the tension in New Orleans had died down. I put together an email with instructions on what and when Alex should pass to Zhilan. Having sent the email, I collected my focus and grabbed a sharp blade before walking back into the smelly house. It was time to help Connor finish off his bottle of Wild Turkey and kill him on the chess board. Sadly, this would be the finale of our earthly friendship. In the back of my mind, I knew this must happen. This was the best thing for the both of us. For this mission to succeed, all loose strings needed to be cut away, no matter who it might be.

"Where have you been mate?" Connor stated with slurred words.

"You aren't trying to leave me tonight, are you?"

"No, Connor," I shot back. "I plan on enjoying every second I have left with you and your silly cats."

Chapter Three

Dangerous Homefront

Jessica sat next to me in the passenger's seat, anxiously brewing within her wall of silence. It was obvious that she was trying her best to put up a good front. From that weird grimace she was unsuccessfully hiding, I knew her back and knees were bothering her. As the months of her pregnancy rolled by, one body part after another have begun to rudely introduce her to her new limitations. The evening walks have long since been cancelled, as are her three-mile jogging sessions. Feeling depressed and unhealthy, Jessica was moody most of the time. I had done well to keep her spirits up, but I hadn't put a ring on her finger. Because of this, her journey towards motherhood was becoming ever more contentious.

Our baby was due to enter the world in January. This brand-new month of November only promised to deliver me more drama. As the baby shower and holidays rolled around with no plans for a wedding, I could tell things were only going to get worse for the both of us. For weeks, we had gone to verbal blows over this trip to Houston. This was my family reunion and it would be her first time meeting many of my extended family members. For everyone outside of my parents, this was to be Jessica's grand introduction. She was eager to make a good impression but was still hung up on not having the official title of Mrs. Jeffers.

"Are you alright baby?" I asked, breaking our hour-long stalemate of silence.

"No," she finally admitted. "I need a bathroom break. Stop somewhere please?"

We were in the outskirts of Houston, driving west on I-10, so there were plenty of places for me to accommodate her request. Taking an exit, I pulled into a Whataburger parking lot and followed her inside. I knew the drill that would soon commence. After finishing up in the restroom, Jessica would inevitably smell the hot food and undoubtedly want a quick bite to nibble on. Preemptively, I bought her an order of fries and a milkshake before finding a spot to sit and wait.

Suddenly my cellphone rang, pulling me away from my state of worry. Seeing the unknown number on my screen, I debated whether or not to answer the call. Then the thought of Anthony reaching out to me using one of his drop phones, entered my mind. He was out on a job in Las Vegas and it could possibly be him calling me for help.

Starting to worry, I pushed down on the answer button and put the phone up to my ear. After offering my hello, I heard a whiny voice that hadn't spoken to me in years. Just hearing the fake thrill woven into Evan's words instantly gave me the notion that this year's family reunion, would definitely be an eventful one.

"What's up A.J.?" he began.

"It's been a minute big cuz. My moms told me you and your baby mama were coming into town this weekend."

We'd only spoke for ten seconds and he was already giving me bad vibes. Evan calling Jessica my baby momma was a clear dig at me as a man, and I had no choice but to eat his punch. I mean, what was I going to do about it? He was only telling God's truth. Yet, Evan was voicing it in a way he knew would burn my chops. I was a former pastor, plus, Evan and I were raised better than that. Our parents had taught us the values of a two-parent home. Hearing Evan mock me, only poured salt in to my wound.

"Hey E," I brushed him off. "How's my auntie doing?"

"You know how my momma is, Achim," he replied. "She's down here trying to run shit like a drill sergeant. My momma's barking orders and buying the grandkids toys they don't need."

"How's the lovely wife?" I shot back.

My abrupt question momentarily quieted the usually confident Evan. His choice of wife was a sore subject within our family circle. Evan's mother felt a certain way about the lily-white woman he chose to marry. My aunt is an opinionated woman that rarely holds her tongue, no matter who it stings. She would often tell me that she didn't raise her son to hate himself. For her, Evan's interracial marriage symbolized a complete rejection of his Black American heritage. This, coupled with his occupation as an employee of the FBI, strained an already tense relationship.

My aunt dabbles in the world of Pan-Africanism and was a new Black Panther back in her younger days. Her deep mistrust of law enforcement was engrained and hard earned. Seeing her only son, seemingly dismiss her own core beliefs, wounded her. The wound caused a rift between the two of them, that ultimately led to my own falling out with Evan.

After the murder of my wife and child, my own faith in law enforcement was fatally severed. In my grief, I became an outspoken critic of Systemic White Supremacy and police misconduct. This put me at odds with Evan, who proudly wore the badge. Our arguments were heated and all of them got intensely personal. We exchanged fiery words that we both knew would mortally damage our kinship. For years, I avoided him like the plague, not wanting to bring our flaming drama upon the family we loved. As it would turn out, my duties with Robert Charles kept me far away from our family get-togethers. Us meeting each other had never been an issue, until now.

"My wife is none of your damn business Achim," he blasted.

"She's the mother of my children, man. You keep her name out of your mouth. Understand!"

"Cool your damn jets," I cautioned. "I mean no harm. It's been years since I've seen you two, and I'm just trying to catch up. That's all."

"OK, big cuz, I just need to make sure we're good before you get here. I'm not trying to cause a scene. I wanna make sure there is peace here today." He explained.

"I come in peace," I confirmed.

Evan let out a long sigh of relief before describing the food our uncles had cooking on the grill. He went on-and-on about the good times we use to have at these gatherings as kids. As he droned on, I got the feeling that something else was on his mind and he couldn't figure out an angle to approach me with it. While listening to him stall himself, I saw Jessica come out of the restroom and knew it was time for me to get moving.

"Alright Evan, I'll be there in a little bit. I gotta get back on the road," I broke in.

"Cool," he softly lamented. "When you get here, swing by and say hello. I need to talk to you about something, in private."

Everything about his request seemed off. Why would Evan want to talk to me? We barely get along, and us having any sort of discussion held potential for disaster. In the back of my mind, the thought of him performing some secret FBI liaison bounced around. If that was his true aim, I'd be pissed, and it would reveal Evan's true loyalties. I shook off the thought. There was no way he could do such a thing and expect me to stay calm. He wasn't that stupid, or at least I hoped.

"I'll come see you E," I answered.

I gathered Jessica's snack and we hit the highway. After an hour, we arrived in Houston. The traffic in north Houston was unusually light, and it wasn't long before we arrived at the public park that played host to our gathering. After parking, I saw familiar faces everywhere. Some of them I hadn't seen since I was a little boy. Excited by all the fond memories, I spoke to everyone, introducing all of them to Jessica before chatting it up about old times. Despite all of her pent-up reluctance, Jessica fit right in among my family. Everyone gave her hugs and smiles when they saw our baby growing in her stomach. Several of my female cousins couldn't contain their happiness, shedding tears of joy as they wrapped Jessica in tight hugs. She quickly became the center of attention. I knew my family was happy to see that I had finally begun the process of putting the pieces of my life back together. I was proud to display her to all I loved, letting them now I was OK.

The brutal murder of my wife and infant son had affected us all. Despite their smiling faces, I could still sense the lingering concerns hidden beneath their hopeful gazes. At one time in my life, I was the brightest star in this family. Becoming one of Houston's most successful pastors was a feat that invoked an immense amount of pride throughout my extended family. Everyone was proud to attach their names to mine and they loved the clout that the association offered within the higher circles of Houston.

After the White Supremacist shooter walked into my church and executed my family, that dynamic changed drastically. For all intents and purposes, the remorse and fear associated with the attack, turned me into a quiet source of pity. More than half of my congregation abandoned our church. Many of them were concerned that our church had become a target for White Identity Extremists. Some of the former deacons publicly blamed me for the shooting, citing my involvement in contentious racial issues.

From my family's perspective, the bright stars that once orbited over my life had dimmed. To them I was a shunned leader and a mortally wounded man; someone that life had delivered a harsh hand to. Quietly, I preferred they view me that way. None of them needed to know the truth about my true calling. They would be horrified if they discovered what I had been up to in this reborn path God had placed me on. Outside of the Italian mob, no sane person would remotely boast about having a hitman in their family.

"Achim, what's up man?" A voice cried out from behind. "Long time, no see."

I turned around and saw Evan standing behind me with a cautious grin. He looked just like I last remembered him, wearing his trademark glasses and close-cut fade. His JC Penny's model outfit gave him the unmistakable look of a proud FBI man. Unlike the other black men attending the reunion, Evan wasn't carrying an adult beverage. Instead, this stalwartly boring man was drinking an ice-cold greater value soda. It was the knock off version of Sprite, and the can's bright colors and cheap tin metal made it an obvious discount purchase from one of our penny-pinching relatives.

"Hey Evan, you wanna talk right now or can it wait?" I bluntly asked.

"If you have a minute, we can chop it up real quick," he responded.

I looked over at Jessica and nodded. Without words, she looked at Evan, offering him a smile before walking away to sit next to my doting parents. I followed Evan as we both walked a short distance away from the picnic area. Satisfied that we had our privacy, he turned around and guzzled down the rest of his soda before smashing the can.

"Word has it that your Chief of Police, Mark "Pokey" Spann, is going to support Governor Clay Lewis's campaign for President." He sarcastically began.

"I've also heard that you and Chief Pokey have become best buds."

"And if any of that were true, what does this have to do with you?" I interrupted.

"It doesn't have a damn thing to do with me," he dismissively replied.

"But it's caught a few people's attention at the Bureau, Achim."

"There are folks at the Bureau who know exactly who you are…..Pokey doesn't know and the damn Governor of Louisiana sure as hell doesn't know either."

I could feel my anger bubbling up within me. This was the real reason he had come here. He hadn't come home to spend time with family or make good on repairing our relationship. For Evan, this was just another business trip. He had allowed himself to become an FBI errand boy. A black flunky they would send my way to deliver a not-so-veiled threat. For years, I had suspected the FBI knew about Robert Charles and my activities as a hitman. Now the FBI had sent Evan here to give a shot across my bow. Yet, I was still confused as to why they would decide to suddenly reveal themselves to me.

"Cut to the chase Evan," I rebuffed. "Why the hell are you here right now?"

"Big cuz, I'm here to visit my momma!" he emphasized, "We both are here for our family reunion, right?"

"I'm just letting you know you got all kinds of eyes on you."

"You may not want to believe me, but I've been protecting your ass."

"A team in DC has been following you for several years now. They know all about your work in New Orleans….how you slaughtered those two white cops."

"The Bureau has even infiltrated your organization, Robert Charles. We know everybody and everything."

"I'm just here to unofficially warn you. The work you've done for Pokey, has brought new sets of eyes on you bruh."

"You are going political now. So, your little silent race war is about to make headlines across the globe. You are stepping into the world of politics, and all kinds of people are going to find out exactly who you are."

Cocky and confident in his superiority, Evan briefly turned his eyes away and suppressed a smile. He had always been a know-it-all. He relished the feeling of lording over others, especially other Blacks. Even as a child, he was addicted to power. Growing up, we were vastly different. While I preferred to spend Sunday evenings alone watching the Chicago Bulls or playing Street Fighter, Evan needed to be outside in the mix with every pencil neck white boy that would accept him.

He needed to be at the front of the line in grade school and volunteered to be a hall monitor in middle school. In high school, he was the captain of the football team and loved to bark out commands to his teammates. He was the quintessential company man, thus the reason he fit in so nicely at the FBI.

It was clear that the FBI wanted something from me. Sending Evan here was their attempt to soften the request and determine if I could be reasoned with. If they didn't need anything from me, they would have arrested me a long time ago. The FBI would have threatened me with all kinds of bogus charges to gain my compliance. From there, they would own me and I knew better than to fall for that scam.

Annoyed with Evan's arrogance, I turned around to walk away, intending to respond to his veiled threat with silence. There was no way I would have a conversation with him about anything involving Robert Charles. I didn't trust him or his claims of having looked out for me. Experience had taught me better. If given the opportunity, he would have used me and Robert Charles to further his own career. The beef between us was no harmless family rivalry. Evan had always been envious of me and my deceased family, mainly due to my early success as a pastor. He quietly hated the attention and adoration our cousins bestowed upon me. In his mind, he believed it should have been him that received all that glory.

"You can't walk away from facts Achim," Evan proclaimed.

"If we have to arrest you to get your cooperation, we'll do it. I'm just offering you a different way out of this."

"I have no damn idea what you're talking about," I retorted. "If you don't mind, I'd rather get back to the reunion and enjoy my time with our family."

"A.J., if you care about your friend Pokey, you'll stop for a second and listen," he blasted."

"I don't care about you E. You're a prick and you've always been a prick," I explained. "You're condescending, obtuse and selfish."

"You happen to be my cousin and that's the only thing that's stopped me from beating your brains out all these years. Consider yourself lucky."

Pissed, I turned around and walked over to my parent's table, leaving a stunned Evan in demoralized silence. I was determined that he wouldn't be scoring any points with his FBI co-workers, at my expense. Arriving at the table, I saw a wave of concern splash across Jessica's face. She knew that my conversation with Evan hadn't been a good one.

"What's the matter with you boy?" My keen mother asked. "You alright?"

"Nothing Momma. Jessica and I are about to leave. We've had a long drive over and she probably needs a nap."

My father looked at me with a gaze filled with quiet disbelief. Despite their reservations, neither of my parents dared to question my judgment. Both of them had raised me and they knew when I had reached my threshold for entertaining Evan's bullshit.

"I guess you and Jessica will be swinging by the house later on tonight?" My mother deftly asked.

"Yes Ma'am, Mrs. Jeffers," Jessica responded.

"We'll swing by for some leftovers tonight. Make sure to save me some of those ribs from Uncle Donny's grill. I'm sure they won't last long out here."

Jessica was playing along. I could tell she would have stayed and chilled with my family, but the sudden change in my mood had alerted her. She knew if something was concerning enough for me to get up and go, it was probably a good idea to just leave. I gave my father the address to our hotel and we said our goodbyes. We hit the Beltway 8 Expressway and drove southwest towards Missouri City. When I hit the far-left lane, I adjusted my rearview mirror and examined each car behind me. Jessica noticed my suspicion and without words, she adjusted her own mirror before unholstering her pistol and chambering a round.

"I take it your cousin Evan didn't come to the family reunion to catch up on old times," she mocked.

"It must be bad if you've decided that running is the only option."

I ignored Jessica's attempt to gain clarity and refocused my eyes on the brown sedan three cars behind us. Its windows wore a tint that was a tad bit dark. To top it off, the way the Sedan purposely kept speed with me grabbed my attention.

"We have a guest," I informed Jessica. "Most likely FBI, but certainly somebody federal for sure."

"You can lose him at the exit five miles down the road," Jessica chimed in.

"That exit ropes into I-10 and I-69. If he loses sight of us, he won't know which way we are going. He'll get caught in all the stop lights and probably give up."

"Great minds do think alike," I softly murmured. "There's a reason I fell in love with your sexy ass little woman."

We were three miles from the exit and in the far-left lane. I hit the gas and rocketed passed the traffic, cutting two lanes over. In the rear-view mirror, I saw the brown sedan increase their speed and fall into my lane, several cars behind. When the exit was less than a half-mile ahead, I hit my brakes and drastically slowed to forty miles per hour. The line of fast-moving traffic behind us swerved as they hastily bolted past us and leaned into their horns for good measure. In a moment of indecision, the driver of the sedan slowed in speed and got close to our bumper. Now the driver knew we were on to them for sure.

"I see a woman behind the wheel," Jessica declared.

"She's a black woman for sure. We should be able to get a better look at her when she passes."

Looking over, I noticed a light skinned black woman sitting behind the tinted front windshield. For some strange reason, the outline of her head and torso felt eerily familiar to me. Yet, I couldn't positively identify the person. Pushing the confusion out of my mind, I focused on the road ahead and put my plan into action.

The exit ramp was right in front of us. Jerking the steering wheel to the right, I pulled over to the emergency shoulder before slamming down hard on the brakes. The sedan motored by, not picking up any speed. As the car approached the exit, it threw on its turn signal and exited the Beltway. We watched as the car came to a stop light and was forced to turn left, towards I-69. I could imagine the driver blurting out curse words in a fit of anger.

"Where is the hotel we booked?" I asked.

"It's just a few more exits down," Jessica replied.

I found a break in the highway traffic and pulled back onto the Beltway. After ten more minutes of driving, we made it to our hotel and I parked in front of the entrance. Grabbing my wallet and cellphone, I walked into the hotel lobby to find a young white woman behind the front desk. She looked to be in her mid-twenties, probably a part-time employee earning some extra cash to help her through some expensive post-graduate program.

"Hello sir! How can I help you?" She recited with polished eagerness.

"Yes, I have a reservation for Achim Jeffers. A one bedroom for two guests." I explained.

The young woman nodded her head before staring down at her computer screen. The sounds of her fingers hastily typing away echoed throughout the empty lobby. As the seconds rolled by, I began to worry as a look of confusion formed on her face. My ears heard her pound on her enter button, getting more frustrated with each unsuccessful keyboard stroke.

"I'm sorry sir. Can I please see your state identification?"

Nothing about this seemed right. Not wanting to alarm her, I dug into my wallet and handed her my driver's license. The young lady looked down at the ID examining it with a consuming expression. Someone had coached her, and the twitch of her lips was a dead giveaway. In silence, she returned my ID and again typed away on her keyboard.

"Mr. Jeffers, you're in room 318 on the third floor. We had to upgrade your room from a queen sized single, to King sized suite due to overbooking."

This was complete horse shit. Nothing about the damn near empty parking lot told me the hotel was even remotely overbooked. With a nervous smile, the young woman handed me my room key and gave me directions to the elevator before quickly disappearing into her office. I knew a set up when I saw it and this was definitely staged. Without protest, I walked out to the entrance before making the decision to play along. Why not see who was behind this? Sooner or later, this would all come to a head anyway.

"Honey, someone is waiting on us here." I told Jessica as I climbed into the car.

"I'll go up to the room to see who's following us. You get behind the wheel and drive off if things get hairy."

"Hell no, Achim," Jessica immediately complained. "We both will go up together. I'm not leaving you here by yourself."

"Jessica, you're carrying our child. I can't risk losing my family again. I need you to listen to me right now."

"No, I'm not staying in the damn car Achim," she cut in. "Plus, you're just being paranoid. What would be the purpose behind ambushing you at a damn hotel?"

"We lost our tail. No one knows we're staying here. Let's just go to our room so you can sleep off all this bad energy, alright."

"Ever since I got pregnant, you've been over the top with everything, Achim!"

Realizing her last choice of words weren't the most prudent, Jessica caught herself and took a deep breath before she went too far. In our moment of silence, I forced the raging emotions within me to a standstill. I knew what she meant with that statement and she sure as hell knew what I had been through.

"I know losing your family has scarred you, but this is different," she softly continued.

"We can't live the rest of our lives in constant fear like this. We have to move on together and believe in each other. I believe in you, now I need you to believe in me."

She holstered her pistol before grabbing her purse. I had lost the argument and Jessica Baker, was going up to that room come hell or high water. Resigned to my fate, I took the handgun from the center console and chambered a round before concealing it underneath my waist band. We walked into the hotel and took the elevator up to the third floor in silence. After walking down a long hallway, we found room 318 near the building's front corner. Pulling the key from my pocket, I scanned it and watched the glowing red light instantly turn green

The electronic door lock made a popping sound, so I leaned into the handle and pushed it half open. Peering inside, I saw nothing but a freshly cleaned room and the end of our tightly wrapped king-sized bed. I pushed the door completely open and walked in. To be safe, I peeped into the empty bathroom before stopping at the end of the bed. Sitting next to the lampstand, was a Hispanic man wearing a brown sports coat and a smile. His thinning black hair was slick and pulled back, while his bushy eyebrows highlighted his brownish skin tone. In his hand, he held up his FBI badge, boldly waving it in the air for me and Jessica to see it.

"Baby, next time I tell you to stay in the car, just do it." I barked in frustration.

"Oh, I see you both are expecting a baby." He proclaimed with fake happiness. "I can only imagine how excited you both must be."

"Go ahead Ma'am…please grab a seat and take a load off. The drive from New Orleans must have been taxing for you."

Annoyed at both of us, Jessica pulled out her handgun and pointed it at him. The FBI man hopped up from his seat and moved his hands, causing me to pull out my own gun and draw down on him too.

"Easy now amigo," I instructed. "No one will believe you shot a black pregnant woman in self-defense… if you aren't alive to tell that lie."

"Achim Jeffers, this isn't that type of visit homie," he laughingly reassured. "I'm here to talk. That's all."

"Well, I'm here to sleep." I replied. "So you can get your ass outta here or get shot to death. The choice is yours."

"I'm willing to bet you have no problem killing a law enforcement officer, do you Achim." He stated with a menacing tone.

"You hate cops, but you sleep with a former cop, a crooked former cop at that. How confused are you, homie?"

"Right now, I'm confused enough to mistake you for an illegal immigrant that's trying to rob my pregnant girlfriend. That's enough confusion to justifiably murder you under the color of law, right amigo?"

"I was clean and you know it," Jessica broke in, interrupting me. "You can make up all the stories you want, but you won't pin that NOPD madness on me, Mr. FBI."

The man laughed before dropping back down on our bed and bouncing like a jovial child. He opened his sports coat and showed me his empty holster before motioning for me and Jessica to put away our weapons.

"Achim Jeffers and Detective Baker, I'm a straight shooter. I'm not here to arrest either of you today."

"So what, you killed a bunch of crooked white cops and saved the Justice Department the trouble of publicly prosecuting our own. Big deal, but I'm not concerned about any of that. Those cops were just as much of a threat to my Hispanic family as they were to you guys."

"Hi, I'm Agent Julian Sanchez. I'm the lead investigator in the Organized Crime Division in D.C."

Standing up from the bed, Julian tried to offer me a handshake. I pulled my gun away and placed it underneath my waistband before looking over at Jessica and waving for her to do the same. Without shaking his hand, I walked over to the desk and rolled out a desk chair for her. Then I heard the room door slowly open and saw another man wearing a sports coat and a badge. This man was short and black. His face was filled with caution as he stood outside of the room. Dangling next to his badge, I saw a gold fraternity emblem hanging from his necklace. Everything about the man screamed, I'm a frat boy. He was a college educated sucker who had to pay for lifelong friends.

"You alright in there Julian?" the man loudly asked.

"Yeah, Agent Porter. We're all good in here. Feel free to join us if Mr. Jeffers will allow it."

The black agent looked at me and pointed at the silver badge hanging from his neck. Shaking my head, I motioned for him to spread his coat. He slowly opened his jacket and displayed his empty holster before stepping into the room and closing the door behind him.

"I'm Agent Chris Porter Jr," the man stated. "I work for the FBI in New Orleans and I'm here with Agent Sanchez."

"Who else do you have out there waiting on me?" I sarcastically asked. "Where's that black woman you had following us earlier?"

"Mr. Jeffers," Agent Sanchez deflected. "Let's cut to the chase."

"We're here because we need your help locating a member of Robert Charles. Her name is Rachel Douglas and we're certain you're familiar with her."

"Word has it, you're the only person that knows her location."

"Who the hell is Rachel Douglas, and why would Achim know where she is?" Jessica bluntly asked.

"Oh, your baby daddy knows where Rachel is hiding. It's his job to know, Ma'am," Agent Porter mocked.

"Rachel reports directly to Achim. He's Rachel's boss."

"They're a hitman couple that's been working together for years now. Their tactic was to use Rachel as bait to lure victims into Achim's trap. First, Rachel disarms them with sex and her beauty. Then Achim here slaughters them in a fit of rage."

Looking into Jessica's wide eyes, I could see the list of questions growing within her. It would have been easier if I had told her about Rachel myself, but having to hear about her from these messy FBI agents, put me on the defensive. I would have no choice but to deny all their allegations and they knew it. For their part, both agents astutely caught on to Jessica's inner confusion and seized upon the moment.

"Yeah, Rachel Douglas," Agent Sanchez piled on.

"We know Achim and Rachel are very well acquainted with each other. Hell, we have videos and images of these two love birds partying together in Biloxi during your little NOPD scandal, Detective."

"Didn't you and Rachel work together in Atlanta some years ago Achim?"

"You guys are making shit up right now," I deflected.

"There is no such thing as Robert Charles. It doesn't exist, so if you're here to spread rumors and lies, you both need to leave."

Both men looked at each other and shared a laugh. They had won the first round and I wasn't sure what they had in mind for the second. Looking over at Jessica, I could see her seething. What was supposed to be a happy trip to my family reunion, might very well end up tearing us apart.

"We can't leave without you telling us the whereabouts of Rachel," Agent Sanchez proclaimed.

"If we do leave without her location, unfortunately you'll be making the trip downtown with us, Achim."

"If you're going to arrest me," I retorted. "Then, come do it."

I mockingly held out my wrists, begging them to place them in handcuffs. Agent Porter's eyes bucked wide and he took a slight step backwards. From his body language, I knew Porter didn't want anything to do with having me arrested. My gamble had worked. Both men's reaction to my gesture told me they had no real intentions of taking me into custody, at least not in these unlawful circumstances. Neither of them had shown me a warrant and if they did take me into custody, I'd walk free on all kinds of technicalities, no matter the evidence they had. Both men also knew that once I left this hotel, I'd be a ghost and they would never catch me nor Rachel. This entire second round, belonged to me.

"I've done nothing wrong gentlemen. We'll see if all the little claims you've made, hold up in court. If you can't arrest me now, then you better come back when you can," I teased.

"Achim, would it matter that you could be saving lives if you cooperated with us?" Agent Porter asked.

"I'm a lowly private investigator gentleman. I'm sure the almighty FBI doesn't need a black man helping them with anything. Right?" I rebutted.

"It's time for you guys to leave and this is my last time asking, so I advise you both to get moving."

"What if the life you were going to save was Mark Spann's?" Agent Sanchez countered.

"I know you and Detective Baker here, are close to the man. The rumors of Pokey joining Governor Lewis's Presidential Campaign have been floating around D.C. for weeks."

"That sort of makes him a high value target, now doesn't it." Sanchez cryptically explained.

He pulled out a small sack and unzipped it. After digging out a stack of photos, he laid them out on the bed in front of me and Jessica. The first few photos were of a heavily tattooed Asian man handcuffed to a metal chair. In front of him sat several strange looking white men with big noses, cheap long sleeve shirts and bad haircuts. My instincts told me that whoever this Asian guy was, he had gotten himself in enough trouble to be interrogated by an angry group of French detectives.

The other photos were pictures of a small hard drive and several screen shots of a long email chain written in what appeared to be Chinese Mandarin. Sanchez grabbed the photos of the email and tossed them towards my edge of the bed. Curious, Jessica grabbed a few photos and gave them a quick once over before laying them back down.

"Our allies in Paris arrested this man. He is a mid-level operative in the Lima drug trafficking ring over in France," Sanchez began.

"Someone named Zhilan has taken over leadership of the Lima gang and made Lima into one of the most aggressive and violent organized crime syndicates in Europe."

"Over the past few years, Zhilan has begun to move his heroin worldwide to places like Paris, London, Madrid, San Francisco, New York and New Orleans."

"When you two gave Pokey that information about those Asian heroin dealers operating in that warehouse in Chalmette," Porter jumped in.

"There was no way you two could have known that the man in charge of Zhilan's New Orleans operation, was his nephew."

"You were doing what the NOPD paid you to do and Pokey simply did his job; getting illegal drugs off the streets."

"But the NOPD raid went bad," Sanchez took over. "It went totally off the rails."

"There was a shootout and Zhilan's favorite little nephew ended up getting shot to death by the hands of a NOPD swat team."

"Then the cops in Paris arrested this gentleman, and found all kinds of interesting evidence in his possession," Agent Sanchez proclaimed while holding up the photo of the Asian gangster.

"If you can read Chinese, this email is mostly about shipments and dirty money. But if you read till the end, you'll find a rumor that Zhilan has put out a contract on Mark "Pokey" Spann's life."

"It's believed that this contract has been assigned to an overseas hitman named, the Tarpon."

Hearing his name and seeing the man's face in my mind, caused me to bite down hard on my lip. Sanchez and Porter were studying my reaction, so I put on a poker face while leaning back in my chair. He was called the Tarpon for a reason. This guy was not just a pro, he was an artist. The Tarpon is one of the most dangerous assassins in the world. Aside from his knack for eliminating hardened targets, the Tarpon was especially brutal to black people. When the Tarpon showed up, black couples would disappear or black teenagers would be found hanging from trees. Black judges would mysteriously commit suicide by jumping into a river or perish in hit and run accidents. Little black girls would suddenly run away from home, never to be seen again. The Tarpon was responsible for scores of black lawyers mysteriously dying in their sleep. If his aim was to make a loud statement, a violent drive-by would conveniently happen at a family picnic or little league game. He was an evil genius who knew where and how to stir death's pot.

The Tarpon was in the rolodex of every White Supremacist group from San Diego to Ukraine. At one point, both the FBI and the CIA had hired the man themselves. If you were a blood thirsty racist and you needed plausible deniability, the Tarpon delivered five-star service. The man could come out of nowhere, then melt away and disappear without a trace. No one knew his real name, or where he had come from. There were rumors that he fluently spoke at least six languages and had the ability to construct near perfect disguises. Nearly everything anyone knew about the Tarpon came from one urban legend or another. In the small world of hitmen, he was a mysterious King Kong or an invisible Paul Bunyan.

"So, I take it you've heard of the Tarpon?" Agent Porter inquired.

"Of course I have," I answered. "I already told you, I'm a P.I. and it's my business to look into people."

"The guy is a hired killer. An assassin from somewhere overseas."

"Heck, didn't you alphabet boys pay the Tarpon to kill Black Lives Matter protestors in Ferguson, Missouri?" I pressed.

"I don't know why you guys need help stopping a man that's been on your payroll for years."

The black agent laughed at my statement. It was obvious that Porter and my cousin Evan were the same type of Negro. To them, massa was never late and always on time. Porter flatly dismissed the notion that the squeaky-clean FBI would deal with such a person, yet I saw the hidden reality in Agent Sanchez's blank stare. The FBI had done business with this deadly mercenary. When paranoia and power are married, it will make space for uncomfortable alliances, which was partly the reason both of these men were standing before me now. The FBI hated Black Empowerment. To them, Robert Charles was no better than a band of Arab Jihadists. Yet, if it meant saving themselves some embarrassment, the FBI would happily sneak into my hotel room and try to bargain with me.

"Your girlfriend Rachel is the only confirmed person to ever have contact with the Tarpon," Sanchez barked.

"We're going to find her with or without your assistance. If we find her without you, it won't be good for you…and that's a promise."

"Achim, this would be much easier on all of us if you just cooperated," Agent Porter jumped in.

"If you don't help us, the FBI will be sure to remember that you didn't lend a hand when we asked."

"So, this Rachel woman is your secret girlfriend, Achim?" Jessica lamented. "Me and you are gonna have one hellva conversation tonight."

She rolled her eyes as she looked away. She was pissed and seemed more than eager to believe the lies agent's Porter and Sanchez were offering. Part of me wished I had told her about Rachel, but I never had the slightest inkling that I might need to. For the most part, my relationship with Rachel had remained a professional one. Trying to explain this to an already emotionally anxious Jessica, would have been a task doomed to fail.

"Spreading lies about my personal life and threatening me isn't going to work," I declared.

"If that's how you guys operate when you need help, it's about time you both got the fuck out of my hotel room."

Agent Sanchez leapt up from the bed and both men walked to the exit. The FBI was pushing a hard bargain and they were clearly desperate. If the FBI was this desperate, they were destined to fail. Pokey wouldn't stand a chance and Rachel would be in serious danger if they found her. She had been the Tarpon's lover and the government was sure to use her as a scapegoat if Pokey were to be assassinated. Worse, Agent Sanchez's not so veiled threat against me and Robert Charles, meant something. I could see the FBI pinning Pokey's murder on Robert Charles, using my association with him to formulate some wild conspiracy theory. Whatever their secret plan happened to be, I needed to stop it or at the very least, confuse it. As Agent Sanchez pulled the door open, I knew it was time to offer my own hard bargain.

"Good luck finding Rachel gentlemen. She's a hard woman to locate and even harder to work with," I began.

"You boys haven't done your homework. You don't even need Rachel, because she's not the only person that's seen the Tarpon up close. Hell, I doubt she'll even want anything to do with the bastard."

"What you boys need is someone who knows just as much about the Tarpon as she does."

"And you idiots happen to be walking away from that person right now."

My hotel room door stopped swinging and both men looked back at me. I knew they thought I was full of shit, but being prudent federal investigators, they had to take my claim with some measure of seriousness. For a few seconds, both men quietly considered my words and waited on me to further explain. Relishing the moment, I stood up from my seat and walked towards them, closing the distance.

"I'm familiar with the Tarpon. I've researched and studied all of his tactics," I continued.

"But more importantly, I've seen the man for myself, and I know his weaknesses."

"Bullshit Achim! Not many people on this earth have ever seen this guy, let alone lived to talk about it," Agent Sanchez declared. "You're a horrible liar!"

"Well, you're looking at one of those people amigo." I rebutted.

"If you want me to work with you, I'll need three things from the FBI."

"One, we leave Robert Charles and Rachel out of this situation entirely. Two, the FBI officially hires me and my wife as Private Investigators, meaning you're gonna pay for my services. I'm not talking about under the table shit, I mean above board with official government receipts…the whole nine."

"No way!" Agent Porter shot back in a fit of anger. "We aren't hiring Robert Charles, you guys are domestic terrorists. The fuckin taxpayers would revolt."

"Did they revolt when you hired the Tarpon to kill black politicians in South America?" I calmly asked.

"Did they revolt when the Tarpon killed those grassroots protestors in Ferguson?"

"You can threaten me all you want, but the truth about your dealings with this monster will eventually come out. This man is a problem you folks helped create. There are quite a few people who have knowledge that this bastard was once a hired gun for the FBI."

"Come after me and Rachel all you want, but you better remember, I know secrets too. You hurt me and I'll definitely hurt your ass right back…and that's also a promise."

Both men cut their eyes away from me. They had me by the balls, but I had also shoved my hand right up their dress. Having to protect Rachel, Robert Charles and Pokey forced my hand. The FBI cleverly used all three of them against me, but I held the ultimate ace up my sleeve. A number of Robert Charles operatives had hard evidence of the FBI's dealings with the Tarpon. They had hired him to unlawfully kill political protestors along with several black South American politicians. The South American incidents were revenge killings, aimed at getting retribution for the brutal execution of two undercover DEA agents, while the Ferguson murders were part of the Blue Lives Matter pushback. Just like the Tarpon, the high and mighty FBI wasn't above sending its own bloody race-based messages.

"OK Achim, what's this third thing you need?" Agent Sanchez pressed, while letting out a loud sigh.

"My final thing is this," I continued while looking right into his eyes.

"I'm not doing this to arrest this bastard. If you FBI fuckers are looking to put the Tarpon in jail, you'll need to find someone else. If I do this, I have to know you boys will go all the way."

The boldness of my last request took Agent Sanchez aback. He struggled to conceal the surprise that splashed across his face. Quickly gathering himself, he ushered Porter back into my room and softly shut the door behind them.

"I take it you're not a fan of the Tarpon." Agent Sanchez cleverly asked. "Is your beef something personal with this man?"

"Does the FBI agree to my terms, Agent Sanchez?" I rebuffed, ignoring his direct inquisition.

"Well, I can't put anything like that in writing. You know the FBI could never do that, so you'll have to take my word on this, Achim." He admitted.

"I'll take a handshake for now and I'll send the government an invoice once you two leave my room." I offered.

Agent Sanchez walked past his stunned partner and shook my hand. His grip was light and weak, so I squeezed hard and looked right into his beady eyes. Sensing my seriousness, he let go first before backing away.

"From here on out, I'm a Private Investigator," I pointedly proclaimed. "That's what you'll confirm with Pokey, your folks at FBI headquarters, and anyone else who asks."

"How do we trust this guy?" Agent Porter opined. "Robert Charles will stab us in the back the minute they get a chance."

"Then don't trust anybody," Jessica sarcastically answered. "Because we sure as hell don't trust you either."

"I'm a former cop, so I know firsthand how low down and sneaky you Federal Agents really are."

"I guess the mutual mistrust in this room will keep all of us on our toes," Sanchez laughingly stated. "And that can be a good thing."

Agent Porter reached into his pocket and gave me a small business card. On the dark blue card, I read his full name and saw a very familiar address. It was the FBI building in New Orleans.

"We are having our first planning meeting on Monday. It will be held on the fourth floor, room 429," Porter explained.

"Make sure to arrive bright and early so you can meet everyone, mister Private Investigator."

Chapter Four

The Snowy Town

I could feel the ferry's engines rattle under my feet as they struggled to fight through the powerful current. The ferry pilot steered us across the cold river towards the snowy banks of Prince Rupert, Canada. The vessel felt overcrowded as its passengers consisted of hordes of natives flying in from Anchorage, Alaska. Behind us sat Prince Rupert Regional airport, situated on a small rocky island. On the other side of the river, the frigid town of Prince Rupert sat in front of snow-covered mountains that dominated the skyline. As the ferry approached its landing, I noticed a rusty tugboat named Alaskan Spirit, moored at an old railroad dock. The crew was alive on the tug's back deck, heaving away at lines and running powerful machinery. They were hard at work pulling several shots of heavy surge chain out of the icy cold water. If the weather wasn't so biting, this would have been a beautiful sight to behold. But the freezing conditions seemed to give this awesome spectacle a harsh dose of suffering. In this part of the world, winter never truly leaves, it just takes a power nap.

This cold weather was a shock to my well warmed blood. I had lived in Southeast Asia for so long that my body had forgotten how to endure this type of cold. During the long flight, I tried to convince myself that I could tough it out. But the reality of standing out in this mess only confirmed how spoiled I had become. Trying to think beyond the numbing pain in my fingers and toes, I wondered if the police in Cape Town had discovered Connor's body. It had been weeks since I left him hanging from his bedroom ceiling. I was sure that the smell of his rotting corpse must have gotten his neighbors attention by now.

Connor had been a childhood friend and was one of the best counterfeiters in the business. If I were to truly disappear after this job, there needed to be no means of finding me. Plus, my trust for Connor had begun to wane. His alcoholism and obesity were getting out of control. He was losing his edge in a fast-evolving world. All the police needed to do was threaten him and he would be so worried about taking care of his damn cats that he'd snitch on me for sure.

Pushing the thoughts of Connor's smelly cats aside, I grabbed the handles on my bags and inched towards the exit before the ferry's crew finished tying us up. At the ferry landing, there would only be a handful of taxis and I wanted to make sure I was first in line to hop into a warm backseat. The crew lowered the gangway, and I scooted across first, beating several native families to dry land. I walked on the icy sidewalk to an idling taxi with a badly faded paint job. White mist poured out of its exhaust pipe while an East Indian driver sat behind his fogged-up wind shield.

"Can I get a ride?" I asked.

Without words, the driver popped open the trunk and stored my luggage while I climbed into the back seat. Inside the taxi, the strong scent of body odor mixed with the hot metal from the taxi's heater. After restarting his toll machine, the driver looked back at me and in perfect English asked for my destination.

"I'll be heading to the Foxtail hotel," I instructed.

We pulled away from the ferry landing and turned onto the main drag. The driver hit the accelerator as the low volume hip hop music gently leaked out of his factory speakers. I could feel the taxi swerve as it glided over the icy road. Concerned, I considered buckling my seat belt, but instead chose to hold firm to the arm rest. The driver glanced back before slowing his taxi down to an acceptable speed given the conditions.

"Your first time in Prince Rupert?" He confidently asked.

"No, I've been here before. It's been about seven years since I last visited," I explained.

"The Foxtail is as nice as it gets here nowadays," he continued. "There isn't much to this place anymore, besides the rail yard and the local gentlemen's club."

"Yeah," I agreed. "Back in the day, I use to come here and hang out with old buddies. We had a dog sled team and we would always meet up here before traveling north to Alaska."

"Dog sledding," he said curiously. "We don't do any sports like that where I come from."

"Where are you from, my friend?" I jumped in.

"I'm from Bangalore, India. I came to Canada for school about five years ago and just decided I wanted to stay."

"I've been in Prince Rupert for about three years now," he detailed. "I live here with some distant relatives on my mother's side. You know, just waiting on my citizenship to get approved."

"Good for you partner. Good for you," I lamented, ending his attempt at small talk.

The driver came to a lonely stop light and made a left towards the river. As we drove past the rustic looking Walmart, memories of the good ole days came flooding back. Buildings that looked new and exciting during my last foray in Prince Rupert, now seemed small and depressed. Gone were the days when proud white men like me could come here and live out our freedom. We once owned this town. It was our little place of solitude, away from the rest of the world. In this place, no one would bother us and everyone here understood the unspoken.

Now Prince Rupert had seen an influx of foreigners from Asia and Africa. Having to share our town with these Non-Whites was infuriating. No matter where we built, these uncivilized beasts will always find a way to force themselves upon us.

The driver pulled up to the Foxtail Hotel and parked in front of the main entrance. He pulled a lever on his meter and relayed the price. I reached into my wallet and handed the driver his fee, plus a generous tip before collecting my bags and heading towards the entrance. As I entered the lobby, I felt my cellphone vibrate. Looking down at my screen, I noticed that my old buddy Alex was checking in on me.

"Hey bro, I made it." I answered.

"Good. Your shipment arrived two days ago," he explained.

"It's being stored at the shipment warehouse. By the way, Diane is on her way to pick you up right now."

"Why is she coming so damn early?" I vented. "I haven't even checked into my room yet."

"Hey, hell if I know," Alex laughed. "Maybe she misses you?"

"Anyway, she's coming early because a few locals have a keen interest in your shipment. According to Diane, she's seen them snooping around. It's probably best that the both of you move it before those foreigners magically make it disappear."

"This isn't the same Prince Rupert we're used to. There are a lot of new players in town, so watch your six."

Alex and I had the same thought. There were indeed a lot of new faces in town these days. Competition in the criminal underworld is fierce. Everyone is trying to carve out their own little territory and ensure they stay cut in. I hung up on Alex and walked to the front desk. An over-anxious Diane would for sure be driving up any minute now, and I needed to hurry.

Diane was a close friend from my old dog sledding days. From the first moment I met her, I've known her to be Rickey's main squeeze. Both were heavily involved in the Canadian underworld and were known to be extremely violent. Back then, nothing about either of them particularly stuck out to me. I suppose we were all dangerously flawed and always in search for some wild new adventure. We fancied ourselves as invincible and if there was a challenge, with enough hard liquor, we'd put our lives on the line to conquer it. Now, Alex's brother Rickey has found himself in Federal prison. With time, we had all grown up and fully grasped our own mortality. Diane had to survive up here without Rickey, and this caused her to have to do some very unsavory things.

I checked in at the front desk and found my room on the fifth floor. When I entered the room, it felt stale and dull. The single window offered a depressing view of the icy roads below, with a backdrop of the freezing river behind them. As I felt the cold air seeping in from outside, I reached down and turned on the room's space heater. Immediately, the machine came on with an annoyingly loud buzz and began the hopeless task of warming the chilly space.

Dumping my luggage on the hard bed, I unzipped its latches, and found my hidden compartment. I reached inside until my fingers touched the cold metal. I pulled the pistol from its secret space and inspected it. As I continued to search through my bag, I found the coat holster and adjusted it to fit underneath my heavy leather jacket.

After placing the gun back in its home, I heard my cellphone ring. It was a number that I wasn't familiar with, so I tossed the phone on the bed and grabbed my shower shoes. As soon as the phone stopped ringing, the sound of a newly arrived text message followed behind it. Once again, I picked up the phone and read the screen.

"It's Diane! It's so good to have you back in PR where you belong! Settle in and I'll be waiting on you downstairs. When you get ready, look for my White F-250," she texted.

Alarmed, I walked back to the window and peeped down towards the ice covered streets. I didn't see a white truck anywhere but I knew she was down there waiting. For some reason, Diane was rushing me. We were supposed to be meeting up tomorrow, but she wanted to get right to business. As I walked away from the window, I determined that whatever her reasoning, it would have to wait until I at least took a shower.

After a lukewarm shower, I changed into my warmest clothes and tucked the holster underneath my leather jacket. Making my way downstairs, I walked out into the cold and paced the sidewalk looking for Diane's truck. I found it in the back of the hotel, parked in a narrow alley way. She sat behind the steering wheel, playfully waving her hands while wearing a jovial smile that reminded me of our younger days. As I approached the passenger's side door, Diane popped open the lock and I climbed in.

"My goodness," I began. "It's been way too long! How's life treating ya?"

Diane looked at me with those blue eyes that could snatch any man's heart. It had been years since I'd last seen her, but she still looked like a young twenty something. She had always been a beautiful woman. For me, she had also been an off-limits beautiful woman. Besides being a sociopath, Alex's older brother Rickey, was also extremely possessive. He once stabbed a competitor sixteen times before a race because he said he caught the man eyeing her. At all of our dog sled competitions, it was common knowledge that no one approached her. If anyone did, they risked their life. Due to this, she barely talked to anyone outside of our tight circle of friends and family.

Despite her lover's jealousy, Diane always found a reason to talk to me. Rickey never seemed to mind me talking to her all that much. In the back of my mind, I knew why he was never jealous of me. I never had any thoughts of ill-intentions, but for some reason, I always got the sense that she genuinely liked me. That always bothered me because her lover trusted me with his most prized possession, yet Diane would try to push the limits of our relationship in roundabout ways. For her, I wasn't sure if it was the game of cat and mouse, but for me, it was about white loyalty. No piece of pussy was worth betrayal and disloyalty. Life had taught me that painful lesson, the hard way.

"It's so good to see you. Welcome back!" She said with an exploding smile.

"It's good to be back," I pretended.

"So, how is Rickey? Is he holding up alright?"

Hearing the name of her lover caused her face to flicker . I knew right then and there that the two were having issues. Putting on a valiant act, I respectfully listened as she tried to tell me how Rickey was adjusting well to life in prison. I knew all of it was hog wash. Rickey was just like me. Neither of us would adjust well to living life like some caged up nigger. .

"I know we were supposed to meet up tomorrow, but I need to make sure your gear is safe and secure, so we'll go do a little pick up before dinner this evening," she proclaimed.

Diane put the truck into drive and pulled onto the street. After the stop light, she turned right and drove down the main drag until we arrived at a large snow-covered warehouse.

"I've seen some foreign guys hanging around here," she said in a serious tone.

"Most of them are from the Middle East. There's a whole gang of them and they like to steal shit."

"The gang started making moves in Prince Rupert several years ago. Drugs, guns, stolen cars, and everything in-between."

"They're probably assuming your box has guns inside and they want a piece of that action," she explained.

"Whatever is in my box is my damn business, not theirs." I warned.

"If they start to play that game with me, they better be ready. I don't extort easy and this ain't some third world shit hole, this is our town."

"That's why we're doing this today," she explained. "We'll take the cargo out to my place. It will be safe and sound there, away from these snakes."

Diane pulled into the warehouse's entrance and we slowly drove past an overweight security guard and his barking dog. She hit the brakes and came to a sudden stop before pulling a clipboard out from underneath her seat. I watched as she carefully examined the notes on the page and looked over towards the Bay 46 sign. Finding the location, she gently pushed down on the accelerator and guided us down a narrow gravel road towards Bays 40-49.

We drove a short distance and the sounds of her tires rolling over the small rocks came to a halt. Diane turned the steering wheel hard left and we coasted into Bay 46. Inside the dim cargo bay, I saw three employees aimlessly standing around as they watched us approach. She put the truck into park, cut off the engine and climbed out to chat with the men. After a short discussion, the men walked over to my wooden crate and used a forklift to load it into the bed of her truck.

One of the men, a rough looking East African, handed me a clipboard and a black pen. After reviewing the documents and confirming that the crate was indeed mine, we departed and headed for her house.

"Now if someone wants to steal your shit, they'll have to come all the way out to my place to do it," she joked.

"You're still a red wine man I assume?"

"Of course I am," I said with a smile.

"Cabernet is king. I'll drink nothing less than that my dear."

Diane teased me with a flirty smile before pulling her eyes back to the slippery road. We were heading away from town and into the dark green hills leading up the mountains surrounding Prince Rupert. I had been up here plenty of times and the old memories of me and Alex racing our expensive sports cars up this road came flooding back. During dog sled season, Rickey and Diane would invite the entire team up to their property where we would fry cod and drink beer in front of an open campfire. Almost everyone besides me smoked weed or sniffed coke, so I was always the designated driver. The night would usually end with all of us jumping into the Jacuzzi, skinny dipping before everyone passed out from exhaustion.

"I bought a special bottle of wine that reminded me of you when I saw it," she explained.

"It's a vintage red. I hope you like it because it cost me almost two hundred bucks."

"I just need something to eat, Diane," I interrupted.

"It's been a long day and I've had several really long flights and layovers. I'm hungry and I need to lay down. That's my focus right now."

Catching the hint, she chose to giggle at me, showing off her pretty red dimples and gorgeous blue eyes. As she eased into her driveway, Diane put the truck into park and turned off the headlights. When the truck went dark, the wild forest surrounding her two-story cabin seemed to disappear into the total darkness of the moonless night. Next to me, I saw the smiling silhouette of Diane lean closer, then I felt her small icy fingers invading my knee.

"You ought to know better. When have I ever invited you out here and not fed you?" She softly asked.

"In the cabin, there's plenty of fresh salmon and fire roasted potatoes. You can eat as much as you want. But before you turn in for the night, we're sharing one glass of wine together, mister."

"It's been years since we last saw each other. You can spare an hour of sleep to catch up with an old friend, can't you?"

"Well, Diane, if you insist. It looks like I have no other choice but to be your gracious guest tonight," I grumbled.

We both climbed out of the truck and I immediately felt the intense silence of the cold forest around us. Following her to the unlit front door, I opened the two bottom buttons on my jacket before adjusting my hidden holster for easy access. When we reached the cabin's front entrance, two motion sensors kicked in, blasting away our night vision with their intense white beams.

"Now if I can only find my keys," Diane joked as she fished around in her small purse.

After a few seconds, she found the right key and jammed it into the bolt lock. With several twists, the lock slid into the open position and Diane pushed in the heavy door. I instinctively wiped my feet on her rather large welcome mat before stepping inside. Both Rickey and Diane used to be very particular about guest walking around their place with filthy shoes, so I did my best to respect them. Strolling into the living room, I quickly noticed that nearly everything about the cabin had changed since I last visited. Gone were Rickey's pool tables and his wall mounted sword collection. A finely polished wood dining room table and several colorful abstract paintings replaced them.

"You can take your jacket off and hang it over there," Diane instructed as she handed me a long coat hanger. "I'll go fix you a plate and pop open our bottle of wine."

"It's rather chilly in this damn house. I'll keep my jacket on until I start up the fireplace," I objected.

"What happened to all of Rickey's stuff?" I quickly deflected.

"All of his stuff is away in storage," she explained

"If he ever gets out of prison, I'll bring it all back out but for now, this cabin is going to have to show a woman's touch."

Diane walked into the kitchen, while I readied her large fireplace in the living room. Next to the fireplace, a neat pile of chopped wood was perfectly arranged for easy access. I tossed several thick pieces of wood inside, stacking a small pyramid before setting the wood ablaze. As the smoke began to billow out of the chimney, I closed the gate and sat down in a rocking chair. She walked into the living room carrying a large white plate in one hand and a TV remote in the other.

"Here's your dinner, caught fresh from the river two days ago," she offered with a smile. "The potatoes were glazed with a bit of olive oil and rosemary before they were roasted."

"If you wanna catch the game, I have the league pass subscription. Just make yourself at home and watch whatever you want, alright."

"Wow," I responded. "You've learned how to make a man comfortable. Are you sure you're the same Diane I knew ten years ago?"

"Because that Diane was a little bit prissy and too much of a self-entitled Feminist to care about the personal comfort of any man, including Rickey's."

"What has caused this young wild lioness to grow into the domesticated house cat I'm seeing today?" I laughingly inquired.

"Rickey going to prison happened," she answered without skipping a beat.

"When he went away, I was lost for the first year or so. After that, I had to learn the hard way that the world didn't revolve around me anymore."

"He had protected me from reality for so long….I lived without consequences, without barriers, without order."

"So, everything that Rickey use to do for me, I made it my mission to learn for myself. The cooking, cleaning, and grocery shopping, all of it."

"You ought to be proud of yourself Diane," I proclaimed. "That type of self-reflection and brutal honesty is rare in this world. I'm proud of you and I'm sure Rickey is just as proud as I am."

Once again, upon hearing his name, she turned away after putting up an uneasy smile. Something was definitely not right between the two of them and Diane was clearly having a hard time hiding it. The house grew silent as I chewed up the fish on my plate, while watching Diane struggle to uncork the bottle of red wine. She filled up two wine glasses before placing a full glass on the lampstand next to me.

"I hope you like it. It's way too damn expensive to be a nasty disappointment." She commented.

"Sometimes, the cheaper wines are a better drink." I explained. "True quality can't always be defined by a price tag. Remember that."

Tickled by my words, Diane flashed a lustful smile as she sat down on her couch. After a small sip, she deliberately crossed her shapely legs and stared at me with fascination screaming from her soul.

"It actually tastes good to me," she stated. "I can taste the wild cherries and the grapes. It's sorta romantic."

Curious, I placed my empty plate on the lampstand and grabbed the wine glass. After a swirl and sniff, I took a gulp and let the wine settle in on my palate. It was nasty bullshit, probably from one of the mediocre wineries south of Napa Valley. Yet, I decided to play along and see how far she would go with her little game.

"It's nice," I lied.

"Good alcohol content. A taste of chocolate, mixed with blueberries, raspberries and pears. Not as smooth as I would prefer but packs a surprisingly nice punch."

"That's why Rickey liked you so much," Diane jumped in.

"You're a guy that can enjoy a fine glass of wine like some rich snob, while devoting himself fully to the primitive world of dog sled racing."

"His other friends were all fake as hell. Rickey saw right through all of them. They would make fun of you behind your back, calling you the silver spoon dog sledder. Yet, Rickey saw you for what you really were," she confided.

"He was able to find out about you. We both just kept that to ourselves. No one else needed to know your business or who you really were."

"Rickey would always tell me how much he respected and feared you. He would tell me that you were the real deal, a true warrior for our people."

"Hearing Rickey and Alex talk so much about you, it instantly made me a little jealous and a tad bit curious. At times, it felt like he loved you more than me."

"I also respected Rickey," I broke in.

"He's a good man. I'm just happy he accepted such a poor sled racer on his team. I'm sure I cost the team more than a few races over the years."

I stood up from the rocking chair and walked towards the kitchen with my empty plate. Hearing the admiration Rickey quietly held for me, only added fuel to my inner resolve to finish this mission. Diane followed, eager to assist and imploring me to hand over the plate so she could wash it.

"I can wash my own plate." I insisted. "Plus, I never felt like a guest when I visited here before. The both of you made this feel like a second home for me."

"We were happy to have you here," she rebutted. "And I'm more than happy to serve you now."

With a strong jerk, Diane ripped the plate from my fingers and walked over to the sink. As the water poured out of the faucet, she scrubbed the dish clean with a soapy rag. A smile beamed from her face as she glanced up, happy to appease my stare of wonderment.

"I've never seen you wash a dish before," I admitted. "I never knew you had that sort of skill."

"Any woman that's worth her salt, will do whatever needs to be done to please a good man," she conveyed. "Even if it means learning something totally foreign."

"By the way, between me and you, what's in your crate? Is it drugs, explosives, guns? Whatever you have in it, you'll need help keeping it safe."

"The crate doesn't matter right now," I blushed. "What matters is that a good man always makes sure to reward a good woman."

In one swift move, I turned Diane towards me and wrapped my arms around her waist. Our lips gently touched at first, before growing ever more curious and cavalier with each lustful excursion. There were no loud cries of protest, just years of pent-up fantasies, finally finding a home in a moment of ultimate privacy. I felt her small wet hands grasp my thick jacket, tugging me closer in her desire for skin-on-skin contact. I moved my lips down to her tender neck, fighting off the urge to dig my teeth into her tempting flesh.

As my tongue tickled her dried sweat, she let out a slight moan of pleasure. On instinct, my hand reached underneath her wool sweater, caressing her breasts and feeling her erect nipples. In response to my intrusion, her hands unbuckled my jeans. I was alive in her hand as she thrust her wet fingers underneath my boxers. She felt my thumping response as I looked into her eyes before diving in for another kiss. Everything about us touching each other felt forbidden. Breaking our silent rules was exciting beyond measure. There would be no coming back now, we both had crossed that barrier together.

In a fit of passion, I unbuttoned her pants and yanked them down, along with her panties. Everything fell to the floor and Diane clinched me close as she stepped out of her thick trousers. Without thought, I rushed in to feel her warmness. She accommodated my curious fingers by leaning herself against the kitchen counter. She began to suck on my earlobe, punishing me with random nibbles in between heavy sighs of pleasure. As my fingers explored her, I felt her small hand wrap around me and began to wildly stroke.

She stopped touching me and tried to pull down my underwear and pants. Feeling her stubborn effort failing, I used my free hand to assist. Seconds later, I was only wearing my thick jacket and the coldness of the house sent goosebumps down my exposed thighs. Feeling me shiver, Diane looked at me with wide eyes while lowering down to her knees. I felt the warmness of her mouth around my hardness. Her boldness and the intoxicating sounds that accompanied her raw display of passion, seduced me. I looked down at her, struggling mightily to control my own ecstasy. Her eyes cut my soul as she stared into my eyes, while pleasuring herself.

The thought of Rickey's unsurmountable jealousy ran through my mind. I was losing the war against my own climax and there was nothing I could do to stop it. At this moment, I knew exactly why he had been a man so crazed and possessed. Diane was a dangerous woman, way too dangerous for one man to try and corral. The overwhelming pleasure rushed over me, so I ran my fingers through her soft hair before attempting to pull her mouth away. She stubbornly thrust her mouth forward, forcing her lips onto me while pulling everything out, taking away my energy to resist. I let out a weak sigh as she continued to pull, then her eyes closed. I watched her swallow before I was released out of her warm mouth, and once again exposed to the cabin's cold air.

I was uncontrollable as my soul recognized my own mortal weakness. Impassioned, I reached down and pulled her to her feet, almost throwing her on top of the kitchen counter. With a knowing stare, Diane leaned back slightly with hazy eyes, opening her legs wider, and inviting me in. I thrust myself into her, taking what was rightfully mine. Grabbing her by her throat, I looked into her yearning soul as I pounded away. Enjoying the punishment, she cracked a smile in between light moans. I felt her digging her long nails into the skin on the back of my neck.

Her wetness increased as I squeezed and pounded harder with each stroke. Droplets of my own blood tickle down my back from the wounds Diane had given me. For this woman, making love was war and the thrill of fighting off death was addictive. Ready for war and needing more leverage, I pulled myself out and picked her up. Wobbling back into the living room, I threw Diane down on the soft couch, making sure my toss was merciless.

"Turn around." I ordered. "I'm about to fuck the shit outta you."

In a fog of lustful obedience, she climbed on all fours and readily opened. I dove back in, pulling her long brown hair and controlling her. I listened as she screamed out, letting all kinds of vulgar words fly. Then, just outside of the large living room window, I noticed a shadow move. Without turning my head to look, I watched as the shadow slowly disappeared into the darkness. We weren't alone out here. This tricky bitch had invited a few guests.

Strangely excited by her little scam, I felt myself stiffen as I pulled her hair harder. Tears rolled down her face as she moaned and asked me to finish inside her. Letting her hair go,

I gripped her waist to accommodate before reaching inside my leather jacket and unholstering my pistol. Feeling my second climax, I glanced out of the window and saw nothing. Now was the perfect time to act and really get this show on the road.

No longer resisting my end, I pounded faster as I began to ejaculate. While I finished, I felt her lean back into me twice, denying me an exit. As she leaned the third time, I pointed the pistol at the back of her skull. The gunshot was loud and sudden. Brain matter covered the bloody couch below her as she fell forward and laid motionless. The feel of her warm urine ran down my leg and created a pool on the cushion. For several seconds, I watched as she involuntarily fought for air before going silent. My old friend Diane was now forever gone and what a way to go.

I jumped up from the couch and ran up to the second floor, turning off the house lights along the way. Soon, Diane's guest would get curious and undoubtedly make their way inside. Creeping through the darkness, I found my way into the spare guestroom with its long window that ran above the front door. Peering down, I saw three dark silhouettes moving nervously towards the house. Several times the moving shadows seemed to stop and retreat, before eventually gathering the nerve to inch forward again. On their last try, they were a few feet away from the front door when the motion sensor sprang into action, instantly illuminating all three men.

Spoiled by the light, all three men gave up on any idea of a sneak attack and began to loudly knock on the door. The group consisted of two black East African men and my East Indian taxi driver from earlier in the day. For about two minutes, the men knocked and knocked, before the taxi driver finally twisted the knob and pushed open the door. Beneath me, I could hear the men calling for Diane before scurrying about in the darkness, looking for a light switch. Crawling over to the overhead rail, I looked down and saw all three men staring at Diane's half nude body. They were in shock as the fireplace cast a dull orange glow about the living room.

Sighting in the supposed leader, I aimed my pistol at the back of the East Indian's head, then slowly pulled the trigger. The report of the pistol broke their shock as the taxi driver crumbled to the floor while I aimed in on my second target. With a quick follow up blast, I hit the second man as he attempted to duck for cover, striking him in his upper back. The third man pulled his gun and looked up at the balcony, squeezing off several wild shots before darting into the kitchen.

There was only one guy left and he didn't stand a chance. I grabbed a pillow and crept to the top of the staircase. Gripping it tight, I reared back and tossed it downstairs with all my strength, knocking over Diane's cheap bottle of Cabernet and her wine glass. The sounds of three panic gun shots rang out from the area near the refrigerator. This African was going to pay for his fear and ignorance.

I bolted downstairs and immediately pointed my gun at the refrigerator. Frozen in fear, the black man stood there paralyzed while looking down the barrel of my pistol. In a millisecond, I collected my aim and zeroed in on his head. I could see him try to raise his gun in response, but it was too late. In that instant, I pulled the trigger and his gun fell from his hands. I watched his blood roll down the refrigerator door, as his body fell to earth in front of it.

Turning my attention to the front door, I crept towards the half open entrance, energizing the outside lights before peering out to ensure no one else was lurking. Satisfied that I was finally alone, I locked the door and walked back into the living room. I was the only one still breathing and that rush of having leveled the ultimate powers of making and taking life, grabbed me. Searching around the kitchen, I opened a cabinet and found a box of Cuban cigars that were mostly old and dried out. Luckily, I was able to find one that was still suitable for smoking. I walked over to the fireplace and lit the cigar as I glanced over at the perfectly cut firewood.

Diane had never in her life cooked a meal, let alone washed a damn dish. There was no way she could chop firewood so perfectly, then stack it up in such a precise manner. Her abject arrogance had betrayed her, leading her to believe that her beauty and sexual prowess could convincingly conceal her true motives. She was indeed a dangerous woman, but also way to naïve to try and pull that game on me. I had fallen for this type of scam in the past, but this time around, fate had totally prepared me for Diane's trap. After enjoying half of the cigar, I piled up the dead bodies and set the corpses next to the blazing fireplace. After scrubbing Diane's body with kerosene, I threw more logs into the fire and turned off all the lights.

I needed to get moving before someone came by searching for her or her partners. Taking her keys, I jumped in her truck and headed back to Prince Rupert. I thought of calling Alex and passing along the good news, but I decided to wait until I was safely out of town. Diane was undoubtedly clicked in with the town's foreign criminals and until this crate was out of Canada, there was no use celebrating an incomplete victory.

Pulling up to my hotel room, I jetted inside and grab my luggage. Once I was packed up, I drove to the old railroad dock near the river. From behind the chain fence, I saw that the tugboat, Alaskan Spirit, was still moored there. It had been years since I had used these guys for a job like this. In the back of my mind, I wondered if the crew would even remember me. Even if they didn't, it was still worth a shot.

I pulled the truck up to the closed gate and an older white man walked out of his guard shack. The security guard shivered as he approached the truck, jamming his bare hands into his armpits. The bottom part of his long beard sported a few frozen ice sickles, and his thin wind breaker couldn't have been of any comfort. Placing the vehicle in park, I rolled down the driver side window and presented the man with my fake identification.

"I have a delivery for the tug Alaskan Spirit from Apex Marine," I stated.

Not allowing himself to be confused, the guard quickly shook his head, while dramatically pointing at his clipboard.

"Nope, there are no deliveries scheduled for the Alaskan Spirit this evening. They are about to leave for Seattle in less than an hour," he explained.

"You probably have your itinerary mixed up with the container ship down river."

"This happens all the time." He continued. "Just keep driving down this road for about three miles and you'll see the ships moored alongside the loading cranes."

"No," I sternly shot back. "This delivery is one of those last-minute deals. I have specific instructions to deliver this to the Alaskan Spirit before they leave for Seattle tonight."

"They're gonna need this fuel pump man. Just do me a favor?"

"How about you call the captain of the tug and tell him Apex Marine is at the front gate with the fuel pump he wants?"

Reluctantly, the guard scampered back into his shack and grabbed his cellphone. As he talked, I saw him peering over at me with confused glances before visibly relaxing and letting out a laugh. Afterwards, he confidently tossed the phone down on his desk and braced himself as he pushed open the shack door and walked outside.

"The captain forgot to tell me about your delivery today," he joked.

"Yeah, he's getting old," I teased.

"Don't worry, he's forgetting a lot of things lately," the guard sighed.

"He asked that you hurry the hell up and get to the pier so he can load his gear and depart on schedule. Just go ahead, I'll officially sign you in and out of the port once you've finished up."

I drove up to the Alaskan Spirit and parked. Grabbing a small duffle bag, I exited the truck and climbed down to the back deck of the tugboat. As I walked towards the main deck entrance, the quick acting watertight hatch sprung open. Crawling out of the space was the captain's tall frame. His thick silver glasses concealed his hardened Germanic features. It had been ten years since we had last seen each other. Despite not quite remembering my name, the wide smile on his old greying face told me he was more than pleased to see me.

"I haven't had a fuel pump delivery in ages," he laughed.

"Hell, I'm surprised you still remembered our code words," I replied. "I figured it was worth a shot to see if you were still working out here."

"Well," he interrupted. "You're sort of lucky. I was supposed to have retired five years ago, but I can't afford to stop working these days. My wife has cancer and if I retire, I'll have to pay for her health insurance on my own."

"My friend, it's good to see you again," he quickly pressed on. "Especially when you have that loaded duffle bag."

The captain waved for me to follow him inside the boat and we walked into the crew's galley. We gathered at a long narrow table and squeezed into two undersized chairs. One by one, four curious looking crew members made their way into the galley while the captain and I chatted about old times. None of the faces were familiar, aside from the Chief Engineer, who had gone bald since I had last seen him.

"Don't worry yourself about all the new faces you see," the captain knowingly advised.

"This is a good crew, they know it's to their benefit to do their jobs and be a team player. We're all God-fearing white men out here. No one on this boat is a loose cannon."

"How's your friends, Alex and Rickey?" He asked.

"Last I heard, Rickey's doing hard time and Alex is living somewhere in the lower forty-eight." I deflected.

"Anyway, this job isn't one of their gigs. I need you to do this delivery for me. I'm flying solo right now and I hope that you can help out an old buddy one last time."

I unzipped my duffle bag and placed it on the table in front of the captain. Without touching it, he looked inside and I saw that familiar look of greed flash into his blue eyes. There was a lot of green inside and if he was a hungry cow, he'd immediately start chewing.

"That's 500K," I explained.

"That should be enough to get you to transport this crate to Seattle without a fuss, I assume."

"Where will you need this delivered?" he asked.

"If I could, I'd like to offload in Tacoma," I requested. "I can meet you at the dock and we can put the crate onto a truck. It will all be done in less than ten minutes tops."

"No, we can't do that," he objected. "Customs has been conducting a lot of surprise visits these days and my bosses will likely be waiting for me at the pier."

"You'll have to get your shit in Port Angeles. I can't risk taking it all the way to Tacoma this time. We'll have to transfer this crate at anchor. That way, nothing looks suspicious."

"I'll claim to have some sort of engine problem, then go anchor in Port Angeles for a few hours to conduct repairs."

"During this window, you'll have to find yourself a boat that is big enough to handle your crate. From there, you can transfer it and sail down to Seattle and disappear among all the recreational boaters."

"If you miss the Port Angeles deadline, I'll tie a buoy to the crate and shackle it into one of the mooring balls in the bay before I leave."

"Either way, we keep the money for hauling it down to Port Angeles. You remember the policy, don't you? No refunds."

The galley grew quiet as every eye examined me. Getting the crate across the Canadian border would be a victory, but finding the means to take this heavy box off their tug was going to be problematic. My mind raced as I considered several viable solutions before settling on one. I'd have to get the crate and break it down much sooner than I initially anticipated.

"Sounds like a deal captain," I agreed. "Let's load this shit, shall we?"

We both stood up from the table and shook hands with the quiet knowledge that we would probably never see each other again, once this was over. I could tell from his probing eyes that the captain wanted badly to ask my name but was refraining himself. It was like two proud white men fighting their own individual wars, while finding ways to look out for each other in the midst of the chaos.

I made my way back to the truck while the Chief Engineer operated the tug's crane. Two of the boat's crew members helped me tie together several straps, before the Engineer lifted the crate and loaded it on the tug's back deck. The crew secured the crate to the deck using two eye pads and the whole operation was over within five minutes. From the pier, I watched as the tug's two main engines were lit off, blowing thick streams of black exhaust into the night sky. The captain was alone on the bridge, and he lowered a side window and shouted down at me.

"You'll be able to follow me by using an AIS tracker. I should make it to Port Angeles in about four or five days, if the currents don't slow me down," he explained.

"I'll keep tabs on you," I responded. "You can bet on it."

"Don't worry yourself about your gear," he quickly replied.

"As long as you show up to Port Angeles ready to go, this ought to be smooth. It will be just like the ole days."

The captain walked the tug away from the pier and turned the bow into the current before heading out to sea. As the tug's silhouette faded into blackness, I climbed into the truck and turned the heater up to full blast. Driving back to the security shack, I stopped and handed the guard my credentials. He took them, placing my fake ID's on his metal clipboard before softly reading out my name as he jotted it down.

"Nathan B. Forrest," he slowly read.

Hearing this Canadian unwittingly read out the name, made me chuckle. He obviously had no clue about the historical significance of Nathan Bedford Forrest. My pal, Connor, had a twisted sense of humor and loved to add subtle pranks and trivia to each of his counterfeit products. Once my mission was finished, it would be too easy for authorities to cite him as the manufacturer of all my fake identities, which is why he had to die.

The security guard filled out his logs and allowed me to leave. I drove away from the railroad dock and headed towards the ferry landing. Looking at my watch, I noticed it was still early enough in the evening to catch the last outbound ferry. The quicker I left Prince Rupert, the better. Parking my truck in the ferry's loading line, I waited patiently as the ticket maids hastily recorded the license plates of the cars ahead of me.

When it was my turn, a young maid walked up to the driver side window, flashing a fatigue filled smile while suffering through the abusive cold. The tip of her pointed nose was bright red, and her hurried manner told me that this evening's trip needed to be her last. I rolled down the window and the truck's warm air escaped as a frosty breeze accompanied the lady's tortured question.

"What's your final destination sir?" She asked while tapping her electronic note pad.

"Anywhere but here my dear," I answered. "Any fuckin where, but here."

Chapter Five

Ghosts Of The Business District

In New Orleans its normal to find tourists browsing the Business District, even during the earliest of hours. Staring through my shop's large front window, I noticed a stampede of white tourists passing by my office. These groups were either working up an appetite or walking off a hardy southern breakfast. Each group passed by the shop without the slightest curiosity about my business. In their world, if I wasn't a black man selling a hot plate of food or playing an instrument, I hardly existed. Strangely enough, that's exactly how I liked it.

There was no better place to hide my operation than the heart of the Business District. In between all the attractions and festivities, my inconspicuous little shop is easily lost. A few blocks from here, other more famous cloak and dagger operations were infamously hatched. In the early sixties, former FBI agent and Cold Warrior, Guy Bannister, operated out of a building just across the street. His office was a place where fanatical Cuban exiles were secretly trained to kill Fidel Castro by the CIA. During Guy Bannister's tenure the infamous proxy, Lee Harvey Oswald, was known to regularly frequent Bannister's office. In fact, credible reports indicate he visited with Bannister months before John F. Kennedy was assassinated.

We had moved the frontlines of our war against White Supremacy out of the shadows and into this public domain. Given the fact that the FBI had noticed our move, I couldn't help but wonder how this would end for all of us. When the details of who we were and want we do eventually surface, will history lionize us or despise us like Lee Harvey Oswald?

Needing to refill my mug, I discarded the thoughts of history and reached for the coffee pot, finding it empty. Frustrated, I opened nearby cabinets in search of coffee supplies, finding none. After cursing under my breath, I grabbed my cellphone hoping to call Jessica to have her stop and buy some. Just as I was about to press the call button, I heard the front door open, followed by a sweet voice.

"You're lucky that I'm actually serious about keeping up this business Achim," Jessica remarked.

"Otherwise, Pokey would come here, and we'd look like some damn fools if he asked us for a cup of coffee."

Jessica walked up to our empty coffee station before reaching into her grocery bag and tossing the needed supplies into a cabinet. Hovering over her, I leaned down and teased her with kisses, before she dramatically pushed me away in mock annoyance.

"Here," she continued. "Get a pot started before he arrives, please."

As she walked away, I noticed the large box of beignets from Café-Du Monde in her hand. Either she was going all out for this meeting, or my pregnant girlfriend's eyes had gotten the best of her.

"Make sure we invoice the FBI for those beignets," I instructed.

"I'm already ahead of you." Jessica stated with a smile as she waved the receipt.

As the coffee began to drip into the pot, I heard the front door open again, so I turned around to look. I saw Pokey's big body walk through the entrance with several black NOPD officers flanking him. His uniform was crisp but tight fitting, as it struggled to cover his massive belly. The black side arm holstered on his waist looked like a small cellphone when compared with his heft. Small beads of sweat had formed below his freshly edged hairline. He and his group of aides had chosen to walk to my office, and the stubborn foolishness of this decision angered me. Upon seeing me, a huge smile splashed across his face as he reached out to shake my hand.

"Achim! My man," he proclaimed.

"What up Pokey," I responded. "You're a bit early."

"Yeah, the FBI folks have asked me to shake up my routine. They say it will help throw this Tarpon guy off, so I decided to get a little exercise and walk over here."

The FBI is stupid as hell. The Tarpon could care less about the victim following some schedule. For him, it was all about seizing opportunities. All he needs is an opening and you'd be dead if he had it. Shaking up routines does nothing but make targets more paranoid. Looking into Pokey's eyes, I could see that apprehension hiding within him.

"Thanks for meeting with us Pokey," I explained. "Sense we are friends, I thought it would be important that we both had a chat before our big meeting with the FBI this morning."

"As you very well know, they recently hired Jessica and I on as investigators. I have prior experience dealing with the

Tarpon, so I wanted to answer any questions you may have about this guy, off the record of course."

"Yep, I knew I was right," Pokey interrupted with a gushing smile.

"If the FBI is hiring you, that means you were definitely CIA or some damn military Spec Op specialist back in the day. I can tell Achim, you don't have to admit it. I already know."

"Outside of the government, we don't build too many black men like you nowadays."

"I'm already feeling better knowing you are on the team. I feel that strongly about your skill set Achim."

Pokey let out a light sigh as he walked past me into the conference room. He was always low-key accusing me of not telling him about my past. Pokey would have bet his life that I was some former CIA operative. He was convinced because, according to him, I talked and moved like one. I never tried to bat the idea out of his head. His belief that I was some type of government issue James Bond was much more convenient then the truth.

Make no mistake, Pokey is cool people, but the traditional black establishment mindset is all too ingrained within him. Blacks like him overvalue their professional titles and only feel a sense of empowerment when they are supported by white dollars or white institutions. For black elites like Pokey, no form of self-validation was greater than the validation that could be obtained from the Dominant White Society.

Pokey and those in his elite black circles view organizations like Robert Charles with quiet contempt, almost embarrassed by our uncompromising existence. To them, motivated black men that fight against White Supremacy are the unwashed and the uneducated. In their minds, white society should only be shown the error of their ways, and never punished. His model for change is to endlessly offer so-called love and understanding to our brutal oppressors. By employing this tactic, Black society could theoretically convert the White Supremacists into human beings.

If Pokey were to find out that I was a leading Counter-Racist Assassin on the payroll of Robert Charles, he'd freak out and probably never speak to me again. For Boule Negroes like Pokey, even the slightest stench of Black Militancy, would forever scar them in the eyes of their white benefactors. Influential white benefactors like Governor Clay Lewis could ill-afford to find themselves in league with Black Empowerment types. For Pokey, the respectability game was his golden ticket to the top.

"Would you gentlemen like a beignet?" Jessica asked as the group gathered around the table.

All three men eagerly nodded their heads and she served each of them their snack on small paper plates. When the coffee finished brewing, I took the full pot over to the table and filled each man's mug. Before officially starting the meeting, I allowed the men to nibble away while Jessica and I secured the entrances to our office. Before locking the front door, I peered out of the window and took note of an unfamiliar white SUV parked across the street.

The FBI was keeping a close eye on Pokey, and I wanted word of our impromptu meeting to make it to the ears of Agent's Sanchez and Porter. I needed them to know I didn't trust them and that I'd tell Pokey their truth if they threatened Robert Charles. After our agreement in Houston, I was scheduled to convene with the FBI's Unified Command at the Federal Building. From what Agent Sanchez told me, the Director of the FBI in New Orleans was scheduled to be there, along with our mayor and other high ranking officials. I thought it was a good idea to talk to Pokey before all the smiling white faces persuaded him to do things that were against his own interest.

I double locked our front entrance and walked back into the conference room. By now, all three men were licking the powdered sugar off their fingers while staring down at their empty plates. Glad to accommodate the men, Jessica opened her box of pleasure and smiled as she reloaded each plate with another round of sugary goodness.

"Make sure you save some for us now," I joked. "We can't be out here feeding the entire New Orleans Police Department."

"Don't worry." Jessica shot back. "I saved us a box in the car."

"You ain't gotta tell a pregnant woman about food bruh." Pokey joined in. "She's gonna make sure she eats, on way or another".

"Jessica," he continued. "Have you given anymore thought to coming back to the force."

"We could use your services as a detective….part-time of course."

"Hell no," she bluntly responded. "You can't ask me to walk back into that Department. Especially the way things went down in my old division. Believe me, I'm fine right where I'm at."

"Plus, what other job could I have where I get to spend most of the day supporting the man I love?"

Seeing that beautiful smile blast across her face caused me to lean down and kiss her on the cheek. Jessica was right where she was supposed to be and there was nowhere else I would prefer her to be, then with me.

"You can stop trying to steal my woman," I teased. "She's needed here and she isn't going anywhere. The NOPD lost her, and now, she's all mine."

"Let's discuss this Tarpon situation," I began while placing a stack of paperwork on the table.

"I invited you here because we need to have a frank discussion."

"First, where is your family? Are they still in New Orleans? What are your plans to keep them safe?"

"Well, they're still here with me," he confidently replied.

"I have three NOPD patrol units guarding my home, alongside plain clothes officers from the State Police."

"If he tries to attack my family, that will be the wrong move for sure. My neighborhood is pretty much Fort Knox right now. Everything that moves in or out is watched."

"Three patrol units and plain clothes officers, won't stop this guy, Pokey," I explained.

"You're gonna have to move your family. The longer they stay hold up in your house, the greater the chance this guy figures out a way to exploit your defenses."

"Achim, I'm the Chief of Police," he sternly rebutted. "I get death threats all the damn time."

"There's no way me or my family are about to pack up and run just because of one freakin nutjob."

"He's one guy, one guy that a bunch of foreign thugs are paying to come shake me up."

"I'm a proud law man Achim. I can't be seen running from criminals. I gotta stand strong, or chaos will prevail in this city. Believe me Achim, that's what these Asian thugs really want."

Pokey leaned back in his chair and wiped a few lingering pastry crumbs away from the corner of his mouth. His eyes cut through me like a laser as he focused in, signaling his intent to stand firm. In the back of my mind, I knew it was suicide to take this sort of position against the Tarpon. If your pride was a weakness, he would definitely try to exploit it.

Resigned to move on, I opened a folder and placed several documents in front of Pokey. The documents were foreign news clippings I found on the gang leader, Zhilan. From the unconfirmed details, Zhilan appears to be a man that is feared all over Southeast Asia. Stories of his body count varied from one thousand to tens of thousands. Pokey picked up the clippings and quickly mused through them before tossing them back at me. We both knew where I was about to go with this. These were questions I had to get answers to, so I could fully understand what I was involved in.

"Pokey, the Tarpon and this Zhilan character aren't the type of folks you want to take lightly," I broached.

"Interpol and the FBI have arrested Zhilan gang members and found them carrying photos of you, your wife and your two sons."

"These are the type of drug dealers who kill police officers for kicks. To them, there is no law, just their power to kill."

"If you want to keep your family here with you in New Orleans, that's your call, but I'm going to ask you some direct questions and I need no-bullshit answers."

Frustrated with my frankness, he shook his head while motioning for me to get to my point. I was sure he had fielded the question before, and I was also sure the mere notion hidden within my inquiry would infuriate him. Yet in the back of my mind, I knew that there could be things going on within the NOPD that Pokey would have no knowledge of. Rogue elements within the NOPD could easily tarnish his reputation, without him knowing it.

"Pokey, I need to know what happened during that raid."

"How did the Asian suspects end up getting killed? How can you as the Chief of Police, be absolutely sure that none of your folks are in business with Zhilan?"

"Achim, those guys shot at cops!" Pokey shouted.

"My folks did everything above board that day! They are all good cops!"

"I'm so tired of you people on the outside using NOPD's old reputation as a crutch!"

"I've worked hard to clean up this department, hell, every chance I get I'm begging Jessica to come back to the badge."

Angered beyond words, Pokey's lips tightened, then he went silent. A part of me wanted to believe him; yet personal experience had taught me better. His emotions were fueled not by facts or logic, but wishful thinking. Someone in his department could have very easily been working with Zhilan, then flipped on him in a move fueled by greed. I knew deep inside not to push this line of questioning too far, so I looked over at Jessica. It was her turn to take over and soften him up a bit.

"You mean well Pokey. You really do," Jessica chimed in. "But not everyone on the force thinks like you."

"It hurts to find out that people you trust….put it all on the line with…that they might be compromised somehow."

"I know that conflicting feeling all too well," she offered. "Don't be like me. Don't let your good heart and trust keep you among troubling company."

"My department is clean, Jessica!" Pokey reiterated.

"My guys aren't involved in any drug trafficking. Those were the old days when you and your dirty ass partners ran the place. Today, none of that shit is going on because I have made sure that won't happen again."

It was evident from their stoic faces, that all three lawmen were offended. They couldn't wait for the right moment to put an end to our meeting and make a hasty exit. Before any of the men could speak up, I leaned towards Pokey and nodded my head, signaling my trust in his word. Although I didn't share his belief, I couldn't very well start snooping around his department to find out the truth. It was too late in the ball game for any of that, and the Tarpon wouldn't care one way or the other. Any attempt to convince a black man like Pokey that he was asleep in a den of vipers, would only lead to him fearfully concluding that I was actually the serpent. I needed to be delicate here, so I took a deep breath and began to relay my truth.

"Before we go to this big-time meeting with the FBI," I began. "I need to advise you on a few things. There is a reason, I'm asking you these pushing questions. There is a reason, I'm recommending you hide your family."

"When we go to that meeting today, you need to know that not everyone's hands are clean in this affair. By everyone, I mean the FBI, the DEA, the state police."

"Not everyone's main priority will be saving your life, Pokey."

"Sitting at that table surrounding us today will be some who have done business with the Tarpon. Some have even sat back and watched as Zhilan grew his organization. You need to know and understand that Pokey."

"The Federal government will be there simply to cover their own asses, and if that means making us into black scapegoats, then so be it."

"You want to believe that no one in your department was dealing drugs, but you damn well better make sure your right about that. If the Tarpon kills you, your friends in the Bureau will find a way to blame the both of us for your own death. I can promise you they will do exactly that."

"You can't allow their titles, the big names, or the white faces to seduce you into your own failure. They are showering you with all this attention right now, not because they like you, but because you are useful."

"These FBI punks like Sanchez and Porter, are born liars," I added. "They can't be trusted."

"Pokey, your life is on the line, and you need to be critical of everyone's intentions…even mine."

He rose to his feet in anger and his black lackeys shot up beside him. In his quietly offended mannerisms, I knew he was done with me, at least for now. I sort of understood how he must have felt in the back of his mind. I had been there once upon a time in my own life, wanting to believe all the hard work and dedication I had poured into this society had earned my black skin, a certain amount of respect. The bloody murder of my family taught me how wrongheaded I had been. I had to learn the lessons of White Supremacy the hard way. Trying to provide Pokey those same precious lessons, was a task doomed to fail. The lie is always sweeter than the bitter truth and too many of us in the black community, prefer the smoothing sweetness of Satan's deceit.

"You don't think I know my life is in danger, Achim," he shot back. "I've been a police officer for twenty plus years. I've put my life on the line every single day."

"This ain't new to me, brother. The only people I trust are my partners that swore to protect me, you and everybody else that enjoy the damn fruits of this great country."

"You might walk around mistrusting the FBI, but I don't believe that's helpful to the black community. You must work alongside them, Achim. You have to show them that you love this country and that you're willing to lay it on the line just like they are."

"Agents like Sanchez and Porter are good people. I trust them with my life because we all come from the same pedigree. A pedigree you wouldn't understand nor appreciate, as a civilian."

"Black people need to learn to leave the past, in the damn past. We need to accept that there is no Black America…there is no White America…. there is only the United States of America!"

"Together, we'll fix our problems. We won't fix them by peddling in wild conspiracy theories around race, or believing that Federal Officers are somehow out to get us because we are Black," he spit out.

Forcing himself into an angry silence, Pokey looked over at Jessica and gave her a fake smile before bolting towards the exit. The tension that followed his illogical outburst was only relieved by the sounds he and his flunkies made while exiting the office. After the encounter, it dawned on me that Sanchez and Porter beat me to the punch. Both men had already gotten to Pokey, watering the seeds of the Anti-Black thoughts that were buried in his soul. The FBI had probably broken our agreement. I could sense that they had revealed something about my past to him.

"Pokey is already sounding like some self-serving member of the Congressional Black Caucus," Jessica astutely observed.

"Whatever Governor Lewis and the Democrats are feeding him, its working like a charm."

"That wasn't just political ambition speaking," I chimed in. "That was the FBI."

"They've gotten to him for sure. He's on their side, and the FBI is a dangerous sidekick for any black person to have."

After a loud sigh, Jessica slowly rose up from her chair and wobbled over to the table. As she reached down to police up the empty paper plates, I beat her to the punch, grabbing them before she could.

"I got this baby," I mumbled. "You go sit down and get off your feet for a while."

Ignoring my request, Jessica stood there watching me smash the paper plates into the nearly full trash bin. The look on her face was one of thoughtful concern and I knew the genesis of that emotion. Despite Pokey being a lost cause, she still cared about the man. I couldn't blame her. I too held within me the very same sentiments, but I didn't have a clue as to how I could feed water to a horse that failed to recognize that it was dying of thirst.

"Is Pokey going to survive all of this?" She bluntly asked.

"I need a straight answer Achim, no bullshit. How does this all play out for him?"

"No," I answered without hesitation. "He probably won't survive."

"I'll be able to keep the Tarpon at bay for a little while, but Pokey will continue to faithfully drink up every lying word these white folks pour out. Eventually, the Tarpon will find a way to manipulate this whole situation and kill him."

"His end will be bloody, vicious and extremely graphic. When it happens, the FBI will come after Robert Charles to distract away from their own failures."

"The narrative of shadowy black militants and a dirty black police chief will be too juicy for the white media to resist, especially when compared to the reality that the Tarpon was once on the FBI's payroll."

"The FBI will fight tooth and nail to cover up the fact that they paid this guy to murder Black protestors."

"That's why they will come after us. We know too much. Robert Charles has become a threat the FBI can no longer idly tolerate."

Frustrated, I yanked the full trash bag out of the can and tied the opening shut. Still deep in thought, Jessica just stood there motionless. Either she didn't like my answer or she still had a question that was burning in her soul. I braced myself for another request as I picked up the bag and walked towards the exit.

"Before you go to that briefing, I need to know about Rachel," she softly demanded.

"Why is the FBI so interested in the both of you?

"And why are you so damn determined to protect this woman?"

I went still and gently tossed the trash bag onto the hardwood floor. Jessica stared without flinching and I knew this wasn't some random question. My vague answers about the Rachel situation hadn't satisfied her, and now she wanted the truth come hell or high water. Right then and there, I decided it was time for the truth. Jessica was going to be the mother of my child, and she deserved my honesty, no matter how painful it might be.

I walked back into the conference room and forced myself into the seat in front of her. After motioning for her to relax, I was finally able to convince her to sit next to me. Ever so gently, I grabbed Jessica's hand and caressed it as I gathered the words in my mind.

"By now you probably have figured out that Rachel works for Robert Charles," I began.

"She's been with Robert Charles since she was eighteen years old. Because of that, Rachel is easily one of our most decorated assassins."

"I met her six or seven years ago while working a case in Atlanta. We both were assigned the task of eliminating this shady European businessman. The guy was making a lot of serious real estate moves all over Georgia."

"We found out that the man was a member of some Eurocentric White Nationalist ring. Later on, we discovered evidence that linked him and the FBI to the murder of a prominent BLM protestor, who died in a mysterious car fire."

"Rachel was able to make contact with our target. Not only did she befriend the guy, but she eventually became his lover."

"The racist bastard fell in love with her, and because of her relationship with him, we were able to gather all kinds of intel for Robert Charles."

"But that's when the trouble started for the both of us," I admitted.

The vivid memories of what occurred during that tragic operation flooded my spirit. Remembering the foreboding darkness of that warm Atlanta night, I could still hear Rachel's faint cries as the words began to flow out of me. My heart could still feel the tingle run down my spine when I saw her handcuffed to that bedpost, half naked with fear boiling in her eyes. Her soft brown arms, legs and breasts were all exposed. Tears were streaming down her face. That panicked look she wore, paralyzed me as I opened the door to her bedroom.

I can still hear her whispering to me through those tears, pleading for my help in one breath while imploring me to leave and save myself in another. A thick cloth satchel was tied around her panty-less waist. It was an improvised explosive device, and it was also the Tarpon's way of making light of his secret fetish. Despite the dimness of the room, I could tell the satchel was packed with enough C4 to level the entire house. The smell of the exposed wire charges was distinct as it hit my nose. For a brief second, I knew I was dead. I knew I had screwed up and walked right into the bastard's ambush.

In a fit of frustration, Jessica interrupted me by jerking her hand away from mine and flashing that all too familiar look. Her eyes cut me deep. She didn't have to say one word for me to feel her anger.

"You were fuckin her weren't you Achim!" She demanded through falling tears.

"You're still in love with this woman. You don't have to admit it, I can tell Achim. I know you…I know you well. I can see it in your eyes."

"You can go to the ends of the earth to protect her, but you can't make an honest woman outta me! I can't freakin believe you right now Achim."

"This isn't about sex or love Jessica," I shot back.

"This unknown client came to Robert Charles, asking us to kill the Tarpon. The client gave us all kinds of information about the number of Blacks he killed."

"Due to the mysterious nature of the client, Robert Charles leadership was split on whether we should pursue the contract at all. Your Aunt Rita was the most vocal about not accepting the work, but in the end, voices like hers were drowned out."

"The client informed us that after killing Black protestors in Ferguson Missouri, the Tarpon had begun assassinating Black's in Brazil and Columbia."

"Rachel was able to find out that elements within the FBI were secretly paying the Tarpon to silence grassroots leadership in the Black Community. We know that was happening because Rachel was able to get copies of the receipts."

"What we didn't know was that the entire campaign was just a ruse. The FBI was using the Tarpon to lure Robert Charles assassins like Rachel and I, out of the shadows. Like flies on shit, we fell right into it."

"Neither the Afro-Latinos nor the Black American protestors were the FBI's real target. It was Robert Charles that was actually on the menu. They needed to find out more about our organization, so they created a way to pull us into the light of day. The Tarpon helped by making himself the bait."

Feeling the old emotions beginning to overwhelm me, I stood up from the chair and took a few paces away from Jessica. Boiling within me was a volcano of anger and shame. The white bastard had gotten the better of me, and I suddenly realized the sting of that defeat had never truly departed my soul.

"What happened in that bedroom with Rachel?" Jessica softly asked.

"Why didn't the Tarpon finish his mission and just kill the both of you?"

"Well…He made a big mistake," I flatly answered.

"Instead of pushing the button and ending the both of us, he made the mistake of feeling his love for her."

"Love caused the man to make his second error. Deep inside, he wanted the opportunity to vent his frustraton at the both of us. Like most White Supremacists, he thirsted to feel power, while within his own shamed heart he was torn and exposed by his own weakness."

"Rachel has ways of manipulating any man, no matter how cold hearted they are, she has the skills to get them to lower their guard."

"Once a man does that, she'll have you in the palm of her hand," I described, as Jessica frowned.

"She really put it on thick with the Tarpon. I believe Rachel had completely fooled that maniac at one point…up until she made the mistake of telling him she had gotten pregnant, and that he was the father."

"Neither of us knew it back then, but the Tarpon is infertile. He'll never be able to have children due to some disease he inherited. All of Rachel's baby talk tipped him off and he got suspicious."

"So, the Tarpon just played along with her, pretending to be a happy soon-to-be father, while secretly researching Rachel and eventually finding out about me."

The news of Rachel having been pregnant appeared to soften Jessica a touch. I watched the angry frown on her face melt away, turning her eyes into a well of sympathy. In that instant, I was reminded of how and why I fell in love with her. She was a compassionate and caring woman. Amid her own fear, anger and frustration, she could still show God-like empathy for another woman that she had every reason to despise. As a soon to be mother herself, Jessica had found a common thread with Rachel that humanized her.

I walked back to my seat and sat down. Barely noticing me Jessica stared off into the distance, refusing to make eye contact with me as she chained herself in her own thoughts.

"Rather than press down on the button and instantly kill us, the Tarpon felt the need to come into the house behind me and attempt to solidify his perceived superiority," I continued.

"I let him run his filthy mouth and work himself into an emotional lather. So, when I saw the opportunity, I knocked the detonator out of his hand and our Super Bowl began."

"I stabbed him four times with my switch blade, once in the chest and three times in the back. The Tarpon cracked my jaw with his brass knuckles before breaking several of my ribs."

"The man is demented. He relished the combat. I could see the thrill in his eyes. His fear of me seemed to motivate him, giving him this extra rush that was hard to counteract."

"Just as I was about to deliver the decisive blow and cut his throat, he managed to slip out of my grasp and kick me away."

"I was helpless as I watched him pull out a small pistol, while he backed away towards the exit."

"Instead of pointing the gun at me, the bastard aimed it at Rachel and pulled the trigger. She was shot twice in her abdomen."

"The smile he wore after shooting her, was pure evil."

"I'll never forget that smile. It was quickly followed by Rachel's loud cries. She was completely covered with her own blood."

"He knew I had to choose between saving her and the child or finishing him off. He knew enough about me to know what I would do next…what I was obligated to do as a black man."

"He ran away. I saved her, but we lost our baby."

"Rachel eventually recovered from her wounds, but the trauma we both shared was too much for either of us."

I looked into Jessica's eyes and saw the tears flowing down her face. Moved by my account, she slowly raised up from her chair and walked over to the coffee station. After wiping her face with tissue paper and adjusting her ponytail, she refilled the coffee maker with fresh water. She was distracting herself with busy work and I knew something else was still on her mind.

"The Tarpon must have found out about what happened to your wife and son. Because of the church massacre, he knew you wouldn't chase after him if it meant the death of Rachel and your unborn child."

"What a sick fuck!" She thought out loud.

"Is this why you're so worried about us getting married?" She asked while cleaning tears from the corner of her eyes.

"I'm not worried about me," I responded. "I'm worried about you."

"I can't afford to lose you Jessica. You're all I have."

"It's my job to protect you and I take that job seriously. Just like me, the Tarpon is a master at finding his opponents weaknesses and exploiting them."

"I'm sure he'll find out I'm involved in all this, then he'll look for some way to make me vulnerable. He knows he can't allow me to get to him first or he's a dead man. This is going to become another death battle, and this time, one of us won't make it out alive."

Jessica walked over to my seat and wrapped her arms around my shoulders, before planting a comforting kiss on the back of my neck. I knew the thoughts that were running through her mind as she held me tight. She was worried and scared of losing me in this mess. This whole thing was taking me back down a dark path and I might never see the light again. I looked back towards her soft lips and gently kissed them. We were letting ourselves feel the love that existed between us. Energized by Jessica's loving spirit, I rose from my seat and grabbed my car keys out of my pocket.

"I can't be late for this meeting," I murmured.

"How can you trust the FBI after they tried to kill you?" She interrupted.

"I don't trust them," I calmly responded. "Like the Tarpon, I'll just have to beat them to the punch."

"Right now, they're desperate. The FBI will do anything to stop this man and spare themselves the embarrassment that is certainly coming."

"Details of his association with them is bound to leak to the media, and a lot of folks within the Bureau will lose their jobs because of it. I knew that the second they came asking for help."

"Well, you do what you need to do," Jessica relented. "And make sure you finish that Tarpon bastard off this time. Don't let anything distract you."

"Your wish, is my command my love," I playfully offered.

I kissed Jessica on her cheek before walking out of the office. As I made my way down the sidewalk, I noticed the same unfamiliar SUV parked across the street. Without giving myself away, I cut my eyes towards them and peered into the vehicle. There were two cleanly shaven white men wearing sunglasses and collared shirts inside. Both were trying their best to study me without being too obvious.

I slowly walked past the SUV, pretending to be ignorant as both FBI scumbags nervously watched. Slipping my cellphone out of my pocket, I typed Anthony a short text message. Once it was sent, I turned up the block towards a parking garage. After a few minutes of slow-paced walking, I entered the garage and took the elevator up to the fifth floor. On the fifth floor, my car sat alone. Nobody liked parking this high in New Orleans. Lazy pedestrians preferred to waste their time circling the lower levels, rather than coming upstairs to take advantage of the vacant parking spaces.

I clicked my doors open and sat behind the wheel. Before starting the ignition, I looked into my rearview mirror, and saw Anthony quietly sitting in the darkness of my back seat. Today, he was on time and was right where I needed him to be.

"I noticed that SUV with the two white boys sitting outside of the office," he whispered.

"Do you want me to take care of them?"

"No," I instructed.

"If they want something to see, we'll give them something to watch."

I reached into my center console, grabbed a clean sheet of paper and scribbled out an address. After double checking for accuracy, I handed it to Anthony, and he reviewed it before tucking it away in his pocket.

"They are probably following me on foot right now," I explained. "That means they're going to be following you too Anthony."

"Go to that address I just gave you and find Rachel. Once you've found her, take her to our safe house in Dallas. Rachel already knows you'll be coming so she'll be ready to move when you arrive."

"Don't try and lose the FBI, but don't be too easy for them to follow either. I need them to follow you and Rachel and believe they are in control."

"If they get too aggressive, lose them, then call me or Aunt Rita. I'll be spending a lot of time with these Alphabet fuckers, and I'll need to know when they've made a move on us."

"When you get to the safe house, both you and Rachel will need to stay put unless you have to ditch your FBI tails."

"Rachel is an insatiable busy body. She loves to party and run the streets. She'll damn sure resist the idea of being locked away inside of a Robert Charles safe house."

"Once you get her inside of that damn house, that's where she stays. I don't care how bored she gets, got it!"

"I got it Achim," Anthony replied with stern certainty.

"You can rely on me. I'll get it done."

With the flip of my wrist, I put the car into reverse and backed out of the parking space. After several tight turns, I followed the exit signs down to the first floor and pulled onto the street. Sure enough, while heading back towards my office, I saw the two clean shaven white punks pacing the sidewalk. Without looking at them, I got Anthony's attention and pointed the two men out. Stopping at a red light, I peered back using my side-view mirror. Both men were turning around and swiftly walking back towards their SUV in a muted panic. When the light turned green, I softly hit the gas and made a lazy left turn before coming to a stop in front of my office door.

"I'll drop you off here," I informed Anthony.

"Jessica bought you breakfast. It's waiting for you in the conference room. Go grab yourself a bite, then make your way to Texas."

Anthony nodded his head and exited the car in total silence. Just as he pulled open the office door, I saw our two nosy FBI agents speed walk around the corner. I pushed down on the gas, pulling off and leaving the two men with no choice but to tail Anthony. Besides, my meeting at the FBI building was due to start within the hour, so following me there wouldn't make much sense.

After hopping onto I-10 east, I headed north towards Lake Pontchartrain and entered the neighborhood of Gentilly. The remote FBI field office wasn't far from the University of New Orleans. Early morning traffic in the area was a bit congested as young white students lazily made their way to class. Arriving at the FBI building, I pulled into the half-filled parking lot, locating a space directly in front of the building's video surveillance cameras. Any evidence of Robert Charles's cooperation with the FBI could be useful to me later. When I reached the front door, I found it covered with all kinds of placards and warnings, almost like I was going into a prison.

Pushing aside a moment of hesitation, I reached for the door handle and ushered myself inside. I was greeted by the bitter cold of the building's well air-conditioned interior. I felt myself shiver as I walked beyond the corridor before turning towards the front desk. Behind the counter, I found a middle-aged black woman, wearing glasses, short blonde hair and a cocky attitude. It was obvious she wasn't law enforcement. She was probably just your typical government employee. A local black hire that was happy to have found a decent government job with good benefits.

"I'll be with you….in a moment," she roughly declared, before I could arrive in front of her desk.

I was blown off when she grabbed her desk telephone and dialed a number. After a long pause, she put on a pleasant-sounding voice and displayed all her teeth as she delivered kind words to the other person on the line. From her considerate demeanor, I instantly knew she had to be talking to a white person. No conversation with any black person would warrant such graciousness from a black woman of her ilk. After a few weird laughs and two unfunny jokes, the lady happily hung up her phone and carefully wrote several sentences down on a legal pad. Upon dropping the pen on the table, she decided to finally look up and honor my dangerous presence in her safe little world.

"Who are you here to see today," she demanded with a mean frown.

"I'm here for a meeting with Agent Porter and Agent Sanchez. My name is Achim Jeffers. I'm a private detective from Silent Endeavors that's working a case with them," I explained.

Examining me from behind her thin glasses, her eyes began telling her my story. The awful expression she made afterwards, told me she wasn't impressed. Annoyed, she grabbed a clipboard and slid it towards me like a dog.

"I'll need you to sign in while I make a copy of your driver's license," she ordered while putting out her hand.

I reached for my wallet and provided her with a photo ID. She took it and held it close to her face in confusion. The lady inspected it for two seconds before angrily tossing it down on the counter in front of me, while letting out a sigh of exasperation.

"Sir, this is a Private Detective's credential. It's not an official state ID," she barked.

"I've already told you once. I'll need your Driver's License to properly sign you in. Either provide identification or I'll have you escorted out of the building."

"Sister, if you try and have me escorted outta here.... you'll regret the moment your pride cost you your little government job," I replied.

"I'm not playing this power game with you today. Call Agent Porter and tell him Achim Jeffers has arrived for our meeting. If you don't call him, I'll call him myself."

The lady rolled her eyes before asking me to have a seat. I walked over to the lobby chairs and planted myself down, making sure to watch her as she put the phone to her ear in a fit of anger. After several moments of her loud talking and making a show, her voice considerably softened, and she hung up without making a fuss. The chime of the elevator broke our silent stand off as Agent's Porter and Sanchez walked right towards me.

"I see you made it, homie," Sanchez greeted.

"Come on up and let's get started."

Agent Porter looked over at the polluted sister, giving her a slight hand wave, informing her that it was all good. In victory, I rose from my seat and shot her a smile that she purposely avoided. The agents and I went up to the fourth floor, then into a small office in the Northeast corner of the building. The room was small, barely wide enough to squeeze in two long desks. Pictures of Asians and Blacks with names stenciled underneath them were posted on all four walls. One of the photos immediately caught my attention, causing me to walk over and focus in on the familiar face.

"We've been on to your boss Aunt Rita for a while now," Agent Sanchez eagerly admitted.

"We suspect she is some sort of grand wizard in your organization. Maybe she could be the lead executive for Robert Charles?"

The FBI was trying to play mind games. They wanted me to know that Robert Charles was on the menu, and this was their crude way of warning me into good behavior. I turned around and looked both men in their faces as they awaited my response. Not wanting to let the FBI have all the fun, I reached into my pocket as both men curiously watched with gated stares. When my fingers found what I was looking for, I unfolded the piece of paper and handed it to a confused Agent Porter.

"I've been hard at work watching you guys too," I mocked. "I believe the eight-digit number above that signature is an FBI accounting string."

"If you look at the bottom there," I pointed. "Five Hundred Thousand Dollars was sent to an account with the name Richmond Drew. Richmond Drew happens to be one of the Tarpon's old aliases."

"You guys paid this monster a half a million dollars, then two prominent Black protestors that the FBI happens to be investigating, are mysteriously killed."

I smiled at the men as they both fumed. Agent Porter crumbled up the receipt, tossing it into a plastic trash bin. Sanchez made a show by rolling his eyes, mocking contempt over my accusations, yet he dare not actually challenge them.

"You just destroyed vital evidence, Agent Porter," I laughingly teased. "I thought the Bureau would have taught you better….brother."

"As a fellow black man, where the hell is your outrage for murdered protestors who put their lives on the line for our people?"

"You don't seem to be outraged by the FBI's misconduct. In fact, if I knew any better, I'd believe that you supported the killing of those black men."

"These men weren't any sort of freedom fighters," he dismissively shot back.

"They were common thugs. Street trash promoting violence against honest cops."

"They aren't my kinda folks and neither are you, Achim Jeffers. You're nothing more than a violent lunatic that kills people for money. So, please keep your insanity to yourself…brother."

Agent Sanchez's face turned to stone before he walked over to a side door and unlocked it. Before the door could swing open, a short light skinned black woman walked into the small office. I recognized her after a brief moment of confusion. She was the light skinned black woman that had followed Jessica and I in Houston, and strangely, I knew her name. It appears the FBI had brought their A-game. Things were about to get really interesting.

"Sharon," I greeted. "It's been a while since we last saw each other, sista."

"I'm sure you haven't forgotten about that night we all shared together over in Mississippi."

"How could I ever forget." She replied with the same distinct valley girl accent I last remembered.

"You and Rachel were a total train wreck in that casino. I lost count of all the drinks you two spilled. Hell, how much money did you lose at the crap tables that night Achim? Was it about ten grand?'

"Yeah. It was about that much, give or take a few hundred," I admitted.

"But it appears you weren't there with us to fellowship. It seems your work was ongoing that whole night, wasn't it?"

Sharon stared at me with those eyes that reflected all different types of colors. A smile erupted across her face before she pulled out her cellphone and loaded a video. She handed me the phone after pressing play and I watched the moving images. The video was dark and a bit hazy, as it had been recorded at night. As it played out, I began to remember the unique features of the Treme neighborhood. Then I saw my own shadowy depiction, as I exited the townhouse that was once owned by the race terrorist Ryan Foster.

"I'm sure you also remember the young white man you butchered that night, before we all got drunk at the casino," Sharon added.

"Nope," I lied. "I don't recall a damn thing about that, except watching you take that man home before the police found him dead. Didn't you two have sex that night Sharon?"

"Very funny Achim," she sarcastically responded, purposely avoiding an answer.

"The FBI was investigating Ryan Foster and those two dirty cops you killed," Agent Porter detailed.

"That's how we got this video of you."

"Instead of arresting you, the FBI did you a favor since you saved us the trouble of having to publicly investigate the NOPD."

"Let me guess guys," I interrupted. "So now you wanna use all of your so-called evidence to try and put pressure on me? How Convenient."

"If the FBI really wanted to arrest those racist cops, you would have arrested them years before they ended up getting killed. So, let's stop with all your childish con-games."

"Look, I'm not gonna cry like a baby if you arrest me. If you wanna play that card, then go ahead and put on the damn cuffs. We'll see how this game plays out for both sides. We'll see who comes out worse for wear when the dust settles, and I promise you, it won't be me."

A sharp silence fell over the tight room as everyone took in my words. They had played their best hand and in return, I had failed to submit to their intimidation tactic. The FBI wanted to control me badly. Once they had their means of control, the evil bastards would take full advantage. I could see the lust in Agent Sanchez's eyes. He was hoping to somehow flip me into a double agent. He would then be sure to use me to take down Robert Charles from there. Yet their attempt to dangle the prospect of hard prison time over my head had failed. From the look in Agent Porter's eyes, I could tell that both he and Agent Sanchez knew that I was becoming a real problem.

These two idiots failed to realize that I had learned that White Supremacy itself is a prison, specifically for people classified as black. The FBI locking me up and throwing away the keys would merely make that psychological reality, a physical one. I'd rather rot away in some cell than find myself totally beholden to the fiendish whims of the FBI. I had decided well before this meeting that I was ready to die for my people. These clowns would get zero cooperation from me.

"Achim, I can promise that you'll spend the rest of your pathetic life in jail if you or Robert Charles try any funny business," Sanchez barked.

"I'll be watching your ass. From here on out, everything you do during this investigation better be on the up and up."

"If so much as a paper clip comes up missing from this building today. If we find out your hiding information from us, I'm coming to see you with a search warrant from hell….got it!"

Both Sanchez and Porter turned away and headed for the exit. After they opened the door, I followed them out into the hallway before looking back into the small room. Sharon stood alone inside, wearing an amused smile as she continued to stare me down. Looking into her familiar eyes, I recalled the mix of terror and focus that consumed her that night we both murdered Ryan. That night she was determined to fight White Supremacy, but now she stood alone in her little room wearing that treasonous FBI badge. The sharp contrast caused me to wonder who the hell this woman truly was.

"Your name isn't really Sharon is it?" I asked.

"I'm Madam Agent to you, Mister," she sternly answered. "You should appreciate that an undercover should never reveal who they truly are. Have a nice meeting, Achim Jeffers."

Agent Porter reached out and slammed the door in front of me, rudely ending my conversation with Sharon. Catching the hint, I adjusted my sports coat and followed the two men down the long hallway. We went down the passageway, passing dozens of open offices until we reached the opposite corner of the building. There was a wide entrance at this corner that led into a large conference room. I followed the men inside and found it filled with casually dressed government employees, many of whom sported black collared shirts and baggy cargo pants.

We found seats near a window and listened in as a preppy looking white boy bullshitted his way through wordy power point slides. Scanning the room, I noticed NOPD badges, Louisiana State Trooper emblems, and a few scattered Secret Service lapels. It immediately dawned on me that I was right in the midst of my enemies. These were

Suspected Race Soldiers, who had dedicated their lives towards oppressing the Black Community. Feeling the determined spirit pulsing within me, I took a brief second to close my eyes and pray to the Lord, asking him for strength. I would surely need his presence in this den of Anti-Black evil.

After a few minutes I noticed Pokey's dark brown face seated near the head of a long table. Alongside him were some very familiar looking dignitaries. His squinted eyes examined the bright screen as the young white man droned on-and-on about surveillance measures implemented at Louis Armstrong Airport.

Sensing me watching him, Pokey broke his gaze away from the screen and looked towards me. After delivering a quick head nod, he returned to reading the screen. He was still pissed, but I instantly knew that in spite of his angst, a few of my blunt concerns regarding his FBI counterparts had hit home.

Next to Pokey, sat the newly elected mayor of New Orleans, Neil Elliot. Neil was a Creole man whose Boule connected family had dabbled in New Orleans politics for decades. He had worked as the press secretary for the D.C. Chapter of the NAACP, before he decided to run for Mayor. For the ever-ambitious Neil, this stint as Mayor of New Orleans was to be a brief stop before he predictably moved on to higher offices. In the world of white political power brokers, Neil was their perfect version of a "Negro Leader". He was eloquent, relatable, smart and most importantly, obedient.

Fully engrossed in the briefing, the mayor leaned back in his chair, softly beating his shiny fountain pen against his bottom lip. From his body language, I could sense that he was very nervous and on edge. He had a good reason to be concerned about this situation. Pokey was his hand-picked guy, and if his Chief of Police ended up getting assassinated, the wound would certainly become a political blemish on his own record.

The Director of the FBI's New Orleans field office, Eve Saunders, sat next to the mayor. Director Saunders was your typical middle-aged white woman from southern California. She had all the features of an athletic jogger who kept herself in shape, yet her manly pants suit purposely hid her womanly features from the world. An attorney by trade, she made a name for herself in the Gulf Region by successfully convicting several popular parish commissioners on fraud charges. On orders from Aunt Rita, I dug into her past, searching for anything we could use against her. No matter how hidden, I'm always able to find something that can protect us from our enemies, but this woman was surprisingly clean. Unlike most senior government officials, Director Saunders ambitions were strictly oriented towards enforcing the law. Aunt Rita and I both knew Robert Charles was on an inevitable collision course with this lady. Sooner or later, this woman would try to sink her teeth into us. Right now, I just hoped her focus was squarely on protecting Pokey, rather than trying to set the table against us.

From across the table where Pokey sat, was a guest that totally surprised me when I first noticed him. Having only seen him on TV, I did several double takes to ensure it was indeed who I thought it was. After thorough examination, it became clear it was him for sure. His name was Travis Chase, a well-known TV pundit and Beltway Insider. Travis happened to be the Senior Manager of Governor Clay Lewis's Presidential Campaign. Pokey had become a big part of Clay Lewis's campaign strategy to turnout black voters in the south, so after more thought, his presence at the meeting became less surprising.

The young white man giving the briefing, quickly flipped through several slides before stopping at one and taking a deep breath. He slowly read off the name Zhilan before descending into very vague details about his Asian gang.

"What do we know about this Zhilan guy?" Travis Chase asked.

"We don't know much," Director Saunders jumped in.

"We know a ton about his gang. Aside from the fact his gang is responsible for a large percentage of the heroin that's entering North America, we've only gotten cold trails on Zhilan himself."

"He appears to be some sort of mystery man. We believe that he's based somewhere in Cambodia, but other than that, our international partners haven't been able to positively ID him."

"Well, I just want to know how this Zhilan character and his gang ended up here in New Orleans, selling dope in my damn city?" Neil Elliot vented.

"From our intel assessments, Zhilan and his Asian gang appear to be a mixture of Vietnamese, Taiwanese and Filipinos. With that wide of a cultural reach, Zhilan's gang likely has access to dozens of cities across the country," Director Saunders explained.

"New Orleans does have a large concentration of Vietnamese nationals that immigrated here after the Vietnam War. It's likely that family ties have brought Zhilan's business to Louisiana. So, they've flooded the drug market, put the locals out of business and are causing a bloody turf war here."

Director Saunders turned in her chair and faced a silent Pokey. Her untanned skin contrasted heavily with her lively blue eyes. Leaning her elbows on the table, she focused in on Pokey as she closed the distance between them. Her body language was bold and rude, visibly disturbing Neil Elliot as she invaded the sandwiched mayor's personal space.

"Pokey, I need to know how you guys obtained the info that led to the death of Zhilan's associates."

"How did your folks know when to raid the place? Did the intel come from someone within your department…or was there an outside source?"

He bit down hard on his lip. I knew what the Director was really going after, and so did he. I asked Pokey the very same thing in my office and he had blown a gasket. Now, White Societies most dominant law enforcement apparatus was wondering if the NOPD had dirty drug dealing cops. Dirty cops that could have deliberately engaged in a bloody turf war with a drug trafficking syndicate. In New Orleans, it wasn't unheard of for drug dealing cops to eliminate their competition, either by arrest or murder.

I knew exactly what Director Saunders was wondering, as she stared into Pokey's soul. She wanted to understand why a successful underground recluse like Zhilan, would risk garnering international attention by assassinating the sitting Chief of Police of a major American city. The very thought of directly attacking an entire Police Department, is extremely provocative. The fact that Zhilan had hired the hyper-cruel Tarpon to execute that thought, conveyed how serious of a threat this truly was. For the mystery man Zhilan, this surely had to be a personal matter. In the world of crime, extreme solutions usually originate from intimate betrayals or dangerous competitors.

"Director Saunders," Pokey gingerly began. "None of my guys are involved in any illegal activities."

"My department is clean. The shoot that night, was totally clean. The officers who performed that raid, are some of my most trusted guys. Hell, I handpicked the team to ensure no one was on the take."

"Everything involving the NOPD is above board, Director." He stated, after taking in a deep breath.

"I believe you Pokey," she softly responded.

"I know it's painful to have to consider that one of your own could be a bad apple, but I know you understand that I must ask tough questions. It's my job."

"Now let's discuss how the FBI plans to keep you alive and catch this Tarpon fellow."

She lifted her elbows from the table and leaned back comfortably into her chair. With a quick gesture towards the young presenter, she summoned him in front of the projector screen and he continued flipping through slides. After finding the slide he was looking for, he began briefing all of us on the Tarpon's greatest hits. His merciless bombing of a government building in Chile. The mysterious assassinations of two West African heads of state. His KGB funded activities in Ukraine and Romania that included the murder of several influential businessmen. The FBI seemed to have an accurate tally of most of the Tarpon's missions, with the obvious exception of their own sponsored murders.

Flipping past his last slide, the young man clicked off the projector before reading a written intel assessment. The assessment described how the FBI strongly believed that the Tarpon would infiltrate into the country via the Texas/Mexico border. The FBI assessed that the Tarpon would illegally arrive in the United States and likely link up with a popular White extremist group in Texas. They believed he would acquire high-grade explosives near Waco, before traveling to New Orleans. Their hope was to use undercover elements in that group to locate the Tarpon and arrest him before he could execute his plan. From there, the FBI believed they could arrest the Tarpon, flip him and ultimately use him to arrest Zhilan.

Their plan was crap and filled with the shit fairy tales are made of. As I quietly sat there taking it all in, I quivered to think that the FBI was this incompetent. All of this had to be some sick joke, meant to provoke me. No hitman worth there salt would risk sneaking into a country by swimming across the damn border like some illegal immigrant. A professional assassin is supposed to be quiet, concealed and stealthy by trade. Low level criminals, like illegal immigrants, are noisy and naturally attract lots of attention. The last thing the Tarpon would do is link up with a wild-eyed White Supremacist group that is almost certainly filled with undercover agents.

"Your report is off the mark big time," I whispered to Agent Sanchez.

"You'll need to can the whole thing and start from scratch, or Pokey's a dead man."

Infuriated by my frank comments, Agent Sanchez hushed me into silence while giving me a contempt filled death stare. After sending his non-verbal message, he looked away, returning his focus to the speaker. The white man described how the Tarpon would likely attempt to plant explosives near each police district office in the city. This entire discussion was nonsensical and it had to be stopped before its illogical ambitions took root.

"Agent Sanchez this is bullshit. You asked for my help, but I'm not going to sit here and silently let the FBI get black people killed."

The conference room went quiet, and I could feel everyone's attention gravitate towards the sound of my voice. Instantly, I knew I had spoken a bit too loud, interrupting the briefing and causing a stir. Director Saunders removed her reading glasses from the top of her hair, planting them squarely in front of her eyes. With a curious squint, she sat up straight in her seat and examined me.

"Who are you and what do you have to add?" She asked in agitation.

I locked her stare with my own, purposely refusing to cower down to her presumed position of authority. Turning myself away from Sanchez, I stood up and faced her presumptions of power head on. Having garnered the rooms full attention, I looked down at the sitting FBI Director and placed my hands into my pockets, purposely dismissing all protocols of professional respect.

"I'm Achim Jeffers and I run a Private Investigative firm here in New Orleans," I began.

"Agent's Porter and Sanchez hired me on to assist in this matter."

Clearly puzzled by the admittance of a civilian in such a top-level meeting, Director Saunders immediately cut her boiling eyes towards both men. She was not amused at all by my presence, and I could see the looming questions exploding in her mind.

"Achim is a civilian investigator we use over at the NOPD from time to time," Pokey interjected.

"He's one of the best P.I.'s I've ever seen, and his work is rock solid."

"Well, Mr. Rock Solid," she cut loose. "You still haven't told us what our report is missing."

"The Tarpon is not going to sneak into the country," I explained.

"He'll walk right up to a customs booth, present his passport and the U.S. Government will happily issue the guy a visa, welcoming him in with open arms."

"And may I ask how you know all this?" She dismissively quipped.

"Because the man isn't stupid, nor is he desperate," I sternly barked back.

"This isn't some wild-eyed Arab Jihadist. This man is an expert at eliminating hardened targets. The Tarpon has perfected the art of shape-shifting and blending into nothing. He's calculating, patient, and extremely intelligent. I'm certain he'll take his time and study our defenses while wearing us down."

"To be frank, he's a white male in North America. You're searching for a needle in a haystack of needles. The man will be sure to use that to his full advantage."

"There's no way this guy is landing at any American airport and not drawing attention to himself," she rebutted.

"While we don't know what the Tarpon looks like, a man like him traveling into the U.S. would be discovered rather easily. TSA and Customs happen to be extremely good at what they do Mr. Jeffers. If he uses any legal means of entering the United States, the Tarpon is as good as caught."

Laughing off her heartfelt bravado, I slowly walked towards the dark projector screen and stared up at it. With my back to the main table, I examined the empty screen and thought it was a much more accurate assessment of what the Tarpon's potential actions might be.

"You'll never catch him thinking like that," I teased.

"This man is a shape-shifter. The Tarpon has mastered the art of changing his appearance, personality, habits, hobbies, damn near everything."

"He has professionally forged passports, along with dozens of hidden ID's locked away in strategically placed safe boxes in almost every country."

"He's made an art of blending into society. Hell, he could be a new hire mopping the floors in this very building and you'd never know it until it was too late."

"And may I ask how you know so much about the man," Director Saunders pointedly asked.

Turning around to look at her, I pulled my hands out of my pockets and presented my balled-up fists. Spooked by the gesture, I could sense the fear within the Director as she watched this black man take a boxer's stance in front of her.

"I know because I've fought the Tarpon and had the opportunity to feel the man's mettle."

"I've taken the measure of the man in real life combat. So, my words aren't just some vague assessments written up by government pricks. My words are hard-earned lessons."

"So, you've seen this guy before," she quipped with a hint of disbelief.

"That means you can help our experts draw a composite of him."

"No," I refused. "It only means I know this animal when I look into his beady eyes. As I mentioned earlier, the man is an expert at changing his appearance, but what he can't change is the burning truth buried within him."

"If given a chance to look at him, I could ID him, but more importantly I can identify the Tarpon by his tactics."

Director Saunders removed her horned rimmed glasses and laid them on the table. Observing her body language, I could tell she was still unconvinced and a bit aggravated by my confidence. Travis Chase looked up at me from his seat and raised his hand. When I acknowledged him, he leaned his elbows on the arms of his chair and looked directly into my eyes.

"Since you've supposedly met this guy, what do you believe he'll do?" he frankly asked.

"The Tarpon won't be coming from Mexico, that's for sure," I reiterated.

"He'll use the northern border, probably someplace in the Pacific Northwest, most likely Seattle."

"During a prior investigation, I was able to discover that the Tarpon always uses the same identity when visiting Canada or Alaska."

"The Tarpon is an enigma. He is many people and then he can become no one. For a man to navigate life this way, you have to have many identities."

"Given the magnitude of this mission, I believe the Tarpon will enter the U.S. using a means he's very familiar and comfortable with. He likely has close contacts throughout that area. Close contacts that won't be suspicious of him because they believe they know who he is."

"The Tarpon is a man whose very survival depends on him being prepared beyond measure," I explained.

"He wouldn't take this job without making sure the odds are completely in his favor. The man won't come here and hope to get it right. He'll come here ready to make it happen."

"This means the Tarpon will likely have to deal with the problem of getting a weapon into the country. The Pacific Northwest is the perfect area to do that, with its wide-open water border with Canada."

"He could easily use a boat to move a bomb, and you'd never catch him."

"Well Mr. Jeffers," Director Saunders sighed. "Let's stop wasting each other's time."

"How about you be a good sport and share this false identity with all of us, since you seem to know everything about this guy."

I turned and looked down at the Director, making sure to put on my biggest smile. Annoyed by my joy, she waved her hand in frustration, imploring me to get to the point. In the background, I could hear Agent's Sanchez and Porter let out nervous sighs as they watched me lower my palms onto the shiny wooden table. Closing the distance with Director Saunders, I fished around in her confused stare and found a bit of weakness within her. She was a woman that didn't like surprises and I had one final surprise that was sure to unsettle her world even more.

"I've been a good sport, Director," I responded.

"In fact, I've already given your agents the name….but your guys saw fit to toss the evidence into a damn trash bin."

I followed the Director's stare as she zoomed in on Sanchez and Porter. In a silent panic, both men quickly realized that there was more than one reason I had given them that receipt. Agent Porter shot up from his chair, bolting towards the exit in a controlled scurry. I could see the sudden importance of the name Richmond Drew finally dawn upon him as he scrambled out of the conference room.

Pleased that I had sent the right message, I leaned up from the table and walked away from the Director. The way Porter had jumped up from his seat and the awkward expression on Sanchez's face, had captured the Director's full attention. At that moment, she realized I wasn't a bullshitter. There was a reason the two men had invited me here. Whatever I knew, both of her subordinates valued the hell out of it.

"So, you're saying we should all make a field trip up to Seattle?" She half asked. "How can you be so sure about this Mr. Jeffers? How the hell would you know if he's going to travel through Seattle!"

Not feeling the need to turn around and address her, I calmly reclaimed my seat. Having captured everyone's attention, I made a show of lazily adjusting my sports coat before providing her with my ironic answer. As the words formulated in my mind, I could barely contain the chuckle that left my lips beforehand.

"Because that's what I would do if I were him," I laughed. "Me and my weapon would already be in this damned country….and that would be a bad day for Pokey."

Chapter Six

Strange Sea Stories

The deep blue waters south of Victoria were choppy, and the lumpy swells felt heavy as they slammed against my laboring vessel. Using this boat's under-powered motor to push against the straits blitzing current was useless. At this point, I was already feeling the exhaustion settling in. I turned my 45-foot sailboat southwesterly in an attempt to head towards the calmer waters near Port Angeles. Pushing the throttle to the floor, I sensed the stern of my boat dig in as the propellers struggled to make way.

Rolling and pitching viciously, I grasped a handrail and held on tight before clipping the engine kill cord into my life jacket. This old sailboat was the only vessel I could find to do this job on such short notice. Having purchased it from an American citizen who lived part-time in Victoria, the boat was already a U.S. registered vessel. After a quick informal tour, I paid the eager seller in cash and bought it on the spot.

Now, out in the middle of the Strait of Juan de Fuca, I was discovering that the boat had more than a few sour lemons. For one, its compass was inaccurate, making steering a steady course in this current controlled waterway, next to impossible. The sailboats motor only ran at half power, and the boat's rudder angle indicator was off by at least ten degrees. There was a reason the seller was so eager to rid himself of this piece of trash, and now I was finding out his secrets. Despite feeling a sense of anger for letting this slick-tongued American con me, I thought it all well and good. Given the amount of money he received, the eager seller would probably never think twice about the unlucky fool who bought the boat from him.

As I turned left and passed behind a fast-moving car carrier, several huge swells pounded my beam, causing sea water to wash over my open deck. Shaking the cold water from my boots, I pressed forward, pointing my bow towards the mountains that towered over the safe haven of Port Angeles.

Having safely crossed the Strait, I anchored my boat in the partially concealed bay. After turning off the struggling motor, I used fresh water to wash the boat's deck before removing the vessel's Canadian flag and replacing it with a U.S. one. On the port bow and stern, the boat's name "Lil Nuts," was plastered on the hull in bold black letters. Climbing down into the cabin, I found the new name stickers that read "Wind Stallion." Given the weak performance of this boat, I laughingly thought the new name was a bit disingenuous.

Leaning over the side of the boat, I placed the new stickers over the old ones. Now that I was inside U.S. territory, it was legally a U.S. flagged vessel and could avoid customs. Logging into my phone app, I searched for the location of the tug Alaskan Spirit. After the program loaded, I saw that the tug was east of Neah Bay and only a few hours away from me. I grabbed a fresh apple from the small refrigerator, wiping it clean with a washcloth. Bored, I decided that I should call Alex to give him the update I owed him.

Scrolling down my contact list, I found his name and mashed down hard on the call button before taking a big bite.

"Hello," Alex quickly answered.

"I'm feet dry," I softly responded while chewing.

"Jesus," Alex loudly proclaimed. "It's good to finally know you made it."

"Rickey and your rice eating friend have called me more than a few times asking all kinds of questions."

"How did things go up in Prince Rupert?" He asked.

"It went just like I thought it would," I tried to deflect.

"I'm sure you and your brother have read the Canadian news reports by now."

"Yeah, we saw them. Rickey was just curious," Alex jumped in. "He wants to know if she tried to fuck you."

The phone went silent and our pause was filled with voiceless tension. The ever-jealous Rickey knew Diane well, so he already knew the answer to the question that was bothering his soul. Even after her death, Rickey was still as possessive and controlling as ever. Knowing better than to tell Alex the harsh truth, I tried to cleverly avoid the question.

"Diane was living with three men, Alex. All of them were foreigners. Two of them were African and one was East Indian," I described.

"I hate to be the bearer of bad news, but in Rickey's absence, Diane was a changed woman."

Understanding my vague answer, I could almost feel Alex considering whether he should ask me the obvious follow-up questions. After passing along Rickey's appreciation, he detailed several conversations he had with Zhilan.

"Your slant-eyed lady wanted you to know that the FBI is on to you. She has sources that are telling her that there is some team from New Orleans hunting you down," he admitted.

"And that's not it. Apparently, the Feds are looking for a woman named Rachel Douglas and have hired a man they believe you are acquainted with. He's a nigger named Achim Jeffers or something like that."

The two names grabbed me, causing me to toss the half-eaten apple into the bay and lean up against the sailboats flimsy side railing. Someone within the FBI was serious, way too serious for me to discount them. This would be a grand reunion for the three of us and I needed to make sure I came to the party bearing the right gifts.

"What do they know?" I asked.

"Not much at all," Alex responded. "All they know is Seattle. Outside of that, they're still in the dark. Your lady wants to know if this occurrence is a showstopper."

"Hell no!" I immediately dismissed.

"Tell her this mission is still on. Have her source provide us with updates twice a day."

"I'll lose them up here and make my way to you. What's the status on my transportation out of town?"

"That's the other problem," Alex conveyed.

"I can't find a truck big enough for your needs. There aren't any rentals, no trucks for sale….nothing."

"I discussed the issue with your lady and she offered to help, if you wanted to continue."

"She has two gentlemen in Seattle that could assist, but she warned me to be careful. Apparently, they aren't the most reliable. She said they are a little young and very immature, but they can get you and your heavy gear out of Seattle and away from that FBI manhunt."

"She was also pretty vocal that this service won't be free of charge," he added.

"The men won't know who you are or what you're doing, they'll only have orders to take you and your gear wherever you need to go."

"OK," I relented. "I'll go ahead and use them. Have them meet me at the lake tomorrow. I'll text you the address once I get moving."

After my conversation with Alex, I put away the cellphone and started the long task of rigging my sails onto the two masts. Minutes after finishing the work, I looked at the horizon and saw a small tugboat towing a large container barge. Pouring myself a warm cup of tea, I sat and watched as the Alaskan Spirit maneuvered into the shallow bay of Port Angeles. The tug slowly shortened its tow wire, before coming to a dead stop and abruptly dumping hundreds of feet of wire onto the muddy bottom. The captain was setting a poor man's anchor and using the wire to do so. As both the tug and barge came to a halt, I reached over and grabbed the sailboat's radio and hailed out to the Alaskan Spirit.

"Alaskan Spirit, this is the Wind Stallion," I recited twice.

"I see you Wind Stallion. Come over when you are ready," a familiar voice responded.

After starting the sailboat's engine, I guzzled down a lemon-flavored sports drink before hauling up my anchor. Putting the rudder over to hard right, I pushed the throttle ahead slightly and turned the boat towards the anchored tug and barge. As I closed in on my target, I felt the power of the breeze pushing me off course. The gusty wind filled my sails with air, causing me to have to make large course corrections to pull alongside the tug.

After increasing speed and calculating my drift, I was able to safely make it next to the tug. Two well-worn deckhands caught my mooring lines as I tossed them over. The gray look of exhaustion on the crews faces told me that they hadn't slept well. I gingerly climbed over to the tug to examine my crate, and I saw that it was still secured to the deck. The bottom of the crate was drenched with sea water and the top layer of wood was covered in salt crystals. Other than being waterlogged, the crate was intact.

"We'll let you have some privacy so you can handle your business." The captain proclaimed while walking up from behind.

The captain had come out on deck only wearing a blue tank top and faded boxer briefs. A lit cigarette hung from his lips and the smell of cheap tobacco seemed to surround him. He held a crowbar in his hand, which he gave to me while displaying a delightful smile.

"If you need anything, we'll be in the galley eating lunch," he advised.

"If I don't see you again, I wanna thank you for thinking of us and giving us this opportunity."

"We had to really hustle to get here on time after getting slammed by the weather offshore," he described. "But we toughed it out and made it here."

After flicking the ash from his cigarette, he looked over at my sailboat and studied it before curiously looking at the crate. Given my tiny sailboat and the size of the heavy crate, I knew the question plaguing his thoughts.

"I plan on making it all fit. I promise, you have nothing to worry yourself about." I knowingly offered.

Satisfied with my assurances, the captain ushered his crew members into the boat and shut the watertight door behind them, leaving me all alone on the back deck. I used the crowbar to lift the top off of the crate and peered inside. Surrounding the Russian built remote controlled gun turret, were piles of 25-pound sacks that gave the crate its heft. After removing a layer of the weights, I was able to lift the gun turret out of the crate and unfold it into a tripod.

The turret's frame was light, but its build was sturdy. This piece of equipment was more than capable of supporting the weight and recoil of a heavy caliber machine gun. The remote-controlled turret could operate using a standard car battery and would rotate 360 degrees on demand, via Bluetooth. I folded the turret back up and tucked it away before fishing for the remote. Underneath the next layer of weights, I found the remote control in a black pelican case. Besides the remote, several pounds of Russian made high explosives were tucked away in protective casings. I took both items and laid them out on the steel deck before diving back into the crate to dig out the final prize. Having removed most of the weights, my eyes finally found the Spetnaz 25mm cannon.

It was a sight of beauty to behold. Taking a few seconds to catch my breath, I simply stared at it, taking in the smooth barrel and dark grey chamber housing. This weapon was a killing machine. One 25mm round was enough to totally devastate an armored car or light tank. With this type of firepower, my human target wouldn't stand a chance.

Using a chain fall, I lowered all the gear down to the sailboat and hid it away in the cabin area. After placing all the weights back into the wooden crate, I lightly hammered the top back into place and prepared to hoist it overboard. I climbed up to the tug's crane and energized the boat's hydraulic pump. After connecting the crate's long slings to the boom, I lifted the heavy crate off the deck and placed it over the side of the tug just above the water.

Eager to get moving, I untied one sling and used a sharp blade to cut the other. The crate tumbled into the water, briefly floating before slipping below the waterline and sinking out of view. Done with this part of the mission, I climbed down to my sailboat and pulled out the long bricks of high explosives. Now, it was time to make a grand exit.

This moment was the exact reason I had the Ukrainian arms dealer add this to my order. There needed to be no evidence that could lead anyone to me, and this tugboat happened to be filled with potential witnesses. As I prepared the explosives, adding fuses and wires, the visuals of the exhausted Captain and his crew's dedication swam into my mind. They had suffered mightily to get here. These were good white men; men who deserved to live another day. Battling the compassion emerging within me, I walked over to the tugs hull and scoped out the perfect place to attach the bomb.

As I leaned over to place the bomb against the cold hull, I took in a deep breath and threw the bomb into the water. None of these men were going to die today. These were loyal white men and if anyone on this fucked up planet deserved to live, it was these guys. The captain would live to take his newfound cash back to his sick wife and somehow, I knew no one would know what all of us had done today.

I started the motor on my sailboat and headed away from Port Angeles as dusk approached. When I was near Port Townsend, north of Puget Sound, I killed the engine and began to sail south towards Seattle. The lumpy seas had calmed significantly but the gusty wind was more than strong enough to slowly push me southward. My destination would be Lake Union, located in the northern portion of Seattle. After calling the marina and reserving a mooring slip, I called Alex to arrange my transportation out of the city.

"I'll be at Lake Union tomorrow morning," I relayed over the phone.

"Make sure our lady has her people there. I'll be ready to move out so we can beat the morning traffic."

"Roger that my friend," Alex replied.

"She told me her guys will be there when you need them. I'll have the beer on ice when you arrive in Phoenix. It will be good to see you again."

"The hell with your beer Alex, let's toss back tequila shots until we pass out." I joked.

Alex let out a pleased laugh, concurring with my sentiments while promising to roll out the red carpet. Before I ended the call, the thought of Achim Jeffers running around the city searching for my whereabouts made me chuckle. As he was trying to give me his final salutation, I interrupted him and asked him a question that re-introduced seriousness to our lighthearted discussion.

"Does our lady have any new information on the FBI and Achim Jeffers?"

For a few seconds, Alex went quiet after swallowing his laughter. On the other end of the phone, I could almost hear his mind searching for the right words to tell me the truth.

"Yeah," he softly admitted.

"You don't have to worry about Achim Jeffers."

"Her contact works in the FBI's Seattle field office and they plan on keeping him away from you."

"If he somehow finds a way to get close, he will be taken care of." He conveyed.

Feeling a profound sense of disappointment, I ended the call and re-focused on steering the sailboat into the wind. I was looking forward to meeting Achim again. I knew that there was no way he would allow the FBI to eliminate him. He was too smart for that, too dangerous of a man. When I made it out of Seattle, he would most certainly be waiting on me in New Orleans.

As my mind raced to find the perfect solution to this Achim Jeffers puzzle, I pulled the sailboat into a shallow cove and dropped the anchor. It had been an early day and I needed a long nap before making a first light arrival at the lake.

After warming up an underwhelming meal of canned spaghetti and boiled corn, I poured myself a glass of white wine. Leaning back into my soft hammock, I set my alarm clock and allowed myself to drift into rest. When the alarm went off, with its loud pulsing rings, I was instantly awoken to the darkness of the rocking sailboat. Jolted, I cleaned myself up before weighing anchor and setting sail for Lake Union.

I arrived at Ballard Locks at sunrise and sailed through to the lake. Without much trouble, I pulled into the

Fisherman's Terminal and found my reserved mooring slip. Once all the lines were secured, I connected my boat to shore power and hastily took down all of the sails. I had made it to the U.S. safely, and now there was this matter of locating my chaperones.

Walking to the parking lot, I looked around for a pickup truck and found one parked underneath a large tree near the sidewalk. There were two Asian men who silently stood out in the light rain, gazing at the ground while puffing away at their cigarettes. This white dominated section of Seattle wasn't their part of town, and the men's nervous body language was an obvious giveaway.

"Are you guys ready," I demanded.

The Asian men looked at me with eyes tortured with uncertainty. I could tell I wasn't the kind of white man they were expecting. My smelly clothes and budding facial hair gave me the appearance of the drug addicted bums they were used to seeing near downtown Seattle. In their silence, they continued to examine me as I slowly closed in on them. When I was a little more than ten feet away, I pointed towards the boat slip, directing their unconvinced thoughts towards my sailboat.

"Come on guys. You're here to help me, aren't you?"

"Alright, I've got some heavy equipment I need to move. Let's go. "

Annoyed with the men's confused insistence, I walked behind the truck and dropped down the tailgate. Hearing the heavy tailgate fall, one of the Asians was spurred into action, causing him to mumble at me in broken English, demanding that I not touch his vehicle. Satisfied that I had their attention, I walked to the pier and both men angrily followed. We climbed down into the cabin, and I pulled out the tripod, remote and Spetnaz 25mm cannon. Using thin blankets, we wrapped up the long cannon before both men carried it off the boat. I walked behind them as the men struggled mightily to move the gear. After pausing several times to allow them to regain their strength, we made it to the truck.

All three of us lifted the cannon into the bed of the truck and tied it down. Satisfied with their work, the men spoke to each other in Chinese. Unaware that I understood their language, they argued amongst each other, debating on when they should kill me. As they loaded themselves into the front seats, the taller man emphatically told the shorter one that they would wait. In that instant, I knew why Zhilan had arranged for these guys to assist me. They definitely weren't trustworthy, hence, Zhilan needed to eliminate them. She thought, Why not have me do the job and spare herself the trouble? Pretending to be ignorant of their scheme, I walked up to the driver side window and pointed at the pier once again.

"Wait," I loudly instructed. "I need to get my luggage, hold on one second."

Unconcerned with their failure to understand, I walked to the boat to get my bag. After stuffing my loaded pistol into the small of my back, I locked up the sailboat and placed the keys inside the marina's drop box. While walking down the sidewalk adjacent to the main office, I saw a dark colored SUV pull into the parking lot and stop in front of the entrance. The driver killed the engine and all four doors popped open. Four men climbed out wearing dark jeans and long sleeve shirts. Three of the men wore badges, while a tall dark skinned fellow looked out of place.

I tilted my head toward the sidewalk and tried my best to examine the man's face using peripheral vision. He was a tall black man and his athletic build rung bells. The man's bald head was cleanly shaven, aside from his long black beard. The awkward presence of his dark sunglasses stood out on this grey morning. This was Achim Jeffers and the concern of how he was able to locate me at this marina, in the wide-open city of Seattle, worried me.

I put away the inner frustration when I noticed three of the men enter the marina, leaving Achim alone to stare out towards the pier. Trying not to increase my pace, I kept him in my field of vision as he scanned the area until he noticed me slowly walking away from him. Feeling Achim's shaded eyes zoom in to inspect, I knew he would swiftly put things together in his mind, so I decided to stop walking and turned to face him. He was around fifty yards behind me and even from that distance, I could sense the look of recognition emerging on his face. Amused by his insightful intelligence, I playfully waved at him before pulling the pistol from the small of my back.

Perceiving my impending action, Achim bolted away towards the pier in a dead sprint. My bullets chased his every step, failing to find their target as he dove into the marina's ice-cold water. Having scared him away, I turned and ran towards the truck. The tall Asian behind the wheel, cranked up the engine before I opened the door.

"Let's get the hell outta here! Now!" I yelled.

The driver stepped on the gas and the truck peeled out of its parking space. As we collected speed and began to approach the Marina's main office, I saw three alarmed men brandishing pistols near the entrance. One of the clean-shaven men was Hispanic, another was white and the last was a short black man. The white man noticed our truck but got distracted as Achim's head finally surfaced above the cold water. While Achim fought to stay afloat, I could hear him yelling at the top of his lungs. The white man disregarded his instructions and ran to the water to save him. The other men seemed to be in a state of confusion as they looked to find the source of gunfire. The black one was the second to notice our truck, and he ran out into the parking lot, wildly waving his badge. Behind him, the Hispanic gentleman cautiously followed with his pistol at the ready.

"Slow it down," I ordered. "We've got the drop on these cops."

"If you guys got guns, now's the time to shoot these cops before they get inside their SUV."

The driver and his partner clearly understood my English, pulling concealed weapons from underneath their seats. Quickly re-racking my pistol, I lowered my backseat window down halfway. As the short black man walked towards our truck waving his badge in wild confusion, I examined my target while my finger eagerly sat on the trigger.

The driver slowed the truck to a crawl and eased towards the Black man. As his eyes began surveying the insides of the truck, several loud gunshots interrupted his moment of fearful confusion. Both Asians let loose a barrage of fire, striking the black man several times in the chest. As the black cop crumbled to the ground, I reached my arm out of the window and aimed towards the ducking Hispanic cop. Behind him sat their SUV, so I aimed and fired four well placed shots, hitting the SUV's two front tires.

In a wild panic, the Hispanic and White man fired shots at our moving truck. Ducking the salvo, the tall Asian driver slammed down on the gas and the truck powered out of the parking lot and turned onto the street. As I looked back, the remaining men were running to the aid of their injured colleague, instead of using the radio that was surely inside their vehicle. We only had a few minutes to put some real distance between us and this marina. Those cops would surely transmit an officer down radio call along with a description of our truck within seconds.

"Where can we dump this truck?" I insisted.

"We have shop near," The short Asian conceded.

"We move to van then we good. We take care of you," he tried to reassure.

The driver avoided the highway and stuck to the back roads, traveling from the heights of Queen Anne to a beat down mechanic shop near Capitol Hill. We pulled up to a closed garage and the short Asian exited the truck, digging for keys in his pocket as he galloped towards the garage's locked doors. Once the gate was lifted, the driver drove the truck into the garage and the gate was closed behind us. Noticing all the tools and ripped apart luxury cars inside this place, I knew these men had taken me to their chop shop.

I could sense the looming arrival of their twisted plans to betray me. How could I not expect it? The hidden looks on their faces when they first saw that cannon, was a gateway into their yellow hearts. For them, this was supposed to be the sudden end of the poor white man and their swift windfall into an unexpected payday. These men who pretended not to understand spoken English, would surely try and double cross me. It was no smal wonder why Zhilan wanted these jackasses dead. If they operated this selfishly, they were certainly a business liability that she wouldn't mind having removed.

What these guys didn't know about me or Zhilan's real intentions, had now led to their own demise. By playing dumb, they thought they had outsmarted me, but life has cruel ways of humbling even the most pious of criminals. Both men talked loudly in Chinese, debating if they should have me help them move the heavy gear into the van before tying me up. While they debated amongst themselves, I exited the truck with my reloaded pistol.

Both men looked confused as I walked over to the driver's side. When they realized I was tightly brandishing my pistol, it was too late. I shot the half aware driver in the back of his skull. The truck slowly rolled forward, softly crashing into a half-stripped BMW parked in front of it. As the short Asian man grabbed me, I easily flung him to the ground. Feeling the limits of the short man's strength, I laughed as he tried wrestling me to the oil-stained floor. Toying with the man, I allowed him to gain enough of an advantage to encourage his continued engagement, only to reassume control of the battle when I felt like it.

Minutes passed by and I could sense his inner fatigue begin to soak up his resolve. He was thoroughly outclassed, so I basked in his physical inferiority. Reluctant to grant this lesser being any sort of merciful death, I kicked him to the floor and watched him labor to catch his breath. Standing over him, I made sure he got a good look at the smile adorning my face. The helplessness staining his eyes was intoxicating. This was the universe's ultimate power, and I was standing in it, taking my rightful position as its arbitrator.

The Asian man begged for his pathetic life in perfect English, hoping his insignificant yellow words could somehow sway the reality I represented. I spat on his face before speaking to him in his native tongue, letting him know that I owned him and his people. Before he would die, he would know I was his God. I was the person he dreamt of and idolized. I was the person he hoped to steal from. I was the person he hoped to be. For that infraction, giving me his life was to be his only path towards repentance.

I reached into a nearby toolbox, picked up a ten-pound sledgehammer and briefly spun it in the palms of my hands. The short man's eyes released tears as he focused on the rusty head of the tool, anticipating the painful blows that were surely coming. Feeling the excitement exploding within my soul, I delivered the first blow to the short man's kneecap, hearing the distinct sounds of his thick bones giving way to the brutal power of my assault.

The high-pitched sounds of his cries caused me to turn my attention towards his loudmouth. After three harsh strikes, his teeth were scattered on the garage floor, swimming in the pool of his dark red blood. His breathing was faint, and he was unconscious. The man was almost at the point of death. Wasting my time to fulfill my own selfish pleasure would be a gross mistake. Tossing down the hammer, I walked to the truck and killed the engine. Inside, the tall Asian man laid still as his bloody head leaned up against the drenched steering wheel. Reaching into his pockets, I removed his wallet and fished out a fist full of keys.

After locating the van both men had mentioned earlier, I tried unlocking the door using the set of keys I found. The fifth key worked like a charm and was able to open the door.

Anxious to get this truck on the road, I started the ignition and felt the ugly vehicle rattle as the engine struggled to turnover. I put the van in reverse and eased the shaky van next to the truck, before using a hanging chain fall to move the cannon.

Ten minutes later, everything was loaded and secured inside. Glancing around the garage, I saw the pools of blood mixing with the dark oil stains on the wet floor. When the police eventually locate this chop shop, they would easily deduce that extreme violence had been employed here.

Aside from the mountain of fingerprints, hair follicles and other biological evidence I'd be leaving behind, the FBI would know that a white man was missing from this murder scene. There was no reason for me to waste my time cleaning up this treasure trove. Besides, when I killed the mark, I'd be set for life. The FBI could have all my fingerprints and DNA. Once my business was done, they'd never find me.

I took the men's ID's and opened the garage door, then backed the van out into the empty parking area. Making sure to lock the garage door, I took one of the keys and inserted it into the lock before breaking it in half. Even if someone else had a key, they'd have to find a way to cut open that lock, which would buy me more time. Pleased with the outcome, I pulled the contemptuous van out onto the road and felt it shake wildly when I accelerated. Looking down at the dashboard, I noticed the orange check engine symbol glowing brightly against the dark background. Next to the light, I also observed that the gas tank was nearly empty.

Frustrated, I drove several blocks before finding a gas station. Pulling up next to a pump, my thin wallet winced when I saw the high gasoline prices typical of Seattle. Quietly enraged, I inserted a credit card before grabbing the nozzle. As the expensive gasoline poured into that thirsty tank, I heard police sirens echoing down the street. Several fast-moving cop cars haphazardly blew past the big red stoplight in front of the gas station. I knew exactly where these cops were headed.

It was time to get moving. Making it out of the state of Washington would be my first taste of salvation. I filled the tank and decline waiting on the machine to print out its receipt. In a hurry, I started the van and felt it shutter as it struggled to come to life. The thought of this piece of junk having to be my only means of making it to Arizona, worried me. Yet, on the other hand, this soccer mom mobile was actually the perfect cover. While driving towards the Interstate on ramp, several cop cars sped by in the opposite lane. None of them had a clue that the white suspect they were looking for, was cruising away in this faded van.

Chapter Seven

Puget Sound Trickers

I absolutely hate being here. There is no place more uncomfortable or frightening, than a hospital. My clothes were still heavy and drenched from my impromptu swim. It didn't help that the buildings air conditioning seemed to be stuck on freezing. If I didn't catch the flu after this, it would certainly be a miracle. Forcing myself up from the wooden chair, I walked over to the large window and stared up at a blanket of greyish clouds. Not one trace of sunlight could be found coming down from the heavens. Every minute I spent in Seattle, made me yearn for the heat and stifling humidity of New Orleans.

The door to our private waiting room slid open and an exhausted Sanchez walked inside. In his hand, he carried a long grocery bag that seemed to float inches above the floor. Stopping at the round dining room table, he briefly glanced into my eyes before lifting the bag and dropping it next to my wet wallet.

"I did the best I could homie." He sighed.

"Hopefully, everything in here fits you."

Reaching into the half-filled bag, I pulled out a cheap pair of blue jeans, a yellow shirt and an undersized Seahawks sweater. As I unzipped my soiled slacks, Agent Sanchez turned his back and slowly paced towards the opposite wall.

Once I changed, I tossed the wet clothes into the plastic bag and tied a knot at the top.

"The doctor says Porter's wounds are superficial," I explained.

"Aside from a few bumps and bruises, his bullet proof vest ate most of those shots. They'll be releasing him in a few minutes."

Purposely ignoring me, Agent Sanchez lowered himself down onto the cheap couch and dismissively stared at his cellphone. I got the sense that this fucker knew what I was about to ask and he was already fighting like hell to deny me his ear.

"Sanchez, you should let me carry a gun," I broached. "Hell, you guys didn't even offer me a vest."

"That fucker could have shot me dead today," I continued. "And you had me out there with no way to protect myself."

"No fuckin way. You aren't getting a gun Achim. Not around me you aren't," he proclaimed with an unconcerned tone.

"Besides, aren't you known for chopping up white people with a machete?"

"The FBI can't have Achim Jeffers, the black hitman, carrying a gun while you're on the FBI's payroll. It's simply a liability thing."

"Aren't you claiming to be a so-called business owner these days? You ought to understand this man, it's business."

"The only thing I understand," I shot back. "Is how corrupt you people really are."

"I looked the Tarpon right in his face and he just smiled while waving back at me."

"He smiled like he knew I would be there looking for him. He wasn't even the least bit surprised to see my black ass."

"What the hell are you trying to say?" He erupted.

"You know what the hell I'm saying," I confronted.

"Someone on the inside is playing for the other team, Agent Sanchez."

"It's as clear as day. The FBI's been infiltrated. Someone is damn sure feeding the Tarpon information on what we have going on here."

Pissed, Agent Sanchez tossed his phone on the couch and sprung to his feet with a seething expression. Trying to blow off my honest assessment, he turned away from me, before throwing his arms in the air in disgust.

"How the hell would you know that Achim?" He replied.

"The FBI is nothing like your Robert Charles crime syndicate. We don't get infiltrated. No one in the FBI sells out information for money. We are dedicated to the great citizens of this country. We have honor, and that is something you don't know a damn thing about!"

The sound of the door opening pulled both of us away from our confrontation. Sanchez and I looked over to see Agent Morgan slowly enter the room. He gingerly carried two large paper bags of Chinese Food in his hands. We watched as he took overly cautious steps towards the round table, before dropping off our precious cargo.

"Lunch has arrived gentlemen," he proclaimed with a nervous smile.

"Let's eat up while it's still hot."

Agent Morgan was our liaison from the Seattle Field Office. Unlike Sanchez or Porter, Agent Morgan was more than accommodating to my presence and went out of his way to make me comfortable. I wasn't sure if the man knew who I really was, but his purposeful hospitality set off all kinds of alarms. He was a chubby white man that went out of his way to regale me with boring stories of his time in the Air Force. All of his smiles and eagerness seemed phony. It felt strategic at times, making me wonder what his real angle was, especially since he was making every effort to slow walk our investigation.

When I ran away from the Tarpon's bullets and jumped into that cold water, I swam underneath the wooden pier to conceal myself from the gunfire. Once I popped up to the surface for air, I cleared my vision and saw Agent Morgan standing near the head of the pier, while the Tarpon was sprinting towards that pickup truck in the background. I yelled like hell for Agent Morgan to leave me and give chase, but he ignored my pleas and tossed a life ring into the water instead. That action alone made me suspicious. His refusal to chase after the Tarpon was revealing and much too easy to discern. If he had chased the man like I had asked, we would have had a good chance of killing the bastard.

I'm sure he knew this, but his weak excuses told me he was on the take from someone. Now, we all sat in this cold hospital, waiting on a comrade who was barely scratched while the Tarpon was probably south of the Washington Oregon border.

"I made sure to order everyone an eggroll," Agent Morgan happily conveyed.

"This place is one of the best joints in town. Tell me what you New Orleans boys think of the shrimp fried rice."

Annoyed with his commentary, Sanchez walked over to the table and pulled the top plate out of one of the bags. After flipping open the lid, he walked away from the both of us and began to feed himself in quiet anger. Feeling the hunger, I followed suit, all the while wondering when this long pit stop would be over. The Tarpon was out there, making his way towards New Orleans and we needed to be doing our damn jobs.

"Alright Morgan, once we finish eating, we're outta here. No more sitting around and wasting time," Agent Sanchez barked with a mouth full of rice.

"Sure," he quickly responded. "But we gotta follow officer safety protocols regarding an officer involved shooting."

"Once Porter is released and given a clean bill of health, we'll all be on our way."

"That's bull," I let loose.

"The longer we sit on our hands, the harder it will be to find this guy. There's no reason for all of us to be here when we are in the middle of a dang manhunt. This is completely ridiculous."

Sensing our combined frustration beginning to brew, Agent Morgan raised both of his palms towards us, silently pleading for calm. Having finished his plate of Chinese food, Sanchez closed the top and tossed the remnants into a large grey trash can.

"We didn't fly out here to take fuckin physicals or fill out use of force reports," he commented.

"You know as well as I do, we can do all that shit once this guy's captured. What the hell do you got going on out here man?"

Angered by Sanchez's unspoken accusation, a streak of fury manifested itself in Morgan's tightly clinched facial expression. The room went silent as both FBI men stared each other down. Just as Agent Morgan was fixing his lips to lob a response, the door of the room swung open and all of our eyes turned towards the noise. The mood in the room changed when Agent Porter walked inside, followed by Director Saunders and her Seattle counterpart. Porter's long sleeve shirt was unbuttoned and several cotton gauze patches were taped over his bare chest.

In his left hand, he carried the bullet riddled vest that had saved him from more serious injuries. The look on his face was one of exhaustion. I was certain that his entire experience hadn't quite sunk in yet, but the sober realization that he had come inches away from death must have been ringing in his thoughts.

"You alright, Chris?" Sanchez cautiously asked.

"Yeah, I'm good," he mumbled.

"I just got off the phone with my wife and she's scared shitless. Other than that, I'll be fine."

He walked over to the hard couch and lowered himself down, before tossing the tortured vest on the floor beneath him. A ghost-faced Saunders sat next to him, gently rubbing his back in her best attempt to offer comfort. Her Seattle counterpart, Director Godfrey, stood next to the couch looking down at the both of them with concerned eyes. I walked over to Porter and offered him a fist bump. He lazily returned the gesture, barely touching my knuckles before ripping his hand away. Despite us both being black, I could tell Agent Porter felt no sense of camaraderie with me. To him, I was just another criminal and wasn't worth acknowledging in his FBI consumed world.

"Porter, the both of us are lucky to be alive," I proclaimed.

"If the Tarpon wanted us dead, he had every opportunity to kill us."

"We better get off our asses and find this guy because he won't be so merciful down south."

"You might be scared of the Tarpon," Porter responded. "But I'm not. I took his best shot and I'm still standing. Wherever he goes, we'll find this piece of trash and arrest him."

Director Godfrey and Agent Morgan both looked at me with eyes filled with disapproval. This officer involved shooting was an embarrassment for them and both men were holding on tight to their pride.

"Your suspect won't be getting away any time soon," Director Godfrey added. "He tried to kill an FBI agent, so we'll respond in kind."

"We have every law enforcement official in the state of Washington looking for this guy. I promise you, he won't get too far before he's caught. He'll be in cuff soon for sure."

"Yeah, Mr. Jeffers." Agent Morgan jumped in.

"I got a good look at his face. His facial composite is floating all over the internet as we speak. Every white pick-up truck from here to Portland is getting pulled over and searched."

"It's only a matter of time before someone recognizes him."

"Plus, we just received a new lead from Canada. Our partners up there believe your guy was in Prince Rupert a few days ago. They sent us a video and it looks like he's been busy." He admitted.

Reaching into his pocket, Morgan pulled out his phone and walked over to Sanchez. I watched from a distance as Morgan unlocked his phone and found a video, before letting Sanchez watch it. Curious, I slipped in behind the men, looking over their shoulders.

It was a security video from a building that showed a muddy truck parked next to an icy curb. The surroundings looked cold as plums of hazy exhaust poured out of the truck's tailpipe. A young-looking white woman sat comfortably behind the wheel, meticulously arranging her hair while looking into a small mirror inside the truck's sun visor. Suddenly, she rolled down her window when a fast-moving male walked into view. From the camera angle, we could only see the figures back, but he was wearing a heavy leather jacket and was clearly a white male. The man opened the passenger side door and jumped inside. Seconds later, the red taillights of the truck lit up and it slowly rolled beyond the view of the camera.

"The Canadians believe this may be the guy you're searching for," Morgan explained.

"That lady was found shot to death in her home, along with three third country nationals."

"Apparently, that woman and her murdered friends had a reputation for running illegal guns and drugs. They were all employed at some bonded warehouse and guess what…that same warehouse has reported that a crate has suddenly gone missing. The missing crate was shipped to Prince Rupert, from Russia."

"We searched the background of the person who signed for the crate and found out that he's some nursing home patient from South Africa. Apparently, the guy has been dead for six years."

With a face full of shame, Sanchez looked at me without uttering a word. I knew he was conceding that I was right, and he had been wrong. Back in New Orleans, the FBI brass doubted my assessment. Now, they had to come to the painful realization that I knew what the hell I was talking about. The video ended and an angry Sanchez shoved the cellphone away with his hand.

"If we continue to make a habit out of being behind this guy," I announced. "Bad things are gonna happen down the road."

Not able to contain my impatience with these men's useless ignorance, I pointed my gaze at Director Saunders. Looking into her eyes, I knew the doubt that once greeted my words had been replaced with a degree of certainty. She had come to Seattle carrying her privately held suspicions. Now, this white woman was a believer, ready to put her faith in my judgement.

"He's long gone," I confidently continued. "We've been sitting on our asses in this hospital for too long, Director."

"I can assure you that he has already changed vehicles by now, so your APB on that white truck is worthless."

"The same goes for your composite drawing as well. The Tarpon will change his appearance at frequent intervals. He does this as a matter of routine. He'll see that composite floating around the internet and just pull out one of his many wigs or simply trim his hair. No one is going to recognize him."

"Our only option is to go back home to New Orleans and wait for him. He's in the U.S. now, so we're totally defensive at this point. We'll have to make hard decisions and try to guess where he'll attack."

Both Seattle men objected to my advice, lobbying Director Saunders to focus on pouring every resource into a statewide manhunt. Their tone towards my assessment was more than condescending as they laid out their plan. Having heard enough from the two Seattle men, Director Saunders stood up from the couch and walked over to Agent Sanchez, who was deep in thought.

"Sanchez," she began.

"What do you think about all of this?"

The room went silent as everyone knew this was the moment a final decision would be made. Avoiding my eyes, Sanchez looked around the room before settling his stare directly at her.

"Achim might be right, but the Seattle guys are more experienced, Director." He softly explained.

"If we go by the book, we need to trap this guy within the state boundaries and keep him here. It's our best chance to stop his plot before he gets too far into it."

"Alright then," she proclaimed.

"Godfrey, we'll go with your plan."

"I'll request every damn resource you can muster. I want to focus our manhunt within the state of Washington. We'll need to send that composite drawing to every law enforcement organization in the state."

"The suits back in D.C. will want to hear this plan from our mouths before they hear about it on the news tonight. Is there a private place where we can start a classified tele-conference, Godfrey?"

Director Godfrey pulled out his huge cellphone and unlocked his screen. After describing how they could call an HQ hotline and host a top-secret briefing within minutes, I felt the eyes of Agent Morgan began to examine me. He walked over to the table and grabbed a sweaty bottle of soda from one of the paper bags.

"You'll need to step outside the room for this, Achim." He admitted while handing me the bottle.

"We're about to hold a secure briefing that's for FBI ears only. Unfortunately, you don't have the clearance for this type of conversation."

"We'll call you back up here when we're finished. In the meantime, keep your cellphone nearby."

I glanced over at Sanchez, noticing that he was still purposely avoiding me. Half hearing Morgan's blunt instructions, the Director offered a half smile followed by a light head nod. Without objecting, I took the soda and also made sure to grab my wallet and bag of wet clothes before exiting the room.

Outside of the hospital, I paced the parking area trying my best to stay underneath the covered driveway as light rain fell from the sky. Thoughts of Pokey's funeral entered my mind, and I began to feel as though I had already failed. While we were up here in Seattle, spinning our wheels, the Tarpon would make it down to Louisiana unabated. It had been my idea to come up here in the first place. Maybe this was the FBI's intention all along. Maybe I had fallen for one of their traps. Maybe these white bastards had outsmarted me, again.

As the negative thoughts coursed through my spirit, I felt my cellphone vibrate in my pocket. Pulling it out, I looked at the screen and noticed Aunt Rita's text message.

"If you are available, please swing by Alki Beach for lunch."

Surprised that my boss would find herself in Seattle, I replied to her message, informing her that I would be on my way. I caught the not-so-subtle hint buried within her words. This was no simple request. It was merely a politely delivered order. As I scrolled through my phone, looking for my Uber app, I wondered why a Robert Charles executive would get this close to a case filled with so much risk.

Agent Porter and Sanchez would eat this up. Both men were chumping at the bit to find a way to connect Aunt Rita to organized crime. Now, she had travelled to Seattle to meet with me, a man the FBI had murder evidence on. As I pressed down on the button to confirm my ride, I began to worry. Despite the trick bag tactic they used to rid themselves of my pesky presence, I knew at least one undercover FBI agent was probably lurking around. The minute I sat down inside the Uber and rode to Alki Beach, I'd be taking them right to her.

Aunt Rita was smart enough to realize this, yet she made the decision to have me come to her in spite of the risk. Whatever she needed to discuss, it was important. With suspicion, I performed a crush and feel inspection on every piece of clothing I had on. Agent Sanchez purchased them outside of my presence, so I needed to make sure he hadn't planted any bugs in my new duds. Confident that no devices were hidden within them, I looked at my phone and monitored my inbound ride.

The Uber was due to arrive within minutes, so I tossed my soda and wet clothes in the trash can before jumping into the back seat of the red Prius. The driver put the car into drive and hit the wet road, heading towards Alki Beach. He was an East African, most likely from Somalia, given his appearance.

From the way he looked at me through his rearview mirror, I quickly guessed that he was an agent or some sort of informant. The whole environment inside the car was uncomfortable as he drove me to my destination in a cloud of worried silence. Finally, he pulled up to a red light and hit the left turn signal before asking me the one question I knew was on his mind.

"You going to Alki to hangout?" He asked with an uncomfortable stutter. "It is cold and wet today."

"Yeah. I just need to see the beach and take a long walk," I lied.

Unconvinced by my misdirection, the driver shook his head dismissively before trying to continue on with the conversation. Using poor English, masked with his heavy accent, the brother volunteered all kinds of information. He detailed how he love to hang out on Alki Beach and barbeque during the summer with family members. All of the driver's talk was nothing more than a filibuster. I was familiar enough with Seattle to know that our immigrant East African brothers would hardly hang out in a place like Alki Beach. They preferred to socialize in the areas near the airport, intentionally keeping themselves away from every other group, especially us native Black Americans.

As the driver rambled on, trying his best to sneak in a few revealing questions, we arrived at the destination. Pulling over to the side of the road, he parked and curiously scanned the area. Nothing was open near us and he re-checked his google maps screen to make sure he had driven me to the right address.

"We're here, brother," I confidently relayed. "Thanks for the ride and God Bless."

Ignoring his hasty follow-up question, I hopped onto the wet sidewalk and calmly shut the car door. I walked fast and watched out of the corner of my eye as the red Uber pulled off ahead of me and made a slow left turn. Stuffing my cold hands into my small pockets, I walked for several blocks before noticing a line of open restaurants down the road. As I approached the restaurants, my phone chimed in my back pocket.

When I unlocked the screen, I recognized that my 6zeros account had just received a direct message. I opened the new message and found new instructions from Aunt Rita. She had sent me a link to an address. I clicked on the address and pulled up new directions. According to my map, she was still several blocks away. After closing the phone, I crossed the empty street and used the other side walk.

I found the bright sign for Alki Sports Bar and turned to walk inside. Pushing the heavy door open, my ears were greeted by the sounds of multiple TV's blasting several college basketball games. Surveying the bar, I noticed Aunt Rita seated at a booth in the corner, sitting across from an older black gentleman with designer sunglasses sitting atop his low-cut grey hair. Even from over ten feet away, I could smell the spicy scent of the man's expensive cologne. He was clean shaven and meticulously manicured; much too sophisticated of a men to be in a sports bar like this.

Confused, I approached the booth while trying to figure out if Aunt Rita and I would ultimately have a moment alone.

As I closed on the booth, my confusion was quickly dispelled when I saw a small emerald earring hanging underneath the old gentleman's designer shades. Openly wearing an emerald is a coded symbol of a covert Robert Charles' operative. Given how chummy and informal Aunt Rita looked in his presence, I presumed that this man must also be a senior leader in our organization. Both rose up from the table and greeted me with wordless handshakes before Aunt Rita, motioned for me to have a seat next to her.

"Achim, this is Mr. James Quest," she detailed with her slow country drawl.

"Mr. Quest runs things up here in the Northwest, so I thought it would be a good idea to meet with him today."

"James, this is my play nephew, Achim Jeffers." Aunt Rita explained with a proud smile.

"Achim and my niece Jessica are expecting a baby. You remember my brother, Darryl, don't you? Well, Mr. Darryl is Jessica's father."

In two moments of recognition, I could see Mr. Quest remember the names Jessica and Mr. Darryl, as he shook his head wildly. He went on to take control of the conversation, using that opportunity to ask roundabout questions about my background. From his deep voice and peppermint breath, I knew this man was some Robert Charles boss, or at the very least, Aunt Rita's equal. I had never seen Aunt Rita so submissive around any man. It was obvious that she was attracted to him.

"May I ask about your background sir?" I boldly questioned.

"Certainly," he responded without a hint of concern.

"Back in the day, I was one of the first blacks to move up here to Seattle and establish roots," he began.

"I was here before the white exodus from California made Seattle popular in the early nineties."

"You see, before Nirvana, Amazon, Starbucks and big tech, the only things up here were Boeing and me. I owned a few businesses and did well for myself."

"Achim, did you know that before the whites came flooding into this very neighborhood, Alki Beach and West Seattle were predominately non-white?" He half asked.

"Years of gentrification have made this area into prime real estate these days. Now they're doing the same in Capitol Hill. The white folks are just running us outta here like rats."

"So, you're the reason I'm here?" I interrupted.

Understanding the hidden meaning sowed into my question, Mr. Quest went quiet for a second before looking up at me and nodding his head, confirming my suspicions. He was indeed a Robert Charles executive. Since he ran the operation up here, I naturally had a burning follow up question that demanded an answer, no matter who it pissed off.

"Do you know a black woman named Sharon?" I pressed.

"She's a short light-skinned woman with low cut hair. She grew up in Seattle. Someone sent her down south to intern with Rachel Douglas a few years ago."

"What about her?" Mr. Quest lamented with annoyance. "Just say your piece and stop dancing around your point son."

Before I could respond, a white waitress walked up to our table with a notepad, causing all of us to press our mute buttons. The waitress's hair was purple, and her arms were covered with dark and gothic sleeve tattoos. Rushing us with her fast-paced speech, she wrote down our orders before giving us all a phony smile and jetting away to the next table. Mr. Quest's gaze returned to me as soon as she left, demanding an answer with quiet frustration.

"Sharon was an intern that was mentored under Rachel." I sternly whispered.

"I did some business with the both of them in New Orleans over a year ago. A case involving Race Soldiers posing as honest cops."

"Now the FBI practically invites Robert Charles into this Pokey situation. The agents I'm out here working with made it their mission to reveal that Sharon was an FBI undercover," I explained.

"They threatened to arrest me after they tried to offer me a deal."

"Sharon has a video and knows names. Now, the FBI knows names too. She has been on the inside and now, she's wearing a badge."

"What the hell happened to our vetting process up here sir?"

"My real question is, who the hell is responsible for letting this damn traitor inside?" I demanded.

Mr. Quest leaned back in his seat and I watched his face turn into stone. My question was rhetorical in nature. I had crossed a forbidden line with a Robert Charles higher up, but I didn't give a damn. We both knew who gave the final approval for new agents coming from each region. Not taking kindly to my feedback, he looked towards the waitress as she approached the table with our drinks. I put on a fake smile as the purple haired freak gave each of us our glasses of ice water, adorned with a crusty looking lemon.

"Easy now, Achim." Aunt Rita cautioned.

"We've been infiltrated by the FBI numerous times before. This isn't the time to start throwing around accusations, whatever they may be."

"I'm not throwing anything around, Aunt Rita." I responded.

"I'm just making sure we have some sort of accountability up here. Especially since it's my ass on the line. Somebody let this fuckin fox into our hen house. When the FBI finally decides to make their move, I'll be the one facing hard prison time, so yeah, I'm gonna question certain people."

I stared Mr. Quest right in his wrinkled-up face, refusing to back down. Either this man was a fuck up, or the FBI had found a way to flip him. Part of me wanted to grab Aunt Rita by the arm and bolt from the table, leaving this asshole alone until we could confirm that he was as incompetent as I believed he might be.

He took a sip of ice water and buried his frustration into the table as he lightly slammed the glass down. I could tell he didn't intend to back away from my serious accusations. The mere thought of profound mistrust between us, had wounded his pride. I could sympathize with the old man's plight, but this Sharon situation was a real nut squeezer. She had been a trusted intern for us, learning under Rachel, one of our most successful field operatives. The amount of private company business this undercover FBI agent had been privileged to obtain, could be enough to easily put us all in jail.

"Son," Mr. Quest replied.

"I can promise you won't spend one day in jail. Whatever happened in New Orleans with those Race Soldiers, the FBI won't dare to come after you."

"You need to trust me when I tell you that."

"I understand that you have a lot on your plate right now, son." He continued. "

"It would be better if you focused on keeping Pokey alive, and keeping the FBI away from Rachel Douglas."

"Trust you?" I shot back with sarcasm.

"How can I trust you sir? Hell, I don't even know you."

"Just because Aunt Rita believes she knows you, means zero to me. I have no idea who you are or what you got going on up here."

Exhausted with our bickering, Aunt Rita used her hands to motion for both of us to shut up. Grabbing me and holding on with a tight squeeze, she looked into my eyes, giving me an unspoken warning.

"I called you here to find out what Director Saunders is up to Achim." She stated.

"How's this investigation going?"

"It's failing," I barked.

"It looks like the Tarpon or the Asian gang he is working for, has sources inside the FBI. A Black FBI agent was nearly killed today and the Tarpon looked happy when he saw my face."

"Someone on the inside is feeding him information, so he'll know every move I make."

"Do you have any idea who is giving him the info?" Aunt Rita followed up.

"I have my suspicions, but nothing concrete yet," I admitted.

"I wouldn't be surprised if Zhilan has a few FBI agents on her payroll," Mr. Quest slipped in.

"The Field Office up here has a terrible reputation. You need to be careful operating up here Achim."

"I'm sure you are very familiar with the inner workings of the FBI," I sharply rebutted.

"Look, I'm trying to help you out young man. That's why your Aunt Rita asked me to come here today." He angrily shot back.

Aunt Rita once again squeezed my hand, forcing me into a state of furious silence. As I fought the urge to construct some smart-ass response, I felt my phone vibrate in my back pocket. Yanking it out, I looked at the screen and noticed it was an unknown number.

"If you both may, please excuse me for a moment. It looks like I'll have to take this call." I declared.

I exited the sports bar and stood alone on the wet sidewalk as the clouds above turned into a darker shade of grey. Pressing down on the answer button, I spoke my greeting into the microphone before pressing the cellphone's speaker up against my ear.

"Achim?" the voice half asked.

"Achim, this is Director Saunders."

"Yes, what do you need?" I asked.

"I need you to catch up with Sanchez and Porter," she demanded.

"They're with Agent Morgan over in Capitol Hill. The locals got a call about a breaking and entering at some Asian chop shop not that far from the marina where you saw the Tarpon."

"Sanchez and Porter are over there taking a look and they've found the white truck," she lamented.

"Like I said Director," I responded.

"There was no way he'd stick with that truck. Agent Morgan and his boss are total morons…."

"That's not all Achim," she interrupted.

"Sanchez and Porter have also found two dead men there."

"Look! Achim, you seem to have a feel for this Tarpon guy and I need you at that chop shop to make sure nothing big gets missed."

"You mean, you need me over there to make sure your people are doing their jobs." I eagerly corrected.

"Look, I'm trying to help you guys out, but my expert assistance doesn't seem too welcome from a few of your employees."

She fell quiet as my words soaked in. I heard her inhale deeply before murmuring a few words to herself in frustration. I wanted to flat out tell her that someone in her organization was crooked, but I didn't know if I could trust this white woman. Aunt Rita didn't trust her and seemed to have this fear that preoccupied her better judgement. Maybe it was Director Saunders who was informing the Tarpon or working for Zhilan? At this point, I didn't know and it was best to assume I was the only honest person with real intentions to protect Pokey.

"I'll have a private talk with Agent Sanchez," she relented. "But right now, I need you at that chop shop pronto."

Director Saunders ended our call and texted me the address. I walked back into the Sports Bar and approached

Aunt Rita's table. Both Aunt Rita and Mr. Quest looked at me with eyes that probed my visible frustration.

"I have to get going." I began.

"Director Saunders just called and requested my presence. So, I'm about to go see what kind of games they have in store for me now."

"Be careful, Achim," Aunt Rita cautioned.

"Saunders is an FBI lifer. If the choice is justice or protecting the Bureau, she'll pick the FBI."

"I know," I softly agreed.

I reached into my wallet and tossed a few dollars on the table, adding to the waiter's tip. Pushing open the entrance door, I walked out into the light drizzle and used my phone to find another Uber. After waiting in the cold for a few minutes, my Uber arrived and a bald-headed white man drove me to Capitol Hill.

Arriving at the address, I left the Uber and walked up a hilly incline until I saw yellow police tape blocking the entrance into a rusty looking mechanic shop. Approaching the tape, I could hear the sounds of men conversing inside. Stopping, I leaned my head over the boundary to take a peek.

"Can I help you sir!" A Seattle police officer demanded.

I turned towards the female cop and slowly pulled out my Private Investigator credentials, lifting them up in front of her so she could read the name. In a moment of disrespect, the white woman saw fit to snatch my credentials from me and examine them in her hand. Outraged by this lady's mean-spirited intrusion, I reached over and pulled my wallet back from her.

"You need to ask before you just decide to take my property," I instructed.

"I don't have to ask your permission to do anything," she yelled back.

"I'm conducting a criminal investigation and right now, you are obstructing. Plus, you just physically assaulted me. Now give me the ID back, so I can run your name."

"I don't give a damn about your phony criminal investigation. Investigate all you want, but you don't get to steal my property, then somehow claim I assaulted you when I take it back," I blasted.

"I'm here on business. Take me to the FBI agents on scene, please."

"I'm not taking you anywhere," she flexed.

The lady cop leaned her mouth towards her hanging microphone and whispered a few coded words. After the radio call, she reached into her pouch to pull out her shiny little handcuffs. As I giggled at her clear intentions, I saw Agent Porter walk around the corner of the building, so I whistled to get his attention. Pointing down at the short lady standing in front of me, I backed away from the aggressive cop as Porter jogged over towards us.

"OK!OK!!OK!!!" He vented as he pushed his way in-between us.

"He's with me. Put the cuffs away and back up please."

The cop holstered her cuffs and took several steps backwards while staring at me through her dark sunglasses. Amused with her race based frustration, I made sure to laugh loudly at her expense as Porter and I ducked underneath the yellow tape. Agent Porter softly apologized while we walked down a long passageway. Without accepting his earnest plea, I followed him into the wide garage.

The dead bodies and the pools of blood snatched the words out of my mouth. I followed Porter over to the white truck where Agents Sanchez and Morgan were taking notes and logging evidence.

"Good to see you've joined us, Achim," Sanchez dismissively greeted.

"Looks like you were right. From the crude records we found in the office over there, the only thing missing from this garage is our suspect and one vehicle. Probably a truck, SUV or maybe a van."

Ignoring Sanchez's sarcastic admission, I walked up to the driver side door to examine the driver. He'd been shot in the back of his head, indicating that the Tarpon likely surprised him. Playing the scene out in my mind, I deduced that the Tarpon either walked up from behind the truck or had fired the fatal shot from the back seat. Moving to the other body, I noticed that the Asian man's face was covered in blood. There was no gun-shot wound to be found. The Tarpon had most likely fought this man, easily overwhelming him, before delivering a cruel end to their hand-to-hand combat.

His teeth were scattered about the floor and his disfigured skull bore the signs of several fractures. This man's murder was an act of pure rage. The Tarpon had enjoyed himself, indulging in an explosion of violence, power and ruthlessness. For the Tarpon, this was but a warm-up before the main event.

"What are you thinking, Achim?" Agent Porter whispered.

"I think Pokey's screwed."

Chapter Eight

Cold Sunny Deserts

Wiping beads of sweat from my forehead, I fought to keep my eyes clear as the scathing sun punished us. The hot weather in Phoenix was a welcome retreat from the cold of the Pacific Northwest. Yet, this welcomed heat served to exhaust me and Alex. Mustering my resolve, I reached into the back of his SUV and unloaded another fifty-pound ammo can.

Carrying it back to the mounted cannon, I sat the heavy can of bullets next to the feeder before flipping open the top. After linking several rounds into the magazine, I turned on the battery and performed a functionality test. Using the remote, I was able to move the cannon's heavy barrel up and down, left to right with ease. The tripods range of motion was extensive, and its reactions to my commands were instantaneous.

"It's a shame when dirty Russians can build shit better than we can," Alex quipped after tossing an empty beer can into the garbage.

"Oh my! I'm sure you Americans have something much nicer. It's just hidden away in a secret military base somewhere," I responded.

"The only difference is that this Russian gear is relatively cheap and you can buy it on the black market."

I walked away from the cannon and found comforting shade underneath the gun ranges long metal awning. Plowing down on the wooden bench next to Alex, I activated the remote-control system and calibrated the HD screen. Looking at the screen, the image of our target, a blue five-gallon bucket of cement, was clear and detailed. Even from just over a half mile, this cannon's telescopic targeting system could read the nearly faded words on the bucket's label.

"Oh, shit man, that's bad ass!" Alex exalted after popping open two more cold ones.

I grabbed a beer and began to sip while adjusting the screen's brightness. Twisting the small joystick, I moved the crosshairs over the center of the bucket. Within a second, the tripod moved the cannon's barrel, adjusting its trajectory. Satisfied with the firing solution, I pressed down on the load button and the distinct sound of the tripods belt feeding a live round into the chamber, rung out in front of us.

Placing the remote down in my lap, I grabbed a pair of ear plugs out of my pocket and donned them. Looking over at Alex, I tossed him my spare set and motioned for him to get ready. He quickly chugged his beer, then tore open the plastic package before jamming his plugs into place.

The firing range was clear, and the cannon was hot and ready. Using my index finger, I flicked off the safety before selecting semi-automatic. My thumb hovered over the fire button, while I waited for a desert breeze to ease up. Once I felt the wind weaken, I pressed down and a bone shaking shockwave, was followed by a loud percussion. Looking at the screen, I noticed that a hazy white cloud had replaced the image of the blue bucket. I cut my eyes towards Alex and watched him pull the binoculars away from his eyes as he turned towards me with boyish happiness.

"That bucket got fuckin waxed," he loudly proclaimed. "I would say that your firing optics are pretty well sighted in."

Taking the ear plugs out, he tossed them on his lap and grabbed another beer. With excitement, he tapped me on my shoulder, motioning for me to rid myself of my own ear protection. Complying with his request, I removed the plugs and leaned over towards him.

"That bad boy's ready to go," he stated with a strong scent of alcohol chasing his words.

"The only thing that would worry me, is the noise. After a couple of rounds, everyone in the world is gonna know where you are firing from. If you miss, your target will damn sure take cover. You'll never get a second crack at it."

"I know," I admitted.

"That's why I'll kill this guy inside the Superdome. Loud noises echo in there. No one will be able to tell where the gunfire is coming from. He'll be blown into a thousand pieces by the time anyone figures it out."

Alex was surprised and puzzled by my admission, and he gently placed his cold beer on the table. I could tell his mind was conjuring up all kinds of questions. Beating him to the punch, I flipped the power button on my remote before tucking it away.

"This will all go down inside the stadium, at close range. I'll need to get that cannon inside the Superdome and mount it someplace high. It will be a two-hour job, at the most."

"I can fire the cannon from a car parked outside the stadium." I described while pointing at the remote.

"That way once it's all done…I can just drive off and be gone."

"How the hell are you going to get this cannon inside the Superdome, let alone, mount it?" He asked.

"Remember that favor you and your brother owe me, Alex?" I reminded him. "Well….I'm cashing it in."

"The Business District is certain to be crawling with cops and all kinds of Federal agents."

"Seeing that you're a disgraced former FBI agent, I'll need you to call up some of our like-minded colleagues and get them to help me out."

His face turned serious as he descended into a deep state of thought. We both knew he had the exact connections to make this plan work, but his body language told me he was more than a bit reluctant. I understood his fears and concerns. After all the bullets were fired, his FBI comrades would eventually become the most logical fall guys. A Russian built cannon finding its way inside the Superdome during an event with heavy security, is exactly the sort of bold statement Zhilan paid for.

When this all goes down, I intend to tell the world that you can't hide or protect yourself from the gruesome clutches of power. This will be my Picasso. My final lesson to my people about the virtues of power and subduing an enemy. Fear is the end result we wish to deliver, and that fear would be painfully introduced to our opponents.

Now, all I needed was for Alex to throw caution to the wind and join our cause. In the back of my mind, I knew I had the trump card. If Alex's spirit of White rebellion was drenched with concern for the meaningless careers of his friends, I was certain that a small piece of the bounty sitting in my offshore bank account would harden the tenderness in his heart. We would send our message of White Male dominance to the world and live the rest of our lives like the kings we were born to be.

Quietly weighing his options, a tortured Alex reached down and flipped open the cooler. With his large hand, he launched his fist deep into the icy water and pulled out two nearly frozen beers from the bottom. In silence, he lightly tossed me another round.

"This is big nuts shit here bud," I encouraged. "We either go big or go home. This isn't cross burning or storming the U.S. Capitol. This is all out war."

"Once this is done, we'll have to disappear for good. I can make all of this really comfortable for you. You'll be paid for life, and you'll be able to leave a little change in your brother's bank account."

"I'm more than down for big nuts shit," Alex agreed. "It's time we stopped playing and send these filthy niggers a message."

"But …..no good deed in life is free. White freedom comes with a cost. This is gonna cost you fifteen million."

Standing up from the bench, I put my beer on the table and wiped the can's cold sweat from my fingers. Reaching out to Alex, he returned my handshake before pulling me close and engulfing me with a tight bear hug. Excited, we both shouted while slapping each other's backs in a moment of mutual appreciation.

"I'll get your money. In fact, I already have it in a bank account for you," I explained. "When our lady friend asked me to do this, you were the first person that came to my mind."

"I'm really honored you thought of me," he shot back. "That really means a lot coming from you, especially given my situation."

"During our time on this earth, we all experience some kind of situation," I calmly deflected. "The only thing that truly matters is where you placed your loyalty and the legacy you leave behind."

We finished several cold beers while watching the sun fall below the jagged mountain tops. Feeling the coolness of night begin to engulf us, we disassembled the cannon and stored it away in the back of Alex's Chevy Tahoe. After policing up all our trash, he went inside the building to shut off the generator and lock the doors. As I waited inside his SUV, I looked around, examining his privately-owned gun range. In retirement, he had done well for himself. This gun range was the perfect spot to get clicked in with all kinds of militias, churches, businessmen and law enforcement. In Alex's mind, this place was a hub for white men. It was a place where we could discuss business and develop allegiances.

Soon the building's lights went dark, and I watched Alex jog towards the SUV. Jumping behind the wheel, he nursed the wide SUV out of the slender back gate before securing it with a lock. We drove into the fading blackness of the dirt road before the lights near Highway 17 came into view.

"Since I'm doing this favor for you, there's someone I need you to meet," he blurted out.

"Do you mind if we have company during dinner tonight?"

"Well, that depends on who it is." I cautiously rebutted.

"She's someone very dear to me," he admitted. "Someone, I want you to meet before I'm gone."

Alex merged onto Highway 17 southbound, driving just below the speed limit in the far-right lane. Unlocking his cellphone, he dialed a number from memory and began whispering to a person on the other end of the line. After making a few arrangements, he ended the short conversation and dropped the phone inside of his coffee-stained cup holder. I felt the SUV begin to accelerate. He hit the turn signal and began sliding over towards the fast lane. Looking at him, I noticed the skin around his eye sockets was a bit puffy.

Concerned with his sudden signs of stress, I placed my right hand close to my concealed handgun and briefly thought of unholstering it. As I continued to watch, I realized why he looked so pale and exhausted. This long trip to the gun range, coupled with the sweaty task of moving all my heavy gear, had pushed him to his limits. Alex was a sick man, afflicted with a rare blood disorder that would soon end his life. Sensing the toughness within him, a white man pushing himself through pain to entertain a long-lost friend, caused me to move my hand away from the pistol. Instead, I reached for the rear seat and grabbed two beers from the slush filled cooler.

"How long do we have you?" I abruptly asked while handing him a cold one.

"Hell, I don't even know. Only God knows," he instinctively answered without a hint of concern.

"My doctor believes I've got two or three years at the most, eight months to a year on the low end. I try not to think about it too much. When it comes, it comes."

Alex took a small sip of his beer, trying to calm his nerves while speeding past a line of slow moving eighteen wheelers. As I watched him grasp his own mortality, I couldn't help but feel a sense of remorse takeover. It was in this moment that I remembered why I had avoided him and his brother Rickey. The moment of reflection saddled me with guilt and a strange sense of regret. I hated experiencing these human feelings. Feelings that weakened me to my core.

"I've been getting my affairs together," Alex stated after dropping the empty beer can on the floorboard beneath him.

"My will. I picked out a grave plot. Planned out the funeral....all that shit."

"Since I'm divorced and I don't have any children, Rickey is my only next of kin, but he's locked up in prison. It doesn't help that he doesn't have any kids himself."

"The woman you are about to meet has been helping me get my affairs arranged. She's a real sweetheart, a former U.S. Attorney that I worked with in the Bureau, back in the day."

"She's retired and owns a few restaurants out here in Phoenix. When I go through my bouts of sickness, she takes care of me."

"Since Rickey will be locked up, I plan on passing down my two houses and my gun range to her. If Rickey happens to get out early, she'll convert back to representing me legally and pass down my legacy to my relatives."

Due to the crackle in his voice, I could hear that fear of not just death, but of an eternal fate that would erase his very existence from the face of the earth. Like me, he was a proud white man fighting not merely for the right to lead the world, but also to continue existing within it. Alex exited the highway and pulled into an area littered with strip malls. After turning into a small parking area, he squeezed into the tight handicapped space, and I followed him into a crowded Mexican eatery.

A young white hostess greeted us near the front door. From the instant sparkle in her eyes, I knew she recognized Alex. Pushing us ahead of the group waiting in front of us, we followed her to a puffy corner booth near the bustling kitchen. We sat down and quickly ordered two sodas in the hopes of offsetting the pool of beer we had drank. Feeling more tipsy than hungry, the unique smell of spicy Mexican food, caused my head to pound. Although Mexican dishes are tasty, there's something about their food that is dirty and nasty to me.

Looking at Alex and his current situation, I was motivated to swallow my discomfort. His plight was much more serious than my hidden distaste for all things Hispanic. He was a white man on his way to his end, and if he desired to ruin himself with spicy grease before his number was pulled, so be it. I listened as his spirit seemed to rise while he explained his boring ventures in Arizona real estate. After ten minutes of hearing his voice mix in with my pounding headache, a woman approached our table with a joyful smile.

From her barely tanned skin, and greying stringy hair, I could tell she came from Swedish ancestry. She was older than me yet the wrinkles crossing her face seemed to portray wisdom instead of old age. This woman was not and never had been, anyone's beauty queen. Her strong face and the tight way she carried her jaw were naturally unattractive features. Yet, the confident manner in which she approached our table caught my eye.

"Hey Susan," a smiling Alex stated from his seat.

"Alex, I hope you and your guest are both hungry," she greeted, while leaning down to hug him.

"I've got my chef back there making you both a sampler platter. Did my niece already get your drinks?"

"Yeah, she took our orders," he reassured. "Susan, this is the friend I was telling you about earlier, his name is…"

"Oh Sir, nice to meet you," Susan rudely cut in. "My name is Susan Wortham, and my restaurant is your restaurant. Whatever you wanna eat, just tell me and I'll make sure it happens."

With a genuine smile, she offered me her hand and we exchanged a light but respectful handshake. From the look of excitement in her eyes, I could tell this woman knew who I was. With giddy ease, she glided an extra chair over to our booth and sat down. I watched as Alex and Susan playfully debated the dates of a country music tour that was scheduled to visit Phoenix.

Failing to agree on the correct date for the event, both of their eyes focused on me as they suddenly went silent, almost begging me to interrupt their useless banter with something a bit more serious. Still feeling the pain thumping in my skull, I gave them both a phony smile before proceeding to lean back into my chair. I could tell they wanted to discuss something but were too timid to broach it.

"Susan, my friend is headed to your old stomping grounds down in New Orleans," Alex finally mentioned.

"Oh gosh!" she exploded. "I absolutely love that fantastic little city!"

"So many old college memories come to mind when I think about the bright lights and stiff drinks of the French Quarter."

"Although, I reckon you're going there on business, I do hope you find time to enjoy yourself, sir."

"I will. I'm certain I'll have a blast." I commented with a fake smile.

"I know you will," she purposely retorted. "I can promise that you will have a whale of a time. Especially, if you hook up with the right people. You know, our kind of folks."

The table went silent and the ringing sounds from the kitchen drowned out other conversing customers. Shooting me a grin, Susan pulled a pack of Virginia Slim cigarettes out of her pocket and lit herself a smoke. On the brown wall above our table, hung a large no smoking sign. Noticing my amusement, Susan chuckled before blowing a cloud out of her mouth.

"It's my place. I own it, so it's my rules here darling," she informed.

"If the city has a problem with that, they can take me to court and sue. Best of luck to them though. I'm a hellva lawyer and I love the courtroom."

"I agree," I replied. "No government should restrict a white person's freedom."

"Exactly," she eagerly agreed. "That's why my associates and I respect you. You're a man our government should be helping."

This lady was no ordinary lawyer. She was clever with her well coded language, and it was obvious she had an agenda. Swallowing my burning mistrust, I responded to her sentiments with a brief smile when our young hostess arrived at the table with our sodas. The pause gave me a chance to collect my thoughts and attempt to decipher her intentions. Susan was undoubtedly a pro and Alex had brought me here on purpose. I got the sense that this was the FBI feeling me out. They had used me in the past, and now they wanted to explore me as an option once more.

"I've done a lot in service of governments," I played along. "And governments are really strange creatures. One minute, they love you and the next they're either running from or after you."

"Nothing given to you is ever as free as they say it is. With every carrot a government offers, there is most assuredly a heavy stick coming behind it."

"Yes," she agreed. "But in this case, that heavy stick may be a beautiful branch you'd rather enjoy."

"I know your little Asian friend sent you here," she continued.

"She's a very pretty woman."

"But she's also very deceptive. No one realizes that this harmless looking little lady is utterly ruthless and surprisingly blood thirsty."

"Hell, everyone on this planet thinks she's a man. Everyone except those who really matter." She cleverly revealed.

I caught her unspoken message, but a part of me was still unconvinced. Sensing the doubt that was surely cascading through my expression, Susan reached into her purse and pulled out a small photo. In the high-resolution image, I saw the unmistakable face of Zhilan as she idly sat in a crowded coffee shop, surrounded by a handful of overdressed bodyguards. Somehow, she had been located and now she was being surveilled. I looked across the table and tried to stare at Alex, but his eyes retreated from mine, guarding his shame. He had given Zhilan up, thus betraying our mutual trust.

"I seriously hope you're not thinking about killing a dying man, are you?" Susan asked.

"You can't blame Alex for looking out for his brother. Try not to think of this as betrayal, but more like Alex giving his brother one last parting gift."

"Alex knows you care about Rickey just as much as he does, so he took the initiative and arranged all of this to get him out of prison early, pending your cooperation of course."

"Lady, what do you people want from me?" I bluntly asked.

Grabbing a yellow saucer from the opposite end of the table, she used it to shave ash from her shrinking cigarette. Alex's timid eyes examined me, fishing for any signs that might convey my thoughts. They had me and Zhilan in a vice grip and they both knew it. If I resisted them, the mission would fail, and my dreams of a comfortable tropical retirement would vanish. On the other hand, if I assisted them, these shady punks would certainly have some life-long price in mind.

"We want you to help us capture your lovely little Asian friend, Zhilan," she boldly declared. "And if it isn't too much trouble, can you see to it that Achim Jeffers is cleaned up as well?"

"Is that too much trouble, my friend?"

"That depends," I quickly deflected. "I need to truly know what I'm getting into here. Last time you guys sent me out unprepared, and Robert Charles damn near got the drop on me."

"This time, I want more information. What's the FBI's business with Zhilan and Achim Jeffers?"

"This isn't the FBI's deal," Alex broke in. "This is just us, our people's business."

"The threat from Achim Jeffers and Robert Charles is obvious. Together with his black terrorist thugs, they have sunk their claws into politics. We have a mutual interest in seeing that both Robert Charles and Zhilan are eliminated."

"Speaking of our lady friend, Zhilan," he continued.

"Together with her slant eyed gangsters, they have begun to interrupt our people's business ventures in Seattle, San Francisco and in New Orleans. She's fuckin with business ventures that are very lucrative."

"She's down in New Orleans overstepping her bounds," Susan jumped in. "And not staying in her place, so we used our folks in the NOPD to send her a little message."

"We don't care if you slaughter Pokey for Zhilan. Killing him would be a hellva blow to Robert Charles, she added.

"Trust me, we are not trying to prevent you from getting paid, but in order for you to get your cash in peace, we'll need Zhilan in return."

"All you have to do is convince Zhilan to meet you in a place where we can extradite her. Once she's there, your work is done and no one will know you were involved."

Now it was all out in the open and everything made sense. Someone in the FBI was setting a trap for Zhilan and now they needed me to help them spring it upon her. I felt a sting of disappointment and shame roll through my consciousness as the table went quiet. We were in a race war and my fellow soldiers, were more worried about drug money and controlling politicians. I had been right about the FBI and predictably, they had taken my bait. Like greedy grifters, these clowns had chosen money and selfishness over preserving the power of our race. Fortunately, I had them right where I needed them. The U.S. Government had unwittingly played into my hands. Now I could execute my real plan, and no one would be the wiser.

"I'll give you Zhilan, but I'll need two things," I responded.

"First, you'll need to provide me with assistance and protection in New Orleans. Once this thing is done, I'll leave the country and give you all the details on Zhilan after she pays me."

"Second, you give me Achim Jeffers and Robert Charles. I'll need you to turnover all the information the FBI has on the group."

Susan smiled as she extinguished the butt of her cigarette. Reaching into her purse, she pulled out a small thumb drive and slid it across the table. I grabbed it, examining it for a brief moment before squirrelling it away. Now physically relieved, Alex allowed a slight smile of satisfaction to splash across his face.

"She just gave you a thumb drive filled with all the information the FBI has on the niggers," he detailed. "There are names, titles, addresses, locations of safe houses, everything you can think of."

"As for New Orleans," Susan added.

"There are some local names saved on there that will be more then helpful. So, whatever you may need to finish off Pokey, you'll find more than a few helpers saved on that thumb drive."

"Also, I'm sure you'll have a ball researching Robert Charles. They are shockingly creative, too creative to allow them to exist."

"We wish you the best of luck." She stated. "We'll talk again once your in New Orleans."

Susan stood up from the table with a victorious smile. She had assured herself that she had control of me. After all, the best opponent to face is an opponent that you can control. In her case, she had miscalculated badly. Not only had the FBI foolishly given me control over them, I also had enough information to sink the FBI if they tried to fuck with me afterwards. Besides, once the blood had been shed, I doubt that anyone would attempt to come after me directly. Every one of these cowards would be covering their own asses once the smoke cleared, and I'd be set for life.

Chapter Nine

Bloody Pelicans

Sitting underneath the thick glass encasement made it look regal and awe-inspiring. It's unmistakable gold surrounded by clear sparkling diamonds, gave this ring an almost magical aura. Out of all the wedding rings in this place, this one looked perfect, almost too perfect in fact. In my mind, I could already see the tears racing down Jessica's face. Her empty ring finger would shake with joy as I slid on this token of my love. It would be a memorable day for the both of us, a day neither of us would soon forget. Arresting my excitement, I forced my eyes past the rings beauty and began to ponder the sobering price tag.

"Sir, I can get you a real nice deal on that ring," the store attendant offered.

"We have a fall special on that particular cut of diamond. If you sign up for our in-store financing, I'm sure we can work out a low interest payment plan for you."

Looking up at the store attendant, I saw the determination in his eyes that was only outdone by the clear femininity in his voice. This black man was trying his best to hustle up an easy sale. His fast-talking gamesmanship made me feel like I was about to be scammed. Part of me wanted to cut the brother off and jet away, but my other half understood that this was simply his job. After listening to the brother's sales pitch, I smiled and kindly thanked him.

Walking towards the mall's front entrance, I reached into my pocket and pulled out my cellphone. After my one-week absence in the Pacific Northwest, it felt good to come home. Given our unfruitful search for the Tarpon, this home field advantage would have to pay dividends if we were to save Pokey's life. The Tarpon had outmaneuvered us in Seattle, but this was my backyard.

Earlier in the morning, Jessica and I visited our doctor for an ultrasound. The news that we were expecting a healthy baby boy had mercifully taken my mind away from the failed FBI manhunt. After leaving her at the clinic, I decided to drive to the mall to grab some lunch. Instead of buying myself a plate of greasy food, my inner thoughts caused me to wander inside the jewelry store.

I desperately wanted to marry her, but I was scared as hell. The memories of how my deceased wife was murdered, pulled me away from what I knew was right. Forcing myself to put away the vivid flashbacks, I opened my phone and sent Jessica a text message. It had been a great day for the both of us, and I knew she would be in a good mood.

"I love you baby. I can't wait to hold the both of you in my arms." I sent.

Longing fantasies of playing catch or dribbling a basketball with this little boy God had blessed us with, flooded my senses. This was my chance to fulfill all the lost opportunities that the White Terrorist had stolen from me years ago. Seconds later, my phone lit up, ringing with its unique chime. Jessica had responded to my text, and I could feel the love we shared interwoven into each of her words.

"I'm so excited! I hope I can be a good mother. I want our boy to be a strong black man, just like his sexy ass daddy."

Jessica's heart felt message brought a smile to my face. Relishing the emotions, I tucked away my phone before walking into the parking lot and exposing my bald head to the rain. In the grayness of my surroundings, my thoughts again wondered if I should turn around and go back inside the jewelry store. In this world of turbulence, Jessica had been my calming salvation. The Lord had deemed it fit to reward me with such a blessing, yet I felt unworthy because of my inner fear.

I was a killer, a man devoted to eliminating the hellish demons unleashed upon God's chosen people. My life was supposed to be filled with raging solitude. Instead, it is an experience of lonely existence, absent of praise or infamy. Yet I had fallen in love, and life on this worldly planet had taught me that my longing for Jessica would only lead to more heartache. I loved her too much to see her suffer because of my own greed. I loved her too much to ask her to risk her life to be my wife. As I unlocked my car, the words of my old mentor Mr. Darryl, suddenly pulsed throughout my spirit.

"Our occupation will absolutely kill your love life. No black woman will support what we do here." The old man would often opine.

Despite the gulf of mistrust between me and my former mentor, his words strangely rang true. In order to keep Jessica safe, I needed to deny not only myself, but her. Just as I was reaching for the car's doorknob, I quickly jerked my hand away when I noticed the torn seal. Refocused, I looked down at the floorboard, examining the carpet before inspecting the back seat. Nothing in the car looked unusual, but when my eyes looked down at the torn seal at the bottom of the driver's side door, I knew someone had been inside.

This broken seal was not the work of some hasty thief or a fumbled attempt to steal my car. Whomever had been inside was a pro and they hadn't gone in there to steal. The first thought in the back of my mind immediately told me it was the Tarpon. He was here and ready to make his presence known to the world. My second thought sent chills down my spine. How the hell did he know where to find me? How did he find out this was my car?

Someone in the FBI was supporting this maniac. If this bastard was able to locate me and my car at a damn shopping mall, then he must have all kinds of hidden advantages. Advantages that could include also knowing the whereabouts of Jessica or Aunt Rita. I was lost in deep thought as I looked through the window, and I began to grasp the challenges the Tarpon was about to present to me. Once again, I would have to choose between two competing interests. On one hand, I'd have to keep Pokey alive, while on the other, I needed to keep Jessica and Robert Charles safe. There was no way I could do both if the Tarpon was targeting them and he knew it.

I calmly stepped away from the car, retracing my path back to the mall's entrance. Under the puffy rain clouds, I discreetly surveyed the parking area, looking for any car with a person sitting alone inside. He had to be here looking and watching, but my pace and the rain made searching much too difficult. The small rain drops seemed to gain weight as I walked, growing into a heavy pour.

Feeling the weathers assault, I used my palm to shield my eyes as I jogged towards the mall's entrance. Thankfully, I slipped inside just before a jolt of lightning made its presence known to the world. Standing behind the long glass doors, I peered out into the parking lot, waiting for a white man to emerge from behind the curtain of rain. After several minutes of fruitless searching, I only saw a group of over eager young black girls racing towards me. Nothing moved in the parking lot, not even one car pulled off. Maybe I was being paranoid? Maybe all of this was an overreaction?

As I pulled my cellphone out of my pocket, it suddenly started ringing in my hand while the screen displayed an unfamiliar number. Cautiously, I pushed down on the answer button and placed the phone against my ear.

"Hello," I barked.

"Achim, this is Director Saunders," she began.

"I'm so sorry to bother you during your lunch break, but I'm going to need you to make your way back to the Field Office ASAP."

"Something important has come up and I think you'll be very interested in hearing about it."

The timing of this call was extremely suspicious. Nothing about it felt normal. I moved away from the entrance doors and walked down the mall's wide corridor, heading towards a large shopping outlet.

"Well Director Saunders," I began. "I'll try my best, but I've got a few more errands to handle before I can head your way, so keep the coffee pot hot for me."

"What do you mean? Where are you?" She followed up.

"I said, I'm running some errands," I forcefully deflected.

Confused by the uncompromising intent behind my words, I could feel her befuddled silence on the other end of the phone. I wasn't going to allow her to ask another nosy question, so I promised that I'd make my best effort before hanging up. Walking into a small shoe store, I pretended to browse while franticly scrolling through my recent calls. This was the moment of choice I had feared, yet in my soul, there were no doubts about what I needed to do. Things were getting urgent, and my heart chose Jessica.

"Hey honey!" She happily answered.

"Jessica, listen up. We have a visitor in town, and he may want to come see you," I cryptically began.

"I need you to go get Aunt Rita and move. Text me when you both arrive and be sure to watch your six. If you see anybody behind you, call me and just keep driving, alright."

She was silent on the other end of the phone. I could sense her spirit of elation plummeting back into our savage reality. The cruel nightmare of my life's calling seemed to be forcing itself into fruition. After a long sigh, I could hear her grunt as she rose to her feet. While she walked, she rattled off a series of unanswerable questions, before dialing it down to just one.

"Are you safe Achim?" She softly inquired.

"I'm fine. I just need you to get going. Your safety is my main concern right now."

"Well, I'm already in the garage, loading up our ditch bags," she explained.

"I need to call Aunt Rita and tell her I'm heading that way. Don't worry yourself about us Achim, just make sure you stay ahead of this guy."

I ended the call while sidestepping a shy looking salesperson on my way out of the shoe store. Despite the raging thunderstorm outside, the mall was abuzz with customers. This particular mall was a popular shopping destination for both black and white residents of New Orleans. Looking out into the horde of focused shoppers, I closely examined every pale face, trying like hell to locate the Tarpon. Suddenly, I felt the weight of my pistol that was hidden away inside the lining of my sports coat.

After passing scores of stores and buying a snack at the food court, it was clear that the Tarpon hadn't followed me inside. For a moment, I reconsidered my initial assessment, wondering if he would actually stick around after booby-trapping my car. My own common sense pushed the doubt away. If I were him, I'd be sitting my ass outside, watching my target's every move. He was a professional and professionals like us would make damn sure that our targets met their end.

He was still out there, and I needed to leave. At this point, the Tarpon probably has figured out that I'm on to him. He had put me in the position of having to defend the woman I loved, rather than concentrating on protecting Pokey. Somehow, I needed to flip the script on him and safely execute a tactical retreat.

Out of options, I made my way back towards the jewelry shop. While every store in the mall was filled with customers, the jewelry shop looked lonely and quiet. Walking towards the store, I saw that the same flamboyant black attendant was still standing behind the counter. He was leaning back against a panel while typing away on his cellphone, trying his best to suppress a giddy smile. When I entered the store, I heard a light bell ring and the attendant's eyes shot up at me.

"Sir, I'm so sorry," he began. "But our store policy doesn't allow customers to eat food or drink beverages in here."

"If you could, please step outside and finish your meal, then you'll be more than welcome to come back inside to shop."

I looked at the brother and laughed before biting off a mouthful of corndog. His face looked puzzled and a bit offended as I walked towards the thick glass counter, chewing loudly with each rebellious step. Noticing the brightly colored emerald necklace at the end of the glass counter, I walked to it and stared down. The necklace was on sale and looked pathetic next to the brilliance of the gold jewelry around it. Curiously watching me, the store attendant walked over while studying my gaze.

"A few minutes ago, you were drooling over that pricey wedding ring, now you're over here swimming in the cheap stuff." He declared with cocky sass.

"Sir, you look lost. How about you let me help you out this time? Whoever you are trying to buy jewelry for, she probably deserves something a lot nicer than this little thing right here."

"I don't know about you bruh," I deliberately began. "But nothing catches her eyes like a shiny emerald."

"It moves her spirit, grabs her attention, and reminds her of her own humble origins."

Somewhat catching on to my true intentions, the store attendant smiled before placing his well lotion hands on the thick glass counter. As he leaned forward, he looked down at the emerald necklace and I could sense that his mind was full of thoughts.

"It's definitely a stone that's made for black folks," he joked. "But we have to make sure that the right black person wears it, otherwise it can be sort of embarrassing."

"Believe me," I quickly retorted. "There would be no embarrassment here…only pride and honor."

"I see," he replied with a shockingly deep version of his voice.

After putting his cellphone into his pocket, the brother made a gesture with his hand and walked to the cash register. Following him, I chomped down on the remnants of my nasty corndog before tossing the wooden stick into a nearby trash bin. He reached underneath the cash register and pulled out a small black binder. Placing the binder on the glass counter in front of me, he flipped through it until a page of photos appeared. On that particular page, an assortment of high-powered rifles were displayed, along with a few handguns.

"Whatever you need, I have it stored in the back," he commented with masculinity dripping from his voice.

"I won't need any of these. I have other problems," I explained.

I reached down and closed the binder before sliding it back at him. Yanking it from the counter, the brother looked at me in a moment of terrified confusion. He assumed that he had made a gross mistake and I could sense his thoughts began to speculate, wondering if I was some law enforcement negro.

"My car has a bomb planted in it," I quickly relayed. "A white hitman is stalking me and our entire Robert Charles operation here in New Orleans, has been compromised."

"What I need right now is a new set of wheels. I need wheels, and for your boss to dispose of my car for me."

Upon hearing my request, I could see blessed relief wash over this brother. He hadn't accidently given away Robert Charles' secrets, he now knew I was on code with him. Then his eyes focused on my problem, and he began to contemplate.

"I can give you my car," he bargained. "Will that work? Where's the guy who's following you?"

Before I could deliver an answer, he smiled and asked me to hold on. His stare shot behind me, glancing over my shoulders, examining the crowd of moving shoppers outside of his store. The brother smoothly twisted around towards the cash register, seemingly placing the black binder in a cabinet, while discreetly pulling his car fob out of his pocket. Turning back to me, he approached the glass counter and slid the car fob over.

"It's a light blue Nissan Altima, parked in the employee parking lot behind the movie theater," He described with the flamboyant version of his voice.

"Please excuse the nasty mess inside….I left a party before coming to work and I didn't have time to tidy up."

"How will you get home if I take your ride?" I curiously asked.

"My boyfriend works at Urban Fashionz, on the other side of the mall," he explained. "He gets off later in the evening, so I'll borrow his car to get home. I'll be fine."

"Don't you worry about that sir, I'll be OK and so will your car. I'll have some of our folks tow it and dismantle whatever was put in there."

"I just ask that you sign this document so that my boss knows who your boss is. That way, we can get reimbursed for helping you today," he lightly demanded.

The brother opened his phone and pulled up a PDF document. He scrolled down to the signature page, placed it in front of me and pointed at a long signature box. I gingerly tapped the screen, prompting the keyboard to pop up. After typing in my full name and using my finger to draw an awful rendition of my signature, I pressed the save button and handed the brother his phone back.

"Wow!" He lamented with a barely suppressed smile. "You're Achim Jeffers!"

"My goodness! You're a legend! I feel so honored right now!"

Using my eyes, I calmed him down and re-focused his attention. Within the tight circles of Robert Charles, I was respected, but none of that meant anything out here on the battlefield. I needed to make it out of this mall safely and I was sure the Tarpon was trying his best to set some sort of trap.

"Did your boss issue you the 6zeros app?" I asked.

"Yeah. I have it on my phone, but I've only used it once or twice. Mainly for work stuff, you know," he admitted.

"But you can find me on Twitter or Facebook if you need me," he offered with a wide smile.

"Well, if you can send a tweet, then you damn sure can use 6zeros." I insisted.

Grabbing myself a pen, I folded a piece of paper in half before writing down two usernames. They were Anthony and Rachel's 6zeros account handles. It was time to take a few extra precautions and do my best to throw our enemies off of our trails.

"Tomorrow morning, I'll need you to make contact with these two associates of mine," I described.

"If they need mission instructions, have your boss provide them with orders, as both Rita and I will be off the grid."

"If I'm killed, instruct them to keep moving and stay away from New Orleans until your boss sends for them. Make sure they understand and follow those orders to the tee."

With seriousness in his spirit, the brother took the paper and folded it up into smaller sections before burying it in his pocket. After a smile and a head nod, I turned away from the counter and headed out of the store. I closely inspected every white male I saw while briskly walking towards the mall's back exit. I didn't recognize anyone, and no one appeared to be following me. Apparently, he was still hiding out in the rain, waiting for me to show myself.

Before pushing open the exit door, I peered out from behind the clear glass entrance and saw that the torrential rain was limiting my visibility. In the front section of the parking lot, I noticed what looked like a bluish Nissan Altima parked near a handicap spot. Bracing myself to get soaked, I blasted through the door and lightly jogged towards the car. The heavy raindrops were surprisingly cold and they encouraged me to hasten my pace.

When I was halfway to the car, I noticed that the Nissan wasn't exactly light blue. Pulling out the car fob, I pressed down on the unlock button and saw no response. The gray paint job and King James Bible sitting on the dashboard told me this wasn't the store attendants' vehicle. My fears were confirmed when I saw a milk-stained baby seat buckled into the rear compartment. Suddenly, I felt exposed so I studied the parking lot again, hoping to find salvation from the monsoon. I spotted a blue Nissan parked several rows in front of me. Once again, I pressed down on the unlock button while jogging towards the next suspect.

This car's headlights burst into action, and I could hear the automatic locks immediately pop to the open position. Opening the car door, I squeezed my legs behind the steering wheel before pulling a lever and sliding the driver's seat backwards. Next to me in the passenger seat was an assortment of bags filled with colorful wigs and female hair care products. In the back seat, there were several Mardi Gras themed costumes and a cardboard box filled with half drunken liquor bottles. On the floorboard, several empty fast-food bags were tossed about, along with a handful of stale French Fries and an open condom wrapper.

This car was filthy, and I felt more than a little bit of shame sneak into my soul once I noticed a half empty weed baggy buried inside the car's cup holder. After pushing the start button, I turned down the loud radio and seated my cellphone into a holder. No matter how nasty this car happened to be, I needed to get out of here. I drove out of the parking lot and took a curvy service road to Veterans Boulevard. When I made it to Veterans, I carefully merged into the slow-moving traffic, making sure to study my rearview mirror along the way. Despite the pouring rain, I saw that no one was following me.

Exiting into a residential area, I took a nearly flooded back road towards the FBI Field Office. The pouring rain slowed my speed considerably, but the tradeoff of ensuring I wasn't followed was the real convenience. Now, I needed to tidy up my plan before meeting with Director Saunders. Despite the risk of FBI spies having tapped my phone, I knew I needed to contact Anthony and let him know what was going on. When I was clear of heavy traffic, I unlocked my phone and opened one of my webcam apps. Once I found his number, I placed a call and listened as the request was sent. After several rings my camera activated, and my screen came to life.

"Hey!" A surprised Anthony answered.

Anthony looked to be in a hotel bathroom. On the screen, I saw his naked chest along with a fogged up mirror behind him. Beads of water ran down his face and I could see a rush of embarrassment blooming within him.

"Get moving now," I quickly ordered.

"We've got problems down here," I discreetly spelled out.

"Where's Rachel?"

Alarmed, Anthony asked me to hold on and the screen became a blur of fast movements as the sound of a door opening ushered in a noisy TV blasting in the background. After a few low whispers, Rachel's unmistakable face appeared on camera. Her natural beauty wasn't the only thing that captured my attention. I could tell from the look in her cutting brown eyes that she was already in rare form. This was going to be difficult, so I braced myself.

"What do you want now, Achim?" she sighed.

"You two need to get moving, Rachel," I replied.

"An old friend of ours is in town, and apparently he's got folks giving him a guided tour."

"Well, if he's down there with you Achim, why do I need to do all the running around? Just keep him down there with you for God's sake," she immediately complained.

"If he's still so busy and obsessed with measuring his dick against yours, he won't have time to worry himself with little ole me."

"You are just overreacting like always, Achim. He's more interested in you. His interest has always been you. I know this man like a book. He wants you, not me."

"Rachel, if you are being followed, I can't guarantee that he won't come give you a visit once he's done with me," I tried to explain. "It's best that you both keep moving."

Annoyed by my insistence, she flashed a look of disgust before abruptly cutting her eyes away from the camera. Frustrated, she handed the phone back to Anthony. I knew she was tired of running from the Tarpon, and she was certainly tired of me protecting her. Rachel wanted this man dead, along with the lingering memories of their relationship. If I were in her shoes, I couldn't blame her. The bastard had shot her in the stomach, killing our child and forever ending any promise of her bearing children. Aside from the re-emergence of the Tarpon, I knew my growing relationship with Jessica had caused a tremendous amount of friction between us. One evening, over drinks, she let it slip that she felt like she was supposed to have been Jessica. Rachel was still suffering in silence. Without Atlanta, life would have been different for the both of us, and having to quietly watch me move on with Jessica, surely didn't help

Deep down, I knew she was right and I understood her plight. If not for the Tarpon, our relationship probably would have manifested into something much more concrete. Back then, we sure as hell motivated each other. Both of us were willing to go to any lengths to punish White Supremacy. Our relationship was intoxicating. It also didn't hurt that we had this crazy, almost animalistic sexual appetite for each other. She was the first woman I truly connected with, after becoming a widower. My time with her helped me realize that there was indeed life beyond my murdered family, and I've always been thankful for that experience. For that gift, I could never truly repay her.

"Anthony, can you please put Rachel back on the phone," I pleaded.

"No," he answered after quickly glancing away from the camera.

"Rachel says she's busy packing her bags. She's really pissed and now I'll be stuck with her bad mood all day. Thanks a lot Achim."

"You're doing a good job," I reassured. "Just get off the phone and keep her moving."

"You won't be hearing from me for a while, so be flexible and stay sharp. You'll be contacted tomorrow by other associates, but I'm still going to need you to make good decisions."

"Think on your feet and stay on your toes. That's the only way you two will stay safe."

"This moment is exactly why I trained you so hard. From here onwards, you need to be on your A-Game. If you aren't, something bad will happen for sure."

Understanding the seriousness of my words, Anthony simply nodded his head in affirmation as Rachel sarcastically mocked me in the background. This mission was indeed a big task for him. From my firsthand experience, Rachel could become more than a handful when she wasn't getting her way. Yet, his ability to appease the ever-insatiable Rachel wasn't my only concern. For all intents and purposes, I was sending Anthony out into this war without a plan, and he was an operator that craved organization. Without any sort of order of battle, Anthony tended to struggle. As we both ended the call, I quietly wondered if the over cautious Anthony, would be up to meeting this challenge.

At the FBI building, I would have my own hurdles awaiting me. The urgency that was in Director Saunders voice was a bit concerning. She had felt the need to call me directly, and my gut was telling me that the cause of her silent panic somehow involved the Tarpon. As the rain began to slow down, I increased the car's pace and plowed through wide pools of standing rainwater. I couldn't help but wonder if the Director and her colleagues were behind this attempted ambush at the mall. It was interesting that she had called me at the very moment that I was supposed to have perished in an explosion. Pondering over these thoughts, I continued to drive, determined to confront the threat in person.

Freeing myself of the maze of one-way streets in the flooding residential area, I pulled the dirty Nissan into the FBI Office's parking lot. After killing the engine, I sat quietly in the car, considering how I might be able to sneak my gun in the building. If I carried the gun inside, I knew they'd arrest me the second their metal detectors alerted them. If I were to pull this off, I would have to go in unarmed. My plan was to get inside and secretly kill one of the agents. I would disown him of his gun, then deliver God's justice upon these demons. Yet, before I took that path, I felt I needed to feel things out to insure I was right.

Unholstering my concealed pistol, I kneeled and tucked it underneath the driver's seat, neatly stuffing it in between two boxes of wet wipes. Just as I locked the car, my phone rung, and I saw that it was Agent Sanchez. I was late and I knew it, but the Tarpon's little ploy at the mall had set me back.

I ignored his call and chose to walk through the building's front entrance instead. Stopping to answer the phone and listen to him whine like a baby would only add to the delay. Additionally, I didn't want him to know I was here. If these FBI bastards were planning something evil, giving myself an element of surprise could help me turn the tables on them.

As I walked into the cold lobby, I felt the contemptuous glare of the blonde-haired black receptionist examine me. When it finally clicked that it was just me returning from lunch, I noticed her snatch the phone and jam it up against her ear. With her other hand, she wildly waved, demanding that I address her concerns.

"Wait right here Mr. Jefferson," she rudely barked. "Director Saunders wants to have you escorted to her office."

Not looking to find myself in another argument with this self-hating mammy, I nodded my head and stood by her desk in silence. As the minutes ticked away, I began to wonder why Director Saunders would want to meet with me. Having me wait down here in the lobby could easily be part of some crude ambush. I examined the surroundings, finding nothing to betray the presence of an impending FBI Tactical Team waiting in the wings with handcuffs. No one in the lobby looked like the Tarpon. Maybe Director Saunders was actually on the straight and narrow?

Just as I was considering any other angles of trickery the FBI could use, the elevator doors parted and Agent Sanchez came waltzing into view. He looked agitated and his movements were rushed. When he spotted me, his eyes zoomed in and he sped over with a sense of urgency.

"Why haven't you answered your damn phone?" he demanded in a loud voice. "I called your ass twice."

"Where's Agent Porter?" I deflected.

Agent Sanchez had to pause to consider my question, which grabbed my attention. His answer wasn't simple, which meant the lying FBI was up to something.

"I was about to ask you the same question, Achim. We're both looking for Porter it seems," Sanchez softly admitted.

"He went out to lunch and hasn't returned yet. That's why I called you."

"Follow me upstairs. Director Saunders and I need to talk to you in private."

We took the elevator up to the third floor before walking down a hallway leading to Director Saunders's office. Entering her suite, I was instantly underwhelmed by her boring white walls. Aside from a series of law degrees, an assortment of honorary awards and a few dull family photos, everything in her office was related to work. This was a woman totally consumed with her profession. Outside of her FBI persona, Director Saunders was an empty shell waiting to be crushed by life's realities. When we found her sitting behind her desk chatting on the phone, I could not help but to feel a ping of sympathy for this white woman. She had totally forsaken life in an attempt to imitate white men, and it was obvious.

"Please guys, pull up some chairs," she asked while hanging up the phone.

"I've got bad news."

I sat down on a chair in front of her desk, while Sanchez rolled one over from a conference table. After Director Saunders placed a few memos inside of a manilla folder, she leaned back into her seat and let out a labored sigh. Her face was visibly red, and her eye lids looked heavy. She clearly hadn't slept the night before, and this afternoon wasn't offering her much of a reprieve.

"Still no response from Agent Porter?" She asked while glaring at Sanchez.

He shook his head signaling no, and I watched the Director's face emote a grin. With a flick of her wrist, she tossed her silver fountain pen skyward. All of us watched as it tumbled earthward before landing on her well-polished desk, ringing out in a sharp clap.

"Achim, Agent Sanchez candidly informed me about your concerns back in Seattle."

"You were worried that we might have a mole within our ranks, someone that was providing the Tarpon with inside information," she detailed.

"Well, I too shared that concern, so I tapped the phones of everyone involved in this case."

"Unfortunately, you were correct," she lamented.

Leaning over her desk, she handed me the manilla folder, while motioning for me to read. I opened it and scanned through a long summary of an FBI phone tap transcript. It was a recorded conversation between an FBI official and his Asian contact in Seattle. The report explained that the Asian man was a senior lieutenant in Zhilan's Seattle operation. The mole had openly discussed our arrival and offered the Asian contact our schedule of events in the Seattle area. I reviewed all the pages and saw that the FBI official had passed along my name and my association with the investigation. The names of Sanchez and Porter were also mentioned, along with the locations of all our hotel rooms throughout the state of Washington.

I knew I had been right. That look the Tarpon had given me at the marina, was a dead ass giveaway. Not only did he know I was looking for him, but he welcomed my participation and was prepared for it. After reviewing the transcript, I closed the folder and gently placed it back on her desk, next to the fountain pen.

"This is why black people don't trust the FBI," I vented.

"This mole has compromised this entire operation. You people let this mole hang around and undermine us for a reason. Now, Pokey's life is in serious jeopardy because of it."

"Hell, the Tarpon had our hotel info. He could have easily stuck around and killed us all."

"We can't protect Pokey like this, not with all this shit going on. So, I'll find a way to protect him my damn self."

"I'm just as upset as you are," Director Saunders replied.

"I need to ask you not to lose focus. We're all in this together Achim."

"Ma'am, we've never been in this together," I countered.

"I have absolutely no faith in the FBI. Every opportunity you guys get, you screw over Black Americans."

"For all I know, this Zhilan guy could be working for the U.S. Government. God knows you people support anything that is Anti-Black."

"That's outrageous Achim!" she shouted. "We are not a racist organization sir!"

"Oh, really Director!"

"Well, who the hell had Malcolm X murdered? Who tried to make Dr. King kill himself?"

"Who purposely fails to charge deadly racists under federal hate crime laws, but eagerly charges Black Americans under laws supposedly constructed to protect us?"

"Who evilly labels all Blacks concerned about rampant police misconduct, as so-called Black Identity Extremists?"

"You can't look me in the eyes and tell me that you have total control over this investigation, can you, Director?"

"Where is Agent Porter at right now? Where is that coon at? Do you even know Ma'am!"

"You're outta line, Achim!" Agent Sanchez shouted. "Remember we're on the same side here!"

I stood up from my chair and walked towards the exit. If I stuck around here any longer, my thirst to kill them both might overwhelm my better judgement. Just as I was about to open the door, I heard Director Saunders speak.

"We have fucked over black people. I can admit that," she stated with a determined voice.

"As an organization, we haven't always done our best to protect Black Americans. We've violated their rights and secretly supported white terrorists. Heck, I can go down the list for the rest of the day."

"But doing so isn't going to help us save Pokey," she pivoted.

"Achim Jeffers, I need your help. This isn't the Director of the FBI in New Orleans asking, it's just me, a regular God-fearing citizen."

"Somehow, you knew that we had that mole in our midst. I don't know how you were able to figure that out, but this Tarpon guy seems to be miles ahead of the FBI, and something tells me that I'm gonna need you to catch up to him."

"So, can you please help us?" she pleaded.

I didn't believe a lying word that left her slippery tongue. She was a very accomplished and calculating white woman. The innocent debris of the lives of many black victims must have surely drowned in her life's wake. Now, she was trying to humble herself and ask for my help. The writing was on the wall and the look in her eyes betrayed her real fear. If the Tarpon killed Pokey, then this career she valued so much would be left in ruins. For white society, her life would simply be another cautionary tale of an ambitious white woman trying to hold suit in the realm of white males.

I took my hand off the doorknob and turned back around. The look on Agent Sanchez's face was one of pure contempt. We both knew what the Director's plea really meant. She wasn't just asking for my help, she was giving me permission to control the investigation. The thought alone must have pissed him off to no end, but at the moment, he was as helpless as his boss.

"I have one question," I stated. "And if I don't get a straight answer to this question, I'm outta here."

Walking back towards the seated Sanchez, I stared down at him, trying my best to hold in my fury.

"We made a promise in that hotel room in Houston," I began. "We both know what that promise was."

"Have you and Porter kept your damn word, Sanchez?"

"Yeah, Achim. We made a promise and we've kept our end of the bargain," he declared.

He was lying through his teeth. Agent Sanchez's well-seasoned expression of earnest frankness couldn't conceal the fact that I already knew the answer to the question I had asked. When pressed, Director Saunders would turn into a bleeding heart, yet this bastard remained a lying sack of shit. His FBI cronies were still following Rachel and Anthony. Now, I had to seriously wonder if he had something to do with the leaks.

"OK. I trust you," I lied.

"Who else knows about this mole?" I asked.

"Just us three here in New Orleans," she relayed.

"A select few in D.C. and Seattle know about this as well. Don't worry Achim, the folks who know are people I'd trust with my life."

"There's a meeting about to be held up stairs," she continued. "Pokey and the city leaders are waiting for us in the conference room."

"I plan on telling everyone about Zhilan's mole, then admitting to the setbacks we've incurred during our investigation."

"Do you have anything else you may want me to add to the discussion with the group?" The Director inquired.

Visions of my booby-trapped car flashed in my mind as both FBI officials waited for a response. In that instant, I decided to keep my suspicions about the Tarpon's arrival in New Orleans, to myself. If they didn't know already, well, they didn't need to know.

"I have nothing to add," I conveyed.

"But we probably should make an effort to locate Porter before we head upstairs."

"I'll stay down here and try to find him," Sanchez interjected. "I'll meet you guys up there."

"With all the heavy rain, Porter probably lost cellphone coverage and might just be stuck in traffic somewhere downtown. I'll locate him and make sure he's alright."

The Director and I both walked by an open elevator, mutually agreeing to take the stairs up to the conference room. As we approached the staircase, I saw the familiar eyes of my mysterious associate, Sharon, descending ahead of us. With graceful respect, she politely smiled at the passing Director. Upon seeing me, Sharon's beautiful smile disappeared into a scowl.

I had seen this sister naked and totally vulnerable. We had shared an intense moment of bonding as she climaxed amid her own drunken and bloody passion. On that night, we both shared the spoils of victory. But here she was, happily working alongside our mortal enemies and offering smiles along with resolute intentions. Despite my efforts in this brief interaction, I still couldn't ascertain what this mysterious sister was truly about. Reaching out my hand to lightly tap her arm, it gently bumped into her, but I got no response. She simply turned her stare away and brushed past me without even saying hello. Shaking off my unease, I followed Director Saunders upstairs to the conference room.

The room was nearly full, and the mood was tense as an exhausted Pokey sat near the head of the table, fumbling through FBI memos. Next to him was Mayor Neil Elliot who sat there quietly engrossing himself in his cellphone. Governor Lewis's campaign manager, Travis Chase, was next to the mayor and he looked impatient when he noticed us walk through the entrance. On the wall, several panel screens showed images from other FBI field offices that were video conferencing into our meeting. Among them were familiar faces from Seattle and a few other agents I had met from the D.C. area.

"Alright, gentlemen!" Director Saunders barked with a voice that put everyone on notice that she was in charge.

"Before we start today's meeting, we have some very important issues to address. So, sit tight and remain silent."

She sat down at the head seat. As she scooted her chair up to the table's edge, her shaking hands adjusted the microphone in front of her. Looking to avoid the spotlight, I found myself a hard seat near the window and gave my butt a home. After turning on her microphone, Director Saunders curiously looked around the room before finding me. After she attempted to wave for me to join her at the big table, I smiled back at her and aggressively shook my head in protest. There was no way I was going to join her at that table. Every ambitious law enforcement official in the room would quickly take note of my perceived rise in status, and the sharp knives would come out afterwards.

"Good afternoon, everyone," she began.

"There's no good way to approach this subject, so I'll just get right to it."

After clearing her throat, a stone-faced Saunders opened her small manilla folder and pulled out three sheets of paper. Everyone in the room and on TV, went silent with anticipation.

"We have a mole in this investigation," she stated.

"Wiretap recordings have found that a trusted member of this team has been relaying classified information to contacts with close ties to Zhilan and his organization."

Low murmurs erupted within the room as everyone seemed to examine the person next to them. As Director Saunders paused, the murmurs heightened to clear muffles. Just then, my eyes found Pokey. I could sense the feelings of betrayal and disappointment within his spirit. He had trusted the FBI, and now he had come to realize that they could very well be orchestrating his demise.

In frustration, the mayor tossed his cellphone on the table while Director Saunders's words seemed to cause Travis Chase to pull his own phone out of his pocket. The political news clippings of corrupt FBI officials somehow being associated with Governor Lewis's Presidential campaign, was something the ever-political minded Travis would need to stay ahead of.

"Who is the damn mole?" Pokey demanded. "I'd like to beat the hell outta them right now!"

"It's me," the speakers blasted. "I'm the mole."

"I'd like to apologize, this wasn't supposed to go this far and I knew better."

On the TV screen, I examined the video conference image that was labeled Seattle. Director Godfrey from the Seattle Field Office was standing, while his subordinates who were seated at the table looked up at him in stunned silence. He looked ashamed and I could sense his embarrassment as he nervously unbuttoned his jacket. Suddenly, a familiar face entered the screen. It was Agent Morgan.

Morgan walked up to Director Godfrey. He whispered in his ear before quickly patting him down and removing his FBI badge. Having finished, Morgan pulled the Director's hands behind his back. The sounds of the metal handcuffs locking, rang out from the TV's speakers. At that moment, everyone attending the meeting surely had the same thoughts. If Zhilan had a Director of an FBI Field Office on his pay roll, then there's no telling who else could be working for him.

As Agent Morgan escorted a disgraced Godfrey out of the room, the video-conference feed from Seattle, abruptly ended. I looked at Director Saunders and noticed a cold and remote look in her eyes. With stern words, she lectured her remaining audience on the FBI's information security policy.

At this point, an exhausted looking Pokey stood up from his seat, picking up his well stained coffee mug before pacing over to the window next to me. He stopped several feet short and we briefly locked eyes before he turned his gaze towards the window. From his demeanor, I knew the thoughts running through his mind. He didn't want to admit that I had been right, yet his physical disappointment spoke louder than any verbal admission he could offer.

Both Neil Elliot and Travis Chase broke the uncomfortable silence when they began to pepper Director Saunders with a myriad of questions. It was mid-November, and a very contentious presidential election was only a year away. Travis Chase was managing Governor Lewis's campaign and they needed the black vote to take the White House. Having two prominent black figures like Mayor Elliot and Pokey available to promote the Governor during Bayou Classic week, was essential. As Neil and Travis loudly disagreed about cancelling all of his political appearances, Pokey just stood there in silence, ignoring all the chaos.

Amidst their asinine dispute, I felt my cellphone vibrate in my pocket. Looking down at the screen, I read the short text Jessica had sent to me.

"We've made it to Tango Bravo," she typed.

Jessica and Aunt Rita had arrived at our safe house in Destrehan, near the Hale Boggs Bridge. As the voices got louder and the tension in the room increased, I decided to type a response and send it to her. I told Jessica to stay put and keep a sharp lookout. There was a lot of confusion in the air, and I had no idea who the FBI was truly targeting.

"Where's your family, Pokey?" I softly asked.

"They're still at home," he answered without even looking at me.

"Now, I'm starting to think I should move them."

"It's too late for that," I whispered. "It's probably better they stay where they are."

"At this point, you can't risk the Tarpon following them. He could use them to lure you into a trap, if they start moving."

"You need to make sure that you are made available to him. Otherwise, he'll kill your family in an effort to smoke you out."

"Whatever your schedule is for the Bayou Classic, you'll need to attend all the events. Every single damn one of them."

"You'll have to trust that I can protect you." I explained. "Don't depend on the FBI. Depend on me," I implored.

"If you cancel one event, I promise he'll go after your family for sure."

"What if I attend them, and make it impossible for him to get to me?" He whispered.

"There are plenty of ways that I can attend these events and ensure that I'm not in harm's way. Will that work?"

"No Pokey!" I loudly blasted in frustration.

The conference room suddenly went silent at the sound of my voice, and everyone's curious eyes instinctively found the two black men having a secret conversation. A curious Director Saunders rose from her chair and walked over towards the window to join us, leaving the Mayor and Travis Chase alone in their angry silence.

"Pokey, you can make yourself a fortress during those Bayou Classic events, but the Tarpon will just target black civilians instead. He'll make sure the Bayou Classic becomes a monumental blood bath and that will become a political disaster for everyone in here, especially when it's leaked to the media that you and the FBI knew of the danger but failed to warn off black citizens."

"We can't have that at all," Travis loudly chimed in.

"That's why neither Pokey, Governor Lewis, nor you Mayor Elliot, can afford to not show up at those events."

"If this lunatic causes a mass casualty event during Bayou Classic Week, then he's basically sunk an entire Presidential Election. My candidate and political party will instantly become radioactive at the polls."

"The Democrat party would never recover in time for the election, and everyone here today can say goodbye to their careers."

"Pokey has to show up and we have to protect him!"

"I'm the Mayor of New Orleans, Travis!" Neil Elliot responded.

"I don't give a damn about your national elections....my job is to protect the citizens of New Orleans ...and that includes Pokey!"

"I'm not gonna force my Chief of Police to attend his own assassination, so you can pick up black votes. You people are fuckin sick."

"Well just cancel the Bayou Classic then!" Travis countered. "Say it's a COVID-19 issue or something like that!"

"If you are that concerned Neil, you should just cancel everything, but you won't. You're too chicken shit to tell your business constituents that they are gonna have to lose all those juicy tourist dollars."

"So, don't come at me with all your self-righteous baloney. You'll have to get re-elected, just like Governor Lewis does."

"Enough with all the damn political angling," I jumped in.

The conference room once again fell silent as my voice resonated throughout the room. Director Saunders looked at me with eager eyes, happily awaiting the moment when I would take control and move the discussion away from this mess. Since I was the only person in the room who could truly do that, she was content to allow me to do so.

"If we cancel anything, the Tarpon will deliver us a racially motivated mass shooting," I explained.

"Our best bet is to make sure Pokey makes it to every single event on his schedule. In fact, doing so might give us an advantage."

"We can control all access points into these events. We can flood them with resources, luring the Tarpon into our noose, then tightening it around his neck once we've located him."

"Otherwise, he'll become a wild card, and none of us want that. We need the Tarpon to stay as predictable as possible."

"Achim's right guys," Director Saunders loudly seconded. "We're outta options here."

"Right now, this Tarpon guy is in control. Like Achim is saying, we need to wrestle control away from him by fighting him from higher ground."

"Pokey, are you going to be able to do this?" She softly asked.

"Because we're really gonna need you to lay it all out there for this to work."

"Yeah," he lightly murmured. "I'll do it."

"The FBI will do everything in our power to keep you safe out there," Director Saunders quickly reassured.

"I promise you, this year's Bayou Classic will be one of the most secure events in the country. It will be all hands-on deck."

Unconvinced, Pokey looked at me and his eyes were filled with mistrust. He no longer believed her white words. I reached over and playfully slapped his thigh, trying my best to pass along some non-verbal swagger. Slightly amused, Pokey seemed to chuckle for a split second before letting his smile disappear into an ocean of his turbulent concern.

A loud knock on the conference room door pulled my attention away from him. When the door opened, Agent Sanchez was standing outside looking unusually nervous. He had his rather large cell phone pressed up against his ear. His shaky eyes were trained on me and overflowing with confusion as he hastily waved for me to accompany him outside the room. As I made my way to him, I could see him whispering hurried words. Despite not being able to hear them, I could sense that the urgency was clearly consuming him.

"What the fuck do you want?" I asked after stepping into the privacy of the hallway.

"We located Agent Porter and it's not good," he declared.

Pointing his watery eyes down the hall, he went back to concentrating on his phone, straining to listen. He turned his back to me and slowly walked down the narrow hallway, leaving me to my own conclusions.

"Agent Sanchez!" I blurted out.

"Where the hell is Porter?"

"EMS just took him to West Jefferson Hospital," he stated after turning around.

"Porter's in critical condition over there. He's been shot. That's all I know right now, Achim."

I felt someone walk up behind me, so I turned. It was Director Saunders. From the stunned look on her face, I knew she had also heard Sanchez's candid words. As our eyes met, she stopped walking and I watched as she pressed both of her hands up against her lips. I needed more information. I needed to know if this was the Tarpon sending us his official notice of arrival.

"Stop with the bullshit games Sanchez! Where did this happen?" I asked.

Purposely ignoring me, Agent Sanchez rudely talked louder into his phone without even acknowledging my question. Angered, I jolted towards him and grabbed his shoulder, pulling him around to face me. When I felt him muster his strength and try to pull himself away, I simply leaned into him, pinning his stubborn ass up against the wall. With a loud clap, his heavy cellphone fell to the tiled floor, shattering into several pieces as it bounced under us.

"You answer me or I'll beat your fuckin ass!" I demanded. "Where did the shooting happen?"

"You can't just fuckin grab me like this Achim,"

"Answer my question Sanchez! Where was Porter attacked?" I shouted again.

"In Destrehan!" He admitted. "He went to Destrehan for lunch!"

"This morning Porter told me he was working some lead in Destrehan. Something involving an anonymous tip from Phoenix, Arizona. He wanted to see if it checked out."

"Other than that, I'm just as much in the dark on this as you."

As my grip on Sanchez loosened, I was flooded with images of Jessica and Aunt Rita hidden away in our secure house in Destrehan. Thoughts of the Tarpon somehow knowing the location of the mother of my child, hit me all at once. Knowledge of the trickster Sanchez breaking his promise, and deciding to stalk Rachel and Anthony, soon followed.

As I let him go, his body fell away from the wall while he softly cursed me out in Spanish. He adjusted his jacket and bent down to pick up the pieces of his cell phone. Before I could stop myself, I kicked Sanchez in his mouth with my foot. On instinct, I delivered several sharp jabs to the back of his head. Our loud confrontation drew everyone out of the conference room and into the hallway. My advantageous assault drew a wild chorus of concerned screams and shouts as a legion of armed officers jumped in to subdue me. Pokey and a group of white State Troopers pulled me away. A now inflamed Sanchez was being held back while his brethren pleaded for calm.

"You bitch!" Sanchez belly ached.

With a large group of officers holding him back and surrounding him, Agent Sanchez continued to make threats, promising to someday get his revenge. Coolly, I allowed Pokey and the State Troopers to escort me to the elevator.

"You alright, bruh?" Pokey half asked. "Because you just hauled off and beat the shit out of an FBI agent for no damn reason."

I stopped and looked at Pokey right in his eyes. The State Troopers surrounding us began to grab me and tried to softly push me towards the open elevator. Without violence, I resisted them, standing my ground before delivering calm words to Pokey.

"I have a very damn good reason, and that reason is the only thing keeping you alive right now."

Chapter Ten

You Can't Stop The Pain

The heavy gusts caused the van to swerve as I plowed across the Huey P Long Bridge. Beneath the bridge, small white caps partially covered the Mississippi River. Tightening my grip on the steering wheel, I shifted over to the left lane and slowed my speed in anticipation of the off ramp. This would be my first time visiting Nine Mile Point, and I was certain that Susan's little FBI buddies were banking on taking advantage of my unfamiliarity.

The thumb drive that tricky bitch gave me was indeed filled with all kinds of juicy information about Robert Charles. Saved on it were names, addresses, bank accounts, relatives, associates, lawyers, accountants, and anyone who had been involved with Robert Charles. In the back of their minds, I knew both Alex and Susan really believed that giving me this precious intel would somehow appease me. To them, I was just another lonely hitman looking to selfishly make a buck. From the look in Alex's jittery eyes and Susan's unspoken conveyances, I knew the score. The FBI would let me assassinate a useless Black Police Chief and earn Zhilan's money, just as long as they could capture her afterwards. In this business, there was no loyalty, only victors and the defeated. Zhilan probably had no idea that her drug selling competitors weren't just a band of crooked local cops. They were also well-connected government agents, with all kinds of political connections at their disposal.

For my troubles, the FBI decided to sweeten the pot with this damn thumb drive, knowing that my bitterness towards Achim Jeffers and Robert Charles runs deep. They were clearly trying to manipulate me. As a proud White man, I knew the game they were playing. True power can't be seen or understood by the weak. Power lives deep in the shadows, hiding its face from the world. True power simply gets things done and doesn't care to offer merciful explanations. The FBI viewed both Robert Charles and Zhilan as growing threats to their power, and now, they wanted me to help them cut both down to size.

I took the first exit after the bridge and made a tight left turn towards Nine Mile Point. Driving next to a tall levee, I followed the narrow road for several blocks before my GPS told me my destination was on the right. Looking out of my passenger side window, I noticed the long light brown Fire Station with its wide concrete driveway. Inside of the garage sat two fire trucks that seemed to shine despite the gloomy skies above.

After double checking the address, I pulled into the driveway and parked in front of one of the fire trucks. Before I could get out, I noticed that the Station had a closed sign hanging from its door. Given that it was a workday, the place was completely dark, which was weird. Determined, I pulled out my cellphone and opened my recent calls. Once I found Alex's number, I dialed it and he answered after six long rings.

"Hey bud," he answered with a groggy voice. "What do you need?"

"I'm at Nine Mile Point," I began.

"It doesn't look like anyone's here. This place is some backwoods fire station. What the hell is going on, Alex?"

He let out an annoying sigh that dripped with all kinds of silent sarcasm. His lack of concern pissed me off and I involuntarily bit down on my lip while waiting for his excuse. He was more concerned about resting than doing his damn job.

"Susan told us they would be there waiting on you…she wouldn't lie about that."

"Wait one second," Alex requested. "Let me reach out to her and make sure things have been properly arranged."

Alex put the phone down and the sounds of him rising out of bed were followed by his heavy footsteps. After several minutes, I was still parked outside of the fire station, quietly boiling in anger. This entire situation was unprofessional and bush league, but I needed to suffer through it. All of this was part of the plan and in order to send the proper message, this had to occur.

"They're inside," a heavy breathing Alex confidently declared.

"She says there will be two men. Both of them are firemen and they have special access to the Superdome during all of the Bayou Classic events. They'll be able to get you inside without any problems."

"Susan's calling them right now. Someone should come and open the front door for you in a second."

None of my concerns were quailed by his answer, but I pretended to be reassured and tried to usher myself off of the phone. Eager to inform me of Susan's long-term plans, a fully woke Alex began to jabber on-and-on about contacts I can use to make my way out of the country once this was complete. While impatiently listening, I saw the front entrance of the fire station slowly crack open. A tall white man sporting a funny looking crew cut briefly poked his head outside.

"Did you make a stop in Texas to visit your old friend, Rachel?" Alex finally asked.

"I did," I admitted. "But it seems like Rachel had several unwelcomed followers lined up to watch her."

"Tell Susan those two FBI guys spying on her, are too obvious. If I noticed their presence, then I sure as hell know that she has spotted them too."

"Rachel and Robert Charles aren't incompetent…even if Susan and her FBI friends want them to be. If the FBI makes a move on her, they'll pay for it. If I made a move on Rachel, I would have been walking right into some Achim Jeffers trap for sure."

"I know better than to believe that he would make the mistake of allowing the FBI to tail Rachel without some plan in place."

Now silent, I listened as Alex loudly coughed into the phone before swallowing and laboring to catch his breath. It hurt my soul to experience the feeling of mistrust for a man that had been my friend for years. He didn't have to try and use his illness to avoid our conversation. I already knew what they were thinking. Him, Susan and whoever they were working for wanted Rachel dead, but they were too chicken shit to do it themselves. That's why they made sure to give me the thumb drive. I was supposed to be their brainless errand boy. The hell with that.

"Well…maybe next time," Alex softly conceded.

"After this is all finished, it will probably be harder to get her…but I'm sure we can find a way to get it done together."

The front door of the fire station swung completely open, and the tall white man walked outside wearing a grumpy expression. Waving his hand, he asked me to join him inside before walking back into the building. Fed up with entertaining Alex's bullshit, I ended the call and climbed out of the van.

"Welcome to Nine Mile Point Station #78," the tall man greeted.

I walked into the fire station and followed him into a lounge area. A shorter white man with brown hair sat on a fake leather couch while Fox News blasted from the loud TV. Without words, both men shook my hand and quietly sized me up. I knew they were trying to figure out if I was indeed the person that they were expecting.

For my own reasons, I also examined them. Both men wore uniforms, and after studying them, they seemed to be brand new. The brown-haired man wore his hair long and I noticed that his stubby chin was partially shaven. His long hair and spoiled chin would easily prohibit him from any sort of firefighting duties. There was no way a self-breathing apparatus could properly seal with all that wild hair on his head. It was my guess that neither of these men were actually fire fighters. They were most likely undercover FBI agents, using this part-time fire station as cover. Alex's little friend, Susan, was attempting to play me, just as I expected she would.

"Here is the schedule of events for the Bayou Classic," the tall one stated, while handing me two memos.

"Pokey is scheduled to participate in several functions during Bayou Classic week, and he will be speaking during halftime on Saturday."

"I'm told you want to get inside the Superdome. We can do that for you…but it will be complicated."

"We can get you up near the balcony, but I gotta warn you, it'll be a hellva shot down to the field to pick this guy off."

"I suggest you look at the schedule and find a more reasonable opportunity."

Without looking at the men, I read the schedule of events and noticed that Pokey and Governor Lewis were slated to be in Champion Square during the football game. Making a mental note of the time and date, I folded up the memo and tucked it in my pocket.

"My opportunity will be inside the Superdome…it needs to be in front of the cameras" I bluntly explained.

"That's where all this will go down. You guys are supposed to be here to help me get it done, not whine about my tactics."

"You help me or you don't. If you won't, I'll find a way to get it done without you."

"Look dude," the brown-haired man loudly broke in. "We aren't here to hold you up but arranging for a secluded gunmen's perch inside of the Superdome, will be like some mission impossible shit."

"Who said I'll be using a rifle?" I sarcastically asked.

Both men looked puzzled as they curiously examined me for any hidden clues to my verbal riddle. Now, I had their undivided attention, and that's exactly what I needed.

"I won't even be in the Superdome when this goes down. I'll be parked outside…and I'll be long gone when the firing stops."

"How in the hell will you be shooting, if you aren't even inside the building!" The tall man blasted.

"Don't think for one second that either of us will be in there doing your dirty work for you."

"Neither of you will have to do a damn thing. Your job will be to get my gear in the Superdome and secure it for me," I quickly rebutted.

I unlocked my phone and showed both men a receipt for one of the stadium's north end box suites. Weeks in advance, I purchased the suite under the account of one of my dummy companies. My company happened to donate tens of thousands of dollars to sponsor all of the events during the Bayou Classic. I also gave money to each school's scholarship fund. Surprised by my foresight, both men looked at each other in shock, before allowing themselves to crack a smile. Showing me all of his perfectly manicured teeth, I was further convinced that the brown-haired man was nobody's fire fighter. These men were lying to me, so I decided it was my turn to paint a little fiction.

"When the game starts, I'll be entertaining a few guests and a handful of dignitaries in my suite. Just before halftime, me and my guest will head down with field passes to watch the bands."

"That's when I'll slip out to my car and remotely activate my weapon system," I explained.

Scrolling through pictures on my phone, I found the image of my cannon and displayed it for both men to see. Expressions of disbelief washed over their faces when they realized what I intended to do and the firepower I planned to unleash. This wouldn't be murder, it would be bloody carnage, and they understood this.

"All you'll need to do is get the pieces up to my suite and hide them. From there, I can assemble the weapon and dress it all up to look like a camera system. No one will be the wiser…and when the bullets start flying…it will be too late for anyone to stop me," I described.

"Not trying to second guess you, but don't you think using a Russian Anti-tank gun is a tad bit much?" The tall man asked.

"Do you really need that much firepower? Pokey is a big man….but even from up in the box suites, he ought to be easy to spot."

"I'm here to send a message," I shot back. "And in this business, simply killing someone is worthless. Delivering the fear of God himself to your enemies, is the gold standard gentlemen."

"All you need to do is get my gear inside my suite. From there, I'll take care of the rest. Can you guys do it for me or not?" I bluntly asked.

With visible unease, both men first confirmed their intentions with each other by using a wordless stare. This was going to be a huge undertaking for them, and after several seconds of thought, both men finally agreed. This mission would be silent and not discreet. It would be bold, while leaving all kinds of breadcrumbs that would lead back to everyone involved. From their subtle doubt, I knew these so-called men weren't committed to doing the dirty deeds required to maintain our race. Like many others, they had tasted and relished the grapes of our forefather's triumphs.

These men preferred the delicious fruits of those victories; over the bloody struggle to plant the seeds. They were Susan's men, and they would surely be ordered to turn on me the minute she had an angle.

"Do you guys want to see the cannon?" I offered. "It's in the back of the van. We can unload it right now and pack it away for transport."

"Yeah, let's have a look at the darn thing," the brown-haired man responded.

The tall man led all of us out of the front entrance and we walked behind my van. As I dug into my pockets for the keys, the thick grey sky let loose a powerful blast of wind. Despite wearing a light jacket, I could feel the small drops of rain start to fall from the angry-looking clouds. Having found my keys, I pushed the open button and the van's trunk began to slowly rise.

When the trunk opened, I observed both men's confusion as they looked into the empty compartment. The only thing the men saw was a thick plastic liner laying on top of the carpeted bed of the van. For a long moment, they seemed to search harder, as if they had missed something that was obvious. Putting the keys away, I reached inside of my jacket and slipped out the knife.

Before the tall white man could ask his silly question, I thrust the blade into his exposed kidney, then yanked his forehead backwards and slashed his throat. As the warm blood poured down his chest, I released his body and felt him crumple to the ground. My eyes met the brown-haired fellow, and I could see him swimming in disbelief.

Instead of challenging me, he turned away and galloped towards the fire house's entrance. I gave chase, determined to subdue him before he made it inside to get the damn gun he sorely needed. Before he could make it to the door, I grabbed him by his collar, and pulled him away from the building. He was unable to free himself or fend me off with his weak punches. Overwhelmed by my power, he began yelling at the top of his lungs, pleading for anyone to call the cops.

I dragged the asshole back to the van before dropping my knee on to his throat. Having taken the air out of his lungs, I shoved my blade into his rib cage. With each stab wound, his strength began to wane. Staring down at him, I could feel his soul slowly give way to his fate. In my disgust, I delivered several blows to his groin, feeling the need to ensure that his inferior version of white genes could no longer pollute my precious bloodline.

Finally, after more than a dozen stabs, the brown-haired imposter exhaled one final time before his bluish eyes went blank. The raindrops gained weight as they came pouring down from above. A small pool of rainwater mixed with his tears, as his lifeless pupils looked skyward. Even in death, the man's face still looked frightened and weak. I used my soiled fingers to close his eyelids and watched the falling rain rinse away the blood.

After loading both bodies into the back of the van, I reentered the fire station. I left both men's cellphones and personal effects inside of an empty locker before wiping down every piece of furniture I touched. Once I was satisfied that every clue had been erased, I locked the stations doors behind me and drove back towards New Orleans. As I crossed the bridge and headed towards Metairie, the heavy rain seemed to subside into a light drizzle. When I neared the old storage facility, I turned off of the main road and drove through the entrance.

My storage unit was in the rear near the properties back fence. Next to the unit sat the food truck I had bought months earlier. Inside, my cannon was arranged so that the barrel and targeting scope could peer out from behind a one-way mirror adjacent to the kitchen. Pulling up next to my unit, I parked and lifted open the storage door. Backing the van into the wide unit, I popped open the trunk and offloaded my grizzly cargo, covering the two men up with a long dark blanket. After finding a dry towel, I peeled off my wet clothes and dried myself.

Once I donned fresh clothes, I retrieved the schedule of events for the Bayou Classic from my wet pants pocket. Each folded sheet of paper was still wet, making them difficult to open. Determined, I carefully opened each fold, taking care not to rip the sheets apart. Having separated all three sheets of paper, I arranged them on a small table and looked down to read.

Long streaks of black and blue printer ink ran down each sheet and covered the words, but looking at the second page, I found what I needed. Both Pokey and Governor Lewis were going to be together for several events, giving me plenty of options.

Inside of a small box on the edge of the table, I pulled out several pieces of old mail addressed to one of my aliases. Recognizing an envelope, I grabbed it and retrieved the city issued permit. This would allow me to operate my food truck in the metro New Orleans area. I took it and walked out to the black and gold painted food truck, taping the permit on the inside of one of the serving windows. My plan was working out perfectly.

Everyone from Alex, Achim and the FBI believed that I would need assistance to do this job, but they were wrong. I was born with everything I needed, which was given to me by a higher power who looked down on my race with gracious favor. I had come to New Orleans shortly after leaving South Africa. Upon arriving here, I set up my food truck business and applied for the proper documents to legally operate during city-wide events. Now, I had the weapon. I had the opportunity and the perfect cover.

There would be no bloody gunfire inside of the Superdome. I could give a damn about Pokey, a token nigger who was just as worthless as these pathetic losers bleeding on my storage room floor. Like all diluted white traitors, Governor Lewis was a liberal cuck. The man thought himself shrewd and untouchable. He was a phony, ready to undermine his own race for personal gain. He went out of his way to curry votes from our black enemies in a vain attempt to elevate his own status. Governor Lewis was weak, and only sought the power of the presidency to advance his own twisted ambitions. While Zhilan rightfully wanted him dead for business reasons, I needed this appeasing asshole gone for much bigger interests.

While walking into the storage unit, I heard my cellphone ring inside of the van. Alarmed, I bolted over to the open door and leaned inside to look down at the bright screen. It was a notification from a locator beacon I had placed on Achim's vehicle. He was on the move, but it was way too late in the morning for him to be heading to the FBI Field Office.

Intrigued, I sat down inside of the van and logged into my tracking program.

Examining the map, I noticed that he was speeding down I-10 west bound. Achim had already passed up the most practicable exits if he were heading to the field office. A consideration that someone else might be driving his car flashed through my mind, but I quickly put it away. Something else was going on in Achim's pathetic little life, and I knew I needed to get to the bottom of it. Before locking up the storage unit, I pulled the bloody plastic covering out of the back of the van and loaded up my tool bag.

The locator indicated that Achim had parked outside of a privately-owned clinic near the airport, so I avoided I-10 and followed Airline Highway towards his location. After thirty minutes of long stop lights and moderate traffic, I arrived at the clinic and found Achim's car parked under a tall shade tree. I pulled the van into a coffee shop next door, found myself a table situated near a window, and quietly observed the scene as the morning traffic cruised by.

After several cups of hot coffee and one small cup of tea, an hour had passed and there was no sign of him. His car still sat alone under the shade tree, protected from the heat of the midday sun. Maybe he knew I was here? Maybe he parked here to flush me out? I couldn't discount those legitimate concerns. After all, he was a shrewd operator himself and that made him a dangerous nigger.

My concerns got the best of me, so I had to do something else besides fill my already loaded bladder. I settled on researching the owner of the clinic and googled the physician's name. True to form, the doctor who owned the clinic was a black lady from Lake Charles. She was a graduate of Tulane University and had practiced medicine in Baton Rouge and Morgan City. Having memorized her name, I didn't recall seeing the woman on Susan's thumb drive, but I still suspected that the doctor was somehow affiliated with Robert Charles.

Just as I was about to do a deep dive into her background, Achim appeared. He smiled as he held the door open for a pregnant black woman that walked behind him. She was a dark-skinned lady, with a pretty face and flowing black hair. Something about this woman's glow instantly reminded me of Rachel, especially the way Achim seemed to be basking in her presence. As she slowly wobbled to her car, Achim cheerfully trotted in front of her and opened her car door like a love-stricken idiot. They exchanged an affectionate kiss before the lady sat down behind the wheel. In that moment, I knew that he was a man in love. My mind suddenly exploded with cruel possibilities. Achim hadn't learned his lesson, and this was something I could use to my advantage.

With that growing tar baby in her stomach, this lady must be his new whore. She might be his legit attempt to reclaim his old life, or she could be his new Robert Charles partner in crime. As much as I hate to admit it, Achim and I had a few things in common. Our racial combat had prevented us both from realizing the true joys of life. We both were wounded men, fighting a bloody war of attrition.

After Achim went to his car, I managed to slip out of the coffee shop without paying my tab. He was driving his black Dodge Charger, while his little lover drove a burgundy Yukon. Both cars prepared to exit the parking lot, so I patiently waited for a break in the steady stream of traffic.

Several blocks away, a stop light turned red and both cars turned onto the road and slowly accelerated past the coffee shop. I put my van into reverse before pulling out and squeezing into the road behind them.

As a matter of habit, I knew the ever-vigilant Achim would surely be checking his six. I kept my distance, making sure not to follow too close. After two red lights, we all came upon the exit that would take us to I-10. The woman's Yukon slid into the far-right lane, preparing to exit Airline Highway while Achim's Charger stayed in the center. Now, I had to make a choice. With the flick of my fingers, I hit the right turn signal and fell in behind the Yukon. I thought it better to follow this interesting little lady for the time being.

The light turned green, and I tailed the Yukon as it merged onto I-10 east bound. After speeding through traffic for fifteen miles, she exited the Interstate near New Orleans East before pulling into a Winn-Dixie parking lot. I found a parking space and watched as the woman pushed a shopping cart into the grocery store. Reaching into my tool bag, I pulled out a remote tracker and tested the device to ensure its functionality. When the coast was clear, I creeped across the half empty parking lot and kneeled next to the Yukon's front tire.

Reaching my hand underneath the chassis, I planted the magnet on a metal frame and saw the tracker display a bright green light. From here on out, wherever Achim's new woman happened to be, I would know exactly where to find her. I trotted back to my van to dial up an updated position for Achim's car. Once my locator system found him, I saw that he was parked outside of the Clearview Mall. After jumping back on the highway, I sped westward to the Clearview area and spotted the Charger parked next to a row of handicapped spaces near the mall's glass entrance doors.

His car was parked crooked, almost like he was in a hurry. I found it intriguing that Achim Jeffers the self-proclaimed counter-racist hitman, would be in a rush to get to a shopping mall to browse the stores like some idle minded teenager. More than a bit nosy, I found an open parking space not far from his car, so I parked. As I sat alone in the van, I could sense his clear vulnerabilities. Whomever this woman happened to be, she had blunted his natural instincts and situational awareness. In short, he had lost his edge. So, killing him would be easy, maybe too damn easy.

While Achim shopped, spending his money with grand thoughts of hugging a brand-new baby, I would take full advantage. Opening my tool bag, I reached down to the bottom and found several pounds of C4 explosives. This would be the perfect way for Achim Jeffers to meet his end. Tucking the explosives into my pants, I exited the van and immediately felt small rain droplets land on top of my head. I needed to move quickly, setting these explosives up in the rain could backfire if the detonator got waterlogged.

With haste, I sprinted over and used my door pick to open up Achim's car. Once I popped open his hood, I placed the C4 near a fuel line and wired it to the electric detonator. After crudely wiring the detonator into the car's battery cable, I re-locked the car before tightening the wires. It was then that I noticed the broken piece of clear tape he had purposely placed outside of the door frame.

If he happened to look down, Achim would surely notice that someone had broken the seal. My heart sunk when I realized that I had no way of replacing the torn tape. I installed the tracking device on his car several days ago, and I didn't notice any transparent seal on the door. Maybe Achim hadn't lost too much of his edge after all. For a second, I considered if Achim was baiting me, knowing that I was here in New Orleans. Activating the device and closing the hood, I dismissed the notion. Surely Achim wouldn't be foolish enough to lead me right to a woman that was pregnant with his child.

Making it back to my van, I climbed inside and waited, as the rain trickled down my windshield. After twenty minutes, wind gusts made the rain pour in from the west and I watched as running customers braved the elements. Then came my first sighting of Achim. At first, he slowly strolled before quickening his pace as the rain poured down on his bald head.

When he arrived at his car, I noticed he paused before his hand pulled the door open. In that instant, I knew Achim had spotted the torn tattletale. He stood there in the falling rain, silently looking down into his car in a moment that was surely filled with panicked realization. He was spooked, and I watched him step away from his car before slowly scanning the parking lot. When the rain began to pour down harder, he turned around and headed back inside the mall.

An angry part of me wanted to follow Achim inside and finish him off, but that would be foolish. I waited in the parking lot for about thirty minutes and saw no sign of him. Given the circumstances, it would be much better to allow the uncertainty of this event to eat away at him. Plus, I was here for a specific mission and no matter how sweet killing Achim Jeffers might be, completing that mission was my priority. There would surely be more opportunities to eliminate him later, I just needed to be patient.

As dark clouds threw down lightening, I cranked up the van and drove away. After fighting my way onto the highway, my cellphone blasted with loud rings as it laid on the passenger's seat. Curious, I picked it up, and examined it while making sure to pace myself with the car ahead of me. It was a notification from the tracker I had placed underneath the SUV driven by Achim's new lady. She was on the move, and apparently, she was heading west on the Interstate, not too far behind me.

If I couldn't get to Achim, snooping around his lady would be a nice contingency plan. It could certainly become a distraction that would put the fear of God into the FBI's new slave. Sensing an opportunity, I slowed my speed and eased myself over to the middle lane while studying my rear-view mirror. Within five minutes, I spotted the burgundy Yukon speeding through the rain. Despite the adverse conditions, I was amazed to see this pregnant woman driving like a madman in such horrid weather.

I pushed down the accelerator and eased over towards the far-right lane as she sped past me. After situating myself several cars behind the Yukon, I paced her car until she left city limits and turned south. She was heading towards Boutte, Louisiana. Not too long after turning towards Boutte, we found ourselves in the city of Destrehan. I watched as she exited the highway and entered a neat looking residential area. Now, it was time for me to fall back and allow my tracker to do its work.

After finding a local gas station, I pulled into the parking lot, and watched my phone as the tracker traced a path towards a familiar address that I had committed to memory. Within the many files Susan had provided, were the locations of several safe houses Robert Charles had sprinkled throughout the Greater New Orleans Area. I instantly remembered that one of those hideaways happened to be located here in Destrehan, near the Hale Boggs Bridge.

Watching the signal, I saw the beacon come to a sudden halt on Oakley Lane and I knew my itching assumption was correct. My car bomb had shaken Achim, and now he was calling audibles to protect everything he loved. I drove away from the gas station, making a quick pass through Oakley Lane as I eyed the small single-story home sitting in front of the large Yukon. There was no gate, screen door or security system. Nothing would stand in my way, if I decided to make a house call. Yet, I knew better than to believe this Robert Charles safe house would be easy pickings.

Aside from what I observed at the residence, a few houses down, I noticed an odd white sedan parked along the curb. Its windows sported a dark tint and its shiny rims were all chrome. In a neighborhood littered with old cars and rusted pickups, this brand-new car and the ladies shiny Yukon were both clearly out of place. The way the sedan was hastily parked and its array of short antennas told me that Achim's lady had an uninvited guest. My thoughts immediately turned to Alex's shady friend, Susan. This was most likely one of her FBI goons staking out the safe house. Instead of just killing these niggers, grifters like Susan were far too interested in protecting their drug money. Grifters like her were far more dangerous than all the Robert Charles operatives combined.

In my curiosity, I drove one street over and squeezed my van into a roadside parking space. I pulled the sharp blade out of a bloody plastic bag, wiping it clean before stuffing it into my light jacket. Popping open the glove compartment, I reached inside, grabbing a 9mm pistol and its silencer. After a quick function check, I loaded a live round into the chamber and stowed the gun in the small of my back. When I stepped out of the van, a heavy gust greeted me, pulling the door hard against its hinges. Despite the angry wind, the cloud ceased to assault us as the rain came to a merciful pause.

As the rainless grey clouds sped eastward through the New Orleans sky, I slowly walked towards Oakley Lane. At the intersection, I turned up the street and saw the nosy white sedan several houses in front of me. Slowing my pace, I examined the vehicle's license plate and quickly confirmed that this wasn't some regular car. This car was most definitely a government owned vehicle.

While walking next to the car, I cut my eyes towards the driver's side window trying to see through the dark tint. Spooked by my abrupt presence, I saw the outline of an image nervously shift in his seat as I examined him. Suddenly, the window was lowered halfway and the eyes of a familiar looking black man focused on me. His chin was cleanly shaved and his long sleeve button up shirt was perfectly ironed. Beyond his annoyed stare, I saw a long black cord dangling from the radio console next to him.

"Can I help you sir!" the black man sternly stated.

In that moment, I made new plans. There was no way I would pass up a golden opportunity like this. This would be the perfect message to send to Achim and his newfound allies. Killing this cop would absolutely inject a lethal dose of mistrust into this new Robert Charles FBI alliance. Susan and Alex needed to realize that there are certain things her FBI pals can't buy with their blood money. Now, it was only a matter of getting this Black cop to lower his guard so I could take him by surprise.

"Yeah, you can help me!" I angrily barked.

"It looks like you don't have any reason to be here…so you need to get moving, buddy."

"We have a lot of elderly people living in the area. I know you're sitting out here casing these houses and it's worrying my neighbors."

"I'm going to ask you this once…so you better listen. You need to leave. This isn't your neighborhood and we don't like you around here."

"If you don't, I'll call the cops. I grew up with the sheriff, so don't test me, OK."

"I don't need to do a damn thing you bastard." He dismissed while rolling up his window. "You can have a nice day, sir,"

"Well, I'm about to call the cops!" I vented. "You thugs are always coming into our neighborhood and stealing shit!"

As I turned and made several steps towards the entrance of a random house, I heard the sedan door pop open behind me. Turning around, I saw the black cop exit the car wearing an angry smile. His hands reached into his pocket, revealing a silver badge with some silly fraternity medallion hanging from it. While he was showing off his credentials, I ripped the pistol from the small of my back and aimed it at his chest. He brought a permission slip to our gun fight, so I immediately vetoed his authority with one pull of the trigger.

His body crumpled to the sidewalk. Blood droplets streamed down the white sedan behind him. Standing over his body, I reached down and took his pistol out of its holster before ripping open his buttoned-up shirt. He wasn't wearing a vest and his chest was bare. The bullet had entered him just above his heart and he was losing blood fast. Grabbing my knife, I quickly stabbed him in his liver to ensure he would meet a certain end. Using the sharp blade, I tore his shirt into long shreds before balling them up and pushing them down on top of the wound.

"With that sucking chest wound, you don't have very long," I whispered. "Maybe five to ten minutes, if you're lucky."

"You'll bleed to death pretty quick if we don't keep pressure on this."

Grabbing his shaking hand, I placed it on top of the balled-up shirt and instructed him to push down hard. Sweat poured down his brown skin, and I watched his chest rise and fall rapidly as he struggled to take in air.

"You're the Tarpon?" he asked in panic.

"Yeah, I…guess I am," I softly acknowledged.

"Achim Jeffers is going to kill your white ass," he declared with an angry smile.

"He might very well kill me," I casually admitted. "Or he might not."

"Either way….I'll need you to do me one favor before you die."

"If you happen to see him before you die, I'll need you to deliver a message from me and Zhilan."

Chapter Eleven

Jaguars & Tigers

A wet and gloomy Thanksgiving came and went, offering no clues as to the Tarpon's whereabouts. Director Saunders gave everyone the day off to mourn the murder of Agent Porter. His private funeral was an anguishing affair, which was held the evening before Thanksgiving.

It was reported on the front page of the Times Picayune that Porter was killed while apprehending a suspect during a botched home invasion. I knew that deceptive narrative was a clever bit of political spin. The FBI had been forced to provide the white media with this false account in order to conceal our operations. Governor Lewis's Presidential campaign applied pressure on Director Saunders, making sure she amended the truth. In the deceptive world of high stakes politics, there would be no raising the alarm or scaring off black voters. Cautious mumbles of a white assassin hellbent on targeting black citizens, would never trump the desire to gin up voters and win elections. After all, the Bayou Classic was a prime opportunity for the Governor to smile in the faces of the black electorate, while giving lip service to our sincere issues.

The myriad of events surrounding the Bayou Classic had all started in earnest the day after Thanksgiving. Despite an overwhelming FBI presence, no one heard or saw the

Tarpon. To our immense relief, Pokey had safely made appearances at several venues and even spoke to a large crowd during the highly touted fraternity line competition.

This grey morning marked the beginning of the last day of the Bayou Classic. Today, we'd all be holding our breath as the football game kicked off inside the Superdome. Due to the large audience and various dignitaries scheduled to attend the event, this would be fertile ground for the Tarpon to deliver his fatal blow. With so many plates to cover, both the NOPD and FBI were going to be stretched thin.

I drove to the 1st Police District near downtown New Orleans, meandering through the early morning traffic to attend our pre-operations briefing. Walking into the dim Police Station, I found the lobby filled with scores of groggy-eyed law enforcement officers. They were all carrying cups of hot coffee and exhausted stares. Most of them wore bracelets around their wrists sporting the bright letters CP, in honor of Agent Porter. I couldn't find their obvious fatigue as any sign of weakness; it had certainly been a draining week for all of us. Now we all were coming down the home stretch, catapulting towards a finale that was sure to challenge us all.

I walked down a long hallway that led towards our briefing room, avoiding the mass of caffeine-filled zombies. Entering the bright room, I found it empty, cold and depressed. I was early, so I spied my favorite seat near the back and claimed the territory for myself.

"You ready Achim?" a voice asked from the hallway.

"Your boy damn sure has to show his face today. He's boxed himself in by waiting this long."

Turning around in my seat, I saw the fatigue in Agent Sanchez's eyes as he strolled into the room carrying his own steaming mug of bean juice. Our eyes met, and I could sense his concealed anger as he looked down at me. He was still pissed about our altercation and I knew he wanted revenge. Due to the simmering tension between us, Director Saunders had done her best to keep us away from each other. The morning of Agent Porter's funeral, Sanchez had called me, attempting to offer some sort of pathetic semi-apology. I heard the man out, letting him try to explain his piece, but I hardly believed a lying word that left his tongue. Now we were face to face, and he was trying his best to pretend like we were still on the same team.

"The Tarpon is never boxed in, Agent Sanchez," I dismissed.

"In fact, we're the ones at his mercy right now."

Without looking at him, I could hear Sanchez chuckling to himself while he walked to the front of the room. He didn't believe me, and I knew that he was way too confident for his own good.

"Achim, my security plan is working out perfectly," he boasted.

"I know it's difficult for an arrogant murderous sociopath like yourself to admit when your wrong, but the FBI is the premier Law Enforcement agency in the world. You're witnessing our effectiveness up close and personal."

"It's in your best interest to remember all you've seen when our business is finished here." Sanchez threatened.

"I damn sure will remember," I replied. "I'll remember everything."

"You can bet your life on it."

Before Sanchez could respond to my not-so-coded threat, a small group of moving bodies entered the briefing room and shattered our privacy. Turning my eyes towards the doorway, I first noticed a strange looking Director Saunders, wearing a tight-fitting cream-colored pant suit. The outfit was cut to match her slim frame perfectly, offering any wandering eye a unique yet classy glance at her petite womanly features. Underneath her thick layer of make-up shined a smile that didn't invoke any sort of happiness. Instead, it was one of those phony smiles that conveyed more than a hint of willful submission and vulnerability.

Behind her, I saw the TV-friendly face of Governor Lewis and quickly realized why Saunders had decided to doll up this morning. Unlike in all of the brushed-up stock videos and campaign ads, Governor Lewis was a noticeably short man. His stringy hair looked to be dark brown and filled with a youthful shine, but as he closed in, I saw stone grey streaks hiding near their roots. His common looking dark blue suit was modest only in appearance, as was his dull looking Rolex that could easily be misidentified as some cheap Timex. The man looked like every part of the typical fast-tongued white politician and his mere presence was enough to unsettle Director Saunders.

While she introduced me to Governor Lewis, I noticed a strain of idolatry waxed in Pokey's beaming eyes as he walked in behind him. He was drunk with inferiority and filled with worthless black fantasies of somehow obtaining a sense of self-importance. This politician wasn't his equal, but his massa in every sense of the word. Pokey was willing to give his life in order to please this white man, while hoping to somehow prove his value to the world in doing so.

My heart ached as I watched him skin and grin for someone who was simply using him as a tool to garner black votes. I knew these were the precious moments that Pokey had silently envisioned and coveted within his hidden daydreams. He held on tight to an incurable thirst to gain some sort of access to a world black people were systemically excluded from. It was his delusion that he alone knew what was best for the black community. With his leadership, us black sheep could live among these ruthless white wolves in peace and harmony. It was all fantasy, yet he had invested all of himself into this make-believe. No matter how painful reality had become, the imaginary sweetness of his inner mirage, had consumed his soul.

All of Pokey's ill-fitting intentions were simply a fairytale. A black fairytale that would ultimately lead Black America to certain doom. Unclouded by worthless pride, I could see the obvious truth as the Governor's shrewd campaign director slowly strolled into the room. Travis Chase looked stone-faced and confident, with both of his hands jammed deeply into the pockets of his designer jeans. He was a man on a mission. That mission involved controlling black voters and capturing power for the Democrats.

"Good Morning Achim!" Governor Lewis smoothly offered.

His well-seasoned greeting was laced with this strange tone of familiarity, speaking his words to me as if we had known each other for ages. We shook hands and I purposely put on a tight grip, enforcing my own non-verbal authority upon his small pale hand. Sensing my increased pressure, Governor Lewis returned his own firm squeeze, while trying his best to unlock details hidden in my eyes. As he released my hand, he finally figured out this Negro that stood before him, was unimpressed. After a silent head nod, he moved on to Agent Sanchez and both men exchanged meaningless introductions.

"I'll need you to be extra vigilant today Achim," Director Saunders softly whispered.

"Both Governor Lewis and Pokey are dead fuckin set on reaching every black voter attending the Bayou Classic today. Pokey will be completely exposed out there, so this whole thing could go south quick."

"Every white face we see, needs to be checked out," she snapped.

"I didn't volunteer to help white politicians win their elections Director," I conveyed in a low tone.

"The safety of Pokey is my only concern, not Governor Lewis's election ambitions."

"Well today, they both are a two for one package deal, bud," Travis Chase rudely interrupted.

As Travis eased up alongside us, I could feel Director Saunders pull herself away. I knew right then that something horrible had transpired between the both of them. Whatever it might have been, it intimidated her for sure. Travis began to ramble on about poll numbers, and the situation I found myself in began to click as I half-listened to his nonsense. Nothing grabs media cameras and voter's like a monumental triumph, or in this case, a bloody massacre. Governor Lewis's campaign could give a damn about Pokey's well-being. If a black campaign spokesperson happened to get assassinated by a white extremist, then Governor Lewis surely stood to benefit at the polls. The media coverage alone, plus the potential to spin the horrific tragedy, would lead to sympathetic voters during the election cycle.

While Travis continued to chat, I knew that if the Tarpon failed to get a crack at Pokey, he would surely shed as much innocent black blood as humanly possible. If I were in the Tarpon's shoes, I'd make sure to have the last-ditch option of killing unwitting Bayou Classic attendees, by the dozens. This heartless last-ditch option itself only stood to offer even more rewards to the Lewis Campaign, giving him the opportunity to paint himself as some blood-soaked "white ally" of the black community. These satanic demons were ready to sacrifice Pokey's life, all in the name of advancing their own political agendas.

Panning my eyes down at Travis, I noticed the light smile that provided artificial life to his meaningless words. In that moment, there wasn't much of a difference between the Tarpon and the Governor in my mind. As a black man, whatever differences white folks claim to have amongst themselves, was of no concern to me. Useless political parties or affiliations mean nothing to blacks imprisoned within this unholy system of White Supremacy. The devil carrying a hot loaf of bread was no different than the devil that swung a cold sword. In fact, the one offering the tempting bread was exponentially more dangerous in my estimation. At least the devil holding the sword was honest about his Anti-Black hatred. I preferred White Supremacy be out in the open, so I can clearly see Satan, and allow the Lord to use me to enforce his will.

"On behalf of the state of Louisiana and the Democrat Party, I would like to thank each and every one of you," Governor Lewis let loose from the front of the room.

"Thus far, you all have done a fine job protecting the citizens of this great city. I have no doubt that with your continued vigilance, peace and harmony will prevail today."

The briefing room was now more than half full, so the Governor thought it prudent to deliver an impromptu pep talk before the start of our briefing. For several minutes, he masterfully sewed more than a few police friendly words into some of his more popular talking points. Governor Lewis openly promised to provide more funding and training to law enforcement, while making certain to water down any hint of punishment. In short, for the mountain of crimes folks in this very briefing room had committed against black society, this Presidential candidate was promising to sanction them with an increased budget and useless training.

All of his cleverly coded words sent the exact message he intended to relay. These white supremacists love to silently wink and nod at each other, while pretending to enact some sort of self-serving reform for black people. The hard truth is there was absolutely no way to reform a white supremacist that hides behind a badge. The police are the Enforcement Arm of White Supremacy. Their main goal is to control the indignant masses of Black Americans and keep them in various forms of duress. The police know this. White society understands this. Governor Lewis knows this, and I damn sure knew it too. For a Race Soldier hiding behind a badge, the whopping specter of performing racial sensitivity training is like being forced to watch an annoying porno video. Racists must be punished severely; it's the only way to cure the disease. If these uncivilized animals want to practice their ideology of White Supremacy, it must come at the expense of their pathetic pale lives.

Black society has coddled and pampered these mischievous demons for far too long. That's why God moved me to join Robert Charles. It's my calling to deliver God's will upon Satan's most treasured converts. After the Governor ended his tricky Pro-Police rant, several onlookers rose from their seats and exchanged grateful handshakes with him. That's when the shiny gold lapel adorning his jacket caught my attention. It was a corny image of a grinning donkey, the symbol and moniker used by the DNC.

As the golden donkey gleamed under the room's bright ceiling lights, the cryptic message the Tarpon passed to Agent Porter ran through my mind. When Jessica and Aunt Rita relayed Porters last words, I initially believed the Tarpon was teasing me. Yet everything about Porter's murder, seemed off. What made the Tarpon pass up the open invitation to harm Robert Charles and choose to kill an FBI agent instead?

Suddenly the golden donkey seemed to relay its truth as I focused in on it. The Tarpon had fooled us and now we were walking right into his trap. I bolted over to the main table and snatched a schedule of events memo out of Sanchez's useless hands. In angry protest, he jumped up from his seat and tried to grab it back as I batted away his weak attempts.

"What the hell are you two doing!" An annoyed Director Saunders vented.

"We need to talk privately Director," I answered.

"No one is doing anything until this fuck-head gives my shit back to me," Sanchez angrily ordered.

Having found the answers I sought, I crumpled up his memo before tossing it down at his small feet. The disrespectful gesture only inflamed his buried passion, prompting him to shove me. I felt myself stumble from the force of his assault, finally regaining my balance after falling backwards several feet. By the time I reestablished my footing, several of Agent Sanchez's crooked allies had come in-between us, urging the both of us to stay cool. Staring into his beady eyes, I could see his inner courage grow as scores of thugs with badges physically surrounded me.

"It's time we diffuse this little beef!" the Director shouted.

"Let's step outside the room. Right now, Achim Jeffers."

I followed the Director into the dimly lit hallway. After shutting the briefing room door, she walked several feet away from the room's thin walls. Even in the misty morning darkness of the hallway, I could see the Directors' plush white face began to turn a light shade of red.

"If you wanted us to talk in private, you don't need to pull a stunt like that Achim."

"Time and time again, I have stood up for you," she went in.

"And now you're in there provoking my agents and making me look like a fool."

"Look, I know all about what happened to your family in Houston. I'm also aware of your storied history with the Robert Charles gang."

"A lot of agents in that room hate the fact that you are even involved in this," she quipped.

"Most of them would rather see you in handcuffs for killing those two cops."

"But I wanted you here, Achim. It was me that reached out to your cousin Evan and asked him to contact you off the record."

"Evan worked for me several years ago when we both were stationed in Tampa. I asked him to talk to you and convince you to help us. Whether you believe it or not Achim, your cousin Evan, really believes in you."

"He told me you're the most upstanding person he's ever known…and so far, I believe he was right."

"But, that's not the only reason I wanted you for this Achim," she admitted while turning her eyes away from me.

"I also knew the white gunmen who slaughtered your family," she softly admitted.

"I had a felony abduction and domestic violence case against the man three years before he shot up your church."

"Unfortunately, due to a few technicalities and other priorities, I made a deal with him because I couldn't get the major felonies to stick. So, my office offered him a misdemeanor, and he walked."

When the words left her lips, I could see the expression of torture in her face. We both knew the origins of those so-called technicalities. The murderer of my family was a violent white male, who had been a career criminal with a lengthy history of arrests. Yet none of that mattered in a system dominated by White Supremacy. People like her allowed this scumbag to roam free and exercise his white birth right, which is 'immunity from law'. Because of that fact, people like Director Saunders had my family's blood on their hands.

Swallowing my anger, I turned away from her and created distance. She had hit me with truth bombs, and I needed to digest them alone. Vivid memories of seeing my infant son choke to death on his own blood, raced through my mind. Sobering thoughts of my wife's shiny gold casket followed. A big part of me wanted to walk out of the station, keeping the knowledge of the Tarpon's secret scheme to kill Governor Lewis, to myself. Yet, another part of me knew this could all be one of the Tarpon's clever manipulation tactics. He was just as shrewd as he was violent, if not more.

"I'm sorry Achim," Director Saunders whimpered.

"I know this may sound trivial and selfish to you, but I've had to carry the burden of that failure with me all these years."

"Achim, I hope our time together on this case will offer the both of us some form of closure. I hope I can somehow earn your forgiveness."

"I'm not interested in your closure," I shot back.

"I'm here to kill the Tarpon and erase him from the living."

"Whatever grief you feel you owe to me and my family, you can keep it."

"Their blood will stay on your hands until I see fit. There will be no painless atonement for your sins, not unless the system of White Supremacy is demolished by your hands."

She walked towards me with sympathy welling up in her blue eyes. From her body language I knew she was about to plead for forgiveness, begging me to offer her an easy way out of the torture chamber of her badly worn conscious.

"That's a really big ask Achim," she softly declared. "Ending racism isn't something I'll be able to do all by myself."

"I don't care about your whining," I let loose.

"Either you're truly seeking atonement, or just hiding behind selfish grief."

"You asked me to forgive you....so I named my price. Now, the choice is yours."

"I'm here to pay whatever price to right the wrong I did," she defiantly uttered.

Puffing out her small chest, and making sure to stand tall before me, I could sense this little lady intended to try and prove me wrong. In those few seconds, I tossed around the idea of keeping her in the dark and trapping the Tarpon all for myself, but I came up with a better idea. An idea that would show me just how much this white woman was committed to correcting her error.

"Alright then," I relented.

"Since you think you want to be on team Black Empowerment, I'll need to tell you that the Tarpon, has been deceiving us all this time."

"I have reason to believe that the Tarpon isn't going to kill Pokey. I believe Zhilan has actually paid him to assassinate Governor Lewis."

Astonished, Director Saunders looked at me with eyes drenched in stubborn disbelief. I could almost feel her mind sorting through the acknowledgement, while she contemplated my conclusion. With several slow shakes of her head, she began to resist my notion before softly voicing her doubts.

"I don't know about this Achim," she stated.

"Every bit of intelligence Sanchez and I have, tells us Zhilan and the Tarpon are going after Pokey. Zhilan believes Pokey and the NOPD killed his cousin. That's more than enough motive for us to be sure he's Zhilan's target."

"The FBI can't afford to screw shit up over some wild hunch, Achim. We gotta keep our feet planted firmly in facts here."

"This ain't a damn hunch," I replied.

"Agent Porter delivered a message to me from the Tarpon, just before he died," I explained.

"The Tarpon told me to not make an ass out of myself, or I'd end up getting broken and bucked."

"Governor Lewis is a lifelong Democrat," I stressed. "Making him a donkey."

"The Tarpon was sending me a warning he knew I would understand. He has an axe to grind with White people like you and the Governor."

"Yes, he despises Black politicos like Pokey, but we all know that it's Pokey's white liberal paymasters who actually calls the shots. Black tokens like him are a dime a dozen. Killing Pokey won't solve Zhilan's problem, but taking out the head of the snake certainly will."

"Zhilan has probably been in business with the NOPD and now feels betrayed. He wants to cut off the venomous head of the American snake that dared to bite him. He paid the Tarpon to come here and eliminate the real muscle behind Pokey."

"This whole situation has nothing to do with him, Director. It isn't about killing some useless black figurehead…. It's about who's actually calling the shots in this crooked system of Anti-Black Oppression. Is it the violent white men. The tricky white women. The so-called conservatives or liberals, Hispanics, Asians, Gays or Straight?"

"It's all about who's in control of black people," I explained.

"Will it be the blood thirsty white men pointing their guns at us…or will it be the devious white men that offer us wine in return for our obedience? That's the real battle here Director, who ultimately controls us as black people."

"Zhilan wants to send Americans a bloody message, and the Tarpon is more than ready to deliver it for him, on behalf of White primacy."

The dim hallway light hanging above her illuminated her uncomfortable silence. I knew Director Saunders quietly agreed with my assessment. The public assassination of Governor Lewis would culminate into chaos almost immediately, throwing U.S. politics into a nosedive.

"We can't risk plunging this country into the abyss over some angry drug dealer," she mumbled.

"I'll need to inform the Governor of the plot and call in more Secret Service for this."

"The hell you will!" I demanded.

"This is our little secret. You keep quiet about this, you understand!"

"The minute his campaign finds out about him being targeted, they'll pull all his appearances and run for the hills like the cowards they are."

"And when that happens….we both know the Tarpon will retaliate by killing as many innocent black people as he can. The Bayou Classic will become a death trap."

"Let Governor Lewis walk around with his pathetic chest out, pretending to be some white hero for the Black Community. Let Sanchez believe he alone is responsible for keeping Pokey alive. Both men are foolish, and I don't give a damn about either of them. My only concern is black people."

"No way Achim!" Director Saunders interjected. "The FBI can't do that."

"We must keep Governor Lewis alive. This country can't allow people like Zhilan and the Tarpon to win!"

"You said you wanted atonement.....didn't you?" I sharply asked.

"Well, this is your chance sweetheart. I'm about to see if you and the FBI are capable of washing the blood of my family off of your filthy hands..."

"America has made me into a ruthless Black man. Being uncompromising is the only way my people will survive in this hell hole."

"The life of Governor Lewis is absolutely meaningless to my people. If the Tarpon kills him, it's God's will."

"As for you...you just better hope I find the Tarpon before he executes the Governor and soils your little career."

"Hell, if this was really a country built on a system of Justice, your career should have been over the minute you cut that white identity extremist loose to kill my family," I declared.

"But it seems, I'll have to settle for this instead..."

Unnerved by my frank words, I could see a white fog of fear trickle down her face, erasing any self-serving delusions of black forgiveness. She understood that if the life of Governor Lewis was worthless to me, then hers wasn't too far behind it. I wasn't a happy bootlick like Pokey. I'm a real black man, and when you fuck with real black men, you earn real consequences. Relishing the moment, I stared at the Director, while offering her a chuckle of contempt before heading back into the briefing room.

Opening the door and walking inside, I noticed that Sanchez had already begun the briefing without us. As he droned on-and-on about individual patrol assignments, I could feel all the angry eyes watching me. Both Governor Lewis and Travis shot looks of discomfort while examining me from their seats in the front row. A confidently coonish Pokey made a show out of his displeasure by wildly shaking his head and letting loose a loud sigh. I lowered myself down and pulled out my cellphone, trying to ignore the simmering hatred surrounding me. As my finger scrolled through my 6zeros app, the dismissive voice of Sanchez pulled my attention away from the secret chatroom.

"Achim, today you'll be assigned to sector five," he relayed.

"You'll be there with two plain clothes officers from St. Bernard Parish. Do you have any issues or complaints?"

Looking up at the force laydown map hanging behind him, I noticed that sector five was the furthest patrol area from the Superdome, encompassing the streets near City Hall. I saw the quiet look of victory hiding behind Sanchez's gaze when our eyes met. This was his twisted version of sticking it to me, making sure to keep my black ass away from the action and more importantly, out of his greasy hair.

"I'm good Sanchez," I lied.

The briefing room door suddenly opened. A disheveled Director Saunders re-entered and quietly walked up to Sanchez. Though she wore a stone-faced expression, I could see obvious signs of tears hiding in her eyes. The change in her appearance caught the attention of more than a few observers, causing the Governor himself to take a long hard look.

"Everyone has been issued their assignments Director," a concerned Sanchez relayed.

"Good. No need for an extra pep talk then. We all know what needs to be done," she stumbled.

"No one lays a damn finger on Pokey today. Let's see to it people."

I jetted out of the room as soon as Sanchez ended the meeting. After grabbing an NOPD handheld radio off of its battery charger, I quickly made my way outside. Jumping into my car, I drove past the City Hall sector and found a public parking area near the Superdome. I didn't give a damn about Sanchez's silly assignments. Today the Tarpon would be near the Superdome, and I wanted to be here to give the tricky bastard a hearty New Orleans style welcome.

The slow rainy morning rolled into a fast-paced overcast afternoon as I chatted on 6zeros. The streets near the Superdome began to fill up with joyous black faces, all of them flossing Bayou Classic T-Shirts. I remembered that just before noon, both Pokey and the Governor's motorcades were scheduled to arrive at the Superdome to attend a luncheon with high ranking HBCU officials. This would be the first real opportunity for the Tarpon to show his fangs and infect us with his madness.

Reaching underneath the passenger seat, I grabbed my pistol, concealing it next to the handheld radio and cell phone. Before leaving the parking lot, I fed dollars into the greedy parking meter and activated my car alarm. After several minutes of walking, I turned onto Poydras Street and walked towards the golden specter of the Superdome. The smell of grilled meat, fried catfish and boiled seafood filled the air. Having arrived at the Superdome, I walked into a half-filled area known as Champion Square and mixed into the light crowd. The sounds of several high school bands added to the scenery, as spectators casually drank while bobbing their heads to their favorite old-school harmonies.

In the center of Champion Square, a raised television platform was barricaded off by a wide circle of iron fences. Several of Sanchez's armed thugs-with-badges patrolled the area, working alongside members of the Superdome's private security firm. The barely noticeable presence of Secret Service officers was light. Thus far, Director Saunders seemed to have made her decision. At least for the moment, she was seeking real atonement on my terms, and not her own. Within the barricade, nervous cameramen worked to position their equipment and find the perfect camera angle. As I walked past the short metal gates, several faces I recognized stood out to me. One was a famous sports commentator, while the other two were former professional football players from the New Orleans area.

During the evening, Governor Lewis was scheduled to appear on national television, before the school's marching bands started their legendary halftime show. Every black alumnus worth their salt would have their eyes glued to the screen, if they weren't already watching from the stands. The Governor and his clever campaign were aware of this and planned to use the opportunity to pander to as many potential black voters as possible.

Walking through Champion Square, I arrived at a long access road that separated the Superdome from the Smoothie King basketball arena. The arena happened to be hosting a lively R&B gala that was packed to the gills. Unlike Champion Square, the wide access road was filled with black bodies, many of them leaving the concert and heading straight for the Superdome to watch the game. Looking towards the back entrance of the Superdome, I could see the yellow barricades sectioning off the paved driveway that awaited Pokey and Governor Lewis's motorcade. Even from the crowded streets, I saw FBI snipers in their perches atop the buildings surrounding the area. If the Tarpon made his move here, he'd be in a tight spot for sure and he might not make it out alive.

The looming presence of the FBI's death squad reminded me to turn on my NOPD radio. Reaching into my jacket pocket, I hit the power button and turned the volume up just enough for me to hear it over the band playing in the background. Several male voices casually rattled off checkpoints before a familiar female voice grabbed my attention.

"What are these damn protestors doing here, Sanchez!" She vented over the radio.

"They can't be here. Get the State Police and the NOPD to move them away from our route!"

Turning around, I saw Governor Lewis's four-car motorcade stalled at the intersection. Bright blue police lights and loud sirens filled the air, as a large crowd waving Confederate flags brought the motorcade to a halt. Behind the motorcade, scores of screaming rednecks boxed in the cars and began to try and pull open their doors. Several officers tried pushing the rabid protestors away, but they were severely outnumbered and quickly overpowered by the violent white horde.

"It's an unplanned protest of Governor Lewis, Director," Sanchez responded over the radio.

"None of this was authorized. They just showed up out of nowhere."

"No shit!" She flatly replied. "Get this street clear now!"

The yells of angry White protestors pierced the air, overshadowing the beautiful symphony of the high school bands. Aside from waving the American Swastika, many in the mob carried placards adorned with right wing slogans like "DON'T TREAD ON ME", "BLUE LIVES MATTER" and "HANDS OFF MY GUNS". Amid the chaos, I saw several meth-head looking men, lobbing bottles at the two limousines in the center of the motorcade. A handful of bottles bounced off the limos hood while one hit its target just right, shattering into dozens of pieces upon impact.

"Oh, hell no!" An angry black male voice uttered from behind me.

Before I knew it, a small group of young black men were trotting down the street screaming threats at the white mob. They were pissed, and I couldn't blame them. These veiled racists had decided to defile the sanctity of Bayou Classic weekend, in order to push their asinine Anti-Black Agenda. This was the perfect cover for the Tarpon. He could be anywhere, lurking in the middle of this perfectly manufactured confusion.

Assuming he was present, I pulled the radio from my pocket and paced myself behind the group of black soldiers. As we approached the white mob, I saw Director Saunders fight her way out of the front seat of one of the limos. She held her radio tight, as a group of elderly white women wearing Oath Keeper T-shirts let loose with a barrage of empty soda cans and gravel.

"Sanchez!" She yelled.

"We gotta get this damn motorcade moving, right now!"

"I'm on it," he answered in frustration.

Out of the corner of my eye, I saw a man standing near the intersection's stop sign. He wore a menacing NRA shirt and a faded camouflage baseball cap. His flabby belly hung over a cracked brown leather belt and his cheap Nike running shoes betrayed his limited social status. Yet, it was the well-oiled M-4 rifle that dangled in front of his chest that immediately captured my worries. The rifle was loaded with a long banana clip. The White Supremacist phrase "We Was Kangz" was stenciled on it in bright red paint.

"Look! Black Lives Matters is here!" One of the White rioters yelled through his missing front teeth.

As the young men closed in on the rioters, both groups began trading verbal jabs before an arrogant white woman decided to push one of the black boys. Within seconds, a full-blown racial melee was underway. An elderly White male attempted to throw a sucker punch at my head. Raising my forearm, I blocked his cowardly blow before returning fire with a crisp jab to his wrinkled chin. The old bastard stumbled backwards and fell to the concrete, having to wipe his own blood away from his busted lip.

As I closed in to finish off my weakened prey, I saw the fat loser raise his rifle up. He aimed it at a lone black teenager who was busy fending off two violent white males. I heard my radio explode with communication as I bolted over to the stop sign. Time seemed to slow down as his knobby index finger leaned into the rifle's trigger. Launching myself forward, I dove into his chest and knocked him down to the ground. The sound of his rifle bouncing on the concrete, followed us both as we hit the hard sidewalk.

"Some of these White rioters are armed!" I screamed over the radio.

After a long pause, FBI snipers all called in from their respective roof tops, hastily relaying sightings of armed men with pistols and shotguns. Seconds later, a large group of State Police and NOPD officers arrived on scene and separated the battling factions. Several heavily armed rednecks were held at gunpoint and eventually handcuffed, as scores of cheering black spectators applauded the officers. Director Saunders ran towards me with her pistol and badge in hand. With hateful indifference, I pushed down hard on the fat fuck's back, ignoring his pathetic screams that his rights be respected.

"Is that him, Achim?" She mercifully asked.

"Nope, but it's definitely one of his distant cousins," I teased.

"Family members won't be good enough today, Achim," she quipped. "We need to find this guy."

"Well….you better get a move on." I advised while pointing at the idle motorcade. "Your boy's a sitting duck right now."

Cutting her eyes away in frustration, the Director waved her hand at two officers, instructing them to clear the roadway ahead. She climbed back into the limo and the motorcade slowly pulled away from the intersection. The black crowd applauded loudly as the limos departed, leaving scores of handcuffed right-wingers in their dust. It was then that I noticed the cameras filming us from within the scores of cheering black bodies. This could all be some clever setup. The footage would surely find its way on the internet or some cable news editing room, providing the perfect back story to spin all kinds of false narratives.

Confused, I grabbed the fat fuck's rifle off of the sidewalk and pulled out his banana clip. Looking down into the magazine, I found that it was completely empty. It was puzzling that not even a single bullet was loaded, yet I knew the exact reason it was dry. My good friends at the FBI were up to their old devious tricks. Smoke and mirror field operations are the perfect way to influence and dictate public perception. Somebody in the FBI was trying to create a convenient fall guy and avoid blame.

"Is that you down there Achim Jeffers!" An agitated Sanchez barked over the radio.

"You're supposed to be at City Hall! That's where were paying your ass to be! Get back to your post, right now!"

"I'm right where I need to be," I lazily responded.

With the flick of my fingers, I muted Sanchez's annoying radio calls and headed back towards the Superdome. I watched the motorcade pull into the Superdome's back entrance driveway. Armed bodyguards quickly circled the cars as the doors swung open, and a figure that looked like Pokey's emerged from one of the limos. With a nervous glance, he looked down the road towards me before several bodyguards aggressively ushered him into the stadium. After Pokey was escorted inside, Director Saunders exited her vehicle and briskly walked back towards one of the limos.

The limo door was opened by a well-dressed secret service agent and Governor Lewis stood to his feet. While waving at excited onlookers, the Presidential candidate deployed a fake smile as he slowly made his way inside while photographers snapped away. Trailing behind him, Director Saunders watchfully followed, ushering him into the Superdome as frenzied reporters screamed loud questions.

Aside from the phony scare at the intersection, everything had gone as planned. Yet, we hadn't seen any indication of the Tarpon's presence. In the back of my mind, I began to seriously wonder when our string of luck would end. He had to be here somewhere; waiting for the perfect opportunity to turn the world upside down. Reaching into my pocket, I grabbed my cellphone and pulled up my 6zeros app. As I reentered Champion Square, I noticed that it was almost filled with people now. Most of them wore the black and gold colors of Grambling State University, while loudly shouting at the TV cameras recording the audience.

The Bayou Classic Kickoff Show went live, and the camera's bright lights streamed down from raised platforms. With faces full of makeup, the on-air talent offered professional smiles while gleefully greeting their television audience. I navigated my way through the fully enthralled crowd, ignoring the white media stage craft on display. When I was halfway through the mass of bodies, I looked out and noticed that Poydras Street was nearly empty. The only sight to be seen was an elderly black couple wearing Southern University shirts .

They were casually walking up to one of the many food trucks that lined the sidewalk near Poydras Street. All of the trucks were facing the Superdome. They had a clear line of sight to watch everything happening in Champion Square. While dodging a sea of cheering fans and hoisted cellphone cameras, I watched as the old couple humbly approached one of the trucks and bought a raspberry snowball. Finally finding a lonely spot away from the crazed TV audience, I sat and examined all six of the food trucks as the first half of the game played out.

From a distance, I could see that all of them were occupied. None of them looked remotely suspicious at first glance. They were either cooking or wiping down small tables, but after thirty minutes of spying, one particular vendor drew my attention. It was a brand-new yellow truck that served vegan food. Operating in the midst of Black competitors, this White owned vegan truck began to look wildly out of place the more I examined it.

It seemed a little too damn obvious to be the Tarpon, but I knew it was prudent to check it out. Scrolling through my 6zeros app, I found our private chat room and sent Anthony a secret message. Seconds later, my phone rung and I quickly his call.

"Where are you?" I blasted.

"I'm in the Superdome, just like you wanted," he declared.

"It's almost halftime and I've circled the whole stadium five times. I don't see anything Achim."

"Are Pokey and Governor Lewis walking on the field?" I asked.

"No. Neither of them are on the field right now, just the two bands sitting behind the endzones."

Pokey was scheduled to speak a few words proceeding the halftime show, while Governor Lewis would sneak out to Champion Square and get some TV time with the sports network. It was a clever political ploy by the Democrats to get as many eyeballs on Governor Lewis's campaign as possible. Meanwhile, when they attracted every black eyeball, the Tarpon would unleash his fury upon a fellow white man he considered off code. My mind raced. I had to make a decision, and it would be a critical mistake if I got it wrong.

"Alright Anthony," I bemoaned.

"Change of plans."

"Make your way out of the Superdome. Walk towards Poydras and find the food truck pavilion across the street from the Arena."

"There, you will see a yellow food truck run by two white people." I explained.

"Go buy yourself a snack and check them out for me. Try not to make it too obvious, stay cool and act normal."

"Security in the Superdome is tight," He responded. "I had to leave my pistol in the car, so right now, I'm naked."

"Should I run to my car and get my tools?"

Looking down at my watch, I realized that the halftime festivities would begin in less than ten minutes. Asking Anthony to walk to his car and make it to the food truck pavilion before Governor Lewis arrived in Champion Square would be a tall ask. On the other hand, this could very well turn into a raging shootout, and sending him to the frontline without protection would certainly cost Anthony his life. For a second or two, I contemplated doing the recon myself but quickly dismissed the notion. The Tarpon would easily notice me. That was the type of advantage I couldn't afford him. We were pressed for time, so I swallowed my concerns and made the decision to put Anthony directly in harm's way.

"No, we don't have time Anthony." I instructed. "You're going to have to fly under the radar as best you can."

"Get to the Pavilion and scout the yellow truck. You'll be looking for the two whites operating it. Use your phone to get a good photo of each of them."

We ended the call, and I shoved the phone in my pocket in frustration. Despite the coolness, I felt the beads of sweat forming on my forehead like it was mid-summer. In the back of my mind, I knew that once Anthony made it to the pavilion, I'd be handing control of this situation over to him. All I could do was try to bury my concerns and trust him to make the right calls.

After five minutes, I watched Anthony walk down a long service ramp leading away from the Superdome. He passed through the police barriers and crossed Poydras Street before entering the food truck pavilion. While slowly scanning each of the truck's menus, he pretended to be engaged in some lively conversation on his phone. Even though the tactic was bold and loud, I liked it. Although the stunt shined attention on him, it was easily dismissible as the sort of typical loudmouth behavior of exuberant black college kids.

After browsing the pavilion, he finally settled in at the yellow food truck and walked up to the window counter. From a distance, I watched as an eager looking white lady pushed the window open and leaned out towards him. They both engaged in a conversation. Both exchanged lighthearted smiles and shared laughs. Suddenly, Anthony lifted his phone and the white woman posed for a picture while holding up a wooden spatula. After taking two photos, a middle-aged white man approached the window and Anthony pointed the phone's camera towards him as well. Without skipping a beat, the white man proudly smiled before embracing the woman in a tight hug.

This was way too easy. The second Anthony pointed his camera phone at the Tarpon like that, he would be dead meat. This yellow food truck was a dead-end, and now we were back to square one. Looking down at my watch, I noticed that the start of the band's halftime show was only minutes away. On the podium behind me, the television lights brightened in Champion Square. The on-air audience cheered as the smiling cable network host began his lead in. Serious looking security personnel began to show their faces, a tale tell sign of Governor Lewis's Secret Service entourage sprinkling themselves among the shouting crowd.

Looking over at the pavilion, I watched Anthony put money into a tip jar before grabbing his sandwich from the window counter. He lazily walked over to a cheap picnic table and sat in front of his meal. Angered by Anthony's ill-logical complacency, I grabbed my cellphone and dialed his number. From a distance, he dismissively pushed the ringing phone away as he chewed his sandwich. After seven unanswered rings, I smashed down hard on the end call button. What the hell was he doing?

The crowd behind me let out a loud cheer which was followed by a long round of applause. Turning towards the TV stage, I noticed the smiling figure of Governor Lewis eagerly waving at the black masses. It was show time for me and the Governor. Either I was right, or the Tarpon was about to kill him and sneak away without a trace. He took his seat in front of the live camera, and I could see Director Saunders standing below the stage whispering into her radio. As the sounds of Governor Lewis and the TV host dominated Champion Square, the roaring black audience went quiet.

Over at the pavilion, Anthony had nearly finished his sandwich when he suddenly picked up his cellphone. He curiously pulled a pair of ear buds out of his pocket and inserted them into his ears. Confused, I watched as he lifted his cellphone and began to talk into the microphone. After a few swipes of his finger, my phone chimed. He had just sent me a photo. I opened the photo and noticed the image of one of the other food trucks. It was the truck that was serving fried seafood. The truck was painted black and gold.

The side door of the truck was open, and an elderly black cook was captured walking down a small ladder. While employing a long blue cane, the cook appeared to be disabled and hobbled. Nothing about the picture looked nefarious until I noticed his wrists. Using my fingers, I zoomed the picture in, focusing in on his hands. On both of his hands the old man was wearing blue latex gloves, but while holding his cane at an angle, the skin under the gloves was revealed. While the color of the wrinkled skin on his face was a dark tint of brown, the skin on his wrist was pale and white.

My eyes instinctively snapped up, focusing in on the strange old man. He locked the door before hitting the sidewalk and limping away from the pavilion. This behavior was more than telling. The halftime show of the football game was the main event of the Bayou Classic. No black person in their right mind would risk missing it, let alone walk away from it. Before I could call Anthony, an incoming call shook my phone.

"Did you see that old man Achim?" He asked in a hushed tone.

"Yeah, I got him," I responded.

"I'm gonna go check out his truck," Anthony replied. "You can follow him, since I'm unarmed."

"Roger," I confirmed. "But, be careful. He may have booby traps inside that truck."

After inserting my own ear buds, I crossed the street and hit the sidewalk, pacing myself as I approached the food truck pavilion. About a block in front of me, the old man limped along Poydras Street before making a right turn onto North Claiborne Avenue. As I walked past his food truck, I noticed the lights inside were turned off. I watched Anthony cautiously approach the truck's back entrance. He carried a small lock pick in his hand, along with a cigarette lighter. Refocusing myself, I turned on the NOPD radio before I closed in on the end of Poydras. Now it was time to roll the dice.

"Director, this is Achim," I spit out.

"Black and gold seafood truck in the food pavilion. Possible sighting, over."

"Achim stand down and keep this frequency clear!" Agent Sanchez yelled over the radio. "Pokey has finished his speech and is secure!"

"Report to City Hall, as you were ordered. Sanchez out!"

As I sped walked towards the end of Poydras, the radio fell into a silent state of confusion. Everyone that heard our two different radio transmissions had to be puzzled. Everyone, except for the Director. When I turned right onto Claiborne Street, I saw that the old black man was no longer limping. He had discarded his blue cane and was now climbing into a beat-up van.

"Achim! Do I need to move the damn Governor or not!" Director Saunders pleaded.

I hugged the sidewalk, trying my best not to be too obvious. Before I could answer her question, my cellphone rung so I answered it. When I hit the answer button, I heard Anthony's voice blast through my earbuds.

"You were right. The food trucks filled with fuckin booby traps. I can't get inside," he shouted. "I was able to crack the door open a little…I see two dead white men inside. They look like they've been dead for a few days."

"Do you see a bomb?" I asked.

"Not a bomb, but a huge cannon's in there…wait a minute…the lights just turned on Achim!"

"Can you disable it from outside?" I screamed.

"No! I can't get near it!" he yelled back.

I took off in a dead sprint towards the van. Pushing the radio up to my mouth, I pressed down on the key and shouted.

"Move him now Saunders! Move him now!"

As I closed in on the van, I heard the loud percussions of a high velocity machine gun rip through the air. The world around me seemed to pop as each round pulsed through the atmosphere. A few seconds into the percussions, an even louder blast punched me in the ears and rattled the earth beneath me. After I fell to the ground, the machine gun fire disappeared. The voices of people screaming in terror were all I heard. The blast was a deep shockwave. Something huge had exploded and in that brief second, I realized that Anthony could have triggered the damn booby trap himself, giving up his life to stop the massacre.

Vaulting to my feet, I shook off the shock and refocused. The van in front of me, cranked up and began to pull away. Angered, I drew my pistol and aimed in as the van's roaring engine struggled to pull away from the curb. With four well placed shots, I hit both of the van's rear tires. Both tires went flat, but the van barely slowed, continuing to barrel down the road. Before I could fire a second volley, the van turned off of Claiborne Street, heading towards Mercy Hospital. As the van limped through its turn and disappeared from view, the sound of a hard impact greeted my ears. The rear portion of the van shot back into sight, followed by the smell of gasoline and melting rubber.

After a tactical reload, I approached the van cautiously, with my pistol ready for action. Slowly turning the corner, I saw the wrecked van, with its front end totally disfigured. The windshield was busted and aside from the deployed air bag, no one was inside. In front of the van, sat a Cadillac Escalade with its front-end caved in. Moving towards the Cadillac, I saw Rachel inside. Parts of the engine had pushed into the front passenger compartment, pinning her in her seat. She was unconscious and from her labored breathing, I assumed she was injured.

As my hand reached for the door handle, I saw a glint of a silver blade rush towards my chest. On the defensive, I galloped backwards using my forearms to block the knife thrusts. The force of the blows caused me to lose my pistol as I staggered backwards to create space. It was the old black man. When the old man looked at me, I noticed his shady eyes and that familiar evil smile. This elderly black man was the Tarpon. With two quick jabs, I assaulted his nose, causing him to retreat several feet. His hand reached up and peeled off the high-definition facial mask, finally revealing himself to me with a sadistic grin.

"We've turned off of Claiborne" I whispered into my cellphone mic.

"Why are you calling for back up?" The Tarpon laughed.

"Why can't I have you all to myself?"

"You can have all this ass whipping, and it will just be me giving it to you," I replied.

I dove forward with a balled fist, missing the Tarpon's head by inches. He tried to counter with a swipe of his blade at my stomach, only hitting air. I stepped back to size him up and we both stared each other down. The Tarpon was playing his little games. He had disarmed me, and I knew he had his gun on him somewhere. He could easily take me out right now, but it seems the ghosts of my past wanted to play themselves out in the present.

"You still punch like a whiny black bitch." He laughed. "My mother hits harder than you."

Taking a quick scan below, I saw my pistol on the ground. It was about ten feet behind the Tarpon, but he caught my glance and knew what was coming next. I rushed towards him, first dodging his knife attack, then engulfing him with hard punches to his head. In a failed attempt to strike a blow, he came at me with his knife. Grabbing his arm, I twisted it backwards, causing his useless blade to fall to the earth as he winced in pain. With a sharp kick to my belly, he dislodged my grip and gasped for air in retreat.

I felt a series of punches pummel my jaw as I lost balance and fell backwards. The shock of the blows was harsh, causing my ears to ring and my vision to blur. During his attack, I saw the faint signs of a wide smile on his face. He now had the upper hand and the thought alone fueled my failing spirit. Mustering my strength, I blocked two of his punches, before wrapping my arms around him and tossing him to the ground in a fit of anger. Stunned by the move, he struggled to try and regain his footing.

Sensing my advantage, I kicked him in his mouth and watched red blood shoot out from in-between his lips. He fell back to the ground in pain and began to crawl away from me.

Chasing him down, I thrust my black fist into his nose several times, drawing new blood with each savage blow.

"Today, you die," I boldly proclaimed.

The Tarpon managed to crack a smile before I saw his eyes shoot up and spy Rachel, who was still unconscious inside of the SUV. I already knew what his plan was, but today, my plan happened to be better. After a chuckle, he looked into my eyes and shot me a determined stare.

"You people are weak. You've always been too damn weak to accept the truth. The truth is your people are too afraid to make the sacrifices that need to be made!" He shouted back in anger.

The Tarpon's right hand suddenly moved towards the small of his back. I was too far away for me to run and grab him. If he got to his hidden gun, he would once again have the drop on me and Rachel. In that instant, I tried to dig out my own spare pistol, which was hidden away in my waist. Before I could aim in and pull the trigger, the loud ring of two successive gunshots shattered my unprepared ears.

Having been shot twice in the torso, the Tarpon failed to rise to his feet before losing his strength and coughing up blood. I watched in shock as Rachel quickly limped over to his bleeding body. She stared down at him with those beautiful eyes that were filled with a special type of hatred. In her hands, she held a heavy Desert Eagle. Placing her finger on the trigger, she aimed down at his forehead. Looking back up at her, the Tarpon's face broke out in an evil smile that expressed a morbid sense of joy. He had come to realize that he walked right into my well-laid trap.

"You're still gorgeous as ever my doll," he admitted.

"From the first day I saw you….I knew your beauty would be my undoing."

"It wasn't her looks that got you caught up…my man," I broke in, while stuffing my pistol back into my waist.

"It's that black fear that lives deep within you white folks. That's what led you here."

"You wanted to find out. So, I decided to show your ass."

The Desert Eagle erupted in Rachel's hand, sending two angry hallow points straight into the Tarpon's temple. Walking over to his corpse, I took the moment to watch the brain matter ooze from his disfigured skull. It was a joyous moment for me; muted by sorrow as thoughts of a murdered fetus dampened my pride. Looking over at Rachel, I saw tears rolling down her cheeks. For her, this was surely a moment of emotional vindication. The spirits of the slaughtered martyrs of her broken womb, had been avenged.

Using my thumb, I wiped the wetness from her eyes and gently kissed her on the forehead. The feeling of touching her skin brought back so many old memories and long forgotten fantasies. When Rachel wrapped her arms around me and buried her head into my chest, I didn't resist her. I couldn't resist her, not now, not ever. She shook as the tears dripped and her voice whimpered. Trying to comfort her, I whispered into her ear, letting her know I still cared. She looked up into my eyes and I could once again see that old longing within her.

All of it brought back memories of those mortal enemies we erased, and the exploding excitement we shared afterwards. All it would take was this very same lustful eye contact, and our plans for the rest of the night would be over.

My flesh wanted to experience it all again. To enjoy Rachel's unique touch and feel. To once again hear that heavy breathing in my ears when I filled her.

The sounds of police sirens broke me away from those unclean thoughts. Finally realizing where we were going, I looked away in embarrassment and I felt Rachel push me in frustration. Thoughts of Jessica ripped through me. I was determined to be a one-woman man, and Jessica was the only woman I needed.

"Why the hell did you shoot him Rachel?" I asked in bewilderment. "You were supposed to wait for my signal, like we agreed."

"Achim, you play around way too damn much boy!" she vented.

"I got tired of waiting in that truck, so I decided to put an end to your little mind game."

"You should have just killed his ass like I told you….but no….you gotta have this mastermind assassin contest with the asshole."

"Plus, seeing the bastard smiling like he was in control pissed me off. I had to pop him."

Several unmarked cars pulled up nearby, along with a NOPD patrol unit. Seeing the blacked out tint and observing their poor parking skills, I knew who had arrived on scene to join us. A driver side door sprung open, and a panicked Sanchez emerged with his service pistol at the ready. Sprinting over towards us, his shiny FBI shield seemed to bounce as it dangled from his neck.

"Is this your guy, Achim?" He asked while examining our handy work.

"Yeah," I admitted. "It's him. He's too busy burning in hell to introduce himself."

"Well, I see why. You've certainly left him in a bad mood," Sanchez joked.

He raised his head and looked at the totaled SUV and the Tarpon's destroyed van. Using his finger, he motioned at the wrecked cars and looked at me. Without words I nodded, concurring with his silent observations regarding my secret scheme. Acknowledging me, he shook his head before turning towards Rachel and giving her a long once over.

"Let me guess. This is Robert Charles's infamous Rachel?" He asked.

"Nope," I warned. "She's nobody."

Catching my drift, Sanchez offered a smile before turning away and slowly walking towards his parked entourage. I felt Rachel's arms wrap around me. She pressed her forehead against my shoulder, and I felt her tears soak my shirt. She was thankful and despite her overwhelmed pride, this was her way of letting me know. Several members of Agent Sanchez's FBI entourage, finally climbed out of their unmarked cars. All of them were wearing dark shades despite the gloomy conditions. The lone NOPD patrol unit's doors popped open, and two Black officers revealed their serious gazes.

Realizing Sanchez's clever ambush, I bolted towards the large SUV, dragging a confused Rachel along with me. Out of the corner of my eye, I noticed Agent Sanchez swing his raised pistol towards us. Before I could get behind the SUV, I heard a series of gunshots. Diving towards the ground, we hit the street and I shielded Rachel with my body.

The gunshots disappeared just as quickly as they had erupted. The terrifying sounds of bullets was replaced by the loud barks of men yelling for people to drop their weapons and get on the ground. Looking up, I saw a legion of mixed law enforcement units descending upon us. The sight of a bleeding Sanchez lying prone on the ground was the first thing that registered. Next, was the abyss of worry on Director Saunders face as she ran towards us in a dead sprint. Behind her, the light-skinned mystery trotted towards Sanchez as he rolled around on the street in pain. Sharon's FBI wind breaker seemed to flap like a cape as she aimed her gun at him, ordering Sanchez to put his hands out to his side.

"You're under arrest," she screamed down at him.

While I was lost in pondering Sharon's true allegiances, Director Saunders thrust her arms out, pushing me off of Rachel. It was then that I noticed the pool of her blood underneath us. Panicked, I helped Saunders turn over her body and that's when I heard Rachel laboring to breathe. Rachel's eyes met mine and I felt her hand clinch my shirt. Sanchez's bullet appeared to have pierced her rib cage. This looked like a fatal wound.

"Get a medic over here now!" Director Saunders screamed.

A Louisiana State Trooper ran over with a first aid kit. I snatched the kit out of his hand without asking and ignored his muted protests. Using scissors and gauze, I open Rachel's shirt and wiped away blood, looking for an exit wound. Understanding my urgency, Director Saunders put on a pair of latex gloves and joined in on the search.

"The bullet must be still inside her somewhere," she concluded. "She could have all kinds of internal injuries."

"We need to get her to a hospital, now."

Just as the words left her lips, the hopeful sirens of an ambulance arrived on scene. NOPD officers waved the incoming truck towards Rachel and quickly made a pathway. The ambulance pulled up next to us and came to a silent halt. Two black EMT's jumped out and rushed over, carrying urgent expressions with their tool bags.

"Please step aside for us sir," the Black EMT ordered with a deep authoritative voice.

Assured by his presence, I relented and made space for him. Both he and his female partner, examined the scene, took Rachel's vital signs and asked her several pointed questions. Having dressed her wounds, they placed her on a stretcher and loaded her into the ambulance.

"Where are you taking her?" I demanded.

"The closest ER is Tulane Medical, sir," the female EMT advised with her distinct New Orleans accent.

"But we'll have to check and see if they aren't already full of patients given the Bayou Classic incident."

The busy lady hopped into her ambulance and started the ignition before slamming the driver side door, leaving me with more questions than answers. Director Saunders and I stood in silence as we watched the ambulance roll out to Claiborne Street, then accelerate away with its sirens blasting.

"She's a fighter," the Director lamented. "She'll make it Achim."

"How's Pokey?" I asked.

"Pokey is more than safe right now. He is locked away, safe and sound."

"How about your fuckin Governor?" I retorted. "Is he in good health?"

"Governor Lewis is shaken…but he's alright and alive."

"Thanks to you and your helper. We were able to clear the stage before anyone was hurt."

"I saw your helper near the food trucks propane tanks. He caused a hell of an explosion, but fortunately, it disabled the cannon fire before the Tarpon could get an accurate shot at us."

"Have your folks found my guy?" I asked.

Director Saunders suddenly looked away. She was gathering nervous words to deliver the bad news. We both had won our own battles today, but my contribution to our victory had come at a great price. Guilt washed through her as she tried to reach with her hands to comfort me. I politely brushed off her attempt and restated my question in a more directive tone.

"My guys are still going through the explosion site, Achim. Most of the other food venders only suffered minor injuries….but your guy was really close when that truck exploded."

"I promise you. We're doing our best to find his remains."

Pushing the thought out of my mind, I turned from her and walked away. I needed my space. There was nothing her sympathy could do for me, even if I accepted it. Despite my wishes, I heard her walking behind me whispering, but I couldn't make out her mumbled words. Stopping and turning towards her, I relented, giving her my ear.

"I do hope you can believe that I'm not a monster. I want to make this right for you Achim….but everything I do only seems to make it worse."

"How did you find out about Agent Sanchez?" I cryptically asked her.

She offered a mixed grin, then pointed at the mysterious woman I knew as Sharon. I turned around to see Sharon and several other FBI agents standing in front of a line of handcuffed men. All six men were on their knees with their heads hanging low. The quiet tension between all of them was evident. The mysterious Sharon was not only just an enigma, but she was also ruthless.

"Last year, one of my private sources caught wind of Sanchez and Pokey's involvement in a nationwide drug trafficking enterprise," Director Saunders began.

"Apparently, a few retired FBI agents over in Phoenix, Arizona are running the whole operation. The sudden emergence of Zhilan in the United States, has angered them and cut into their profits."

"Sanchez was able to extort Pokey and keep him quiet, blackmailing him with evidence that members of his special NOPD drug task force were selling Zhilan's drugs. That's when Pokey called you and had you investigate Zhilan's nephew."

"From there, things spiraled out of control….and Pokey was too involved, too power hungry and too scared to do the right thing," she explained.

"This was a very sensitive mission, so I had to put my best and most trusted undercover agent on the job."

"And now she's over there putting the finishing touches on her work here in New Orleans, before she heads out west to Phoenix to mop up the ring leaders."

Totally surprised by the Director's killer instinct, I couldn't contain my admiration behind a stoic stare. She had known the score the whole time and was simply using this incident to draw Pokey and Sanchez into her own shrewd trap. Both men's greed had started this whole mess. They crossed Zhilan and had more incentive than anybody to spoil the Tarpon's plan, but in doing so they exposed themselves. After a chuckle, I shook my head and smiled at her. The Director's eyes beamed with pride as she reached out again, this time touching my hand. Sensing her curious touch, I decided to play along.

"How did you figure I wasn't in on all of this with Pokey?" I inquired.

"I didn't….but after Pokey and Sanchez sent Agent Porter after Jessica and your Aunt Rita…I assumed that you weren't on their payroll."

"That's why I had your cousin contact you in Houston once we found out about the Tarpon's hit," she admitted. "I needed to try and feel you out first…off the record."

"But it seems Sanchez and Porter got to you first, so I had to change my plan and show patients."

"I believed in you Achim….can you trust me now? I'm fighting like hell to make all of this right for you."

"Don't try to make it right for me," I shot back.

"You fight White Supremacy among your own people….and if you defeat it…all will be right between me and you."

Looking around the crime scene, I noticed the media cameras starting to surround the area. Large groups of black people were briskly walking away from the Superdome, many of them in a quiet state of shock. Several officers began passing the news that the rest of the football game had been cancelled due to security concerns. Hearing the update, I walked over and picked up my pistol before holstering it and making my way back towards city hall.

About halfway to my car, a limo swerved out of the bumper-to-bumper traffic and pulled up to the curb next to me. As I watched the passenger window slowly roll down, I saw a familiar face that made me smile wide.

"Hey sexy! Good to see you're still alive," Jessica teased.

"Did you finish your job?" she asked.

"Yeah," I answered. "He's gone and our check should be in the mail any day now."

Her eyes lit up with approval. She was proud of me, and we both knew the death of the Tarpon was a big step towards securing our future. The limo door swung open, and I curiously watched as Jessica sled aside to allow space for me. As I climbed inside, I noticed Aunt Rita's smile. Her face shined like the sun as she sat next to another familiar face.

With his corny gold jewelry, loud cologne and aura of cockiness, Mr. Quest from Seattle was a hard man to forget. I wanted to see Jessica and was more than happy to see Aunt Rita, but this negro I hardly trusted had no business here.

"It's good to see you again Achim," he offered. "I see that you've done very well during this mission…so far."

Combined with the unimpressed look in his eyes, I was pissed by the way he said it. All of it nearly made me boil over. I slammed the passenger door shut and leaned over towards his face to close the distance.

"We lost two of our best agents today, yet we were able to expose criminals in the FBI and kill a renowned white assassin. So, what in the hell do you mean by so far, sir?" I asked.

"Oh, I understand. Your one of those old civil rights negroes who refuses to give the younger generation any damn credit for cleaning up the mistakes you made?" I continued, not allowing him to answer my question.

"Achim, did I not just say you did well?" He lobbed back. "Maybe you're one of these young cats who's hard of hearing and stays caught up in his emotions."

Jessica grabbed my forearm as I felt myself raise up to confront him. Her touch warned me off and caused my tamer side to prevail. Then my eyes focused on Aunt Rita who was still sitting there, calm and cool as ever.

"You should conserve all that righteous energy young blood," Mr. Quest advised with a cocky smile. "This is only the first battle for you, and there's plenty of war left."

"There are many enemies out there still angling to harm us, son."

"I bet your very familiar with them, aren't you sir?" I responded.

Mr. Quest laughed my accusation off before pulling a can of breath mints out of his pocket. After pouring a few pebbles into his mouth, he leaned over and offered me the can while staring me in the eyes.

"I think we're all about to get to know Zhilan after what you did today, Achim." He laughed.

"And I'm sure she'll be more than happy to acquaint herself with you real soon."

This was the second time I heard this guy refer to Zhilan as a woman. Deep in his serpent like eyes, this old man knew more than he was willing to admit. I hardly trusted him and now he was giving me more of a reason to believe that he wasn't on the up-and-up. Looking over at Aunt Rita, I noticed that she remained stoic. In Seattle, she cautioned me to stay cool in spite of my legit concerns. Robert Charles had been infiltrated before, she told me. There was no need for me to get angry or overplay my hand. In war the most logical general's win the battles, not the most motivated.

Following her silent cues, I reached over towards Mr. Quest's can of mints. After taking a few into my hand, I tossed them into my mouth and felt the powdery candy crunch in-between my teeth. The mint's coolness engulfed me and soothed a wild tongue that yearned to be let loose. Now was not the time, nor was it the place. Mr. Quest smiled and nodded his head as he watched me chew, surely believing that he had lowered my guard.

"In this race war, we can't afford to have permanent friends or enemies." He relayed.

"We, as black people, must only have permanent interests, son."

The Coup

After years of living here, I have grown to love the first two weeks of December in New Orleans. When the seasonal chill of late November passes, December's warm blue skies reward our patience. Aside from the thankful appearance of a bright sun, this clear morning also filled my heart with a new kind of energy. Adjusting my sunglasses, I silently listened as a nervous white Pastor stood over a cheap wooden casket. This grave site was small and cramped, too small to host anything bigger then what we were doing today. Looking in the Pastor's eyes, I could sense his desire to do right by the deceased, then swiftly go back to offering salvation to living souls.

As a former Pastor myself, I knew the poor man's task would be a difficult one. In his commitment to the Lord, he had volunteered himself to officiate this lightly attended service in remembrance of a man no one truly knew. There is nothing in the world more tedious than having to speak for a dead man you never met. The Pastor's only solace was the fact that the few people in our audience, were just as detached from the deceased as he happened to be. The only exception to this, was me. As soon as he started his service, the Pastor began shooting his eyes towards my seat. Someone undoubtedly told him that I knew the guy, and now he was feeling me out.

"Sir, if you may," he began, finally motioning at me. "I'd like to offer you the floor to say a few words on behalf of the deceased."

Put on the spot, I nodded before walking up to the dull casket and staring down at it without removing my glasses. No one needed to see my lack of remorse, as they would soon feel the truth in my words. Turning towards the hesitant gathering, I made no pretense and jumped right in.

"He was a man no one knew. That's how he lived his life on this planet. The world will never know his real name, nor his life story. We'll never know what created this monster or understand the journey that brought him to lay before us today."

"But we do know that he was an evil man… a filthy White Supremacist, possessed by ancient spirits that will be cast into the fire by God himself."

"Now that God has removed him from the living, this cruel world is a little bit more tolerable without his presence…just a little bit more tolerable…. not much though. For that, we all should praise Elohim. God Bless you all."

As I walked away from the Tarpon's dull casket, I could see the surprise riddled in the eyes of the Pastor. The silent stares of Director Saunders and the ever-mysterious Sharon betrayed their quiet distaste for my remarks. Jessica, on the other hand, was visibly pissed. Upon walking back beside her, she looked up at me with eyes that could cut. She preferred that I lie to the world instead of delivering hard truths about the deceased. Ignoring her critique, I looked away from her and boldly stood tall as the confused Pastor asked us all to join him in prayer.

The Pastor concluded and several Hispanic graveyard attendants opened the non-descript sarcophagus. After the men loaded the Tarpon's casket inside, the Pastor sprinkled blessed water and bowed his head in prayer as the graveyard workers locked the lid in place. Director Saunders and Sharon walked over, formally introducing themselves to Jessica before turning their attention to me.

"Well, you didn't say a lot. Your words weren't flattering, but at least you told the truth," the Director commented.

"The truth doesn't require a long sermon, Director. Truth tends to speak for itself," I coyly replied.

"How about you Ms. Sharon?" I purposely deflected.

"What happens to be your truth today?"

With a dismissive laugh, Sharon shot a glance over at Director Saunders before tossing the long strap of her designer purse over her shoulder. She didn't appreciate my question and this was her way of telling me to fuck off.

"If you had clear vision Achim, you would be able to see my truth," she retorted.

"The Tarpon is dead. Agent Sanchez and his cohorts are all on administrative leave pending our investigation. Even your crooked buddy Pokey resigned. Yet, you and your Aunt Rita still walk free. Isn't my truth easy enough to see?"

"Truth doesn't always need words, Achim. Our actions send all the truth you seek. You need to trust us."

"You're right," Jessica interrupted. "We'll have our eyes on you and you can count on it."

"What the hell do you mean", Sharon retorted in disgust.

"We've seen what you two have done so far." Jessica shot back. "As much as I love Pokey, he needs to be arrested for what he did, not hidden away to help Governor Lewis avoid embarrassment."

"And we all know Sanchez will get a slap on the wrist, despite him having killed that innocent black woman named Rachel, in cold blood. Plus, you haven't done anything about those two former FBI agents in Arizona, which makes us wonder why they are suddenly off limits."

"Achim, you and Jessica will just have to trust the FBI to do the right thing," Director Saunders replied.

"We'll clean all this up….it just takes time. Justice always takes time."

The Director looked around and examined the area around us, waiting for passers by the walk beyond the sound of her voice. When the coast was clear, she leaned towards my ear and started to whisper.

"This is why I'm promoting Sharon." She relayed.

"Sharon Quest will now serve as my official Chief of Staff. She's one of you and she's going to be my right hand man. I need someone close to me that I can rely on, and she's the only person we both can trust," the Director added.

Hearing the last name Quest made my ears perk up. Looking at her with enlightened eyes, I noticed all the facial similarities and could somehow smell James Quest's odorous cologne seeping from her veins. Aunt Rita's wannabe boy toy had infiltrated the FBI, and before me sat his daughter. Sensing my realization, Sharon looked at me with a familiar stare that I recognized from our murderous night in Treme. For a brief second, I felt myself beginning to believe the spider web that Director Saunders was trying to spin.

Yet, the charges the Justice Department decided to press against Sanchez were meaningless. He was merely charged with illegal wiretapping, misappropriation of government funds, and misconduct. None of the charges came anywhere close to addressing the widespread corruption within the FBI. Once again, the FBI was doing its best to protect itself from embarrassment and Director Saunders appeared to be leading that effort.

It was at this point that I realized that her and Sharon had been the ones who set up that right wing protest during the Bayou Classic. Instead of protecting Pokey or the Governor, Director Saunders chose to protect the FBI. The White Media had promoted the half-truth that Right Wing Extremists who were affiliated with the Republican Party, were responsible for the riot outside of the Superdome. All of it was a well-manufactured FBI lie, but having the advantage of truth and receipts to back it up, now made us practically untouchable. The FBI would have to walk softly for the time being. A war with Robert Charles would have to wait for another day.

"Congratulations Sharon," I stated, while offering her a handshake.

"Since your days as an undercover agent are over, I wanna say it's a pleasure to finally know your real name," I explained.

"Thank you, Achim," she replied with a cute smile. "It's been a pleasure working with you all this time…and I do hope we can somehow continue our professional relationship after all of this."

I could feel the eyes of Jessica burning holes into my head as Sharon's handshake got a bit touchy. The sound of my cellphone ringing in my pocket was my salvation, allowing me to rescue my hand from her flirty grasp. I helped Jessica out of her seat and pulled the ringing phone out of my pocket as we walked away from the grave site.

"Hello," I answered.

"Achim, we're in the parking lot. You and Jessica should meet us there please," Aunt Rita instructed.

Jessica and I slowly headed for the parking lot and walked up to our SUV. As Jessica popped open the locks, a stretched Lincoln Navigator pulled up alongside us and parked. Trying to peer through the heavily tinted windows was useless. After a few seconds, the back passenger door opened and I saw Aunt Rita sitting with a glass of wine in her hand.

"Come on you two," she ordered. "We're about to make a block."

I assisted Jessica as she climbed up in the Navigator before following her inside. Once I sat down, I realized that Aunt Rita wasn't alone. In the rear seats next to Jessica sat Anthony and, Rachel. Closing the door, I heard Aunt Rita's driver engage the locks and put the SUV into drive before slowly pulling off.

"Oh, my goodness Achim!" Rachel let out with a clever smile.

"You two have a child on the way?"

"How far long are you girl?" She asked.

"I'm going on eight months," Jessica proudly answered. "It's a boy."

"Y'all are having a boy!" Rachel proclaimed with phony happiness.

"I'm so happy for the both of you. I am really…. please let me send the baby a gift."

"First," Rachel paused, catching herself in the moment. "Let me introduce myself. Hi, my name is Rachel Douglas, and I've known Achim for years."

Jessica's eyes quickly examined Rachel before they turned towards me, harboring all kinds of malice hidden behind her own cleverly constructed smile. Next to Rachel, a nervously amused Anthony did his best to find a rock to hide under. In those first few seconds, the unspoken dominated the air, and you could sense discomfort growing wings among us.

"It's nice to finally meet you, Rachel. I'm Jessica Baker," she politely responded in a purposely professional voice.

"Achim and I will be more than happy to accept your gift. Whatever you send, we'll take it. I'll be sure to send you my mailing address."

Rachel's face flinched as she smiled, and I knew Jessica's words had wounded her, yet she was determined to keep up the front. Feeling the tension begin to boil, I turned to an entertained Aunt Rita and helplessly watched as she sipped on her half-empty glass. Unlike the uncomfortable Anthony, Aunt Rita appeared tickled to death by all the drama.

"Achim, I'd like to know why the hell you felt you needed to fake our deaths." Rachel snapped.

The tone of Rachel's question was filled with doubt and concern. It was a miracle that her and Anthony had even followed my orders. Looking back on it, I'm glad I decided to use the gay jewelry's shop attendant as my conduit to organize my plan. Between the ambulance service and transporting their fake remains to Georgia and the Bahamas, our secret jewelry shop connection hit a home run for Robert Charles. Since the FBI has dug its claws into us, our little trick allows us to hit the reset button and take away all their advantages.

"Rachel, if the FBI thinks you and Anthony are deceased, they will be less inclined to perceive Robert Charles as a critical threat," I explained.

"I made sure they followed you and wasted their own time for that exact reason. Now that they've seen you both die, they've totally lost your scent."

"Plus, they can't arrest someone who is already legally dead, especially if they believe you two might know a lot of their embarrassing secrets now."

"You ought to be thanking me, Rachel. I've just made you untouchable. You both are off the grid, and like the Tarpon, neither of you will ever exist."

"So, what's our next move, Achim?" Anthony curiously asked. "I know you have something else in mind after all of this."

Smiling at Anthony, I reached into my pocket and pulled out a small box. Anthony watched as I handed it to Jessica. Confused, Jessica looked at it like a ticking time bomb before asking me what it was. After some encouragement, she mustered up her nerve and lifted open the top. Inside, she saw her engagement ring and before words could leave her lips, tears came streaming down her face.

"If Jessica says yes," I started. "Anthony, your next move will be to attend our wedding, and make sure no one ruins it."

"Yes! Yes! Hell yes baby!" She blasted in tears.

She hugged and held on to me while a tipsy Aunt Rita smiled in silence. I kissed her on the forehead and felt her lips move up to mine, delivering a passionate tongue kiss. She was happy and I was proud to be her fiancé. Shocked and a bit rattled, Rachel offered her congratulations with a blank smile.

"So, it seems I'll get to plan your engagement party, right?," Rachel joked.

"Girl, no," Aunt Rita quickly retorted. "You'll have more important things to do for us."

"Now that Achim and my niece are getting married, I'll be retiring."

"Achim will assume my position as Executive of Robert Charles South and voting member in the Robert Charles National Leadership Council."

"When Achim moves up, he'll need you and Anthony to start carrying a lot more weight around here."

"Rachel," I added. "You'll be getting a promotion as well. I trust and need you."

"You're now my Chief of Operations and Anthony will be your lead assassin. I'll be depending on the both of you to make things happen."

"So this means Achim and I will need to discuss the terms of my raise and increased benefits," Rachel spelled out to Aunt Rita.

"Yes, we'll be getting together on that," I sheepishly jumped in. "You and Anthony can both expect raises and more perks."

Rachel's face lit up with a real smile and I could only imagine what her inner thoughts happened to be. The flames in Jessica's eyes easily told me her joy had been tempered. She wasn't happy at all that Rachel would still be a part of my world. Displaying her own version of a muted smile, Jessica congratulated Rachel and they both exchanged catty stares. I understood her concerns, hell, I even had my own. Yet, in this war, there were no two people I trusted more than Jessica and Rachel. For now, all of this had to work out. This was the way things had to be. We were in the middle of a race war and I needed every soldier up front, no matter the strings attached. The fate of our people depended on us somehow making this uncomfortable situation work.

"Make sure you two are ready," I explained to Anthony and Rachel.

"Robert Charles needs to do a little house cleaning. That will be our first order of business after the wedding."

"I believe we have a black traitor hiding among us, and it's time we eliminate that cancer."

"It will be painful. It will be bloody. It will be gut-wrenching, but true power requires decisive action. It requires us to prioritize cold logic over hot emotions."

Looking over at Aunt Rita, I watched her place her empty wine glass into a cup holder. She knew who I was talking about. She may have love for the man, but I didn't trust him or his daughter. None of us are above respectful vetting or examination, no matter their position. We, at Robert Charles, hold each other accountable and enforce our own code of conduct amongst ourselves.

"The empowerment of Black people on this planet, has very stiff demands." I explained.

"Obtaining that power and delivering Justice, has harsh requirements. I intend to grab that power, whatever the price."

"I am on a quest to protect our people from White oppression…. I humbly ask each of you to follow me onto this dangerous battlefield. We are all we got. We are all we need."

Follow Spirit of 1811 Publishing, LLC on Instagram, Facebook, Twitter and TikTok. Visit our website at www.spiritof1811publishing.com and sign up for books specials, newsletter updates and exclusive offers.

Be sure to purchase "War of The Heart", the 1st novel in the Achim Jeffers series. Available in Hardcover, Paperback, Audiobook and also available on Spotify. Pick it up at Amazon, Google Play, Barnes & Nobles and other retailers.

Visit www.spiritof1811publishing.com for a full list of retailers.

Download the 6ZEROS mobile app and join the 6ZEROS online community. Communicate personally with the author and experience/contribute to the book writing process during conferences.

Upcoming Projects from Spirit Of 1811 Publishing LLC:

"The 13ᵗʰ Floor" – Donald London is a black man that seemingly has it all. He's well-liked, highly educated, good looking, and has all the right connections to win the upcoming Louisiana Senate Race. His election day victory appears certain, as the white media has showered him with adulation and national prominence. Suddenly out of nowhere, comes a polarizing racial scandal that disrupts the momentum of his campaign, presenting Donald with a critical life-changing decision that tests his loyalties. How does Donald reconcile his political ambitions, while advocating for the Empowerment of the black community he comes from? (Urban, Romance, Drama)

Tentative Publishing Date: Winter 2023

"Spirit Of The Trembling Prairies: The New Orleans Slave Revolt of 1811" – The 1811 Slave Revolt was one of the most captivating moments in Foundational Black American history. Sadly, it is also one of the most forgotten and racially suppressed moments in American history. Relive the revolt and feel the revolutionary spirit of the "trembling prairies" in New Orleans, Louisiana. (War & Military, Black Historical Drama)

Tentative Publishing Date: TBD

Visit our website and signup to receive our newsletter for more details at: www.spiritof1811publishing.com

Released Novels Available Now – Buy Your Copy Today

"War Of The Heart: An Achim Jeffers Novel" – Mold breaking debut novel of the Achim Jeffers Counter-Racist series. Rated 4.7 out of 5 stars on Amazon/Goodreads. Available in Ebook, Print book or Audiobook, at Amazon, Google Play or any place books are sold.

"Nothing Will Come Between Us" - It's a dangerous post-Reparations world, but Nuria Sellers is no stranger to war and sacrifice. After losing her left arm battling White Extremists, the brave amputee, instantly became a Foundational Black Americans hero. Despite all the glory and acclaim, Nuria's professional success has come at a tremendous personal price. Physically disabled and suffering from PTSD, she struggles to find happiness in a floundering marriage that is totally consumed by mistrust, jealousy and painful conflict.

Her personal life is in utter turmoil, but for Force Protection Agent Nuria Sellers, ensuring the safety of her California based Reparations Colony is what defines her existence. A lethal attack from shadowy Anti-Black forces challenges Nuria to find her inner strength and somehow protect her colony's political gains. While pursuing the culprits, Nuria's already battered spirit comes face to face with the hidden demons of her personal life. Join Nuria Sellers as she embarks upon a turbulent journey towards self-realization and God's truth.

Explore a post-Reparations society that is rife with calculated deceit, forbidden technology and competing value systems. "Nothing Will Come Between Us" is provocative, aggressive and uncompromising. Reader discretion strongly advised. Available in Ebook, Print book or Audiobook, at Amazon, Google Play or any place books are sold.

Visit our website at www.spiritof1811publishing.com and sign up for books specials, newsletter updates and exclusive offers.
Follow Spirit of 1811 Publishing on Instagram, Facebook, Twitter and TikTok. You can also contact Spirit of 1811 Publishing and its authors on the 6ZEROS app.